HEIRS ON FIRE

JON PEPPER

More information is available at www.jonpepperbooks.com

Printed in the United States of America

First Printing: October 2020

ISBN: 9798684048500

This book is dedicated to the meek, who shall inherit the earth, but not much else.

PART ONE

Bad Matches

EARLY JUNE

1.   AN AHI MOMENT

Thirty-nine thousand feet over the thumb of Michigan, the slumbering chairman of the Crowe Power Company found himself stumbling through a meadow in pursuit of an exotic beauty.

Her name was Natalia, a barista he had recruited from the coffee counter at Café Che to work side-by-side with him as he transformed his family's iconic company into... something else. Robbie Crowe was running as fast as he could but still losing ground. Why was she so hard to catch? She glanced behind her, smiling and beguiling, then disappeared into a throng of protesters in front of the company headquarters on Broad Street in New York City. Suddenly the mob of raging Planetistas turned in his direction and marched toward him, chanting, *Hey hey, ho ho! Robbie Crowe has got to go!* Natalia emerged from the demonstration, clad in her old commie coffee fatigues topped by a black beret with a red star, her fist raised in a revolutionary power salute. The smile was gone, and she regarded him with contempt and disappointment. As she drew near, she put her lovely lips to a megaphone and spoke in a voice loud enough for all to hear:

"Mr. Crowe. Are you thinking about lunch yet?"

Startled from his dream, Robbie opened his eyes to see his hands loosely holding his phone in his lap. He snapped his head back and blinked. Where the hell was he? He looked across the aisle to see Digby Pierrepont, his phlegmatic brother-in-law and General Counsel, with his nose buried in the salmon pink pages of the Financial Times. Okay. He was on Crowe Bird I. They were going, where? Dallas? No. *California.* Some sort of conference in the East Bay. He looked up and saw Charles, the slight flight attendant, standing before him, bug-eyed and ashen.

"I am *so* sorry, sir," Charles said. "I did not realize you were napping."

"No. I was just—" Robbie licked his lips and blinked away the sleep from his eyes. "Forget it."

"I was wondering if you were considering lunch, sir."

"Um. Yeah," he said. He stretched, yawned. "I guess so."

Charles smiled. "Very well." He reached over to unfold a birdseye maple table, straightened the legs, and carefully laid down a leather placemat in the company's trademarked color, Broad Street Blue. He set out the sterling silver flatware and a linen napkin monogrammed "LRCIII" for Lester Robertson Crowe III, the Roman numerals signifying that he was born a very important baby. With trembling fingers, Charles adjusted the place setting just so and summoned a weak please-don't-hit-me smile as the jet hit an air pocket, rattling both the table setting and Charles' frazzled nerves. "We'll have something for you in a moment, Mr. Crowe."

"'Something'?" Robbie asked. "What does that mean?"

Charles took a deep breath and stood as straight as a chopstick. "Mr. Crowe. Sir." He cleared his throat. *Ahem.* "I deeply regret to inform you that we, we, we—" His voice escaped him. His mouth opened but nothing came out, except for an unfortunate squeak.

"Wee-wee-wee, *what?*" Robbie demanded. "All the way home?"

"We... don't have any sushi."

Robbie's body jerked in a spasm, as if Charles had stabbed him with the fork. Now, the chairman was fully awake. "You are kidding me."

Digby, sensing imminent danger, dropped his newspaper to his lap and sat forward, in case he was needed to step in to save poor Charles' life.

"Apparently," Charles said, "we had a teeny little mix-up with the catering crew back in Teterboro. Your lunch was loaded onto Mr. Padden's plane. Mr. Padden's lunch was loaded onto your plane. And, and, and... I'm just at a total loss as to how something so, so, so catastrophic could have happened. I mean, how anyone could be so utterly careless with something as important as *the chairman's lunch?*" He said it seriously, reverentially, as if he were a deacon speaking of Jesus and the Last Supper.

Company. That, in turn, would leave the company vulnerable to a takeover by longtime rival Staminum Energy, led by Robbie's former CEO, Walker Hope. And, amidst all this turmoil, he was vilified daily as a climate criminal by the Planetistas, the radical environmental group that pasted "WANTED" posters with his picture on light posts all over New York's Financial District. *Robbie Crowe!* The one business leader in America who actually *cared!*

Robbie sighed, picked up his phone, and reflexively plugged Staminum Energy's ticker symbol into his browser, only to feel the screws tighten on his rack of mental torture. Obsessed with Staminum's stock rise since Walker left Crowe Power to become Staminum's new chief executive, Robbie checked the price compulsively, desperately hoping for a collapse that never came. Staminum had missed on their earnings for twelve straight quarters, yet there again on the screen was a thick green arrow pointing up. Staminum had risen another dollar sixty-five just that morning! Clearly, the market was expecting the same managerial magic from Walker that he had conjured at Crowe before Robbie pushed him out. Should Staminum's share price continue to rise, Walker would have plenty of equity to use in a bid for Crowe, and Robbie could lose the company. How could Robbie live with himself then? Everyone would regard him as a failure. He'd have to leave New York... move into the woods... grow a wooly beard... forage for food...

Robbie looked across the aisle to Digby, who had inserted his AirPods in his ears and played white noise as a defense against Robbie's incessant chattering.

"Digs," Robbie said. Hearing no response, he repeated his command, more urgently. "*Digs!*"

"What?" Digby mumbled, continuing to read.

"Jesus, man, can't you hear?"

Digby removed the AirPods. "I was listening to, uh...something."

"Did you see this crap?" asked Robbie, holding up his phone. "Staminum's up twenty-one percent since Walker joined them."

Digby turned the page. "Twenty-two."

"And?"

"And what?" Digby asked, annoyed.

"That's insane. That company hasn't made money in years."

"Market's betting Walker will figure out a way."

Robbie blinked slowly, trying to comprehend. "So…"

Charles head swayed to and fro like a weathervane in a windstorm, tryi catch Robbie's drift. "So?" he repeated, squinting.

Robbie's words spilled out in a torrent. "So don't just stand there jackass," he said. "Go get it."

"Get what?"

"Tim's lunch. What do you think I'm talking about?"

"You want Mr. Padden's lunch?"

"Yes, I want his lunch. Damn it, man. Are you dense?"

"Sorry, sir. I'll warm it up right away." Charles turned back to the galley a panic that he slammed into the doorframe, damaging his knee, his shoul his sense of job security. He whimpered in pain and closed the door beh Why had he taken this gig? Travel was supposed to be fun. *See the wo glamorous people.* Oh, dear God. It was nothing like that at all.

Robbie watched Charles' clumsy retreat with disgust, throwing up h and flopping in his leather seat like a freshly boated flounder. "I giv muttered. "Can you believe this crap?"

"Robbie, you need to calm down," Digby said. "You're going to worl into a stroke. It's just lunch."

"Just lunch? Is that what you said? Just lunch?"

"You want to make it something more than that?"

Robbie shook his head. "See? That's what you don't get, Digs. It's not It's a symptom of everything that's going wrong right now. Everyon one!—disappoints me."

Digby looked at him dully. "I won't take that personally."

"You know what I'm saying."

"I certainly do."

Digby retreated into his newspaper as the chairman threw his h his seat, staring at the cabin ceiling, the whine of the engines boring i like a drill as he clicked through his growing inventory of personal the top of the list: His twenty-four-year marriage to Lindsey, in which loving, faithful and true for at least eight nonconsecutive years—oka four—was on the precipice of a ruinous divorce. This was no time for that would divvy up his stock holdings and threaten his grip on the

Company. That, in turn, would leave the company vulnerable to a takeover by longtime rival Staminum Energy, led by Robbie's former CEO, Walker Hope. And, amidst all this turmoil, he was vilified daily as a climate criminal by the Planetistas, the radical environmental group that pasted "WANTED" posters with his picture on light posts all over New York's Financial District. *Robbie Crowe!* The one business leader in America who actually *cared!*

Robbie sighed, picked up his phone, and reflexively plugged Staminum Energy's ticker symbol into his browser, only to feel the screws tighten on his rack of mental torture. Obsessed with Staminum's stock rise since Walker left Crowe Power to become Staminum's new chief executive, Robbie checked the price compulsively, desperately hoping for a collapse that never came. Staminum had missed on their earnings for twelve straight quarters, yet there again on the screen was a thick green arrow pointing up. Staminum had risen another dollar sixty-five just that morning! Clearly, the market was expecting the same managerial magic from Walker that he had conjured at Crowe before Robbie pushed him out. Should Staminum's share price continue to rise, Walker would have plenty of equity to use in a bid for Crowe, and Robbie could lose the company. How could Robbie live with himself then? Everyone would regard him as a failure. He'd have to leave New York... move into the woods... grow a wooly beard... forage for food...

Robbie looked across the aisle to Digby, who had inserted his AirPods in his ears and played white noise as a defense against Robbie's incessant chattering.

"Digs," Robbie said. Hearing no response, he repeated his command, more urgently. "*Digs!*"

"What?" Digby mumbled, continuing to read.

"Jesus, man, can't you hear?"

Digby removed the AirPods. "I was listening to, uh...something."

"Did you see this crap?" asked Robbie, holding up his phone. "Staminum's up twenty-one percent since Walker joined them."

Digby turned the page. "Twenty-two."

"And?"

"And what?" Digby asked, annoyed.

"That's insane. That company hasn't made money in years."

"Market's betting Walker will figure out a way."

Robbie blinked slowly, trying to comprehend. "So..."

Charles head swayed to and fro like a weathervane in a windstorm, trying to catch Robbie's drift. "So?" he repeated, squinting.

Robbie's words spilled out in a torrent. "So don't just stand there like a jackass," he said. "Go get it."

"Get what?"

"Tim's lunch. What do you think I'm talking about?"

"You want Mr. Padden's lunch?"

"Yes, I want his lunch. Damn it, man. Are you dense?"

"Sorry, sir. I'll warm it up right away." Charles turned back to the galley in such a panic that he slammed into the doorframe, damaging his knee, his shoulder, and his sense of job security. He whimpered in pain and closed the door behind him. Why had he taken this gig? Travel was supposed to be fun. *See the world with glamorous people.* Oh, dear God. It was nothing like that at all.

Robbie watched Charles' clumsy retreat with disgust, throwing up his hands and flopping in his leather seat like a freshly boated flounder. "I give up," he muttered. "Can you believe this crap?"

"Robbie, you need to calm down," Digby said. "You're going to work yourself into a stroke. It's just lunch."

"Just lunch? Is that what you said? Just lunch?"

"You want to make it something more than that?"

Robbie shook his head. "See? That's what you don't get, Digs. It's not *just* lunch. It's a symptom of everything that's going wrong right now. Everyone—*ev-er-y-one!*—disappoints me."

Digby looked at him dully. "I won't take that personally."

"You know what I'm saying."

"I certainly do."

Digby retreated into his newspaper as the chairman threw his head back on his seat, staring at the cabin ceiling, the whine of the engines boring into his skull like a drill as he clicked through his growing inventory of personal disasters. At the top of the list: His twenty-four-year marriage to Lindsey, in which he had been loving, faithful and true for at least eight nonconsecutive years—okay, maybe just four—was on the precipice of a ruinous divorce. This was no time for a settlement that would divvy up his stock holdings and threaten his grip on the Crowe Power

Robbie protested. "But the guy's an asshole."

"Maybe. But he's their asshole now. There's nothing you can do about it."

Robbie massaged the back of his neck and twisted his head around, trying to undo the knot at the base of his well-coiffed skull. *Was that a tumor he felt back there?* He turned on his phone's camera and reversed the focus to study his image. Since moving out of the house he shared with Lindsey, he had been working desperately to look more youthful—with his carefully colored reddish-brown hair allowing only a dash of silver at the temples, a spray tan applied at the club spa, and regular workouts on his bicycle to keep his paunch in check—but the constant anguish on his face was etching deep crevices in his brow. As he turned from side to side, evaluating his visage, he had to acknowledge that Digby was right: stress was taking its toll. *Face it, man. You look like shit.*

Digby reached blindly behind him to the credenza and picked up a copy of the *New York Post*, emblazoned with a headline in World War III type: COPS BUST PERVY ELMO. He regarded the pathetic heap of a man to his left. "The truly amazing part is that Walker just started last week," Digby said. "The stock run-up is all built on expectations. Imagine how it will go once he makes some progress."

Robbie stretched out his arms, palms facing up. "What do you want me to say, Digby?" he asked. "I made a mistake?"

Digby scoffed. "I know better than that."

Robbie stared blankly at the bulkhead. "This has got to be driven by institutional investors, right? Spearhead Partners? Gemstone? Fourth Street?"

"Probably."

"Don't they understand it's not just about profits anymore? It's about people, right? And planet, and… and… you know, all those other 'p's people talk about."

"Purpose?"

"Whatever. I *hate* these short-term thinkers on Wall Street, always focused on nothing but the bottom line. I mean, even if you accept the premise that money is the only thing that matters—which I certainly do not—Walker doesn't deserve all the credit for Crowe earnings the past four years. You know that, right?"

Digby suppressed a yawn. "I've heard it said once or twice."

Robbie sat up, animated with indignation. "Go down the list, man. Who approved his strategy? *Me!* Who made sure the board got him every damn thing he needed? *Me!* Who rallied the family to hire him in the first place when everyone thought he was just some g-droppin' goober? Again... *hello!* But do you hear anyone give me credit for all that?" He hit his phone screen with the back of his free hand. "It's like I wasn't even there."

"You were there. Saw you myself from time to time."

Robbie shook his head, soaking in self-pity. "I worked my ass off."

"In by the crack of ten, sometimes three days a week."

"Four, most of the time." He looked skeptically at Digby. "You know what? Enough of your sarcasm. I don't need to justify how I do my job to you or the media or investors or anybody else. Hell with you all. Where's our damn lunch, now? Did Charles fall out of the plane?"

"He probably has PTSD from serving your cappuccino this morning."

"Good! He deserved it! Did you see that mess? Foam dribbling over the side, no little heart thingy on the top. It was a complete disaster," Robbie said. "Now he can't even catch some dead fish? I'm about done with that guy."

"Impossible to find good help these days."

"Tuh! Don't I know it." Robbie sighed. "I'm so sick of the failures in this company. Our stock's falling like a rock and nobody—*nobody*—is doing a damn thing about it. Did you see we're down almost sixteen percent this month?"

"Seventeen as of yesterday."

"I don't need heckling."

"You're the one who's always insisting on hearing the ugly truth."

"Okay. Fine. *Fine!* It doesn't matter, because we're moving on! We're going to forget all about Walker..."

"As if."

Robbie nodded vigorously, talking himself into a proposition. "We're going to do better than ever with Tim Padden. That guy's the real deal."

"Uh-huh."

"I know he can do it."

"Right," Digby sniffed. "Tim."

"What?" Robbie said, alarmed. "You don't like him?"

Digby gave up on reading the paper and tossed it onto the table in front of him. He crossed one gabardine leg over the other, pointed his Berlutti loafer in Robbie's direction and peered owlishly at him through his rimless glasses, which rested just under a mop of wavy brown hair. "I don't like to contradict you,

Robbie, because I know it only incurs your wrath, so I'll say this just once: I have no idea why you picked him. There's nothing in his background to suggest he can lead a complex global company like ours. I get that he's deferential and subservient. Sort of like a border collie with male pattern baldness. I'm just not sure he's got the stuff to run off and fetch some success."

Robbie sank back into his seat. "You've got this all wrong. All Tim needs is a chance. And, damn it, I'm going to give him all the time he needs."

"Uh-huh."

Robbie, now in full agitation, sprang out of his chair and jumped into the aisle. "But here's what I don't understand. Why doesn't he get off his dead *ass* and do something about our share price? Staminum's going up and we're… I mean, it's been six fucking weeks already. Where's the big plan for our future?"

Digby leaned forward. "That's what this *Power to the People* offsite is all about. We're supposed to coalesce around a plan, or plan to make a plan, or, I don't know. Sounds to me like everyone's going to gather 'round the campfire and sing the Barney song. You know: *I love you; you love me*? Maybe that way, we'll give each other a nice big group hug when we don't hit our numbers."

Robbie leaned over and looked out the window to see silvery clouds stretched thinly over a patch of blue water. What if he parachuted out of the plane? Was there a way to somehow open the door and leap? Maybe he'd land on a fishing boat and live on the Great Lakes, away from all these decisions and all this pressure to be another legendary Crowe, like his great-great-grandfather, and his great uncle, and his not-so-great-grandfather, and his absentee dad. *Yeah. Living on a lake might be better than hiding out in the woods.* "You guys coalesce, or confer, or—for all I care—congeal. I personally don't give a shit. I'm not going to sit in a stifling meeting room all day long going over one slide after another with a bunch of engineers and finance people. God! They're the most boring people in the world. I never understand what they're talking about and they sure as hell don't understand me."

Charles, at last, reemerged from the galley holding a silver serving tray.

"It's about time," Robbie muttered.

"I'm sorry, Mr. Crowe."

Robbie drew the linen napkin from the ivory ring and put it on his lap. He regarded Charles peevishly. "All you say is 'sorry,' Charles. Do you notice that?"

"Sorry sir. I won't say it again."

"Stop it!"

"Sorry. *Argggh!*" He recoiled and looked at Robbie. "Sss...."

Robbie glared at him as he removed the cloche plate cover, displaying a gigantic cheeseburger the size of Robbie's two balled fists. Robbie looked at it, then at Digby, then back at Charles.

"I see," Robbie said, speaking slowly as he tried to contain himself. "Instead of the nice, healthy seafood lunch that I wanted, you're offering me this... this... *cowpie*?"

"It's what Mr. Padden ordered, Mr. Crowe. I'm so... um, nothing."

"*Sorry?*" Robbie appraised the attendant with disgust. "Goddamn right you are." He picked his napkin off his lap and tossed it on the table. "Enough screwing around here, Charles. Get this steamy pile of poo out of here and tell Mark I want to land at the nearest airport. Then tell him I want Tim's plane to meet us ASAP. Understood?"

Charles adopted the face of a guilty dog who just chewed up a pillow. "Of course, sir. Thank you so much for your patience. I know I don't deserve it." He snatched the tray and disappeared, shaking his head sadly and mumbling to himself.

Digby looked at Robbie in wonder. He had performed many childish maneuvers over the years, but this might beat them all. "I hope you're not doing what I think you're doing."

"I'm retrieving my lunch," Robbie said with a huff. "If numbnuts here can't figure it out, I'll do it myself, just like I do everything else in this company."

Captain Mark Livengood, a sandy-haired former fighter pilot in a tight white short-sleeved shirt with epaulets on the shoulders, ducked his head under the doorway and into the cabin. He had flown more than a hundred sorties dodging anti-aircraft fire in Iraq, which proved necessary training for flying around the world with Robbie. "Hey, Mr. Crowe," Capt. Mark said. "Real sorry to hear about that lunch snafu. Not sure what you have in mind, sir. But Mr. Padden's plane is about forty miles ahead. I can have them circle back and get both birds into Chicago in about twenty minutes if that works for you. We'll have to refuel, so that will delay our arrival into SFO by an hour or so."

"Fine," said Robbie petulantly. "I don't want to go anyway."

Capt. Mark looked confused. "You want me to head back to New York?"

"No, Mark," Robbie said, exasperated. "I want my *LUNCH!*"

"Loud and clear, sir. We'll have you on the ground in a few."

Digby looked over at Robbie. "You know, we could have avoided this problem entirely if we all flew out on the same plane. You, me, Tim. Your sushi. His cow pie. Would have saved on carbon emissions, too, which I thought was some kind of big deal with you."

"Oh yeah. Great fucking idea. I can't even think with Tim pestering me for three thousand miles with questions about this and that and the other thing. He doesn't seem to understand I can't hold his hand and explain everything to him. He has to figure it out for himself. Otherwise, what the hell do I need him for? I may as well do it myself."

Digby couldn't resist. "Maybe it's time to consider that. I don't know if anyone can satisfy you. Five minutes ago, you were Tim's biggest cheerleader. Now he's a complete doofus."

The plane descended through the thin layer of clouds over Chicago, landed flawlessly, and taxied toward the Signature terminal for private jets. Charles clambered down the steps and, bruised from his encounter with the cabin doorframe, galloped like a wounded antelope across the tarmac toward Crowe Bird II, which was taxiing to a stop nearby. Through the window, Robbie could make out Charles talking animatedly with Tim Padden, and see Tim bolt from his seat, scurry down the steps, and walk hurriedly toward Robbie's plane while Charles trundled off in another direction.

"Oh, for Christ's sake," Robbie moaned. "Tim's coming over."

Digby looked past Robbie out the window. "Doesn't look like he packed a lunch."

The Chief Executive Officer of the Crowe Power Company entered the cabin, stooped over and breathing hard. "Robbie, gosh. I am so sorry."

Robbie's shoulders fell. "Don't tell me."

"I'm afraid so."

"You ate my lunch?"

"Just north of Cleveland," Tim said sheepishly.

Robbie writhed in his seat. *God!* He wanted to roll up Digby's newspaper and savagely beat Tim about the face and shoulders. "Well that's just *fine*," Robbie said bitterly.

"Obviously," Tim said, "if I'd known..."

"Well, now, here's the thing, Tim. This poor attention to detail—I'm not saying by you, of course, but by people on your operations team who failed to load the planes properly—means we're all going to have to wait for someone to bring me something to eat. And that means we're all going to be delayed, needlessly burning jet fuel here on the tarmac. Not only is that a huge waste of money, it emits CO_2, destroying our planet. And it did not have to be this way."

Tim nodded, dutifully. "Believe me, I'm going to get a team on this as soon as we land. We're going to find out exactly how they screwed up your meal. I guarantee you, as God is my witness, you'll never go hungry again."

Robbie arched an eyebrow. "I certainly hope not."

Tim took a deep breath. "Well, boss, as long as we're both here, maybe you have time to run through a couple of things regarding the offsite? I haven't had much luck getting on your calendar to fill you in."

Robbie spoke between clenched teeth. "Not a good time, Tim."

With a look, Tim appealed to Digby. Digby shook his head and silently mouthed, "Don't."

Tim nodded. "Okay, chief. We'll catch up at the hotel."

As Tim left, Charles limped across the tarmac and struggled up the stairs with two containers of sushi. He reentered the cabin and put one on a plate in front of Robbie, the other in front of Digby, and clasped his hands together. "Lunch," Charles said triumphantly, "is served."

Robbie surveyed his plate and nodded, as if in approval. "One last thing, Charles," he said softly. "Digby and I require privacy. I'd like you to step outside."

"Right-o," Charles said cheerily. "I'll be up in the galley if you need me."

"No, no, Charles. I mean outside the *plane*."

"Of course, Mr. Crowe," he said, puzzled. "Whatever you wish."

Robbie watched Charles hobble down the stairs to the tarmac, turn, and face the plane. Through the window, Robbie motioned with the back of his fingers for Charles to step further away from the jet. Ever obsequious, Charles nodded and took two steps backward. Robbie gave him a thumb's up through the window and called out to the captain. "Wheels up, Mark."

Capt. Mark came on over the intercom. "Mr. Crowe, Charles is still outside."

"It's an airport, Mark," Robbie shouted. "He can find a ride home."

Robbie poured soy sauce into a small dish, swirled in wasabi mustard with his chopsticks, and picked up a piece of ahi tuna, dipping it into the sauce and plopping it into his mouth. He didn't bother to note Charles' astonishment as the stairs folded into the plane, the engine revved, and Crowe Bird I rolled toward the taxiway without him. For the first time in a month, Robbie felt like at least one small part of his world was back in charge. He was the Supreme Leader for these turbulent times.

Digby said drily, "Maybe you could mention Charles in your 'People Before Profits' speech tomorrow."

"I'm drawing the line, Digby." Robbie said, picking up a shard of pickled ginger. "There's no room in this company, in my life, or on this plane for people who can't meet our standards. Not if we're going to maintain control." And certainly not if he were to win over the lovely, elusive Natalia, who remained just beyond his reach.

2.   THE B WORD

Lindsey Harper Crowe rummaged through the refrigerator in the kitchen and found a half-filled bottle of Pouilly-Fuissé. Had that been what she was drinking last night? It was hard to remember. All these days and nights ran together since Robbie left. She pulled out the stopper and poured some wine into a juice glass. No need to use stemware, which would alert the staff that she was drinking in the morning again. Especially since this was no big deal. All she needed was just a little something to take the edge off and steady her hands in advance of a very important meeting.

She tipped the glass and drained it, the alcohol dripping through her system like a warm glaze. The sensation was so comforting that she knew another splash wouldn't hurt. She poured another.

"Mrs. Crowe?" a voice called from the foyer.

Lindsey gulped down the wine. "Coming." She rinsed the glass in hot water and left it in the sink, then walked to the foyer, where she grabbed her purse and met her driver, Anton. "Good morning," he said, opening the door, then rushing ahead of her to open a rear door to the Land Rover parked in front of her five-story townhouse on East 67th Street. She settled into the back seat and reached into her purse for a piece of Trident spearmint gum. That should mask the scent of wine before they reached her destination.

The vehicle turned left onto Fifth Avenue and headed south past the apartment towers and hotels on the east side of Central Park, then glided past the flagship stores of fading retail empires as Lindsey anticipated the day ahead. There were so many implications to consider. How does one end a marriage?

Anton turned right on Fifty-First Street, right again on Sixth Avenue, and rolled to a stop after crossing Fifty-Second Street, where he jumped out and opened the door for Lindsey. Her heart pounded as she stepped onto the crowded sidewalk, already filling with office workers, delivery people, and tourists.

She pushed through a revolving door to the lobby of the black glass office tower, quite uncertain as to where to turn. Divorce deliberations were uncharted territory, as were these marble monoliths of Midtown. To her left was a Starbucks, which was familiar enough. To the right was Anthropologie, a newsstand, and a chocolate shop, and straight ahead, several clumps of people engrossed in their phones, waiting for elevators. *What,* she wondered, *did all these people do?* As Lindsey stepped uncertainly toward the security desk to ask for directions, she was intercepted by an attractive young woman in a business suit.

"Mrs. Crowe?"

"Yes," she said, then added with a wistful smile, "for now."

"I'm Miriam, with Glickman, Edwards & Stein? Mr. Edwards asked me to show you to our office."

Lindsey nodded gratefully and followed her past the guards to an express elevator, which whisked them to the thirty-sixth floor, whose sole tenant was the law firm known as Glickman Edwards. There, they were met at a desk by three receptionists smiling with the bright intensity of game show panelists poised to hit a buzzer for the next question. In the face of such exuberance, Lindsey felt a sudden urge to flee. Bergdorf Goodman was right down the street. She could lose her anxieties for an hour or so weaving through the tables of shoes.

"Right this way," Miriam said, indicating a hallway.

Lindsey followed with increasing trepidation. Until Robbie's serial infidelities had become too blatant to ignore any longer, Lindsey's toughest decisions revolved around juice cleanses and Botox injections, finding the right dresses and accessories for social occasions, and learning about obscure humanitarian causes in remote parts of the world that she could alleviate with a single check. Even her recent discussions with the Harper family attorney, Bentley Edwards, felt abstract, as if they were talking about the devastating circumstances of someone else's life. *Do you know what her husband was doing behind her back? Everybody knew about it except her...* Now, she was beginning to accept that the tragic star in this Manhattan melodrama was her, and that she had to learn new lines quite apart from her old script. One was well-practiced already: *Robbie and I are taking a little break right now.* What would she say if the break were to become permanent?

Lindsey wobbled in her red Louboutin heels as alternative plots swirled in her mind. Could she avoid the pain of divorce by pretending that Robbie's long parade of girlfriends and hush money payouts never happened? Was it reasonable to believe his insistence that his philandering days were over and he was on the straight and narrow? Could they wind back the clock and recreate some semblance of a loving couple? Or had the foundation of the marriage crumbled away so long ago that there was nothing left to build upon? The answer was becoming obvious—and unavoidable. Their marriage was a failure. And so, now, was she.

Miriam led Lindsey into a large conference room. She sucked in her breath at the sight of a huge team of lawyers and advisors finishing the buffet breakfast they had just enjoyed on her fast-swelling tab. *How many people,* she wondered, *did it take to address her situation*? As linen napkins were discreetly picked up by busboys and carts of dirty dishes were wheeled out behind her, Lindsey was met by the comforting presence of distinguished attorney Bentley Edwards, sporting a light gray pinstripe suit with a pink pocket square and a tie featuring little blue whales, a graphic totem that whispered East Coast Establishment. Bentley, appropriately enough, was named for the greatest love of his parents' life: their car, a 1954 Bentley R-Type, in which he was conceived as it was parked on a remote beach in Nantucket. Bentley grasped both of Lindsey's hands in his and smiled warmly, soothingly, with the stolid earnestness of an undertaker, reinforcing the notion that her marriage was dead and they were now making arrangements for its cremation.

"Lindsey, my dear," Bentley murmured. "So glad you could come in. I do hope it was no trouble finding us. You look wonderful, just *wonderful.*"

Lindsey certainly didn't feel that way. Despite wearing a stretch knit dress by Victoria Beckham, she felt bloated, awkward, and out of place among all the sleek dark power suits. "I hope for your sake, Bentley, you're more convincing in court," she said.

"Come now," he said with a guffaw. "I absolutely mean it." He went on to introduce his team: four lawyers, three financial consultants, two investment bankers, a public relations advisor, an equities analyst and... a *chef?* "I thought perhaps you would like something to eat," Bentley said. "Philippe could whip up an omelet for you or, perhaps, an avo toast? Anything you like."

Lindsey would have considered triple homicide for a single strip of crispy bacon, but she was mindful of her appearance, given her possible reentry into the dating market and her overreliance on Spanx to keep things in order. "Thank you, Bentley. Maybe a cracker to nibble on if you don't mind. Gluten free."

Bentley signaled to a server—*chop-chop!*—who broke into a fast trot from the room. He showed Lindsey a seat at the head of the long table, where business cards aligned with the placement of each person in attendance were arrayed before her in a 'U' shape. There was a Robert to her left, a Thomas, a Gail, and a Larry over there somewhere. Bentley, standing nearby, explained that all these specialists were required to consider her best interests from every conceivable angle. No stone, he assured her, would be left unturned. Nor, she suspected, any billable hour.

"I am not an expert on matters of the heart, as my ex-wives could attest," Bentley said, splaying his fingers over his breast pocket. "Only you can decide what's best for you and your sense of emotional well-being. Yet, as I began to study your situation, it became obvious to me that I would commit grave malpractice if I didn't help you understand the massive financial implications of your decisions. As a friend of your dear family for eons, you know I simply could not let that occur. I owe you this, Lindsey, which is why I've put together the best support team on Earth to walk you through your options."

Lindsey smiled. "I appreciate that very much."

As Lindsey's crackers were delivered, Bentley asked, "May we begin?"

"Certainly."

Bentley turned to Miranda Vasquez-Gillis, head of Glickman Edwards' family practice, who nodded respectfully to Lindsey and slid across the table a one-page biography listing degrees from Oxford and Yale. Lindsey glanced over the long chronicle of achievements and noted that Miranda was just the sort of smart, beautiful woman who attracted Robbie. As she appraised her fine features and thick cascade of long brown hair, Lindsey couldn't help but wonder: *are you sleeping with my husband?* Since the split, Lindsey saw Robbie's girlfriends everywhere, as ubiquitous in Manhattan as Sabrett umbrellas.

"Mrs. Crowe, I know there is so much for you to consider and it can all feel a bit overwhelming," Miranda said. "I've been there. Like you, I'm a mother who found herself facing difficult choices prompted by her spouse's bad behavior. Like you, I also had other lives to consider besides my own. Decoupling is never pleasant, but by examining all your options, I believe you can take heart in knowing this short-term setback could become a long-term gain."

Following an inventory of shared assets—such as their homes in Manhattan, East Hampton, Palm Beach, London, Tuscany and Montecito—she directed Lindsey to a screen at the back of the room where a chart depicted an overview of the Crowe family's interests in the company that bore their name. While the descendants of Homer Crowe owned only a fraction of the company's common stock, they held the entire bloc of privileged shares that gave them control over the board. Within the family, Robbie and Lindsey together held the biggest chunk at twenty percent. Robbie's Uncle Chuck owned fifteen percent and Lindsey's parents held an additional ten percent, purchased as a favor to her when Robbie was dueling his cousin for the chairmanship.

"As you know," Miranda said, "the proxy for your parents' vote is held by your husband. But it is reassigned to you in the event of a divorce."

Lindsey's head turned away and her eyes widened. *What did she say?* She turned back to Miranda. "I, uh—*Really?*"

Miranda smiled faintly and slid another sheet of paper her way. She tapped it with an index finger. "It's all right here."

It took a moment for Lindsey to absorb this bulletin. She sat up in her chair. "I assumed I would inherit their shares eventually," she said, glancing at the paper, "but I never thought about votes. That was always Robbie's department."

Miranda nodded. "The implications are potentially game-changing. If you combine your parents' shares with those you would receive in an even split of your marital assets, you become the Crowe family's single largest and most powerful shareholder."

Lindsey fell back in her chair. "I don't know what to say."

Miranda continued. "We assume Mr. Crowe wishes to remain chairman of the company?"

"Of course," Lindsay said. "He couldn't exist without it."

Miranda sat back. "Then his desire to maintain control gives you enormous leverage to extract a very favorable settlement."

Bentley walked around the table and addressed Lindsey from the back of the room, near the screen. "There's another way of looking at this, too, Lindsey. I'm going to ask Irene Chang, our equities analyst, to explain."

Lindsey turned to see Irene, a thirtyish woman who stood at the far end of the table in a simple black dress, which displayed a fabulously trim and toned figure. *Oh yeah*, Lindsey thought. *She's definitely sleeping with Robbie.*

"Mrs. Crowe," Irene said, "You're undoubtedly aware that Crowe Power stock traded at a premium when Walker Hope was CEO. You may also be aware that CRO now trades at a discount because of investor doubts in the company's current leadership."

Lindsey pursed her lips. "Can you be more specific?"

"To put it bluntly, Mr. Crowe is a drag on the company. His dismissal of Walker Hope as CEO, his selection of the deeply underwhelming Tim Padden as replacement, and his own record directing the company's strategy years ago demonstrate a serious lack of judgment. If Mr. Crowe were removed as chairman and Tim Padden were replaced with a more credible CEO, we believe the share price would rebound rather dramatically."

Lindsey scoffed. "You know that can't happen. Robbie has control over the board."

Bentley rose to his feet and interjected, "For the moment."

Irene continued. "That brings up another issue holding down the stock."

Lindsey sucked in her breath. *There's more?*

"Mr. Crowe has made it clear many times that Crowe Power will never be sold," Irene said. "By foreclosing that possibility, the company is like a painting in the Louvre. There's no way to establish a real market value. All possible bidders, such as Staminum Energy, know a bid for Crowe Power would be messy, expensive, and ultimately futile."

Lindsey sighed. "If I'm understanding correctly, you're saying Robbie is a millstone around the company's neck."

Bentley said. "Your words, my dear, not ours. That said, we don't disagree."

"Do you think he should be removed as chairman?"

17

Bentley somberly shook his head. "That's not our call. We're simply saying his continued employment comes at a very dear price to you and everyone else in the family."

Lindsey exhaled. This was all too much. Divorce Robbie *and* try to remove him as chairman? And open the door to selling the company that's been in the family for more than a hundred years? She wasn't even a Crowe by blood. It was heresy, wasn't it? "I feel uncomfortable even thinking about this."

Bentley shot a look to Miranda, then back to Lindsey. "Of course, you do. That's quite understandable. But, as you ponder your decisions in the days ahead, know this: our analysis suggests that the difference between a settlement in which he buys you out to maintain the status quo and one in which you assert control to move the company in a new direction would exceed a billion dollars."

"Billion? With a 'B'?"

"Yes, ma'am."

Lindsey never regarded herself as a mathematical wizard, but she understood that a billion dollars was a great deal of money. Was keeping her lying, cheating, back-stabbing husband worth a billion dollars or more? Was one last-ditch effort to revive the corpse of their romantic life more important than ensuring the wealth of her children and grandchildren and great grandchildren for the next hundred years? Left to his own instincts, Robbie could squander the entire fortune and leave them with nothing. She'd seen it before in other wealthy families, who were left with little but a storied name and a big tax bill after some ancestor blew their inheritance. "I'll admit you make a compelling case," she said, "but it seems rather academic. I don't know of anyone in the family who's capable of replacing Robbie as chairman. My children are too young. Uncle Chuck is too old. Most of the others in the family have only a remote interest in how the company operates."

Bentley walked over to Lindsey and squatted low on his haunches to look up at her. He patted her arm. "What about you?"

Lindsey burst out laughing. Such a preposterous idea! And so thrilling, in a way. Wouldn't that be a comeuppance for that rat bastard? Still... she needed to be realistic; she could barely decide what to wear these days, much less select a board of directors for one of the largest companies in the world. "That's *well* outside my expertise."

Bentley stood up. "You'd be amazed how many people in family companies suddenly find themselves thrust into a position of power without any experience and do quite well. A death in the family, a disability, a divorce—any number of things can cause one to suddenly assume large responsibilities. As chair, you wouldn't have to actually run the company day to day. You would have to find the right people to oversee the business and make sure that management does its job." He gestured toward the team assembled around the table. "We have experts in this room who have advised many boards and large shareholders in similar situations. They can help you sort out your options and execute a strategy, if that's the course you choose to take."

Lindsey sat back. "Even if that made sense to me, I couldn't exercise these prerogatives without the support of others in the family, right?"

Bentley said, "Perhaps some of them would side with you."

Lindsey shrugged. "They can't be happy with the way things are going." Still, the thought of attempting a coup was staggering. Was it worth leading a mutiny for a bounty like this? What would the children think? And what if—and this seemed the thorniest question of all—the Crowe name were to slip away into history? What if it became no more relevant to the modern world than names like Woolworth or Studebaker? "Bentley, you know there's a part of me that wouldn't mind bringing Robbie down a peg. But there *is* the larger family to consider here. And he remains the father of my children. I don't want to go out of my way to humiliate him... necessarily."

"It's not about revenge, Lindsey. It's about a simple value proposition: can you afford to keep him?"

3. LOSS LEADERS

Walker B. Hope, the newly-installed CEO of Staminum Energy, prowled the perimeter of the company's "Natural Gas Room" like a panther stalking white-tailed deer. Meanwhile, the unsuspecting leadership team casually nibbled on the data strewn about in one presentation after another, oblivious to the imminent danger.

Marty McGarry, the company's new head of communications, had seen this movie before and had a pretty good sense of the outcome. He had followed Walker uptown from Crowe Power, where Walker turned a perennial money-loser into a top performer and made CRO the preferred stock in its sector. Now, as Marty watched Walker circle the mahogany conference table assessing the herd, he couldn't help wondering: *who is going to die?*

The company's Chief Operating Officer, Fred Crispin, seemed a likely candidate as he staggered through a forecast calling for sustained periods of underperformance followed by intermittent bonfires of cash. Staminum Energy hadn't met its budget in years and was apparently in no danger of doing so now. Marty knew from experience that this forecast would probably not last, and neither would Fred.

"Let me know if I'm in the way," Walker said as he crept close to the screen, put on his reading glasses, bent at the waist, and squinted at Fred's chart. "I can't read all this itty-bitty type from the back of the room." He ran his index finger along a line at the bottom of the screen and moved his lips as he read silently before turning back to the presenter. "Now I see why. Guess that's on purpose, right?"

"Well..." Fred stammered. "I, uh, wouldn't put it like *that*, exactly."

"Gotcha," Walker said with a wink. "How would you put it, Fred?"

"It's just that... we don't want to overload anyone with too many details."

"Oh, no, no, no!" Walker protested. "I guarantee you, detail is not goin' to bother me. I find the most interestin' information is often down in the footnotes. I especially love asterisks. Don't you?" He looked up toward the ceiling and stretched a hand in its direction, as if reaching for the heavens. "They're like a, a guidin' star, directin' you to buried treasure on a desert island. There was this one time? At Crowe Power? I found seven hundred million dollars hidden in some sort of 'contingency fund' at the bottom of a slide. Marty, you 'member that?"

Marty cleared his throat. "Vividly."

"Who put that slide up there? Was that Jerry Adler, the fella who ran Asia?"

"Indeed it was."

Walker snapped his fingers. "He left not long after that, didn't he?"

"Yes, he did," Marty said, clearing his throat. "That afternoon."

"Good ol' Jer," Walker said, shaking his head. "Wonder whatever happened to him."

"I saw on LinkedIn that he's doing charity work," Marty said.

"Oh, that's just wonderful. Non-profit is a perfect fit for him." Walker slapped his hands together. "Okay. Back to it."

Walker resumed his saunter around the room, patting the backs of chairs, searching for signs of intelligent life, or at the very least, some modicum of interest. Even the worst meeting at Crowe had been better than this lethargic slog through cost upturns, revenue downturns, malfunctions, malfeasance, soaring debt and sagging profits. The presenters droned on, talking over slides packed with factoids and charts in typefaces too small to read, while colleagues blinked hard to stay awake or engaged in whispered commentaries. No wonder some senior leaders didn't bother to show up at all. Group Vice President Fritz Stamper, son of company chairman Steadman "Steady" Stamper, was ostensibly in charge of Public Affairs, which he pursued from a yacht in the Mediterranean. Margaret Hathaway, the head of Corporate Citizenship, was said to be taking a "mental health" day with her personal shopper at Saks Fifth Avenue, as was customary on Thursdays. And Hollings Jenner, the august head of Investor Relations for three-plus decades, had yet to emerge from the executive washroom, where he had taken the Wall Street Journal forty-five minutes earlier.

As Marty noted how little stamina there was at Staminum, he wondered how he could craft a narrative for the media that covered this company. This was a stunningly unimpressive crew. Hank Schilling, head of North American operations, yawned so intensely during a video presentation by Wolfgang Reuter, the dapper Frankfurt-based head of Europe, that Marty wondered whether someone should wheel in a cannister of oxygen. The Chief Strategy Officer, Kip Stamper, a fifth-generation member of the founding family and Steady Stamper's nephew, blithely shuffled shoeless to the back of the room for rice crackers and La Croix, untroubled by the ongoing discussion of a credit downgrade from Standard & Poor's that could sink the company's debt into junk territory. And while Kaitlin Whitmore, the beleaguered head of Health, Safety & Environment, ticked through a long list of recent plant accidents and explained how they could have happened to anybody, the Group Vice President of Human Resources, Jack Harding, was whispering, chuckling and playing footsie under the table with Kimmee Brewster, the comely young Vice President of Marketing.

Did these disengaged executives somehow mistake Walker's aw-shucks Midwestern personality and off-the-rack suit for a lack of ruthlessness? If so, they hadn't done their homework, perhaps believing that great patriarch Steady Stamper would swoop in and protect them if Walker moved too aggressively. Marty, who had watched Walker shear through executives like a Weedwacker during his tenure at Crowe Power, could have told them that Walker's determination to hone his reputation as America's foremost turnaround executive should not be underestimated. He wasn't here to fail.

"Go back to that slide talkin' about second quarter results," Walker said to Jim Haliburton, the chief financial officer. "I want to ask everybody a question." Walker stood next to the screen, staring at the wide delta between the revenues that had been forecast and those that had actually come in. He wheeled back to the room, scanning the blank faces. "How do we feel about this?"

Walker sensed a collective shrug. How were they supposed to know what he wanted them to think? To avoid getting called on, executives slumped in their chairs, checked phones, and nodded their heads subtly in the direction of Fred Crispin. After all, he'd already been beaten like a dusty rug.

As the silence gathered around him, Fred sensed there was no escape. "Well, Walker," he said, blowing out his cheeks, "the business environment was brutal in the second quarter. We had serious headwinds."

Walker nodded sympathetically. "Headwinds. I hear that a lot when companies don't hit their numbers. They ran into these—*oooh!*—mysterious headwinds." Walker waved toward the windows. "So, tell me Fred. Were these so-called headwinds just blowin' on *us*? Or did they hit *every*body in our business?"

"I suppose they were tough on everyone," Fred conceded.

"But they made money and we didn't."

"I kinda get where you're going with this." Fred said. He leaned back in his chair, grimly gripping the armrests, as if he were clacking slowly toward the peak of a rollercoaster, bracing for a harrowing downhill run. "It's just that, you know, some issues probably hit us harder than the other guys. We got locked in on long-term contracts for materials, labor... things of that nature."

"Did we try to figure a way out? Maybe renegotiate those contracts?"

"Oh sure. I mean... we can certainly look at it."

"You mean *now?*"

"Well, we just didn't think at the time, that, uh—" Fred's mouth went dry as he looked for help from his teammates, none of whom would even glance his way. *Could he have some water? Coffee? A loaded pistol?*

Walker crossed his arms and bore in on him. "Didn't think what, Fred?"

"I, well, you know, it's kinda hard to, uh, in retrospect, to, um—"

Walker resumed his tour around the table, and said loudly: "Anybody want to help our friend Fred with this?" The execs looked around. *Fred who?* "Alright then." Walker continued. "Let me tell you what I think." The assembly prepared for the worst. "I *love* this slide."

Jaws slackened. Eyes widened. Even the executives conferenced in from overseas stopped scanning news sites and real estate auctions to pay attention. *Is he kidding?* "This is the best slide I've seen today," Walker said, heading back to the screen. "And you know why? It's the brutal truth, which is what we all need to accept if we're gonna turn this thing around. Start with where we actually are, not where we wish we were. And the truth is: we stink. And I'm not talking about the air around our refineries."

"Now, wait a second," interjected Kip Stamper, the only one in the room with the sort of job security that comes from the right name, massive amounts of stock, and significant voting rights. "That's hardly fair."

Walker looked at the floor, folding his arms across his chest. "No?"

"Well, for one thing, you're only looking at the numbers."

Walker scratched his head. "Maybe I'm missin' something. Is there something else I'm supposed to look at?"

Kip regarded Walker with pity. How could this man be so backward and unenlightened? "You may not fully appreciate this, Walker, but we don't judge ourselves on a quarter or two. You have to look at the long-term record. We've survived two world wars, the Great Depression, the Great Recession, and every other disruption over the past century."

"Okay. Can the company survive our management?" Walker glanced back toward the screen. "Based on what I'm seein' here, if Staminum Energy were a hospital patient, the doctors would say 'Pull the plug.'" He sauntered slowly over to the wall adorned with black-and-white photos of Staminum's most notable assets from its long history. "Look at these properties, will ya? The Trans-Pakistan Pipeline. The Loire Valley Nuclear Plant. The Refinery de—how do you say it?—*Nuevo Revolucion* in South America. We can't make a profit with assets like these? What's wrong with us? Maybe it's time to sell 'em to somebody who can. Anybody know how to open these blinds?"

A collective shrug suggested this was a task below both their pay grades and their knowledge. Fortunately, Kaitlin, the head of Health, Safety & Environment, popped out of her chair and went to a control panel near the door. "I got it," she said in a tone that suggested long-standing annoyance with her sluggish colleagues. She pushed a button and the blinds rose on the eastern windows to unveil a sunlit panorama of the Midtown skyline. Walker wandered toward the windowsill, sending a roosting pair of pigeons fluttering away.

"Look at that, will ya?" Walker said, his arms outstretched. "All those monuments to success. And all them mausoleums of failure. Amazin' to think about how so many once-great companies are gone. Remember PanAm? It used to be right over there on Park Avenue where it says MetLife. When Juan Trippe was runnin' them, they were the best airline in the world. Then—*boom!*—hit a patch of turbulence and crashed into bankruptcy. No survivors." He shook his head. "PaineWebber was over there," he said, pointing down Sixth Avenue. "How about them commercials? 'Thank you, PaineWebber?'" He chuckled. "No need to thank 'em now. They're dead." He waved a hand over the horizon. "Bunches of other big businesses like us got swallowed up by other companies when they stumbled. RCA. Union Carbide. Sperry. They've got big tall tombstones all over town."

Walker sat on the window ledge. "Sometime, just for fun, take a look at the Fortune 500 list from fifty years ago. You'll be impressed how many companies looked a whole lot like us. Nice big headquarters on prime real estate. Lots of cushy creature comforts for the rulin' class. Everybody livin' the dream on fat expense accounts and high salaries and big bonuses. They all ate at fancy restaurants with French names. Took two or three hours for lunch and drank martinis. Man! Those were the days. They were at the pinnacle. And then it all collapsed underneath them. *Oops!* Where the heck did our dang company go?"

"Are you suggesting that could happen to us?" Kip asked, sharply.

"No," Walker said. "I'm not suggestin.' I'm tellin' you as plainly as I can that it will happen to us if we stay on this course."

"That's just it," Kip said, his impatience evident. "We're not standing still. We're investing aggressively in the future. That's what our Greeneron subsidiary is all about. We've acquired twenty-one small companies focused on alternative energy."

"I saw that. We're gonna extract energy from sun and wind and water and algae and I don't know what all. Fantastic stuff. How'd it do last quarter?"

Kip guffawed. "You can't evaluate it based on a single quarter."

Walker sat on the edge of the conference table and fixed a stare at Kip. "How about the past year?"

"I couldn't say off the top of my head."

"Let me help you. Greeneron lost eight-hundred and forty-six million dollars last year."

"So what are we to do?" Kip spat. "Keep on with the same old, same old? People demand more from companies these days than just profits. We have to be stewards of our planet."

Walker said. "We can't be stewards of our planet unless we're stewards of our business first. If you want to save the world, or at least live long enough to fight another day, we have to serve the people who keep us alive. Investors, customers, employees, suppliers." Walker stood up and resumed a slow walk around the table. "Anyone here want to save this company?" He looked around the room. "It really doesn't matter to me."

Kip looked at Walker incredulously. "You don't care?"

Walker kept moving. "Nah."

"Not at all?"

Walker stopped at the head of the table and faced his team. "Listen, folks. I love my wife. I love my kids. I love my dogs. I don't love companies. They never love you back. They're just vehicles to help us reach our dreams in life. And the only dream I have for Staminum Energy is to make it work for everyone who has a stake in it. If we succeed, a whole lot of people succeed. If we don't, then a whole bunch of people who depend on us get hurt. I can't make you care about that. It has to come from here." Walker tapped the area over his heart. "Maybe you all think I was just pickin' on Kip and Fred, but I'm tellin' you, whether Staminum Energy lives or dies is up to all of us. And as of this week," he said, raising his hand, "that includes me. Are you in? Or aren't you? Let me know right now so I can plan accordingly."

Walker looked around the room. Nearing sixty, he recognized that of all his turnarounds, this could be the heaviest lift. These people were fat and happy. If these executives weren't going to shake off their apathy and do their part, he would rather pack it in early and go home to Michigan. Yet, slowly, one by one, the hands went up around the table and on the monitors. Kip was the last to raise his hand.

Walker sat down in his chair at the head of the table and folded his hands in front of him. "Alright then. Here's the deal. This Leadership Team meetin' is the most important one in the company. We start at nine o'clock sharp every Thursday morning. If you're on the Leadership Team, you're here and you're on time. If you can't be here because—I don't know, you're havin' open heart surgery—you send a substitute. Nobody, no-*body*, gets a pass."

Walker stubbed a finger into the table. "Everyone reports on the progress in their area in type big enough for everyone to see, even in the back. You have bad news? Tell us. You've got a problem? Tell us. You're not making plan? Tell us. Bring it to your teammates in bright bold letters and we'll see how we can help you out, 'cause we're all in this together. When we're here, nobody's lookin' at their phone, unless they need to call their spouse to say they're comin' home early—for the rest of their life. If you can't give your full attention to your colleagues and the subject matter before you, let me know and we'll find some other accommodation. Jack, you run HR. We have outplacement programs, right?"

Jack, focusing on something other than Kimmee for the first time that day, nodded his head rapidly. "Oh yes. Very good ones."

Walker continued, "There will be no empty chairs. This is Staminum's adults table. We won't have disrespectful side conversations while our teammates are presentin'. No secrets. No hidden agendas. No more shruggin' off bad results or pretendin' it's somebody else's problem. Everything we've got is going to be devoted to turnin' around this company." Walker looked around the room. "Are we good?"

"Not just yet," Marty said.

"No," Walker said, slapping the table. "But we're gonna be."

4. A DOCTOR IN THE HOUSE

Robbie Crowe trailed a chatty porter into the lobby of Berkeley, California's Claremont Club & Spa, picking through the bills in his wallet, searching for a suitable tip. Couldn't this guy shut up? He must think Robbie should give him a twenty because he's rich. Well, *fuck that.* As the chairman settled on a couple of singles, he noticed a woman across the lobby who looked remarkably like Dr. Kristi Kramer, the noted TV commentator, celebrated author of best-selling business books, and Founder and CEO of The Mission Institute for Higher Corporate Purpose. Was she walking toward him? And *smiling?*

"Why, I believe you're Mr. Crowe," she said grandly.

Robbie hurriedly shoved the miserly tip into the porter's palm and turned to the woman. "I certainly hope so," he said.

"I'm Kristi Kramer."

"You don't have to tell me, Dr. Kramer," Robbie said, stepping around the leather bags that had been abruptly dropped at his feet. "I'm a huge fan."

Kristi blushed. "You're so sweet," she said, offering her hand. "Call me, Kristi, if you will? And, between you and me," she said, looking around conspiratorially, "I use 'doctor' in quotes."

"Oh?"

"Well. It's not like I'm going to perform surgery or anything," she said with a wink. "Maybe a Heimlich Maneuver. You're not choking, are you?"

Robbie laughed. "Thankfully not," he said.

"My doctorate is in Missionology."

"Ah," Robbie said, mulling the concept. "I've never heard of that."

"I invented it," she said brightly. "You come on down to the Mission Institute in Chapel Hill and I'll give you a private tour of my laboratory."

Oh yeah, Robbie thought. He'd love to see her by the light of a Bunsen burner. What a multi-sensory delight she presented. There was sight: an enormous frosted-blond mane framing a perma-tan face, designer apparel of ivory silk and satin, a robin's-egg-blue scarf cascading into her décolletage, and a shimmering collection of jangling silver jewelry. There was the fragrance of freshly applied cologne—was it Bottega Veneta that his former mistress Maria Territo used to wear?—that made Little Robbie bark in his shorts like Pavlov's dog. And there was the soothing tone of her voice, a warm butter-honey drawl suggesting the Mid-South.

Robbie's reverie was rudely interrupted by the approach of Tim Padden, freshly attired in his new resort wear from Macy's, duckwalking over with a massive white vinyl binder under his arm. *Oh, please, Tim. Not now...*

Oblivious per usual, Tim clapped Robbie hard on the shoulder, as if they were old pals. "I see you two have met," he said.

"Why, Timmy, we're just getting acquainted," Kristi said.

Robbie looked to her in surprise. "You two know each other?"

"Kristi's our speaker tomorrow," Tim said. "She's going to be with us for a couple days to help us plot the next steps in our corporate journey."

"Oh, right. Of course," Robbie said, tentatively.

Kristi's eyes widened. "You didn't know?"

"Maybe you just haven't had a chance to see the briefing book yet," Tim offered.

Robbie flushed red and stared at Tim with such ferocious intensity that the CEO thought the plastic covering on his binder might melt all over the creases in his khakis.

"Kristi," Robbie said, deliberately. "If you don't mind, I would like a word with Tim. Then perhaps you'll join me for a drink?"

"Of course," she intoned, fluttering her eyes. "I'll meet you in the lounge?"

As she sashayed away like a runway model, Robbie clutched Tim by his upper arm and perp walked him to a corner of the lobby. "What the fuck, man. You don't tell me you've got Dr. Kristi Kramer coming to the offsite? That's not something your company chairman should know?"

Tim was genuinely baffled. "It's right on the front page of your briefing book," he pleaded. Hadn't Robbie even looked?

"That thing's heavier than my suitcase. I'd need a fucking hi-lo to wheel it in here, which is why I left it back in New York. You should have told me personally about something as important as Dr. Kristi Kramer attending our conference. But no." Robbie crossed his arms. "You make me look like a complete dope who doesn't even know what's going on inside his own company."

"Honestly, Robbie, I tried. I couldn't get in to see you. Winnie told me you were busy—I mean, like, every day for the past two weeks."

"What? Your fingers were broken? You couldn't email me?"

"I *did.* Repeatedly, with no response. Winnie finally told me on Friday that the best way to reach you was through your private account, but she wouldn't give me the address. She said I would have to get that from you." Tim bowed his head, deferentially. "So, do you think, like, maybe I could have it now?"

The brass of this guy! Robbie shook his head in wonderment. How thick could he be? "Well, Tim, that would kind of defeat the purpose of a private account now, wouldn't it? I mean, if everyone and their brother has it—"

"I'm not just *any*body. I *am* running your company."

"Oh. You are, are you?" Robbie said, with a bitter laugh. "That puts you on some sort of equal plane? Well, guess again, buddo." He stuck a finger in Tim's chest. "You report to me. I don't report to you. Understood? You've got some serious balls to leave me out of the loop on something as big as this, and then—on top of that—to blame me. *Wow.* That's all I can say. Just one big fucking *wow.*"

Robbie turned away, deeply wounded yet again by the carelessness of a minion. Tim waltzed around him, trying to look him in the eye. "Robbie. Believe me. I'm not pointing fingers at all."

Robbie shook his head. "I am so disappointed. You just don't fucking get it, do you, Tim? By chance, have you ever looked at the company logo? Do you see the name 'Tim' in there? No. This company has my name on it. That means I need to know what's going on *at all times!* Do you read me?" Tim nodded dolefully as Robbie continued. "And you need to make sure you do whatever it takes for me to know. I don't care if you have to hire an airplane with a banner and fly it around the building. Send me a raven with a message. Whatever. You can't keep me in the dark. Do you understand?"

Tim dropped his head, exasperated. "I'm doing what I can, Robbie. You're extremely difficult to reach."

"And why do you suppose that is? I've got a company to oversee. A board of directors to manage. A family that's nagging me about the sinking stock price of the company you claim to run. I have to fend off a possible threat of a takeover from my former CEO. And, to top it all off, I have a wife who's threatening to divorce me over... well, certainly nothing that *I* did." He trailed off, pondering the mystery of it all, then refocused on Tim. "Where, exactly, in this chockablock schedule of running pillar to post every damn day of my life do I need to carve out time for you in case you feel like telling me about my company business? *Hmm?*"

Tim blanched. Was he about to be fired? "I'm very sorry, Robbie. I—"

"Don't apologize to me," Robbie said sharply. "Apologize to *her*."

"Kristi? I don't get—"

"Tell her it was your fault that you didn't let me know. Right now. I want you to clear the air before I go over and have a drink with her."

"Actually, I was supposed to have a drink with her to go over the program." He held up his binder. "That's why I came down."

Robbie considered a swift kick to Tim's nuts. "You want a drink? Have it in your room, with your binder. After you apologize to Kristi."

Tim took a deep breath. He hadn't been this depressed since he and his wife put Pickles, the family dog, to sleep. "Alright," he said with a sigh. "Again, Robbie, I'm sorry."

Robbie regarded him with contempt. "You sure as hell are."

* * *

If nothing else, Robbie had to give Tim credit for knowing how to take a good beat-down. It was for Tim's own good, Robbie knew, for him to learn early on where he stood in the pecking order vis-à-vis the chairman. Robbie had made the mistake of not putting Walker in his proper place right from the get-go and it had come back to haunt him, with Walker regularly overstepping his boundaries. Robbie was never going to allow that to happen again. He would put a virtual electronic fence around the chairman's office and shock the dumb bastard every time he crossed the line.

And, yet, he couldn't help losing a bit of respect for Tim in the process. Seeing the CEO of his company curl up into such a meek little ball and offer so little defense of himself was sad in a way. How would he stand up to competitors like Staminum Energy? True, fighting back against Robbie could cost him his job, as it had many others over the years. But did a job and a paycheck mean more to him than his self-respect? Robbie couldn't understand an attitude like that. It wasn't his fault that Tim hadn't built himself a little financial cushion. *Blame your parents, dude.*

Robbie headed for the lounge to meet Dr. Kristi Kramer, stopping on the way to check the phone vibrating in his pocket with a new text message.

Natalia

Protest outside HQ today.

Natalia! Oh, my *lord!* Just to see her lyrical name sent his heart aflutter. It almost made news of yet another protest worth it. He stepped into an alcove for privacy, tapped her name with his thumb, and then the phone icon for a call. "Hey, it's me," he said. Would she know his voice without saying his name?

"Hi Robbie."

She did! Oh joy! *Rapture!* "Wow. You do know my voice."

"Kind of," she said, awkwardly. "You're the only one who shows up as 'caller blocked.'"

"Ah, right. So tell me. What's going on?"

"You told me to let you know when the protesters were back at it," she said. "Well. Here they are. I'm outside watching them now."

"The Planetistas?"

"And a few of their friends. We've got Anarchy Malarkey out here. Communist Plot. Let's see... We Mean Green. They all seem to have amped it up a bit this time, maybe because the weather's so nice. You recall there was a Climate Calamity scheduled last week, but the cold spell caused them to postpone. Today's beautiful, and they're out in force."

"Oh, no. That's horrible. How many people?"

"Maybe forty?"

"Forty *thousand?*"

"No. Forty. Four-oh."

"Ah." He exhaled. "So, it's not like millions of people."

"No," she said. "But it's still quite a scene. And a lot of noise."

"I don't get this. Didn't we just write the Planetistas a check?"

"A hundred thousand dollars. Looks like they used a chunk of it to buy new props. They've got some hinky-looking inflatable dinosaur in front of our doorway that keeps falling over. They're dripping fake blood on the cobblestones and laying down like they're dead, at least long enough to get pictures. They're blowing airhorns, banging on plastic drums, rattling cans, and chanting over a megaphone: 'Death to Crowe Power.' Some group from China looked absolutely terrified and took off before tanks rolled in. I see a few other tourists out there posing for selfies in front of the mayhem. A genuine New York experience, I guess."

"Yeah, but... we can't let this go on. It's embarrassing to have that on our doorstep. People will blame me."

"That's the idea."

"So what are they saying about me?"

"Well, let me think," she said. "From what I've heard, you haven't been mentioned."

"That's a relief." Still, *shit,* Robbie thought. *Don't they think I'm important anymore?* "What do we do now?"

"We can always write another check, but that just seems to whet their appetite for more," Natalia said. "What I'm hearing from Ernesto—"

"Who's that?"

"Ernie Rothstein. He's the assistant manager at Café Che. He's calling himself Ernesto now. Some sort of *nom de guerre,* I guess. They're not going to go away for good unless they can claim a victory. That means we have to do something bold for which they can claim credit. I'm thinking we need a big public statement about our climate policy."

"I'm working on that."

There was silence on the other end of the line. "Seriously?"

"What?"

"I mean, still? That's incredibly lame, Robbie."

"Well, of course I know what we need to do *generally*. I've just got to bring the rest of the people on our leadership team along. They'll have to execute whatever I decide, and you know how resistant to change they are. Why don't you tell the Planetistas to go uptown to Staminum? We know Walker doesn't give a shit about sustainability. They should protest in front of his building. Tell 'em we'll give 'em fifty thousand dollars. They can buy another dinosaur."

She sighed. "You know, Robbie, the reason you were able to induce me to come back to corporate life was because I thought you were actually committed to doing something about climate change. If all we do is pay people off, I may as well go back to making lattes. At least it's an honest living."

"Stop," Robbie said. "Don't even think about that. I will get this done the right way. I promise. I'm working on something very big and very, very bold out here." He looked in the direction of the lounge, where he could see Dr. Kristi Kramer smacking her lips together in the mirror of her compact. "Just bear with me a bit longer, will you?" He lowered his voice to a near-whisper. "Natalia. The last thing I want to do is make you regret your choice."

"Then you really need to do something."

"I will," he said. "And I'm going to make you proud."

5. TEA TOTALING

The woman who suddenly held the fate of the Crowe Power Company in her hands settled under a canopy of mostly-sunny skies, with chandeliers dangling from clouds and cherubs flitting about playing harps. Safely back in her world of long, languorous lunches, Lindsey Harper Crowe found safe harbor from the momentous decisions ahead. Here, in the Astor Court at the St. Regis hotel where she often had lunch or tea, her toughest call was typically the choice between the Champagne Risotto and the Tuna Niçoise.

Her lunchtime companion, the perfectly coiffed Bits Pierrepont, patted the back of Lindsey's hand. A Crowe family scion, Bits was Robbie's older sister and the wife of company General Counsel Digby Pierrepont. She was also perhaps the world's foremost expert on how to drink exquisitely at lunch. "How about some wine," she asked.

"I'd *love* some—"

"They have a very nice Chablis."

Lindsey made a pouting face. "But I don't think I should."

Bits withdrew her hand. "What?"

"I *know*," Lindsey said, sheepishly. "That makes me boring, doesn't it? It's so tempting. But I think it has to be this way, at least for now."

"Oh, come now. I thought you were over that. Didn't you try going dry already? When you gave Robbie the heave-ho?"

"I did. And you know what? It helped. I think I have to try it again. There are some things I'm working through that just... I can't be in a fog." Lindsey sighed as the waiter approached. "Iced tea, unsweetened."

"My word. This is *serious!*" Bits said. She turned to the waiter. "I'll have an Aperol Spritz." She added in a whisper, "And, since I'm apparently drinking for two, just a teensy bit of Grey Goose on the side. Neat. In a coffee cup. And not *too* teensy, if you know what I mean." As the waiter nodded knowingly and turned away, Bits said to Lindsey, "What's wrong with being foggy? It's kind of the point. Who wants to be alert with all the nonsense in the world today?"

"Believe me, I know," she said. "I have nothing against day drinking and I'm certainly not judging you..."

"...Which means you are."

"No." She said emphatically. "Not at all. Really. I mean, it has been totally fine for me as long as all I have to think about is lunch and shopping and playing hostess and serving on volunteer boards. Not to say all that's not important—it is, of *course*—but I can do all of that on autopilot. I'm in uncharted waters now and I've got to try to keep my wits about me."

"God, Linz. Please don't go all holy on me. Nothing worse than somebody who just gave up booze or cigarettes. I don't want to have to start hanging out with Kay Rochester and hear about her fucking cats. Do you know she has them see an ophthalmologist twice a year?"

"You are kidding."

"You watch. They'll be wearing designer glasses before you know it."

As the waiter brought their beverages, Lindsey said, "Well, put all that out of your mind. You're not getting rid of me that easily. And you're certainly not dropping me for Kay."

"I won't. Pinky promise, as long as you can keep it sort of real," Bits said, offering the hook of her little finger. "Well. As real as we ever get. So tell me. Why do you feel like you need to drop out of our little conga line? I mean, obviously, there's my bratty brother to deal with..."

"Job one."

Bits sighed. "You don't have to sugarcoat a thing with me. I *know* he's a little shit. Always has been. If you decide to go ahead and divorce him, be my guest. The way he treated you, I'd like to push him down the stairs again. That's how he got that thing on his chin, you know." She pointed to a spot under her own jawline.

"Could you do it again? I wouldn't mind."

"So, is that it for your marriage? You're done? Or are you going to give him one more chance?"

Lindsey sipped her tea and gently patted her lips with the napkin. "Bits, I *have* given him one more chance—about forty chances. The thought of forty-one is exhausting. I hate to say that because at the end of the day, he's still your brother, and I know that blood matters, regardless of how much he annoys you from time to time."

"True. But I don't have to live with him anymore. And, frankly, neither do you."

Lindsey sighed and her eyes watered. "I'm so sad about this. It's not what I ever expected." She took a deep breath and sat up, banishing the tears. "But I've known for a long time it was inevitable. There's nobody in his life he doesn't dispose of eventually. Sooner or later, everybody's an idiot." She looked at Bits meaningfully in case she didn't get the message.

Bits' eyes opened wide. "Including *me?*"

Lindsey nodded. "Everybody."

"That asshole!"

"It's easier than facing up to his own foibles and follies. Just blame other people for your shortcomings." Lindsey sighed. "I feel sorry for him, in a way. Measuring himself against all those legendary Crowes who came before him is an impossible burden."

"Crowes, schmoes. You know it's all mythology, right? I grew up with the gods from the Hall of Fam. They make better statues than relatives."

Lindsey chuckled. "I know that. And you know that. But they remain larger than life in this family. And they cast a very long shadow over Robbie. It's not enough to follow in the footsteps of Homer Crowe and Charles Crowe and Lester and the rest. He has to make his own footprint, one worthy of the gods."

"Any idea what that imprint is going to be?"

"No," Lindsey said. "That's part of the problem. He's tormented by it. He has no claim to greatness."

Bits sipped her vodka and signaled for another. "I suppose it's worse when you're a boy. I got a pass, on account of my girlie parts. Don't ever tell anybody I said this but thank God. All I had to do was get good grades, keep my thighs crossed, and play a decent game of tennis. The rest would take care of itself. He was bred to run the company, even if he had no interest or aptitude. It was his obligation. The greatest success my parents had was raising Robbie to be a genuine prick."

Lindsey laughed. "The funny thing is, when Robbie works a crowd, he can appear completely charming. Stick a glass of wine in his hand, and he's talkative. He's funny. He can act like he's genuinely interested in you."

Bits scoffed. "That's just a strategy to make people think he's not a sociopath. Think about it. You notice how the reporters and commentators always say, 'Robbie Crowe may be inept, but at least he's a nice guy?' Uh, no, he's not."

They picked up their menus and glanced over the selections. "What are you thinking?" Lindsey asked.

Bits ran a finger down the list of entrees. "I'm thinking forty-eight dollars for a lunch portion of sea bass is excessive," she said. "But I do like the way it filters out the riff raff who can't afford it. What are you getting, besides separate maintenance?"

"Tuna tartare, I suppose." Lindsey placed her menu on her plate.

"So what's next?" Bits asked. "Have you told Robbie what you want to do?"

"I don't know what I want to do. Exactly."

"But you're leaning, obviously. I can tell."

"Well, actually, I'm debating. I'm not sure whether I should divorce him or fire him."

Bits dropped back in her chair. "You lost me, honey, on the 'firing' bit. I don't think that's how it works."

"Hear me out." She sipped her tea, then leaned close, speaking in a conspiratorial whisper. "On one hand, I'm trying very hard to put aside for a moment the emotional wreckage Robbie has caused in my life. On the other hand, he is costing me —and my kids and you and Digby and all of us in the family—a great deal of money. Do you have any idea how much that is? Bentley Edwards just ran me through the numbers, and when you add them all up, they are simply *staggering*. And I'm not talking about Robbie's salary and stock options and his corporate jet and the payouts to his girlfriends that the company picked up. I mean what he's doing to the value of our holdings. The experts who know an awful lot more about this than me say it is costing us all a *fortune*. If I settle now, I will shortchange myself by a billion dollars."

Bits fell back in her chair. "*Billion?*"

"Maybe a lot more than that."

Bits dismissed the idea with a wave of her hand. "Oh, come on. That can't be!" She glanced up at the chubby angels on the ceiling, then back to Lindsey. "Can it?"

"I believe it. Our company—."

Bits cut in. "*Our* company? I've never heard you say that before."

"Yes, *our* company. It's deeply undervalued because of Robbie. Crowe Power would be worth so much more if he weren't in charge. That has implications not only for me and my children, but for you and Digby and your kids, too. We need to think about that."

"Can't we do it with a little drinky-poo?"

Lindsey paused, her resistance weakening. "I can't."

Bits lifted her coffee cup and sipped, then exhaled, with a long, slow and exaggerated "*Ahhh...*"

Lindsey watched her with envy and took a deep breath. "I shouldn't do this, but, you know what?" she said. "Maybe one little glass wouldn't hurt."

6.   THE OFFICE BUZZ

With his first leadership meeting behind him, Walker believed he had a pretty good sense of who could play and who couldn't. Now it was time to move on to the next critical phase: finishing his plan for an organizational structure that was fit for purpose.

He looked at his watch and saw that he had eight minutes before he was scheduled to pee, which would provide just enough time to complete his diagram. He grabbed his accordion folder of notes, clippings, and filings, a short stack of white copy paper, and a purple Sharpie from the top drawer of his desk. He sat at his conference table, facing north up Sixth Avenue toward Central Park, and prepared to add his last scribbles. This was gonna be so much *fun!*

To Walker, every corporate reorganization was like tearing down an old house to its foundation and rebuilding in a smaller, tighter, more modern and efficient way with new gizmos and gadgets. Fortunately, his experience in restructuring three other broken companies helped him quickly spot which parts of Staminum were essential to the business and which were a drag on performance and had to go. He had studied every financial filing the company had made over the past ten years, detailing what the company did right and where it went wrong. The plan that Walker would put in place would simplify the jury-rigged corporate structure, align the company's resources around its most essential lines of business, and jettison the junk that just didn't belong. The structure he envisioned would fit neatly on a single sheet of paper, so that anyone viewing it could understand in an instant how things would operate.

There was just one glaring problem that Walker couldn't get his head around. Why did Staminum shovel so much money into its alternative energy subsidiary, Greeneron, when it was so obvious the strategy wasn't working? It didn't really fit with anything else the company was doing. So why were people like Kip Stamper passionately devoted to seeing the cash burn continue? From what Walker gleaned from company publications and filings, the subsidiary was dedicated entirely to the highly risky development of alternative sources of power, with investments in everything from compressed hydrogen to the capture and sequestration of cow farts. Greeneron had made twenty-one acquisitions over the past five years, none of which were profitable, and all of which were sucking up valuable capital. Yet the acquisitions continued unabated. Was there a point at which the Stampers would give up? *Somethin' stinks about this,* Walker figured, *and it ain't just cow poots.*

"Knock, knock," a woman's voice called out cheerily from the doorway.

Walker turned to see Steady Stamper's in-house proxy, the company's notorious gossipmonger Margaret Hathaway, at his door. The Queen Bee of Staminum didn't usually buzz around the C-suite until after lunch. What in the world was she doing here now? Walker turned over the paper on which he was drawing and stood to greet Margaret. "So good of you to stop by," Walker said, summoning a forced smile. "Please have a seat."

Margaret, swathed in a black Chanel suit, a yellow-and-gray Hermes scarf, and a tinkling collection of golden necklaces and bracelets, parked herself regally in a chair at the conference table, sending a puff of Prada perfume wafting over Walker's papers. She was a corporate officer, but Walker knew she derived her power less from her formal role than from her long-time relationship with Steady Stamper, who relied on her as a messenger, gatherer of executive information, and general enforcer of the family's interests. That made her virtually untouchable, a member of Staminum's protected class, allowing her to work without a formal job description, to come and go as she pleased, attend only the meetings that interested her, and adhere to no calendar other than Steady Stamper's. Nobody besides the chairman himself could tell her what to do, and even he seemed afraid of stepping on her pointy toes. Walker had been advised before he started: regard the Queen Bee as a bug in Steady's ear. And watch out for that stinger.

"Your office looks lovely," she said, looking around at the massive display cases of grip-and-grin photos with presidents and popes, magazine covers, trophies, plaques, and other mementos behind Walker's desk. "Your glory wall is *very* impressive."

Walker turned toward the display and blushed. "Oh. Well, that's not about me, exactly."

She scoffed. "No? Looks like you're in every picture."

"It's, aw, I don't know. Just things I like to remember now and then." Walker shrugged, uncomfortable with being called out, then turned the focus away from himself. "We missed you at the Leadership Team Meeting this mornin'."

"Oh, I *am* sorry," she said, shaking her head sadly, a maneuver which failed to move a single lacquered hair in her Wintour-esque pageboy bob. "I *so* wanted to be there. The traffic on the Upper East Side was complete gridlock. What is going on in town today? I haven't seen anything like it in my life."

Walker shrugged. "Couldn't say. Haven't been out of the buildin' since six."

"You're *kidding!*"

"About what?"

"You *really* got here at six? Oh my! Up with the chickens? Is that what they say where you're from? Where is that anyway?"

"Well, if you really want to know, I was born in Kentucky and grew up in Michigan, a little steel town south of Detroit. Raised mostly by my grandmother."

"Why, that's lovely. I just adore Lake… oh, what is it? Lake… *Winnebago!* That's it, isn't it?"

"Naw," Walker said, shaking his head. "Nothin' like that in Michigan I know of. There's one in Wisconsin."

"I know. Lake Woebegon."

"That's Minnesota. And it's make-believe."

"Oh, I don't know." She waved the idea away. "I was out that way once as a child. A funeral for an aunt or an uncle or somebody. All those states run together for me. Especially the ones that start with 'I.' Anyway, I certainly wish I'd gotten here at six. When I realized I would be late for your little powwow, I nearly got out of the car and ran down Fifth Avenue, but I don't think these shoes would have gotten me very far," she said with a chuckle, nodding toward her high-heeled Jimmy Choos and turning a shapely ankle in Walker's direction. "The last thing in the *world* I wanted was to miss your first meeting."

"Here's the good news, Margaret," Walker said, leaning across the table. "There's another meetin' next week. And the week after that. And every week from here on out. Really important for you to be there and show support for your teammates."

"Teammates?"

"Yes, ma'am. We need everyone on board to grab an oar and pull in the same direction if we're goin' to get this big ol' boat turned around."

Margaret looked as if Walker had told her he was undergoing treatment for head lice. "Wouldn't you know? I'm in London *all* next week. Steady needs me to check out venues for a board meeting next autumn. I was thinking of a dinner at something very classic, like Rules. It's more than two hundred years old, but then, so are some of our directors." She laughed at her little funny. "Do you have a favorite place you like to go in London?"

"Honestly, I'm fine with a half-sandwich and a cup of soup. But I'm sure you'll pick out somethin' nice," Walker said with a tight smile. He slapped both hands on the table. "Hate to rush you, Margaret, but I've got a deadline to meet. You want to talk to Heidi and get on my calendar?"

"Of course," she said, remaining firmly seated. "But this will only take a minute."

Walker sighed. "What's on your mind?"

Margaret looked over her shoulder toward the door, then back to Walker. "I heard you really shook things up in the meeting this morning."

"Aw, I don't know about that," he said.

"Well, they're rather shaken *and* stirred out there. And I just want to say: good!"

"Good?"

"Oh, yes! We need this, *desperately*. I've been saying for years that this company had better wake up. Tom, your late, not-so-great predecessor, just didn't get it. He was an arrogant idiot, if you ask me. I have no idea what went through that man's head. I tried to tell him: '*Steady's not happy,*' '*Steady's worried,*' '*Steady needs to know what you're up to.*' But did Tom listen? *No!* And where is he now? I have no idea. All I can say is, 'good riddance.' He never fit. I don't know why Steady hired him in the first place. It was a mistake and I told him so right from the beginning."

"Well, Margaret, I suppose that's why I'm here."

She clapped her hands together excitedly. "Ex-*act*-ly! And that's why I am your biggest cheerleader. Not only do I want you to succeed in this job, I desperately need you to succeed. I have virtually all my life savings invested in this company." She studied a fingernail. "Well, some of them, anyway." She turned back to him. "Regardless, you can understand why I'm concerned."

Walker looked puzzled. "About what?"

"Just some of the buzz I'm picking up in the office. People talk, you know."

"I do know. It goes with the territory," he said, checking his watch again. *Three minutes to pee...*

"Look. I know you have to go," she said.

"You have no idea."

"Can I just offer a little friendly advice? If you're going to rattle the cages around here, make sure you've got the ringmaster upstairs to back you up," she said, pointing to the ceiling in the general direction of the chairman's office. "You know what I mean? People, especially people named Stamper, are used to running to the chairman whenever they're unhappy. And, unfortunately, he can be a bit of a sucker for a sob story. I can hear them now, 'Walker's a big meany. He's making me do—I don't know—my *job*.'" She made a face to suggest she was offended by the thought of such treachery. "I suggest you keep Steady apprised of what you're doing, preferably in advance, especially when it comes to anything involving the family. He may not show up at the office very often, but I guarantee you, he's paying attention. And, believe me, he hears *everything*."

"Imagine that," Walker said, drily.

"It's *true!*"

"Well, I've got to be honest with you, Margaret. Based on the results we shared this mornin', I'm amazed that anyone has time to complain. We have so much to do."

She leaned in, coyly, batting her eyes. "I'm not saying anyone's complaining, per se, Walker. I'm just saying you'll want to tread lightly as you organize things. I'd hate to see you step in doo-doo, and believe me, there's plenty of it around here. You don't even see it, and then, *oopsie!*"

"Is there somethin' in particular you have in mind?"

"Let's just say there are certain lines of business that the family is very fond of. Steady doesn't necessarily like them or even understand why they're part of an energy company—I mean, why do we own a company that harvests *seaweed*, for God's sake? But Steady tolerates them to keep the peace. You know, the younger generations are very eco-savvy. They don't like all this dirty business around gas and oil and coal and so forth. You can expect them to make quite a fuss if you make any moves that involve their pet projects."

"Like what?"

"Like Greeneron, number one."

"What if it doesn't fit the company?"

She swept the idea away with a flourish of her hand. "Doesn't matter. There are just some things you probably shouldn't touch, and that includes some of the assets from the olden days. Like that stupid Trans-Pakistan Pipeline. It was developed by Steady's father. I know it doesn't make money anymore, but it holds a great deal of sentimental value to the family. Steady went to Quetta with his father when he was a child on their one company trip together and, well, I guess they bonded and it was a special moment or something."

"I can understand he loved his father. But who loves a pipeline?"

"Walker," she said, leaning forward, "please understand me. I'm not saying it makes sense. I'm just telling you it's the way they *think*. They regard the company as their personal property. That's why they get first dibs on the corporate jets, all the tickets to the Giants games, all the say on what's on the menu in the cafeteria and the kind of coffee that's served in the pantries. This is their baby. It's personal to them. It's like a second home. And when someone tries to move things around, look out. They're very proud people, and they believe in a traditional hierarchy. Any threat to the established order is unsettling, especially when it comes from an outsider—which, I'm sorry, darling, but you are and you always will be. That's why you need to go *slowly*."

Walker peered at Margaret. How much of this B.S. was he supposed to take? "Well, here's the thing about goin' slowly, Margaret. They've been goin' slowly out of business for a long time. If things don't change, the pace is gonna pick up and they'll start goin' bust a whole lot faster. And then it will be over. I'm sure Mr. Stamper understands we can't keep doing the same old, same old and expect a different result. That's the definition of stupidity."

"I believe it's 'insanity.'"

"That, too. This company won't survive."

"You need to survive first, my dear," she said. "You're not going to do anyone any good if you're fired."

Walker laughed. "Fired? Don't you think they ought to wait at least until I clean up this big ol' mess?"

"All I'm saying is, be careful. I'm sure you know some of the family members don't actually show up for work. I mean, take Fritz Stamper. Useless, right? Flunked out of Brown. Had a baby with his girlfriend when he was still married to his second wife. In and out of rehab. The works. Hasn't been seen around here since February because he's too busy cavorting with supermodels in Ibiza. But Steady gave him this job to provide him with some structure, some sense of *purpose*. It's the only hope Steady has that Fritz will do something productive with his life. I wouldn't push him too hard to come to your little meeting every week."

Walker bristled. He'd finally heard enough. "Alright. Let's get somethin' straight here, Margaret." His eyes narrowed and he leaned forward. "That little meetin', as you put it, is how we run the business. You can't be on the leadership team if you don't attend. That includes Fritz. And, just so we're clear that nobody's exempt, Margaret, it also includes you."

Margaret's mask of collegiality fell like a failed souffle. "Walker. Dear. I don't *do* meetings."

Walker stood, dismissing her. "And I don't do payroll for people who fail to show up for work."

She laughed bitterly as she stood, glowering at Walker. "You do realize I report *directly* to the chairman."

Walker nodded. "You're also a member of the management team, and you have an important role to play. I need you at the table, deeply involved in our leadership decisions, so you can understand our strategy and help us effectively convey it in our conversations with others."

"Or... *what*, exactly?"

"I'm sure a person with your skills could certainly find another job, although I honestly don't know what that would be in my organization. I don't need a messenger service. I don't need career counselin'. And I don't need anyone to tell me that I should somehow fix this company without makin' big changes. It can't be done."

She looked him up and down. "You may want to advise the chairman," she said, tartly. "Better he hears that from you sooner rather than later."

Heidi appeared at the door. "Walker," she said. "Mr. Stamper's calling for you. Line One."

Margaret smirked. "As I said, Walker. He hears everything."

7. GOODNESS GREATNESS

From a sofa in the lounge, Dr. Kristi Kramer locked the approaching Robbie Crowe squarely in her sights. *Lasso this little lost lamb,* she told herself, *and she'd hold the Crowe Power Company in her consulting stable for years.*

She rose to greet him as he moved in for air kisses. She held both his hands in hers and pulled them close, between her breasts. "I can't tell you what a pleasure it is to meet you," she said, purring the word "pleasure" as if she were narrating a late-night TV commercial for sex toys.

He took a seat on an adjacent easy chair, so close to her that their knees touched. He inhaled her lovely perfume, luxuriated in the soothing tones of her voice, and let his eyes wash over her like a bucket of warm sudsy water. That this highly regarded author and counselor would greet him so enthusiastically was surely a compliment of some sort, wasn't it? An endorsement of his purging Walker, the supposedly great CEO? Or maybe it was support for his magnificent green vision, such as it was.

"So," Robbie said, as they clinked glasses of Pinot Noir from the Russian River Valley, "how did we ever convince you to join us out here for our conference?"

"Oh, stop. It didn't take a whole lot of convincing," she said. *A hundred thousand dollars for three days' work certainly helped!* "I'm sure Tim must have told you: I don't normally work with energy companies. I mean, I really don't believe in fossil fuels. But I've always thought your company was, you know. *Different.*"

"Really?" Robbie said, settling back dreamily into the cushions of his chair. "Why?"

"Because of you."

Me? Dr. Kristi Kramer wants to work with our company because of me? Well, now! Robbie was dizzied by the thought. "You're putting me on."

"Don't be silly. It's true! I heard your TED Talk a couple of years ago—you know, where you spoke about your amazing vision of a carbon-free future—and I must say, I was blown away. You, my friend, *get it*."

Robbie sighed. "Can you convince my management team of that? They think I'm from outer space."

"That's exactly why I'm here," she said, putting her hand on his knee and looking deeply into his eyes. "I want to help get them into your orbit. That means we need to bring them up here, with you." She held a flat hand at eye level. "Know what I mean?"

"Yes! Totally! We are so on the same page," Robbie said. He ran the palm of his hand over his forehead. What a relief to hear her talk this way! "So many of these guys are dull, linear thinkers. They can't see any farther than their spreadsheets and PowerPoints. 'Boil more oil. Pipe more gas. Burn more coal.' I look at them and think, 'Guys. Stop for a second. Ever heard of, like, solar power? Wind power? *Helloooo.*' We need to move not only in new directions, but in new *dimensions*." Coincidentally, a portion of him was doing that at this very minute.

"Oh my god! I *love* that," she squealed. "You are soooo profound! And so right. They are not on your level." She reached over and lightly tapped his temple. "We need to make all those brilliant thoughts in that noggin of yours clear enough for the simple folk to understand. This is going to be a *riot!*"

"Or," he said, his voice dropping, "how about this: a *revolution.*"

"*Si! Si! Si!*" she exclaimed. "*Viva! Viva Robbie Crowe!*"

Robbie scanned the growing crowd of people milling about the lounge for a waiter and signaled for more wine. "So tell me," he said, turning his attention back to the divine Dr. Kramer. "How'd you get where you are?"

She sat back in full seduction mode, batted her long false eyelashes, and fiddled with the pendant between her breasts. "You mean sitting here with the chairman of the Crowe Power Company? Lordy! I wish I knew! I mean, if you were to tell me twenty years ago, when I was a divorced mother of two young children eking out a living by day and going to school by night that I would be here today, with this, this *genius* of a business leader, I would say you're absolutely crazy. But here I am and there you are."

Did she just wink at him? Robbie was absolutely dazzled by this woman. He'd read, or at least skimmed, several of her books. Well, the dust jackets anyway.

Kinda got the point. He was generally familiar with *Great Halls of Hire*, the seminal book about corporate virtue as the basis for creating wonderful places to work for millennials and Gen Xers, and *Getting Real—and Spectacular,* which was all about helping companies pretend they were authentic, or something.

"What did you do before this?" he asked.

"You mean, before I became a missionologist? Robbie Crowe, let me tell you what I did: I cleaned houses. Waited tables. Sold time shares in Mexico. Ran call centers for a plaintiffs' law firm. Whatever it took, I did it. And you know why? Because I had a *mission:* to take care of my babies in any way I could. No matter what I did—whether it was slingin' cheeseburgers or signin' up retirees in Cleveland for condos in Cancun—I had this incredible sense of mission. That's what we have to find here. What's the mission for your flock? What makes everyone passionate about Crowe Power and gets 'em to jump out of bed in the morning sayin', 'I can't *wait* to get to work?' We need people who are jazzed about Crowe, people who are driven. We want them running through walls for you."

Robbie nodded vigorously, although he was having trouble tracking what she said. His sense of mission at the moment had nothing to do with Crowe Power and everything to do with Dr. Kristi Kramer. "I couldn't agree more," he said. "You and I—wow. We're going to be a terrific team."

She blushed. This was going to be more financially rewarding than she thought. And maybe she could squeeze another book out of it and make even more money. She could be set for life! "You are *so* sweet," she cooed, running her fingers through her thick hair and flopping it all over to the other side. "Now. Tell me all about you. How did you get to be the supreme leader of this ginormous company? It must have been an awful lot of work."

Robbie looked at her incredulously, his eyes welling, as he struggled for words. He said, quietly, "Thank you."

"For what?"

"Nobody—and I mean nobody—has ever asked me that. They see my name and think, 'You're a Crowe. Of course you got the top job.' Like it was just handed to me or something. They have no clue as to how difficult it was and how hard I had to scratch and claw and fight my way to the top."

She sipped her wine, folded one Pilates-toned leg over the other, and lightly bounced it up and down. "Tell me about it."

"Well, when I started out," Robbie said gravely, "everyone was against me. I had just finished my MBA at Harvard, and they said, 'Let's throw this kid in the deep end and see if he can swim.' So they sent me to Aruba to work at our refinery."

"Aruba doesn't sound too tough."

"Well, no. But I had no experience in a refinery. And they knew that, the bastards. So I go down there and they've got this grizzled old prick, JR Flagemon—I'll never forget that guy. He was in about his hundredth year as the superintendent and I can see he hates me from 'hello.' First thing he says, 'Don't touch any fucking buttons, Junior.' I say, 'What do you mean?' He says, 'You meddle around in this plant and you could blow the whole island to kingdom come.' I said, 'Okay. What am I supposed to do?' He says, 'Go to the beach.' I thought, 'Fine. Fuck 'em. I'll never go in again.' And I didn't. And that's how I spent my first six months at Crowe."

Kristi wanted to laugh but stifled it. She patted the back of Robbie's hand. "How did you ever recover?"

"I made up my mind right then and there that I wasn't gonna take shit anymore. When I got back to the States, I marched straight to the CEO's office. The assistant said, 'You can't go in there.' And I said, 'Oh yeah? Watch me.'"

"*Wow.* That takes some serious brass," Kristi said.

Robbie nodded. *Damn right.* "So I go in and I say, 'You know what? This is bullshit. I didn't work my ass off in grad school to do some fake job. I want real work.' And Dad said, 'Okay. Fine. If that's the way you want it, you're gonna get it.' And they made me a Vice President and put me in charge of our Washington lobbying office."

"That had to be a huge challenge. I mean, lobbying for fossil fuels. Especially when that's not what you're about *at all.*"

"It was freaking brutal. Breakfasts, coffees, lunches, receptions, dinners. Morning to night. This club. That club. Handing out checks like coupons for a dollar off on… whatever people get coupons for. Almost never got a break to go bike riding or skateboarding. Worse, I had to argue for policies I didn't even believe in, like more lax pollution laws. I didn't know why then—and I don't know why now—we can't be the 'and' company."

Kristi made a rolling gesture with her hand. "Elaborate, please."

Robbie struggled to remember. His head was swirling. "It's like I was just telling Digby, our general counsel." *Shit. What was I telling him?* "I was saying I, I want us to be green *and* profitable. Global *and* nimble. Or maybe it was agile."

"Oh, who cares," Kristi said, dismissing his confusion with a furrowed brow. "Keep going. This is good!" she said, flopping her hair back again to the other side.

"Decisive *and*—" He paused and blew out his cheeks. "I'm not sure."

"It doesn't matter," Kristi said. "You know what I'm thinking?"

He dropped his voice to a growl. "I hope it's the same thing I'm thinking."

She raised a finger and put it to his lips and looked deeply into his eyes. "Hold that thought. Let me tell you mine first."

Robbie's heart was swinging on a trapeze, careening wildly through his rib cage and thumping off the sides. "I'm all ears."

"I'm thinking I would like to feature you in my next book, *Goodness Greatness.*"

Ha! Now *there's* a thought! Goodness Greatness! At last, somebody understood him! "Am I the goodness or the greatness?

"Both."

"Oh my god! I love it! Fill me in."

"Well, it's about how a few enlightened companies, led by those extremely rare visionary leaders, like you, pursue greatness through goodness. See? My working theory is that it's not enough to produce a widget or a barrel of nails or a box of chocolates. You need to produce these things for the right reasons and in the right way. That's how history will judge you. And, here's the best part: in the end, you achieve far more than you ever anticipated, financially and socially, blazing trails to go places no one has ever gone before."

"I like the sound of that."

"Once we get through this conference and we start making Crowe Power into this incredibly good company, and you are well on your way to being acknowledged by one and all far and wide as a truly great corporate leader, I could *easily* see you on the cover of the book, a shining example of and a beacon for the principles of higher corporate purpose. And that, in turn, could be your platform for... everything."

"Like what? What are you thinking?"

"You could keynote at Davos. Send a public letter to all stakeholders extolling, I don't know, let's call them *The Goodness Principles.* There could be more TED

Talks, and op-eds in the *New York Times*, and podcasts, and seminars at Harvard and Oxford and Cambridge. Oh! And how about this? Do you know how much I would treasure having you as an honorary member of the faculty at the Mission Institute for Higher Corporate Purpose down in Chapel Hill?"

Robbie fell back in his chair. Dr. Kristi Kramer had arrived at exactly the right time in his life. For the moment, all his doubts were gone, his own sense of purpose reignited by the sparks flying in his mind and the raging fire in his loins. Wouldn't a book like *Goodness Greatness* flip the bird to Walker and all the doubters and heretics who said he would never make the grade? *How do you like me now, suckas!* And what would they think when they heard he was speaking at Davos, telling all the other big thinkers how to put good intentions into action? "I've gotta tell you," Robbie said. "I'm gobsmacked."

Kristi looked with pride at her fresh catch. She'd pursued a dozen executives for features in her book and got nothing but vague promises to get back to her. There was no such problem here. Robbie Crowe was the biggest fish she'd had on the line in months. Now she just had to haul him into the boat. "So what do you say?" she purred. "Want to do it?"

"Well, yeah. Of course!"

"Then let's go."

"You mean *now*?"

"Honey, once I've got a plan of action, it's time to stop all the thinkin' and start the *doin'*."

8.   GOLD COASTING

A black Cadillac Escalade exited the HOV lane of the Long Island Expressway with Walker in the back seat, anticipating his meeting with his boss, Staminum chairman Steadman "Steady" Stamper, the company's biggest shareholder. If even half of what Margaret Hathaway said was true, Steady would be the biggest obstacle to fixing the company. It was time to find out why and map out a way around him.

As they slalomed through traffic toward Exit 40, Walker removed the phone from his satchel and tapped Moe Klinger from the top of his list of recent calls. Moe, who rose from poverty in Brooklyn to become one of the world's most successful hedge fund managers, was Walker's steadfast patron for good reason. Once Moe took a position in an underperforming company such as Staminum, he needed a leader like Walker to help turn its fortunes and drive up its value.

Moe listened quietly as Walker recounted his conversation with Margaret.

"I have to tell you, Moe, I'm at a loss."

"So's the company," Moe said, flatly. "Eight quarters in a row. They're burning more cash than coal."

"Does Steady want me to fix the company or not?"

"Personally, I don't give a damn what he wants. You're there because I want you there and I was going to run a new slate of directors against him unless he hired you. And he knew I'd win," Moe said. "It's not terribly surprising he sent in one of his flying monkeys to deliver a message. And make no mistake: That message came directly from him. It was a test. He wants to see if you're as much of a pushover as the last guy they stuck in there. What was his attitude like when he called you?"

"Couldn't have been more pleasant. Just asked how things were goin'."

"Here's your answer: 'They're going great. Now back the fuck up.'"

"Honestly, Moe, I'm not lookin' for a fight. I just want to get this thing turned around. This is on me now. And I don't have time to slow dance with the chairman. I told him I had a few things to discuss and he invited me out to see him in a few weeks. I told him it couldn't wait that long. I'm on my way there now."

"Going to The Castle?"

"Is that what they call his house?"

"It's not just a house, Walker. It's more like a medieval resort. Do you joust?"

"Not lately," Walker said.

"Then keep your mace club handy, just in case," Moe said. "You might need to clock him if he doesn't listen. Look, I agree with you. We don't have time for fun and games here. He's handed you a big bag of money for a reason, alright? He needs you more than you need him, and deep down, I suspect he knows that whether he lets on or not. So don't ask for permission to change things. *Tell* him what you intend to do, and say you expect his support to keep the rest of his family in line. He may think he's got a leg up, but anatomically speaking, you've got him by the short hairs. Remember that. And if push comes to shove-it-up-your-ass—in an upper-crusty sort of way, of course—I can work things with the rest of the board. I've run a coup before. I can do it again."

The driver exited the freeway and snaked through a series of towns toward Oyster Bay. He brought the Escalade to a stop at the iron-gated entrance to Steady's Gold Coast estate, pressed a button on the intercom, and exchanged words with security. Massive electronic gates slowly swept open, inviting them onto the manicured grounds. The SUV rolled up a winding oak-lined road to the front door of a palatial limestone mansion on a bluff overlooking Long Island Sound.

Walker exited the back seat and stretched his legs on the cobblestone drive. He inhaled deeply from the salty air drifting in from the sound and walked to the front door. There he was greeted by Waldo, Steadman's inscrutable butler, who ushered him in through a foyer and a long corridor to a two-story library and offered him a beverage. As Walker awaited Steady's arrival, he perused the stacks, stopping at a shelf of presidential biographies. He pulled out a massive thousand-page tome on Theodore Roosevelt and flipped through the contents.

Someday, after this Staminum job was finished, he might find time to read a book like this...

"Greetings!" a voice called cheerily.

Walker turned to see Steady, as he had been known since childhood, enter the library in his tennis whites, a towel draped around his neck, and no sign of perspiration. His silver hair plugs were aligned neatly across his scalp like sentries, repelling the advance of a prominent forehead. At 69, the man's lack of facial lines, bags or wrinkles made Walker understand why Steady was a perfectly appropriate nickname. Life on this side of the moat was on a very even keel.

Walker purposely retained the deferential title from their first meeting months earlier and offered a handshake. "Mr. Stamper," he said, smiling broadly. "What a pleasure to see you again."

Steady declined to suggest Walker drop the formality and call *him* by his first name, given the obvious social disparity. "Walker, my dear fellow," he said. "Sorry to keep you waiting. We were engaged in a rather vigorous tiebreaker."

"Did you win?"

"That can't be a serious question," Steady said with a hearty laugh. "I was playing my personal trainer, who apparently concluded there was greater valor in falling on her racket than taking down a poor old man."

"A wise decision, I suspect."

"She's keeping her job another week," Steady said. He nodded toward the book. "I see you're getting reacquainted with Mr. Roosevelt—a very good friend of the family. His estate is just up the road, don't you know."

Walker shook his head. "I didn't."

"Didn't what?"

"Didn't know."

Steady squinted at Walker. "I don't follow."

"You said, 'don't you know.' I didn't know."

Steady absolved him for whatever infraction he was confessing to with a lockjaw smile and a hearty clap on the back, and they walked slowly toward a seating area. "It's quite alright," he said. "You'll catch on."

Walker, settling into a club chair, looked up at the walls of shelves. "This is bigger than a branch of the New York Public Library. I could spend a few days in here, just browsing through the shelves."

"Oh, you'd have to take more time than that to catch me," Steady said grandly. "I've read every one of these books, many of them twice."

"That is absolutely incredible," Walker said. *Why, Steady couldn't have worked a full day in his life!* "How in the world did you manage that?"

Steady shrugged, almost modestly. "You know, Walker, I like to think it comes from all the old-fashioned values considered so passé these days. Commitment. Discipline. Intellectual rigor." With a slight wave of his hand, Steady brushed aside any further inventory of his virtues for the moment. "Please. Let's talk about you. How are you settling in?"

"I'm just fine. Not sure the troops are. As you may have heard, I'm rufflin' a few feathers."

"Yes, indeed," Steady said with a chuckle. "So a little bird told me."

"If it's the same little bird I think it is, her feathers might have been twisted a bit, too."

"I never give up my sources," Steady said. "Let's just say I've known everyone on the team down there for a long, long time. They're not used to change. But, let's face it, Walker: we need somebody to stir up things. That's why you're here, right? Give 'em all a good swift kick in the slats? We pay them damn good money." He laid his head back on the pillowy club chair. "Nobody gets to loaf."

"I appreciate that, Mr. Stamper. It's important to know I have your support. I need to move fast and things could get a bit rough."

"Oh, don't I know it. Management requires tough decisions, and our people are just going to have to accept that things are going to be different," Steady said. "Of course, the changes have to be strategic. They need to make sense with the long view in mind. We can't just go off willy-nilly."

"Certainly not," Walker said.

Waldo entered with a tall glass of iced tea and placed it on a monogrammed leather coaster next to Walker. Steady regarded the beverage with a disdain bordering on disgust. "Good God, man. Don't you want something stronger than that?" he asked. He looked at his Rolex Yacht-Master watch. "It's several minutes past five. How about a stiff belt? Scotch for both of us, Waldo."

Waldo scurried off as fast as his stiff stork legs could carry him while Steady parked his elbows on the armrests and tapped his fingertips together in front of his chest. With a rip-roaring tennis victory under his Burberry belt and the company he was charged with overseeing destined to rise under new management, Steady was the very picture of self-satisfaction. "I must say, I'm quite pleased with our share price," Steady said, bobbing his head up and down. "Twenty-two percent! We haven't seen a jump that high in some time. *Very* impressive."

Walker shrugged. "I wouldn't put much stock in that."

Steady laughed. "I have nothing *but* stock in that! They're betting on you, old boy. Just as I am. What do you say?" He leaned forward, clutched Walker's knee and grinned at him. "Are we ready to make a run at Crowe Power? I'd love nothing more than to take down those smug bastards. They've been a thorn in our side forever. My great grandfather couldn't stand them, and I can stand them even less."

Walker regarded Steady incredulously. Did he have any idea how badly Staminum had slipped on his watch? While Steady was holed up in his castle reading books and beating the help at tennis, his unsupervised executives were reenacting *Lord of the Flies* back in Midtown. "We need to take over Staminum first."

Steady looked genuinely befuddled. "Say that again?"

"Mr. Stamper, we're a long way from fightin' shape. The company's in no condition to take on anyone until we get our own house in order."

As Waldo reappeared, Stamper looked like he'd been told they'd just run out of Grey Poupon. "I knew things weren't quite up to snuff, but—seriously. That bad?" Steady snatched a Lalique crystal tumbler of Dalwhinnie scotch from Waldo's silver tray and hurriedly clinked glasses with Walker. "To your good health." He sipped his whiskey and sighed, "Give it to me straight."

Walker summarized his evaluation: billions of dollars squandered on money-losing acquisitions in new technologies, a disengaged leadership team, and a structure that allowed autonomous fiefdoms around the world to do as they pleased with zero accountability. There were no economies of scale, rewards for success, or punishments for failure. The company seemed to have been running on autopilot for many years and it had strayed far off course. "The fact is, Mr. Stamper, our company's been adrift a long time."

Steady flushed red, looking more embarrassed than angry. Clearly, he didn't miss the point: this was an indictment of his leadership. He held up his index finger to stop Walker from speaking further and cocked an ear toward the hallway outside the library. Hearing the voice of a woman nearby, he said, "Let's take this outside, shall we?"

He briskly escorted Walker by the elbow through French doors to a long veranda at the crest of a hill and guided him down the brick steps to a terrace and a pair of Adirondack chairs under an ivory canopy. In the distance, over the sycamore trees, the summer sun sparkled off the sound while sailboats glided between Oyster Bay and Connecticut. "I don't need Alice overhearing our conversation," Steady said. "Things could be... misinterpreted. And I need to manage the messages to the rest of the family about your activities very carefully."

"I'm sure there are many sensitivities," Walker said.

"You have no idea," Steady said, with a sigh. As Waldo set two fresh scotches on the table between them, Steady nabbed his second drink with the speed of a frog snaring a passing fly. He gulped it down, blinked hard, turned back to Walker, and burped softly. "This is all very sobering."

"Sorry to be the bearer of bad tidings," Walker said. "The good news is that we can fix it."

With a shrug of his shoulders, Steady dismissed the idea that "we" were involved. After all, what are hired hands for but to lift the burden of labor and responsibility off more exalted people like Steady, freeing them for sports and scotch and books and whatever moves them at any moment in time? "I'm sure you'll figure it out," he said, looking away.

"As a matter of fact, I have," Walker said. "I'd like to share my plan with you right now."

Startled, Steady sat up straight. "Walker, please. I'm sure you're a wizard. Your reputation as a turnaround specialist precedes you. But you've been on the job for less than two weeks," he said. "With all due respect to your considerable talents, I don't see how you can possibly produce a credible plan that quickly.

Staminum's been part of my life for nearly seventy years and, I'll confess, I still don't understand it all. There's enormous complexity in a company like ours."

"Right," Walker said. "We need to reduce that complexity and streamline the company so it can be managed properly, with clear lines of accountability." He reached into his satchel, pulled out the single sheet of paper, and handed it to Steady.

Steady looked at it, then back to Walker. "This is it?"

For the first time, Walker noted a little tremble in Steady's hand as he fumbled with his reading glasses and peered down his nose at the array of purple circles, lines, triangles, squiggles and handwriting scrawl. He turned the paper around several times to make sure he wasn't seeing it upside down. At last, he put the paper on the footstool in front of him. "I can't make heads nor tails of this. What am I looking at?"

Walker used the capped end of his purple marker to point out elements of his plan, which entailed closing operations, selling subsidiaries, and focusing their management and their capital on a few essential objectives. As Steady realized where this was going, he looked up at Walker with alarm.

"You want to sell *Greeneron?*"

"First order of business."

Steady shook his head. "You're touching the third rail here, Mr. Hope."

Mister Hope? That's a switch. "Why is that?"

"It's our hedge," Steady said. "Fossil fuels aren't going to be around forever. We need to build a sustainable future. There's no way of knowing yet which new technologies will make the most sense for the future. It could be one, or two, or three, or a combination. That's why we bought all the start-ups we could get our hands on."

"But—" How to put this delicately? "They're not businesses, Mr. Stamper. They're more like ideas. Science projects."

"Sci... *what?*"

"I could understand placin' a couple of high-risk bets. Every company needs a moonshot or two. But we've got twenty-one. And every one of these—from microbes and methane to tidal turbines—loses money that we don't have. We're takin' cash away from our profitable operations to fund Greeneron, which might never pay off."

Steady sat up straight and wriggled his neck as if he were getting ready to go the next round in a prize fight. "I certainly understand what you're saying, Walker. But you need to understand something here, too," Steady said. "Our family was instrumental in the development of the energy industry more than a century ago. It's partly because of us—four generations of Stampers—that the world built an unhealthy dependency on oil and gas and coal and all these other dirty fuels mined from the earth." He made a face as if he smelled something bad. "Now we have a chance to rectify that, to take responsibility for the consequences of the threat to our world." He stubbed a finger into the armrest of his chair. "It's up to us to find new ways to reduce the world's dependency on fossil fuels."

Walker fought the temptation to roll his eyes. "Yeah. Okay. I mean, I've seen the commercials on Sunday mornin' TV."

As Waldo appeared with more drinks, Steady fixed Walker with an icy stare. The impudence he saw in this man was breathtaking! "This is more than public relations, Walker. These young people in the fifth and sixth generations of our family feel very strongly about this. And I must tell you: they've opened my eyes. All it takes is for one of these 'science projects,' as you put it, to take off. We could define a new way of living. Not only can we save the company, we can save our Earth. Think about that, why don't you."

Walker nearly burst out laughing. This was the same serving of sky pie that Robbie had liked to dish out. What was it with these rich families and their guilt over how they made their pile? Didn't their companies provide *some* useful product or service? All this pearl clutching must salve their consciences as they sit behind the gates of massive estates with the carbon footprints of a small town. "Mr. Stamper, if you've got a better idea, please let me know what it is. Otherwise, somethin's gotta give, here—the quarterly dividend, or the share buyback program or all this capital gettin' sucked up by Greeneron. We can't fund everything. Not when we're losin' so much money."

Walker realized Stamper wasn't paying any attention. He was lost in a distant world. Walker followed his gauzy gaze to the hill, where a lovely young woman in yoga pants, a sports bra, and a bare midriff laid out a mat and began a series of elaborate stretching exercises. Spotting Stamper watching her, she offered a smile and a wave, then spread her feet apart and bent at the waist, touching her head to the ground and casting a moonbeam in Stamper's direction.

"Elyse," Stamper said, with a sigh. "My personal trainer. A very fine young woman."

"I can see that." *Why, she's not even as old as your scotch,* Walker mused.

"I think she went easy on me today."

"She doesn't look any worse for wear."

"Oh, she broke a little sweat. See there? Just enough to make her glisten in the sunlight..." He snapped to. "Alright. You lost me for a moment. I'm going to need time to think about all this, Walker. You can't just spring it on me as a *fait accompli*. There's a good deal to consider here. Alice and I are heading to Europe tomorrow for three weeks. We'll talk about it when I get back." He rose to his feet. "That will also give you some time to reconsider some of these... suggestions. Then maybe you can get back to me with a better plan."

Walker stood and squared his shoulders with Steady's. "A better plan? No, no. With all due respect, sir, these are not 'suggestions.' This *is* the better plan. And these are actions needed to save your company from goin' down the tubes. I've got things to do in the next three weeks that can't wait for you to get back. If we don't move quickly to staunch the bleedin', you may not have a company to come back to."

Steady sighed. "Alright," he said. "You can move ahead with—" he flicked his hand as if he were dispatching a booger, "—all this other stuff on your paper there. But don't you dare touch Greeneron. You'll have a war on your hands that you can't win."

Walker bit his tongue. *Wanna bet?*

9. BOOBY TRAP

Robbie and Dr. Kristi Kramer were barely over the threshold of the Presidential Suite when they began to molt. A silk scarf fluttered to the vestibule floor. A kicked-off loafer crash-landed with a clatter on the glass coffee table in the living room. A helicoptering thong touched down on a lampshade, while Robbie, shedding his slacks, staggered like a potato-sack racer toward the bedroom, striving for the finish line.

They tumbled onto the king bed in a ravenous heap, clutching, grabbing, pawing, pinching, and kissing with manic urgency. Robbie, dumped in recent weeks by both his mistress and his wife, had never been more ready. Clearly, he had already blinded Kristi with the brilliance of his mind. Now he quickly considered how he could further impress in bed, mentally turning pages through his well-thumbed catalog of astonishing techniques. In a premature miscalculation, he decided to skip the preliminary events and go straight to the finals, rolling on top of her. Kristi, however, had him, quite literally, by the balls.

"I'm sorry," she whispered in his ear, "but we can't go any further."

"*What?*" Robbie said. "Why not?"

"I don't do this sort of thing without a commitment."

Robbie was dumbfounded. "I'm in no position to make a commitment right now. I'm still married."

She kissed the right side of his neck. "You have budget, right?"

He was having difficulty following. "Budget? At the company? Of course. What does that have to do..." he trailed off. *Jesus.* She was holding his boys for *ransom!*

"You do realize I run a business," she said.

"Yes, of course, as do I. But... you're driving a really hard bargain."

She smiled and grasped his southern peninsula. "So it seems."

"Okay. What are we talking about here?"

"Consulting retainer. Three years. Fifty thousand a month."

"Seriously?" Robbie said. "That's... almost two million dollars."

She cooed, "You don't think I'm worth it?"

"I'm not saying that."

"Consider the possibilities, Robbie. You and me? Together? We could do so much *good* and so much *great.* For the company. For the country. For the *world.*"

Robbie's idea of greatness at the moment was focused more locally. "Can we talk about it later?"

"*No,*" she pronounced. "We need a deal before we move on. But I tell you what. Because I like you and I believe in you so much, and I want you to be recognized for the incredible genius that you are, I'll give you my special friends-and-family discount."

"What's that?"

"One point five million, even."

Robbie rolled off her and on to his back. "I can't believe we have to go over this stuff right now."

She reached an arm across his chest. "This *stuff*? Robbie, darlin'. We're talkin' about my *livelihood* here. What kind of woman do you think I am?"

He was getting a pretty good idea. "Okay. Fine. *Fine.* Say I can find the money somewhere. What does that get me?"

"Access."

"To what?"

"Well, all my ideas, for one thing." She reached down again between his legs and grabbed a hold of Little Robbie, who was all grown up now. "And I've got lots of good ones."

"Your first one's okay."

"I *knew* you'd appreciate it." She slowly slid down his body and buried her head in his lap. "Tell me if this works for you, too."

Robbie let out a long sigh. "You've got me licked."

Just as quickly as Kristi went down, she popped back up. "Not entirely," she said. She moved on top of him, straddled her legs around him, grabbed the top the headboard, and waggled her breasts in his face. "Some services are *a la carte.*"

"Like what?"

"Like *Goodness Greatness.* The publicity you're going to get is priceless. You know how much other companies would pay for prime placement in a best-seller like this? Gazillions. And if I offered them the cover, too? Why... it would be in the kajillions!"

Robbie was wearing down. "How much are you charging me?"

"Another one-five."

"Three million total?"

"It ain't cheap, Robbie. And neither am I."

"Of course not," Robbie said. "I would never say you were. It's just that at this particular moment, I don't happen to give a fuck."

"No, sir! And you won't until you and I have an agreement in principle." She whapped the side of his face with her breasts. "Do—" She swung back the other way. *Whap.* "We—" And again. *Whap.* "Have—" And again. *Whap.* "A—" *Whap.* "Deal?"

Good lord! Had Robbie been in an accident and the airbags deployed? It took a moment to get his bearings, but he recognized further resistance was futile. Who knows how she might abuse him next? He held her by the side, rolled her onto her back and smoothly entered into a mutual agreement. "I'm all in."

"Yes you are!" she said, as he further pressed his point. "Yes. Yes. *Yes!*"

* * *

Robbie donned one of the hotel's monogrammed robes and staggered into the kitchen, searching for something to nibble on besides Kristi's ear. He found a massive fruit basket on the counter and dug through the grapes and oranges to find an energy bar. Hmm... acorns, vegan caramel, and hay. That had to be healthy, right? He tore open the wrapper and walked over to the large orange sofa in the living room to consume his snack and contemplate his evolving circumstances.

Regrets, he had a few. A voice in the back of his mind said the last thing in the world he should do right now is take another plunge into the dating pool. With Lindsey's lawyers circling and his marriage gasping for air, evidence of another splash in the extramarital pond could pull it under for good. Against his better judgment, he let himself get seduced by Dr. Kristi Kramer, who was possibly the most expensive prostitute in the world. A one-time event cost three million dollars? Holy *shit!* Now, he'd have to continue the relationship just to improve his cost basis. Even if he got three more humpy pumpies out of the deal, they'd still run seven hundred and fifty thousand dollars each. That's insane! Was there a sensible way to amortize this? Maybe he should talk to somebody in Finance…

"Say cheese!" Kristi said. She had come up behind him, wrapped an arm around his neck and held her phone in front of them, smiling and snapping a selfie before he had time to react.

"Jesus *Christ*," Robbie exclaimed. "You gave me a heart attack."

"Oh, you!" she said, playfully slapping his back.

Kristi stood, checked that the photo had met her satisfaction, sent herself a copy, and bent over and kissed him on the forehead. Then she pulled her robe a little tighter and shimmied into the kitchen. There she managed to locate a bottle of Dom Perignon in the wine cooler and a pair of champagne glasses to toast their richly rewarding new partnership. She popped its cork as authoritatively as she had popped Robbie's and joined him on the sofa. Robbie looked at her and sighed. *I hope she doesn't want more,* Robbie thought. *I don't have the energy or the budget.*

Kristi poured a glass for Robbie and handed it over, and poured another for herself. "*Cin-cin,*" she said, clinking glasses.

Robbie managed a wan smile. "Oh yeah."

"I have a little present for you."

"Another one?"

She reached behind her into her briefcase and pulled out a paper, then a pen.

"What's this?" he asked.

"It's our Master Services Agreement," she said proudly. "It lays out all the particulars of our partnership. You know, terms and conditions, that sort of thing."

Robbie picked it up and flipped through it. "It's fourteen pages long."

"You don't have to *read* it, silly," she said with a laugh. "You just have to *sign* it."

He put it on the coffee table. "Later."

"Ahem," she said, drumming the pen on the coffee table. "*Now.*"

He sighed as he scribbled his name on the back page. "Happy?"

She took the agreement and put it in her briefcase. "Extremely." She folded her legs up underneath her, draped an arm over the top of the couch and looked at him with a deeply serious expression. "I hope you understand why we did what we just did back there in the bedroom."

Robbie sipped his champagne. "I have a pretty good idea."

She shook her head and smiled. "I'm not sure you do. See, there was a lesson there. I was trying to demonstrate one of the core principles in my books."

"I must have skipped the best parts."

"Think about it. What we did was all about *mission*, right? When somebody wants something real bad—like you did just now—look how motivated you were! You'd do *anything* to reach your goal. That's what we need to instill in the people of the Crowe Power Company. That overwhelming sense of desire. To want success so much it hurts." She leaned over and reached down into his robe. "When they feel that fire downstairs in the boiler room, they'll blow the roof off."

"Have you seen our leadership team? I don't think they've ever had sex."

"Oh, *you.*" She slapped his knee and sat back. "I'm not talking about doin' the deed, honey."

"That's a relief. The breakout sessions would be appalling."

"I'm talking about the yearning for something beyond the ordinary wants and needs of everyday life. We need to give your people the opportunity to find emotional fulfillment through the company. It can't be all about the paycheck. They spend the better part of their waking hours every week at work. There's got to be something bigger, deeper, more meaningful to the time they spend. Know what I mean?"

Robbie nodded. "I do." Throughout his life, he'd been bored by the routine demands of daily life, which tended to shoehorn people into little boxes. Why should he have to learn in a conventional classroom like everyone else, sentenced to sit in a chair next to dull people who could only learn by rote when he could grasp abstract concepts without thinking twice? After joining Crowe Power, he thought it beyond absurd that some of his alleged "superiors" expected a royal to keep office hours like the plebeians from undistinguished bloodlines and middling colleges. And, as he became chairman of Crowe Power, why in the world would he follow in the same deeply-rutted tracks as his forebearers, who built the company for an unenlightened society slurping up fossil fuels for cars and boats and planes without giving a thought to the damage they were causing? Robbie saw things differently. He was exceptional, as his adoring mother made clear from the time he was in diapers. He should follow his own divine inspiration and let it guide him to a higher existence. He could change the world, somehow.

The next phase of this charmed existence started right here, with Dr. Kristi Kramer. Here they were, in matching robes: celebrated author and industrial titan. She had interviewed dozens of chairmen and CEOs. Obviously, she knew what a prize he was. Still, contract or not, he needed to nip the sexual aspect of this relationship in the bud. If Lindsey ever got a whiff he was fooling around with Kristi, any chance of reconciliation was out the window. No, for once in his life, he would deny himself a pleasure that was rightly his. He would exercise the steely discipline embedded in his genes and demonstrate the self-control that enabled him to best all competitors to reach the pinnacle of Crowe Power. From now on, the Robbie-Kristi "partnership," as she put it, would be strictly professional.

Except that, damn, she sure looked fabulous in that white robe, which set off her tan in a lovely way…

"You are so right about finding inspiration for these slugs," Robbie said. "I've been thinking about something along these lines for years. I've just never known exactly how to put it."

She poured him more champagne. "I've got an idea about not only how to put it, but where." She reached back and dimmed a light. Then she pulled a vial of essential oils from her pocket, poured some on her hand, reached inside her robe, and applied the oil to one breast, then the other, then in a trail down to her abdomen. She looked at him and coquettishly cocked her head. "Think you could give me a hand?"

He'd have to defer that steely discipline for now. Little Robbie was breaking out.

10. CADDY SACK

For most of his career at Staminum Energy, Fred Crispin was known as "a Tom guy," one in a retinue of executives hanging onto the coattails of a rising corporate star named Tom Flaherty. It was a rewarding association, since Tom took Fred with him every step of the way to the corporate summit, helping him climb up and over the stalled "Bob guys" and diverted "Jim guys" and other guys' guys, male and female, whose champions faltered, leaving their followers to plunge into the career abyss, forlorn and forgotten.

When Tom became the company's CEO, he naturally enlisted his devoted caddy Fred to become his second-in-command. They made a strong one-two punch, since Fred was good at taking direction and Tom was exceptionally good at dishing it out. Better still, Tom provided cover for Fred as a master schmoozer, giving protection to his team by deftly handling relations with the Stamper family. Tom knew instinctively how to show proper deference to Stampers at all times by nodding his head at inane remarks, chuckling at clumsy attempts at humor, and acceding to their every wish to spend company money on their pet projects and personal comforts. For Tom and Fred both, it was a long, profitable ride, at least until Moe Klinger came along. The activist investor noticed how sleepy Staminum was run, saw an opportunity to wake it and shake it and make some money by pushing a recalcitrant Steady Stamper to give Tom the heave-ho in favor of Walker Hope.

Could Fred now make a deft pivot to become "a Walker guy"? Odds were not good. Given an opportunity to impress the new boss in the team meeting, Fred knew in his bones he had failed. It was obvious he had stumbled with his lame response to Walker's question regarding the company's poor performance. Worse, Fred *knew* the right answer. Staminum *could* do better! Fred knew people sniped that he'd never had an original idea in his life. But that was so unfair. Nobody ever *asked* him for one! He could probably come up with some really good stuff if he only had a minute to *think*.

Fred tossed and turned in his Westchester bedroom throughout the night, flipping his pillow over and over, throwing off the blanket and pulling it back on, slipping on an eyeshade and then tossing it to the floor, all the while replaying the meeting with Walker and his mistakes. *Was it tough just for us? Or for, I don't know... everybody?* When Fred finally drifted off to sleep, he dreamt that Walker stopped by his home in Scarsdale and asked Fred to drive him to Arthur Avenue in the Bronx to buy cannoli. Fred, looking in the rearview mirror, pleaded with Walker not to sit behind him because he was blocking the view. *Please, Walker. Don't shoot...*

Fred shot up straight in his bed. It was 4 a.m., and he gave up on sleep. He trudged quietly into the bathroom for a shower, careful not to wake Maggie, who had already been up half the night reading a bodice-ripper. Word was that Walker was in the office every day no later than 7 a.m. Fred was determined to be his first meeting of the day. Now that he understood Walker a bit better, maybe he could press the reset button.

Fred turned on his radio to WOR and drove his Mercedes S-Class sedan down the Bronx River Parkway, the Cross County Parkway and the Henry Hudson Parkway, before turning onto an uncrowded West Fiftieth Street toward headquarters. He left his car with the valet in the executive garage and rode up the elevator to the dimly lit fifty-first floor, which smelled of freshly brewed coffee from the pantry. Other than the uniformed service crew and security, nobody was around but Walker, who Fred could see was already at his whiteboard, writing and drawing. Fred knocked on the door frame and Walker wheeled around.

"Good morning, Walker. Got a sec?"

"Heck, yeah," said Walker, holding a black magic marker. He looked at his watch. "Is it that time already?"

"I wanted to get a jumpstart on the day," Fred said.

"Another hour earlier and you would have beaten me to it," Walker said. "Glad you're here, big guy. I'm just workin' on the org chart. Have a seat."

Fred took a chair at the conference table. He studied the boxes and lines on the whiteboard and felt a shudder go through his body. "Is that the whole thing? Or just part of it?"

Walker grimaced. "Why do you ask?"

"Well, to be perfectly honest, I don't see my name on there."

Walker stood back and appraised his work. "By golly, I see what you mean." He flipped the board over and sat down in a chair at the end of the conference table. "Work in progress. What's on your mind this morning?"

Fred gathered himself. "I just wanted to say I thought it was a great meeting yesterday."

"Really?" Said Walker in surprise. "Why?"

"First of all, I appreciate your candor. You told us exactly what you thought and, frankly, I find that 'brutal truth' concept very refreshing."

"Like a bucket of ice water over your head, I'll bet," Walker said with a wink.

"It was bracing, for sure. You really shook up some people on the team. But, you know, I think that's for the best. We could use a good rattling."

"So glad to hear you say that, Fred," Walker said, leaning forward. "Really appreciate your support. As you know, this transition is goin' to be difficult."

"Understood, Walker. I just hope you didn't, you know, take my comment in the meeting about all the external challenges the wrong way."

Walker's expression turned blank. "What way is that, Fred?"

"Well. I didn't mean to sound like I was blaming our sub-par performance on issues outside the company."

Walker scratched the back of his head. "That's kinda what you said, if I heard you correctly."

"Technically, yes. That's true." Fred found his breath a little harder to catch. "It's just not what I meant exactly."

"Uh-huh. And what exactly did you mean?"

Uh-oh, Fred thought. *Be careful. You're not even on the org chart yet.* "I meant that I know we have to improve our performance. That's obvious. What you saw yesterday in our results does not meet the standard needed for us to turn this company around. I certainly know that."

Walker nodded thoughtfully. He leaned back in his chair, locking his hands behind his head and propping one foot up on the edge of the table. Behind him the lights of Rockefeller Center were starting to flicker off as the sun rose in the distance over the barrier islands on the Atlantic Ocean. "Let me ask you somethin', Fred. You have a family?"

"I do. Married thirty years."

"Nice!"

"My wife, Maggie, does a lot of charitable work around town. In fact, she chairs the fundraising committee for the Sisters of Mercy."

"Aw. That's so sweet. Kids?"

"Three: one at Dalton, one at UVA, and the other at Duke."

"Oh man." Walker clapped his hands together. "Sounds like everyone's doin' just great. And that's because you helped them. You gave them the air cover to succeed. And let me tell you somethin', Fred. I'm all for givin' people a chance. I totally believe in that."

Fred exhaled and settled a bit in his chair. *Phew! Coming in early was so worth it!* "I'm very relieved to hear you say that, Walker. I've been thinking for some time now that it would make sense for me to put together a comprehensive new plan for operations. You know, review everything we do, top to bottom, and lay out a timeline on how to hit our numbers."

"Fred! I love, love, love it! How long will it take to put your plan together?"

"I'm thinking... six months?"

"Uh-huh," Walker said, looking out the window for a moment before looking back at Fred. "I'm thinkin' somethin' different."

"I could do it faster, of course. Maybe... four months?"

"How 'bout next Thursday."

"Thurs... uh, *what?*"

"That's six whole days, brother."

"Well, yes, but... I mean, I've got to gather my thoughts, get input from the team—"

"If I'm not mistaken, Fred, you've been at this company for twenty-eight years. Am I right?"

"Correct."

"And you've been the Chief Operatin' Officer for the past three?"

Fred gulped. "That's right."

"Now... people tell me you were 'a Tom guy.'"

Fred guffawed. "I know others say that, but I never saw it that way. I've always thought of myself as my own man—a 'Fred guy,' if you will."

Walker fixed a steely eye on Fred. "Then help me understand somethin' here. With all that experience and all that knowledge you've gained over the years, and you bein' 'a Fred guy' and all, why don't you have enough to tell me a plan *right now?*"

"Don't get me wrong. I have lots of ideas. They've been percolating in my head for a long time."

"Good. Like what?"

"I've been thinking we could combine some divisions, consolidate operations here and there, maybe incorporate disruptive technologies from some of those Greeneron companies into the mainstream of our business."

"Which ones?"

Fred took a deep breath. "That part, I don't really know just yet. Greeneron's never been something I had to pay attention to. And, you know, there are so many moving parts at a global company like this." Fred sighed. This was going nowhere. "It's just really, really complicated."

Walker nodded. He walked over to his desk, pulled a paper from his briefcase, and brought it back to the table. "I hear you," Walker said. "That's exactly why I need leaders who can make it less complicated, like I did in this plan I showed our chairman yesterday." He slid the paper across the desk to Fred, who could quickly grasp the genius in its simplicity.

"You did this in nine days?"

"Eight and a half."

Fred studied the paper, then looked back to Walker. "I, uh—" His throat went dry. "I..."

Walker sat on the edge of the table, looking down at Fred. "Let me ask you another question, Fred. If you've had all these great ideas over the past three years, why didn't you put them in motion? I mean, you're one of the big dogs in this pound."

Fred felt the room grow dim. "Well... I guess the first reason is: it's hard."

"Hard? Like, 'difficult?'"

"Well, yeah. I mean, to come up with a big company strategy on top of my day job, which is to make sure everything's running like it's supposed to—"

"That's the point, Fred. It's not runnin' like it's supposed to. It's runnin' in a way that doesn't make any money."

"I know what you mean. But you still have to keep it going."

"And make up for losses with volume? Is that what you're thinkin'?"

"No. Not exactly. I mean, I—I know things aren't going well. I've just never had the time to pull my head up from the day-to-day grind and see everything at once and say, 'I'm going to have to figure out a better way.'"

Walker slapped the tabletop. "You know somethin'? I really like you, Fred. You are one stand-up guy. Hard worker. Family man. Not someone who's afraid to admit their mistakes. Just the kind of fella I'd like to grab a beer with some day. And that's why I want to tell you: there's absolutely no shame in you comin' in here this mornin' and sayin', 'Walker, this just isn't the right job for me. I'm in way over my head and I'm drownin' here.' And I appreciated you tellin' me that, Fred. Really. It's okay. No hard feelings. Alright?"

Fred couldn't feel his fingers or his toes. Was he paralyzed? Was he having a stroke? "That wasn't quite what I was saying—"

Walker stood and extended his hand. "Oh, no! No need to apologize. I know exactly where you're goin'."

"I, uh… I'm goin'?"

"I guess you are." Walker looked at his watch. "Just glad we sorted it all out right out of the chute here, Fred. Spares everyone a lot of confusion, and I really appreciate it. Speaks to your character to stand up like you did and say, 'I'm out.'"

Fred stood, wobbly. "Maybe I didn't explain quite well enough."

"No, no, no," Walker said, clapping him on the back. "You nailed it, buddy. See Marty sometime this mornin', will ya? He'll figure out a press release around your departure that honors your service in just the right way." Walker offered a handshake. "Fred, I salute you. And I want to thank you *so* much for helpin' me with this org chart. Think I got a really good handle on how to finish it."

11. TOGETHER FOR GOOD

I f Robbie wasn't sure before that he'd made a mistake in selecting Tim as Walker Hope's successor, he was certain of it now. The poor bastard was supposed to fire up his team with the opening remarks at the *Power to the People* offsite conference, but he was putting everyone to sleep with his trite homilies and corny analogies. How long should Robbie ride it out with this loser? Another week? Who should he get to take his place? Would he have to jump in and do it himself? *Lord.* The thought of it made him sick. Why does it always, always, *always* have to be him riding to the rescue?

"So when we think of our guiding principles, let's think of the letters in our name: C-R-O-W-E," Tim said, spelling it out as if he had discovered some mystical formula that eluded company leaders for generations. "'C' is for constant improvement. Got it? 'R,' robust returns. I guess you could say that's actually two Rs, but you get the point. Now 'O'—I know that's a letter 'O' and not a zero, but still—is for zero safety problems." Eyes glazed over in the audience as Tim trudged ahead, blazing a trail no one could follow. "'W' is, of course, winning, which is what we're all about. Winning. And, 'E'—extraordinary. Now, why we're extraordinary, well, that's exactly what we're going to figure out today. Okay?" He paused a moment for his profundity to sink in. "Easy enough to remember, right, gang?"

Oh, for crissakes, Robbie thought. *Where's a gong when you need one?* He looked over at Dr. Kristi Kramer, who was standing in the back, raptly watching Tim speak as if he were actually interesting. He had to admit: she certainly knew how to service a client. Maybe she and Robbie should re-enact their demonstration of how a sense of mission can drive people to exhilarating performance. *That* would get the crowd engaged.

Tim continued. "So listen, people. We have a wonderful speaker coming on now to set the tone for the next couple of days, a woman who can get us all fired up about the essential role that each of us has to play in shaping the future of Crowe Power," Tim said. "And, from my perspective, we're incredibly lucky to have her."

Kristi came running down the risers like she had just been called as a contestant on *The Price is Right*. Dressed all in white, befitting a high priestess of higher purpose, she arrived on stage jiggling and jangling, beaming from ear to ear, as if this were the most stupendous moment of her entire life. Kristi bowed to the applause and then rose up, extending her arms, and with a jerk of her neck, threw her massive mane of blond tresses back over her head.

"*Whew!*" she said. "My goodness. You are a-*may*-zing!" She walked along the front rim of the stage, applauding back at them. "I *love* this team!"

Robbie leaned over to Digby. "What the hell, Digs? The chairman of the company doesn't open the conference? I thought I was on now."

Digby opened a tab in his conference binder. "No. This is right. Looks like you're not up until after dinner."

"When everyone's plastered?"

Digby nodded. "Might be better that way."

Kristi struck a humble pose, one adapted from Sunday morning TV preachers. She bowed her head slightly and held her hands together in front of her, almost as if she were in prayer. "I am so *deeply* honored to be here," she said. "You know, I normally don't offer private counsel to businesses. My study of missionology—which is all about what makes companies super successful—just doesn't allow me the time to give one-on-one advice." She walked slowly across the stage toward Robbie. "But I made an exception in this case because I get the chance to work closely with visionary leaders like Robbie Crowe, who told me personally that he wants to direct this iconic company's energies to seeking a greater good. And I find that stimulating in ways you can't imagine." She looked at Robbie and smiled. Surely, *he* could figure it out. "I ask you: what could be more exciting than a company that's been so successful for so long harnessing all its magical powers to create a better world?" She turned back toward the center of the room. "And it all starts right here, with us in this room, right now. Think of it. To be a part of something so much bigger than ourselves? Why, I get *chills.*"

Digby leaned over to Robbie. "Maybe we should turn down the air conditioning."

"Don't," Robbie said. "I like the cold air indicators turned on up there."

Kristi went on to extoll the utopian company that Crowe Power was about to become through the discovery of its executives' shared interests. Together, they would turn employees from sluggish drones scrolling all day through Facebook and Pinterest into highly engaged warriors, fearlessly charging up every hill their newly dedicated managers pointed out to them. They would convert the residents of every community where the company operates stinky refineries and leaky pipelines from crabby neighbors complaining about fumes and fireballs into enthusiastic supporters, ready to approve every pollution permit as a happy win-win for all concerned. They would even link arms with the pesky Planetista protesters picketing in front of the New York headquarters to find mutually agreeable solutions for a cleaner, greener planet where all species can live in harmony and peace and utter awesome-osity. It was all going to be *soooo* wonderful!

"And do you know why?" she said. "Because, today, we are going to find the one singular mission that binds us all together in our sense of common purpose, something far more meaningful than the pursuit of profit. And I can't *wait!*"

As the tepid applause petered out entirely, a woman in the front row raised her hand. "Dr. Kramer, I read *Great Halls of Hire* and I'm puzzled by something. Half the companies you use as examples of success for mission-driven companies no longer exist. They either went out of business or were sold."

Kristi nodded vigorously. "That's right."

The woman looked confused. "So... what am I missing?"

"The *second* edition."

"I'm pretty sure that's the one I read."

"*Okaaay,*" Kristi said patiently. "You may not be aware, but there's a *third* edition with a whole bunch of *new* success stories. And when I write my next book, I'm counting on Crowe Power to become the shining example of how a company turns goodness into greatness through a fantabulous new mission. Do you mind if I ask your name?"

"Lucy Rutherford."

Robbie leaned over to Digby. "Complete shit stirrer."

Digby nodded. "She has a point."

Kristi continued from the stage, "And what do you do, Lucy?"

"I'm president of the Americas."

"My *word*. That's like a couple continents, right?"

"Last I looked."

"I'm *soooo* impressed. That's *huge*! Like an entire hemisphere! Now let me tell you, Lucy, the number one problem for companies that I wrote about that are no longer with us is: they didn't *stick with the program*. They thought getting a mission was some sort of check-the-box exercise. You know, 'We've got our mission statement. It's done. We can just go back to jackin' up profits and bein' a big ol' greedy corporation.' But, see, that's a *perversion* of my concept. What I'm talking about is finding the real meaning that goes deep into your core. We're talking about the very *soul* of your company. Do you follow me?"

Lucy shrugged. "Not really. I've seen a lot of company reinventions that do little more than embrace the latest fad and conjure up a slogan. That makes the people at the top all giddy, but the people down below never get what the fuss is all about. It's pretty much forgotten before the ink is dry on the banners. Eventually, when they see nothing's really changed, it makes them cynical and the whole exercise does more harm than good. Maybe I'm just overly skeptical."

Kristi turned away for a moment, thinking, then turned back to Lucy. "No, no. I'm so glad you shared your feelings, Lucy. That's the *only* way we're going to arrive at a consensus. Let's get all our cards out on the table and show what we've got. Here's one of mine—and why I think Crowe Power is different. You have what I think is the secret sauce that very few companies have. You have real ownership because of the Crowe family. And best of all, you have L. Robertson Crowe, III." All eyes turned to Robbie, nearly dozing, sat up straight at an elbow from Digby. "See, there's no worry he's going anywhere else. You know that he has staying power, which means your chances of success rise exponentially. Are you with me?"

Given the pressing agenda before them and the breakout groups to come, Kristi cut off further questioning and directed people to her website, where they could find oodles of videos and other supplementary materials, as well as merchandise—like coffee mugs inscribed with pithy inspirational sayings to keep people going past 10:30 in the morning. As executives applauded the fact that the presentation was over, Digby stood up and stretched. "When do they pass out the Kool-Aid?"

Robbie stood. "Make sure you get some. This mission's going to last for some time."

"That sounds ominous."

Said Robbie, quietly, "I made a deal with her last night."

Digby's face fell. "You didn't."

"Three years. Three million dollars. It includes a book."

"Were your pants on when you struck this bargain?"

"Let's just say I was in no position to prolong a negotiation."

"So we're paying for sexual harassment in advance rather than in one big lump sum at the end? I suppose that's some sort of progress."

"Good for the financial forecast, don't you think?"

Digby didn't hide his disgust. "Frankly, Robbie, I don't think there's anything good about it."

"And I don't believe I asked your approval," Robbie said peevishly. "I don't know where you get off as the moral arbiter of my life. I agreed to a deal and that's that. Isn't living up to our promises a core value of our company? As far as I'm concerned, this is putting our values into action, which is what I'm all about."

Digby sighed. *This will end well.*

12. A NUMBER OF PROBLEMS

Marty McGarry apologized to the woman on the other end of his line for mistakenly calling her number. He hung up the phone and punched a button on his intercom. "Brenda? Can you come in here for a moment?"

Marty looked up to the ceiling and listened for a response. He hit the button again. "Brenda. Are you there?"

Hearing no reply, he grabbed the yellow message slip and walked to his outer office to find his executive assistant, Brenda Pachulski, yawning in her chair, holding a phone to her ear with her left hand and using her right hand to fluff up her thatch of frosted curls. She turned toward Marty, a faint flicker of recognition in her eyes. *Oh, right. The new guy, What's-His-Face.* "I'm on hold," she said with a hopeless shrug. "Stupid cable company. What's up?"

He handed the phone message to her. "You gave me this message to call Tilda Ecklund at *Buzzniss?*"

Brenda squinted at the message, as if deciphering an intercepted code. "Oh yes. I remember that. Tilda. The reporter. Uh-huh. Told her you were in the bathroom."

"You told her—*what?* Brenda, please. Don't do that. They don't need the visual."

She turned away with a sneer. *What's with him?* "Oh. Hello? ... Yes, this is Brenda. I'm having problems with my Hulu..." She sighed and glanced back at Marty. "I'm getting terrible service."

Marty ran his hand down the back of his head. "I know what you mean."

Brenda looked at him blankly. "What did you want again?"

Marty leaned over her desk. "The message you gave me. Tilda Ecklund?"

"Right. *Right!* I remember now. She wanted you to call her. That's it. And she told me to give you her new number. Uh-huh."

"That's what I'm saying. You gave me the wrong number. I got me some nail salon in Chinatown."

"That's funny," she said with a chuckle. "I wonder how I did that." She bit a knuckle on her thumb. "How many numbers did I get right?"

Marty took a deep breath and counted to three, lest he overturn her desk. "I don't know, Brenda. Maybe nine out of ten, but it doesn't matter. You need to get them *all*. In order. It's kind of the deal with phone numbers."

Brenda, struck by a brainstorm, sat up straight. "You know what I'm gonna do?" she announced in triumph. "I'm gonna Google her!"

Who'd have ever thought of that? "Brilliant," he said.

"Soon as I get off the phone—oh, hello." She turned away again. "Yes. This is Brenda. Well, as I've told just about everybody in your company, I can't connect with my Hulu and there's a show I want to see tonight..."

Marty slunk back to his desk. At least one message from Brenda was clear: she didn't care nearly as much for her job as she did for her favorite shows. Brenda had worked in the Staminum C-suite with top executives for more than a decade, perfectly fitting the unaccountable culture Marty had witnessed throughout his first two weeks at the company. Nobody was responsible for *anything*.

Staminum, it seemed, was on cruise control for a long, slow journey to nowhere. And while the company's lack of focus made his workday a life-sapping series of long, pointless meetings, Marty remembered the mantra that guided his career: *If this company weren't so fucked up, it wouldn't need me.* And, if they didn't need him, he couldn't generate the money he needed to support his dependents: his ex-wife and her boyfriend shacking up in the family home in Westchester; his kids in college; his mother in a nursing home; and the landlord of his walk-up apartment on Bleecker Street that was, appropriately, bleaker than anyplace he'd ever lived before. Yessir, he was *livin' the dream...*

Based on conversations with his financial advisor, Marty needed to hang on to this gig for five more years to meet all his financial obligations before he even considered a new job. In the meantime, Marty's survival at Staminum would depend on his ability to continue selling Walker Hope to the press as a colossus of American business without alienating the founding family. That would be tricky, given that Walker was hired to fix problems that festered under the family's lackluster leadership.

Marty hadn't yet met Steady Stamper, but he suspected a splashy story about the wonders of Walker—and the implicit shortcomings of the Stampers—wouldn't be the best way to meet him. During his Crowe Power days, Marty had set Robbie's hair on fire by placing Walker on the cover of Fortune Magazine with a headline suggesting he was the best CEO in America. The text of the story incensed Robbie even more with its pointed conclusion: Crowe Power was led by Hope... and a dope. The ensuing rage set in motion all the events that led to his firing and executive exodus, with Walker, Marty and Maria Territo heading uptown to Staminum. A similar story would not help here. Somehow, Marty would have to help the media find an angle that extolled Walker's leadership capabilities while still making the Stampers look good. Surely, they had *some* skills besides yachting and tennis.

Tilda Ecklund was his first challenge. Formerly a star reporter at the Wall Street Journal, she was lured to Buzzniss.com, the start-up online publication, with *carte blanche* to cover whatever piqued her interest. She hovered over the business landscape and swooped in on the stories that most intrigued her, often prompted by a tip from her well-cultivated network of sources among the city's business and cultural elite. Known as a tough contrarian, she tended to go against well-worked storylines and break new ground.

"Marty McGarry," Tilda said, grandly. "Thank you so much for returning my call. You know I thought of you just the other day when I saw that Gino Morelli from Hearthside Financial was paroled. So glad you didn't end up in jail, too."

"Aw. Thank you, Tilda. That's very sweet of you."

"Kind of a close call for you, wasn't it?"

"I was never indicted, you know."

"Right. You were just the PR guy. So: tell me about your new position. What's it like having another front-row seat to Walker Hope working his turnaround magic at another big company?"

Marty summoned his most enthusiastic tone. "Oh, gosh! Early days, of course, but it's very, very encouraging. Staminum has so much going for it in terms of assets and history and wonderful, hard-working people." Marty paused, marveling at his own capacity for bullshit. *How do these words come out of my mouth?* "The Stampers have so much to be proud of in terms of what they've built over the years. I mean, the results haven't been great lately, but that's why Walker's here, right? There's still passion. Commitment. And, of course, energy. It's inspiring, really. Now it's just a matter of getting everyone to pull in the same direction."

"Yeah, well. That's kind of boring."

Marty gulped for air. "I don't know why you'd say that."

"That story's been done to *death*, Marty. 'Walker Hope does it again.' Whoop-de-doo. I mean, I get why that was news at BFC, and Goliath, and even at Crowe Power. But this is getting to be old hat. I think it's time for a fresh appraisal of the Walker way. I'm looking at how companies perform after he's gone."

Uh-oh. "And?"

"The answer is: not so hot."

Oh Lord. If a story like that got out, Marty might not make it a month in this job. "Let me get this straight. You attribute a company's bad results to Walker—when he's not even there any longer? That hardly seems fair."

"I didn't suck this out of my thumb. People I've talked to say he mortgaged the future of those companies to get short-term results. That's why Walker's meeting resistance this time around."

Marty reflexively guffawed. "Resistance? Where in the world would you get a notion like that?"

"Let's just say I have very good sources," she said. "And they're saying Walker is moving too fast for his own good, making snap judgments to drive financial results without considering what they mean for the future. The Stampers have been at this for a hundred years, and they've built a reputation for doing things the right way. This is about more than profits, Marty. They're proud of their name and they don't wany anyone sullying that. I wonder whether Staminum will be Walker's Waterloo."

Marty could imagine an illustration of Walker astride a horse, wearing a Napoleon hat, with a hand stuck inside his Jos. A. Bank suitcoat. That would *not* go over well with the boss. Nearly as troubling, Marty would now have that stupid fucking ABBA song stuck in his head all day. *Waterloo. Couldn't escape if I wanted to.* "That sounds more like water cooler than Waterloo, Tilda. Are we talking off the record?"

She sighed. "For the moment."

"I would caution against paying undue attention to gossip. There's always resistance to change inside companies. I saw it at Crowe Power. I've seen it everywhere. A certain amount of that is expected. To cobble together a story out of the usual grumbling seems like quite a stretch."

"A significant difference here, Marty, is that the 'grumbling,' as you put it, is coming from the founding family. Walker's not their guy; he's Moe Klinger's guy, and they don't like Moe either, with all his focus on quarterly results, cash dividends and stock repurchases. And while Klinger may have the muscle right now, the Stampers have plenty of staying power. They could kill Walker's regime change if they want to."

Marty looked up at the clock. *Was it time for lunch yet?* "I can say unequivocally that Walker has nothing but respect for the Stampers. Their stewardship is without parallel." *Who else could lose so much money for so many years?* "Surely, they see their interest is tied to Walker's success. A turnaround benefits them more than anybody. Look at the stock price. It hasn't been this high in years. If you ask around, I'm sure you'll find plenty of support for Walker."

"I have. And I didn't."

"Tilda, please," Marty said. "We're not even two weeks into this. Doesn't he at least get a chance?" Marty's voice dropped to a near whisper. "I trust you're not writing anything soon."

"As soon as I get a response from Walker. When can I get a sit-down with him?"

There was no way Marty would offer up Walker for a hit piece like this. His best hope was to delay as long as possible. "I'll certainly see what I can do, Tilda, but you can imagine how busy he is right now. In the meantime, maybe we could discuss this further so I can brief him. Are you free for breakfast sometime in the next few weeks?"

"I'm not waiting that long, Marty. I want to write."

"I understand. Let me just check my calendar—"

"Don't stall for time, Marty. I'll write without him if I have to."

"Of course not. I'm just looking for the next opportunity. How's... hmm. Looks like I'm free two weeks from today."

"Tomorrow," she insisted.

"I have a conflict—"

"Bubby's in Tribeca."

"I can't do it then."

"See you at nine." *Click.*

Marty hung up and wondered whether he'd hit a nice, cushy awning if he jumped out the window, or land on a shish-kebab skewer at the Halal Shawarma stand. The last thing he needed was a critical story to feed the Resistance, pissing off Walker and inspiring other media to advance the storyline further. The second-to-last thing he needed was a visit from Brenda, who appeared at his door, triumphantly waving a message. "I have the number," she cried.

"For what?"

"Tilda Ecklund."

Marty tried to comprehend. "I just got off the phone with her."

"So you *found* the number yourself?" she asked, astonished. *How was that possible?*

"Apparently."

"Well I am sorry," she said, putting her hands on her hips. "I'm a little out of practice, you know. We didn't return media calls before you got here."

"I hope you're kidding."

"Andy always said it was better they reported that the company couldn't be reached for comment. So when reporters gave me their numbers, I never bothered to write them down. I'd pretend I was writing them—you know, 'did you say two-one-two?'—but I was faking it."

"I'm sure you were convincing."

Brenda sniffed, "Andy approved, and he was a very, *very* good man. He always treated me with the utmost respect." She turned to leave, then looked back. "Oh. By the way, Toni called from Kip Stamper's office. They want you in a meeting in the Coal Room."

"When?"

"Well, let's see..." She glanced at her watch. "Five minutes ago."

Marty felt like he was going to lose it. "Were you going to tell me?"

"I was on *hold.*" She shook her head as she walked away. *This guy's a real dodo.*

13. LINDSEY, INC.

Maybe getting hammered with Bits at the St. Regis was the best thing that could have happened, Lindsey mused. Still wobbly from her five-round bout with a vintage Saint-Estéphe, followed by a shot or two of tequila, Lindsey decided she had truly touched bottom this time. She resolved, as firmly as she could, that today was the day: no more drinking. Not with Bits. Not with her other friends. And certainly not in public. Had she really fallen down on her way to the restroom? Or was that a dream? The blurry memories were painful, as was her hip. Starting here, starting now, she would direct all that energy wasted wallowing in her past toward finding a better way forward.

After a shaky morning spent restoring some chemical balance, she devoted the afternoon to overseeing the conversion of the fifth floor in her Beaux-Arts mansion on East 67th Street from Robbie's unused workout space into an office. Out went the dusty Peleton, floor mats and weights; in came furnishings for the next stage in her life. This room was just right, with plenty of natural light coming in through the casement windows and peeking through the mansard roof, easy access to the elevator and an adjacent bathroom, and a pantry that the house staff could stock with healthy beverages and snacks. She wouldn't even *think* of having them bring wine.

The furniture, an eclectic collection of one-off chairs and lamps from basement storage that didn't fit anywhere else in the house, could use an upgrade at some point, but the prize piece was a lovely desk that once belonged to her grandfather, Albert K. Harper, the Chicago retailing magnate, along with his lovely Art Deco reading lamp. Best of all, it was her own space, like her dorm room at Wellesley, except this sanctuary had a Monet on one wall and a Renoir on the other, rather than peace signs and posters.

The staff shoved the last cabinet into place as the late afternoon sun bent its rays over the roofs and treetops outside, casting the room in a lovely tangerine incandescence. Lindsey excused Frederick and his assistants and settled into the big leather chair behind the desk, basking in the glow of a fresh start. Now what? What would it be like to make decisions that decided the fate of such a large and historic company as Crowe Power? The idea was overwhelming and exhilarating at the same time, but there were many questions to answer before she let herself get carried away. First, she had to understand more about Robbie and his role at the company. Was it fair for her to move against him now just because she could? Why was he regarded so poorly by investors? Robbie was certainly intelligent, IQ-wise. Had he scaled the corporate ladder too easily? Did he not try hard enough? Or was he distracted by his extracurricular pursuits?

The best person to answer those questions might be the woman who was instrumental in setting all these changes in motion: Maria Territo, Robbie's mistress when she had worked at Crowe Power. Lindsey had summoned her to tea when she learned of the affair and graciously suggested Maria could have Robbie, but he dumped Maria first. Now Lindsey strangely felt a bond with Maria: they were both victims of the same man.

How, Lindsey wondered, could Robbie have put so much time and effort into romantic liaisons and still have time to run the company? Can someone who incessantly lies to his wife and everyone around him still hold the moral authority to lead? And what, pray tell, did he do all day?

Lindsey opened her laptop computer and composed a note, taking nearly an hour to strike the right tone.

> Dear Maria,
>
> After a good deal of reflection, I want to express my thanks to you for being so candid with me about your relationship with Robbie. I hope you are moving on with your life in a positive way and that your future holds more satisfying adventures ahead.
>
> I, too, am working through a transition and would appreciate your perspective from your time at Crowe Power. Please let me know if there is a convenient time for us to meet again in the near future.
>
> Sincerely,
>
> Lindsey Harper Crowe

She stared at the note and reread it one last time before hitting the "send" button. She heard the whoosh of the email flying off through cyberspace, sat back in her chair, and exhaled. What a crazy, upside-down world she inhabited these days, when one of the few people she could trust was the woman who had been sneaking around with her husband not too long ago.

Next, Lindsey needed to gauge whether her children would support her if she challenged their father's leadership of the company. Neither Missy nor Chase showed any pride in Crowe Power, which they dismissed as an industrial relic with little social cache in the technological age. Nor did they seem to appreciate how much the company's performance impacted their fortunes. Their trust funds were magically replenished with Crowe Power dividends four times a year. And their net worth was calculated largely on the price of Crowe Power stock, which was sinking again after a brisk rise. Did they understand that? How would they feel if the company were sold? For older generations, Crowe Power was a central component of their self-identity, both in the way they saw themselves in the world and the way others saw them. Would a sale bother her children at all? Would it foreclose any future career possibilities they might see for themselves?

Lindsey knew there was no hope of calling her daughter on the phone, a pathetically old-school means of communication that Missy found intrusive, alienating, and 'sooo Nineties.' Lindsey typed her daughter's name in her text messaging app and tapped out a short missive asking her if they could connect on FaceTime. Within moments, her daughter's face was displayed on the phone, calling from the house she shared with four other girls in New Haven.

"What?" Missy demanded.

"Hello, darling," Lindsey said, cheerily.

"What's with the FaceTime, Mother? I mean, like, you never FaceTime. Is this, like, some new drunk dial?"

"I'm not drinking," Lindsey said calmly. "Haven't had a thing all day." *We'll ignore yesterday for the moment.* "I just wanted to see your smiling face, dear."

"O-kaaaay," Missy said, skeptically. "Here it is. Are you going to complain about my hair again?"

"No, no." She regarded the odd smudge of purple at the front of Missy's head of wavy blond hair. "I've come to terms with it, I think. It's just so good to *see* you. You haven't been home in ages."

"Busy. What can I say?"

"Oh, I know. And I'm sorry to bother you."

"So… can we get through this? I thought maybe you were calling to say you and Dad are getting a divorce."

"We haven't decided anything just yet. We both just want to do what's best for everyone concerned, including you."

"Well, I don't know how you can stay with him. He's treated you like total shit forever."

"Let's just say we're working through things."

"Okay. Fine. *Fine,*" Missy growled, picking up one of her father's verbal ticks. "Mother, please. If it's nothing," She sighed, stressed. "I'm just really super busy. Finals start next week. And I gotta get ready for *The Bachelor* party downstairs."

Lindsey could feel her heart pounding. How was she going to put this delicate issue without giving away her own thoughts? "I won't keep you, darling. I just wanted to ask you a couple of questions about the company."

"Crowe Power? Who cares about *that?*"

"Well, your father and I care about it a great deal. And, you know, it's quite important in terms of our family's income and net worth."

"Like, we don't have enough money already? I mean, seriously. How much do we need? We're hearing all these reports in class about income inequality. We are, like, so privileged. We ought to just give it all away. I'm sick of hearing about it."

"You may think the company doesn't matter to you now, dear, but it very well could down the road. Not just to you, but potentially your children and your grandchildren."

"Uh, not happening, Mom. I'm not having any children. They emit CO_2. There are *way* too many people on the planet already."

"What about your career? Do you ever think you might want to follow in your father's footsteps and work at Crowe Power?"

"Oh, Mother. Puh-*leeze.*" She laughed. "Is that some kind of joke? I'm studying art history. You think I want to labor in that tar pit with all the other dinosaurs? It's, like, the furthest thing from my mind."

Lindsey was getting annoyed with all the blowback and attitude but took a deep breath and held her emotions in check. "Wouldn't it make more sense to work inside the company for the changes you would like to see?"

"Mother. I want to live in Florence, okay? I don't want to be in New York. It's too embarrassing when people learn you're a Crowe. They're like, 'Oh, yuck. Kill any polar bears today?' They think we're these horrible, terrible people, and I'll be honest, I think so, too. Just saying my name to anyone around here is considered a micro-aggression."

"Dear," Lindsey said firmly, "you've never killed any polar bears and you never will. The company actually provides a very useful service. Everyone uses energy."

"Yeah? Well, we're not making the right *kind* of energy. I saw this thing on YouTube that says we should get all our power from composted garbage. Why don't we just do that? Who needs smelly old gas and oil and coal?" Missy turned to someone off screen and called. "*Coming! Be there in a minute.*" She turned back to the camera. "Mom, I have to go. Can you wire some money to my checking account? We're all going to Cuba for the weekend."

"Can't you just move money from one of your funds?"

"I told you, Mother, I have to get ready for a *party*. I don't have time to play around with that banking crap. Just send twenty thousand, okay? I'll pay you back. *Jeez.* Why do things always have to be so difficult?"

"Okay," Lindsey said tartly, eager to conclude. "I'll take care of it."

She hung up and wondered: twenty thousand dollars… for *Cuba*? Missy must plan on giving the money away, which probably seems like a sensible idea when you have no idea where it comes from or why it's even valuable. Lindsey pushed away from the desk and sauntered over to the pantry for some wine. *Stop!* Sparkling water. Yes, that's more like it. She found a can of berry-flavored LaCroix and returned to her desk. Much to her astonishment, Chase happened to be calling her mobile phone.

"Chase, darling. What a pleasant surprise," Lindsey said. "I was just planning to call you."

"Hey, Mom. You good?

"Everything's just… tickety-boo. Where are you?"

"Bunch of the guys decided to take a little break from school. We're in the Algarve."

Lindsey settled back in her chair. "Portugal should be lovely, I would think."

"It's okay, I guess. We're just having a little trouble getting back in time for class on Monday. Some of the guys got stuck in coach, which really sucks for a long flight. I'm wondering if you could send one of the company jets to pick us up."

"Have you talked to Winnie? She should be able to arrange that for you."

"She said there was only one plane available and I could have it if you weren't using it to go shopping in London or West Palm or something."

"I have no plans, dear."

"What about Aunt Bits?"

"No. I'm quite sure she'll be in town this weekend."

"Cool. I'll grab it then. Thanks, Mom. Good to—"

"Wait, Chase. When am I going to see you?"

"I don't know. July, possibly."

"Okay. Before you go, I want to ask you a question. I know you've talked with your father about working at the company someday. Is that something you're still considering?"

"Yeah. I guess."

"Is that a long-term plan?"

"Not really. I mean, I was thinking about working there for the summer. Maybe as, like, a roving vice-president of some kind. Long term, I want to do something else. That industry is doomed. It's going to be regulated out of existence."

"So Crowe Power's not where you plan to spend your career?"

"Not really. We've all been kicking around an idea of starting an artisanal rum business in Dumbo called Rumbo. Is that a cool name or what? We even sketched out a label on the beach and asked some of the girls we met what they thought. Everyone dug it. So we asked Buckley's dad to get it trademarked. Now all we have to do is find somebody who knows how to do the other stuff, you know: make it, package it, market it, distribute it and all that jazz. We're having a rum punch party tonight to celebrate our launch."

That was a *launch?* A half-baked idea? Oh well. With neither of her children considering a job in the family business, Lindsey concluded they did not depend on Robbie retaining his position at Crowe Power to help them slide up the corporate ladder. And if they didn't need Robbie as chairman, why did she? Was he the best person to look out for the broader family's best interests? Or would they be better off with someone else? This would require some more conversation with Bits, and perhaps Digby, as well as Uncle Chuck. If they took her side, she could move mountains—and the board.

As she sat up to put her computer to sleep, an email dropped into her inbox from Maria Territo.

How about the bar at 21 Club @ 6:30 tomorrow?

Lindsey quickly typed her reply.

See you then.

14. MORTAL DANGER

The mysterious letter was sent through the U.S. Postal Service to Robbie Crowe at the Crowe Power Company without a return address. Inside was a sheet of paper with letters cut from magazine covers glued on to the page.

yoU RuinED CroWe Power
You oWe ME $200 thousand

Sensing imminent danger, Robbie's dutiful executive assistant, Winnie, immediately notified Crowe Power Corporate Security. Within minutes, two former G-Men were in her office with latex gloves, studying the missive from various angles and taking photographs.

"Was there any powder in the envelope?" one asked.

"No," she said, uncertainly. "Do you need some?"

"Sorry?"

"I have a little powder in my compact."

"I'm asking about anthrax."

"Oh no," she said. "I wouldn't have anything like that."

"Thank you, ma'am. You've been very helpful."

The security agents deposited the letter and the envelope in a plastic bag and whisked it downstairs to their office on the first floor. There, using the latest detective techniques from the 1920s, they steamed the letters off the page, flipped them over, and pieced together enough elements of various address labels to determine that the magazines came from the office of a Midtown dentist by the name of Dr. Stuart Littmann.

A PDF of the document was dispatched to Tom Michaels, a former Secret Service agent now heading Crowe Power Corporate Security, who was travelling with the chairman in California and keeping an eye on the hotel lobby for suspicious characters. Advised of the threat, Tom instantly endeavored to alert the chairman.

He first searched for Robbie at the *Power to the People* conference room, where executives had broken into roundtable groups to consider Crowe Power's "One True Mission." Next, he looked backstage, where Tim was huddled with Dr. Kristi Kramer to review the afternoon's agenda; Tim said he hadn't seen the chairman since the first morning session; Kristi didn't admit to seeing him at all. After checking Robbie's suite and the inn's bars and restaurants, Tom at last found the chairman lounging by the Claremont Club's main pool, where he was evaluating the varying degrees of fitness displayed by the ladies on deck and checking his Fantasy Baseball scores.

"Mr. Crowe?"

Routed from his daydreaming by yet another rude interruption, Robbie looked up, eyes flashing with anger. *"What?"*

"We have a situation," Tom said somberly.

Robbie, alarmed by Tom's Joe Friday mien, sat up from his chaise lounge with a start. "Tell me."

Tom detailed the communications from Winnie and the follow-up investigation. He showed Robbie a copy of the letter on his phone and outlined his findings about its origin.

"I've never heard of this dentist," Robbie said. "Do you think he's the guy who sent it?"

Tom shook his head. "At this point, we simply don't know for sure. Our records indicate that a Dr. Stuart Littmann is in fact a company shareholder with a sizable position."

"How much?"

"About twenty thousand shares."

Robbie scoffed. Compared to what *he* owned? "A piker."

"Might be a lot to him."

"Could it be someone else who took magazines from his office?"

"Possibly. We think this a matter best handled by the police."

Robbie was incredulous. "Are you out of your *mind?*" he said. "That would put it in the public record. Imagine the press getting a hold of that. *'Robbie Crowe gets death threats for ruining the company.'* The media would have a field day. They already hate me." Robbie leaned over, scratching the back of his head as he deliberated. After a moment, he came to the only logical solution. "Call Howie-Do-It."

Now it was Tom's turn for head-scratching. Howard J. Doolin, AKA Howie-Do-It, was Robbie's off-the-books black-ops henchman, a guy with an office in a dark corner of the headquarters basement who would do anything for Robbie and never worried about company procedures or criminal statutes. An amateur detective at best, Howie was a devoted Robbie loyalist who stood ready, if not eager, to take a bullet for the boss. There were many times when Tom wanted to give him one, preferably in the temple.

"Mr. Crowe, Howie-Do-It could complicate matters."

Robbie seethed with impatience. "Tom, listen to me. It does not appear there is time for debate. Guy like this?" he said. "He's obviously unhinged. He could be anywhere right now with a scope rifle, ready to take me out."

Tom looked at the tall trees and evergreens around the pool. "Low probability, sir."

Robbie flushed red. "See? *See?* This is exactly why I want Howie. He'll take this shit seriously. And he'll do whatever it takes to deal with it."

"That's what concerns me Mr. Crowe. Howie's not always mindful of the rules."

Robbie slowly shook his head. "I'm not worried about rules, Tom. I'm worried about a homicidal maniac who blames me for all his troubles. He could strike at any moment." Robbie regarded Tom with disgust. *Why won't these people simply do what's necessary?* "You know what, Tom? Fine. *Fine!* I'll call Howie myself."

Tom sighed. "Mr. Crowe, I'm not trying to be difficult—"

"Well, you are, and I really don't understand why," Robbie said, looking up Howie's listing on his phone. "So how about this? You do things your way. I'll do things mine."

* * *

Howie-Do-It was enjoying a typically productive day in the basement of Crowe Power headquarters. He had responded to every criticism of Robbie Crowe on Twitter with a series of vile counterattacks and smears under a variety of pseudonyms. He had sold his entire weekly supply of weed to the building crew at a tidy profit. He had photoshopped some celebrity faces onto naked bodies in lewd poses and uploaded the images to porn sites. And, in a nod to company procedures, he had belatedly filled out his annual Self-Assessment from Human Resources, contending he had met all his objectives for the year and that he deserved a high ranking and a raise because he "Exceeds Expectations."

In fact, there were no real expectations for Howie other than that he was on permanent standby to do whatever Robbie Crowe needed done. Spy on Crowe Power executives? *Yessir!* Intimidate social media critics of Robbie Crowe? *Okay!* Deliver hush money to those who might have been party to one of Robbie's amoral adventures? *What's the address?* Such dedication made Howie a genuine FORC—Friend of Robbie Crowe. As a result, he was impervious to the usual strictures of employee conduct and thoroughly insulated from the possibility of dismissal, despite flunking out of four departments for general indolence regarding his assigned duties. Unlike the corporate drones who passively followed rules, regulations, and instructions from supervisors, Howie was an independent man of action who reported only to Robbie. No one seemed to know which department he was in any longer, but he still retained a paycheck, as well as a desk in the basement bullpen, lodged with a dozen other misfits and untouchables who, for various reasons, also couldn't be fired under any circumstances.

Howie's hotline—one in a series of burner phones that could not be traced to Robbie—rang just as he launched a rerun of *WWE Smackdown* on his desktop computer. He gladly hit the pause button to speak to his revered patron. "Yo," he answered.

"Howie," Robbie said gravely, "I need your help." He explained the letter and its vaguely suggested threat, his disgust with Corporate Security for refusing to do their jobs the way he saw them, and his worry about a possible assassination. "You're the only one I can trust," Robbie said. "These people on Tom's team are completely dead on their ass."

Howie assured the chairman that he was in safe hands now. "Don't worry, boss. I got you covered. I'll get a copy of the letter from Security and start my own investigation. We'll get to the bottom of this pronto."

"Let me know what you find out as soon as you can," Robbie said, anxiously. "We can't have some nut job out there putting me in his crosshairs."

"Seriously, dude, don't worry. I got it. Focus on what you do best and run the company."

*　*　*

Robbie hung up and headed to the whirlpool, while Howie called Dr. Stuart Littmann's office and spoke with the delightfully accommodating receptionist, Chanisse, who managed to squeeze in this promising new patient with a toothache, a Cadillac insurance plan, and a willingness to pay his out-of-pocket charge in advance. Howie rode the 4 train up to Grand Central Station, walked a couple blocks to an office tower on 44th Street, and took an elevator to the nineteenth floor, where a glass door led to the office of Stuart Littmann, DDS. After checking in with the large but lovely Chanisse—*was she flirting with me?*—Howie took a seat in the reception area, where an ancient man with a walker was dozing in a torn pleather armchair. Quickly deducing that this nonagenarian was probably not a suspect in *The Case of the Threatening Letter*, Howie discreetly pulled from his jacket pocket a copy of the partial mailing label pieced together by Corporate Security and carefully compared the typography, coding and layouts to the labels on the well-worn magazines tossed into a pile on the coffee table. Based on his forensic examination, as well as some wild guesses, Howie concluded that the label probably came from a combination of *Us*, *Glamour*, and *Fortune*. He quickly texted Robbie: *We're getting closer.*

"Mr. Doolin?" a woman called from the doorway to the inner sanctum.

Howie, carrying a two-month old copy of *Us*, was escorted by Emilia, a masked hygienist wearing powder-blue scrubs, to a cubbyhole at the end of the hallway where he was offered a dental chair and asked about the tooth that was troubling him. Howie indicated that a lower left molar was at issue, but the pain had subsided with Tylenol. Nevertheless, he thought it important to get it checked out, and Emilia obliged by probing for soft spots with a pick, shooting an x-ray, and promising the doctor would see him shortly.

Dr. Littmann entered briskly and barked out, "*Mis*-ter Doolin." He grabbed the chart off the credenza and studied it. "Good to meet you. What brings you in?" Howie appraised the would-be assassin as five-foot-six and approximately one-hundred and forty pounds, without the lab coat and magnifying eyeglasses. With thinning, dyed-black hair, bushy eyebrows, teeth as ivory-white as piano keys, and a concave build that suggested he might have trouble lifting a magazine and a pair of scissors at the same time, Littmann did not strike him as an obvious menace.

After Howie explained the pain he had experienced, Dr. Littmann said, "Let's have a look." Littmann yanked on Howie's chin and peered into the void, poking here, prodding there, and scraping enamel with his scaler, before wheeling back in dismay. He turned and peered at the x-ray brought in by Emilia and shook his head. "Mr. Doolin, when is the last time you saw a dentist?"

Howie shrugged. "I dunno. Two years. Three. Maybe four."

"Uh-huh. Uh-huh. It looks it," he said, spinning around and casting a hard look at Howie: his thick neck, corded like a tree stump; his forearms covered with ancient tattoos that had mottled into a blue-green swamp of illegible drawings, proclamations and 2 a.m. inspirations; his choppy buzzcut that looked like something he did himself, possibly with the lights off. His neglected teeth fit the picture of a man who might be operating a meth lab in the Poconos. "Your insurance pays for dental care. Why don't you use it?"

"Ah. You know, doc. It's hard to find time."

"Well, now you're going to need a series of appointments for cleaning and repair—and not just the tooth that was bothering you. Do you work nearby?"

"I work downtown. Crowe Power, on Broad Street."

Dr. Littmann visibly jerked, like someone had stuck a fat Novocaine needle in his neck. "So," he said, recovering, "what brings you all the way up here?"

"Somebody referred me."

"Marty McGarry?"

"Is he a patient?"

"He was." Littmann scribbled a note on Howie's chart.

"That figures." Howie picked up the magazine from his lap and held it for Littmann to see. "I thought maybe you could tell me something about this?"

Littmann looked at the cover, which bore a photo of a distraught celebrity.

JEN'S LATEST HEARTBREAK
Dumped Again!

Littmann shrugged nervously. "I had nothing to do with it. I don't even know her."

Howie sat up and pointed to the mailing label with Dr. Littmann's address. "I'm talking about this," he said sternly. "Somebody sent a threatening letter to our chairman with letters cut from magazines mailed to this office. This caper's got your name written all over it, doc."

Littmann pushed back in his chair and spoke in a staccato stutter. "That, that, that, that, that's just one heck of an accusation, Mr. Doolin."

"Yeah? Well I have proof."

"I never threatened anybody."

Howie pulled his copy of the letter from his pocket. "What do you call this?"

"I call that a, a, a complaint," Dr. Littmann said, his register rising.

"So it *was* you."

"You're, you're, you're *damn* right it was me! I foolishly believed in your company. I thought the Crowes were good people. I thought Walker Hope was a great CEO. I liked the fact that they were based right here in the city and that some of their employees were my patients. That's why I invested my entire inheritance in Crowe Power Company stock. One million dollars, all on CRO. And you want to know what it's worth now, just six weeks later? *Eight hundred thousand!* I've lost twenty percent in little more than a month! That may not be a lot of money to a rich man like Robbie Crowe, but it's a hell of a lot of money to me. I borrowed against my stock and now the bank wants its money back. I have nothing to give them. I could lose everything, including my practice."

"And you blame Robbie Crowe for that?"

Littmann's eyes rolled as his blood pressure rose. "Who else should I blame? He's destroying a perfectly good company. The public needs to be warned about this man."

Howie folded the letter back into his pocket and shrugged. "You'll keep your opinions to yourself, if you know what's good for you."

"You're *threatening* me?"

Howie shrugged. "Call it 'advice.'"

Littmann rose to his full five-foot-six and pointed with a shaky finger to the door. "I want you to leave."

"I bet you do," Howie said, yanking off his plastic bib, tossing it aside and scrambling to his feet. Littmann snatched a drill and pointed it at Howie. "Stay back," Littmann warned. He stepped on the foot pedal, eliciting an electric whine. *"Chanisse!"* he called toward the hallway. "Get security up here. *Now!*"

Howie, looking for a weapon of his own, found only a plastic cup with mouthwash. He grabbed it and held it up, ready to toss the luminous blue liquid. Littmann countered by grabbing the water pick in his other hand, poised to shoot a stream at Howie if necessary. They stared at one another, crab walking, in a toothless standoff.

"I want my swag bag," Howie said. "Or this mouthwash goes all over your nice white coat."

Keeping his eye on Howie, Littmann carefully put down the water pick and reached blindly behind him to the credenza, fumbling for a white plastic bag stuffed with a toothbrush, floss and travel-sized package of toothpaste. He tossed it to Howie.

"Take it and get out."

Chanisse appeared at the door. "Dr. Littmann, you want me to handle this?" she said, her voice suddenly dropping an octave or two.

Howie quickly reappraised Chanisse, whose gender transition looked like it may have occurred very recently, possibly this morning. She was six-foot-two and two hundred and twenty pounds of rippling muscle; very possibly, she had been a linebacker for the Giants in an earlier life. Regardless, Chanisse was not the hill Howie wanted to die on. "I'm leaving," he announced. He pointed a finger and snarled at the dentist, as he slid past Chanisse for the door. "You need to be careful, pal."

* * *

Howie found a pocket park a half-block from Littmann's office, where workers from nearby office buildings were having afternoon coffee together, eating a late lunch from the Shah of Shawarma food truck, or sitting alone, texting their friends. Howie grabbed a metal mesh chair and table under a locust tree and phoned Robbie.

"I got a make on this guy," Howie said. "It's definitely Littmann. Looks like we've got ourselves a disgruntled shareholder."

"And he's pissed at me? I'm the only one around here trying to do something."

"I know. It ain't fair, man."

"Damn right."

"And get this: Marty McGarry was one of Littmann's patients."

"Ah! Well, no *shit!*" Robbie said. "It's all coming together now. You think he put him up to it?"

"Wouldn't be surprised. You got nothin' but crappy media coverage when he was running PR. Nobody gave you the proper respect."

"Oh my god," Robbie said. "You may have to kick his ass, too."

Howie sighed. Robbie's list of people whose asses needed kicking was growing longer by the day. There was the guy at the newsstand in the headquarters lobby who looked at him squinty-eyed one day. There was the lady in New Jersey who criticized him on the Yahoo! message board for firing Walker. And there was Ernesto, field comandante of the Planetistas, who bitched about carbon emissions to Natalia. How many more of Robbie's demons could Howie take on? "How about if I pay Marty a little visit and rattle his cage? We can take things from there."

"Get on it," Robbie urged. "Do whatever you need to do to get this dentist off my ass. I don't care what it takes, Howie. I'm sick of this crap and I'm not going to take it anymore."

15. OUR SLIME HAS COME

Marty headed down the hall toward the executive conference rooms, named for various fossil fuels. Peering in through the long vertical window next to the door to the Coal Room, he saw people milling about with coffee and bagels. Kip Stamper, suspected leader of the Resistance, was walking around shaking hands, looking very much in command of his insurgents.

Marty entered the room and was met by Kimmee Brewster, the head of marketing. "Marty, so glad you could make it," she said. "We're just waiting on Hatch."

"Hatch? Who's that?"

She looked at Marty as if he'd just dropped in from Pluto. "Hatch *Peterson?* Are you kidding?"

"Should I be?"

"Well, yeah. He runs Plan9 Interstellar in Brooklyn? *C'mon.* He's like this incredible branding genius. We're so lucky to get him. You must have heard of him. Aren't you the communications guy?"

She abandoned Marty for someone who could actually help her career, leaving him to meander among the people milling about, walking in little circles, sipping matchas and nibbling multigrain crackers. Those who bothered to look up quickly appraised him as an alien being—*dude's, like, wearing a tie?*—and looked away again. At the refreshment station, Marty tried three different coffee urns before finding one with a little liquid left, swirled in an ounce of soy milk apparently flavored with dirtballs, and grabbed a seat in the back, where he could doze off as needed.

"It's important you're here, Marty," said Kip Stamper, who had come up behind him and leaned over the back of his chair. "Despite what Walker Hope might think, quarterly results aren't what drive Staminum's reputation."

"Thank god for that, eh?" Marty said.

"It's all about doing things the right way." Kip patted Marty on the back and went off to join the commotion at the door, where the exalted Hatch was making his entrance to a fawning crowd. Donned in a standard Brooklyn uniform of black boots, skinny jeans, a white shirt buttoned halfway up, and a purple velvet blazer, Hatch pulled off his aviator sunglasses, revealing red-rimmed, hazy eyes, and ran his hand over glistening black hair that looked like it had been used to mop up an oil spill in the East River. The brand genius of Plan9 Interstellar moved slowly to the front of the room, followed by a posse of young creatives, ever eager to touch the hem of his garment. He barely acknowledged the existence of the Earthlings he encountered with a faint nod, but assiduously avoided their cooties.

At the head of the conference table, Hatch turned his back to the room. He buried his face in his hands, as if in anguished thought, while the assemblage went still and an assistant dimmed the lights. At last he turned to the group, and in volcanic fashion, spewed his pitch.

"*Fuck* your stupid power plants!" he said, pounding a fist on the conference table. "*Fuck* your greasy pipelines!" He hit the table again. "*Screw* your refineries!" Once more. "And to *hell* with your stinkin' profits. That's *not* who you are."

He's got us pegged, Marty thought.

Hatch pulled out a vial of green slime from his pocket and placed it delicately, reverently, on the conference table. "This," he said, "*THIS* is what Staminum is all about." He looked around the room, waiting for the gravity of his pronouncement to sink in. "It's fucking algae, man, and it's the new image leader for this company, a company that's built for the *future.*"

The silence that followed was quickly broken by rapturous applause, most enthusiastically led by Kip Stamper, who put his index finger and his thumb in his mouth and whistled. Grinning, he looked back at Marty. *See? This is what I'm talking about!*

Hatch continued. "I have no idea how this shit works, man. None. But I know that you've got people in this company developing, like, these amazing microbial fuel cells that will power the world. It's nature, man. It's real. It's *green*, for fuck sake! And as far as your corporate marketing goes, it's fucking *gold.* Even better, there's more where this came from. You've got all kinds of little projects coming up with weird new energy shit that's going to make all these fossil fuels go away.

That needs to be the conversation you have with America. Staminum..." He paused, then softly. "The Power to Dream."

Hatch collapsed in the chair at the head of the table, drenched in a drizzle of sweat from his passing brainstorm as the applause rolled like thunder. Now it was time for his acolytes to follow up with how this concept would come to life through creative applications on TV and the internet. There were short videos about hydrogen cars that could be flown to the moon and tidal energy that generated electricity for entire cities and cow poofs that powered tractors and combines—all against a backdrop of rolling hills and acres of corn, sylvan glens and dandelion spores drifting in the breeze, happy horses grazing in meadows and ducks and swans splashing merrily in ponds. It was all so wild and weird and wonderful. And not remotely close to what Staminum actually did or where it operated.

This, Marty figured, was what the Greeneron subsidiary was all about: investing big on science experiments to find alternatives to fossil fuels, rehabilitating Staminum's reputation, and salving the consciences of a family that made an enormous fortune off the business they now found socially embarrassing. None of Greeneron's projects were ready for prime time, but no matter. Marty decided the best policy for the moment was to go along with the gag. Pretend this all made sense and clap. *Bravo, Hatch! Bravo!*

As the meeting ended and Marty returned his coffee mug to a bus tray, Kip approached him from behind. "Is that great stuff or what?" he said.

Marty nodded. "Oh yeah. Are you kidding me? PR brilliance."

Kip shook his head. "No, no, Marty. It's much more than PR. This is about our direction as a company."

"Better living through pond scum?" *Ah, shit.* He shouldn't have said that...

Kip squared his shoulders with Marty's. "I don't care if it actually works or not. *Something* in here will work. It has to. And that's all it takes. I want to change the conversation about this company."

"I don't think there is any," Marty said.

"Then we need to start one," Kip said. "I hear your boss is not a fan of Greeneron."

"Walker? I don't know whether he's a fan or not. I do know he's not just my boss. According to the org chart, he seems to be everyone's."

Kip smirked. "I know all about you, Marty. You're a CEO whisperer. Well, whisper something nice about this campaign. We're presenting to him tomorrow and we need him on board, quickly. This train's leaving the station."

Marty wondered: *powered by what?*

16. A FRED IN NEED

Hours after losing his job, Fred Crispin remained in mouth-breathing shock, staring out the window of his corner office, trying to process his disastrous encounter with Walker.

How could he have miscalculated so badly? Didn't his track record count for something? He had done pretty damn well as COO, by Staminum's low standards. True, they never met their objectives in his three years at the helm, but they came mighty close once or twice, and the shortfalls couldn't be attributed entirely to him. Surely, his old boss Tom Flaherty bore some responsibility. After all, Fred was merely charged with *executing* the game plan, not conceiving it.

Now the rich life as he enjoyed it was over: The extraordinary pay—*seven million dollars last year!*—gone. So, too, were the perks, the prestige, and the notion that the gravy train would keep rolling as long as he wanted. He had always assumed he'd leave the company on his own timetable, with all the proper honors and salutations. What a stupid mistake to reach out to Walker! If he hadn't, he might have hidden in the woodwork a while longer and Walker wouldn't have noticed him. But, *no.* He had to go out and do the right thing, the responsible thing, the *Fred* thing. It made him sick.

His admin, Ellen, appeared at his door. "Fred, your nine o'clock is in the Natural Gas Room."

Fred stared dully. Ellen, sweet, sweet Ellen. Such a helpful partner, she suddenly seemed a distant, unknowable figure. Fred felt himself drifting into the darkness of deep space, like an astronaut cut loose from the tether to his rocket ship, while Ellen gazed at him through the window of the module, pounding on the glass. A voice crackled in his head: *ground control to Major Fred...*

"Fred," Ellen said, cocking her head. "Did you hear me?"

He blinked hard, searching his jumbled brain for a response. "I, um—" *Why was Ellen even there?* "What did you say?"

"The Logistics meeting. It's coming right up."

"Oh. Right." He fumbled around his desk, looking for... something. He couldn't remember what. His keys? A pen? "I, uh—I'll head down in a minute."

She stepped closer. "Are you okay?"

"Sure," he said with a forced laugh. "Why not?"

"You don't seem okay."

He brushed it off with a wave of his hand. "No worries. I'm fine." He took a deep breath. "Seriously." As Ellen returned to her desk, Fred thought of the big jobs he'd passed on over the years out of loyalty to Tom Flaherty and Mother Staminum. Was that gig in Wichita still available? Would he want to live there? Where was Wichita, exactly? Somewhere in Kansas, yeah, but Fred's whole life—not to mention his mistress—was here in New York. Aw, hell. Maybe he was better off moving out to the prairie, taking his girlfriend with him, and downshifting to a more manageable speed. Guy like him might be a big deal out there in the hinterlands. Maybe he wouldn't have to work so hard.

He pushed himself away from his desk and headed toward the door. Outside his office, Ellen was back at her desk, typing away on her computer, unaware of the tsunami that was about to slam her world, too. Once he was gone, she'd never work again for an executive with a rank as high as his, and her standing in the executive assistant pecking order would fall with her. She'd even have to sit at a different table in the lunchroom. As Fred passed, she reminded him, "You're going to Gas."

Fred sighed. Aren't we all? He stepped into the corridor of the fifty-first floor and moseyed down the hall past Natural Gas to proceed to the office of Marty McGarry. "May I come in?" he asked, tentatively.

"By all means," Marty said, indicating a couple of chairs at a small conference table in the corner.

Marty couldn't help thinking Fred was perhaps the most singularly unimpressive top executive he'd ever met outside the Lucky Sperm Club. Fred didn't look the part of a penultimate corporate leader, with a mismatched wardrobe of purples and browns, a horrendous case of spider veins on his face resembling a Waze map of Manhattan gridlock, and dull dyed-brown hair. Nor did he sound the part of a corporate poohbah, with a wheezy twang that suggested he might have a couple of cotton balls lodged in his sinuses. And Fred certainly didn't demonstrate the level of command that a CEO like Walker would demand, with no ready diagnosis of the company's problems, an essential prerequisite to prescribing a cure. Fred's reputation as a CEO bag carrier with no ideas or leadership skills of his own was apparently well-deserved. Nevertheless, Marty had to feel for the poor bastard. He, too, had been fired not so long ago. It wasn't fun.

Marty shut the door behind Fred and they both took a seat. "You've worked with Walker before," Fred said. "What just happened to me?"

"I don't know any details," Marty said, with a sympathetic shake of his head. "All I heard is that we need to work on a press release announcing your, uh, retirement? Is that what we're calling it?"

Fred laughed mirthlessly. "Retirement? Hell. I went in to tell him he had my full support and I walked out without a job."

Marty reflected on his own painful encounters with Walker. "I know what it's like. Walker can remove your spleen without making an incision. Next thing you know, it's sitting on the table."

Fred shook his head, bewildered. "He didn't even give me a chance to prove myself. Once we got acquainted a little better, I could have helped him just like I helped Tom."

Okay. *That,* Marty thought, *was a problem.* "Sometimes that happens when you're too closely associated with the last CEO," he said. "The new CEO can't get that out of their head. They see you as an officer in the last army. If there's any good news in all this, it's that you can frame the story of your departure pretty much any way you want."

"How do you mean?"

"You decide why you've elected to leave Staminum. It could be for personal reasons. Maybe you have a health issue or you want to spend more time with your family. Maybe you're planning to pursue other opportunities. We don't have to say what they are exactly."

"But that's just it: I didn't decide to leave," Fred protested. "And I don't have any other opportunities. Walker decided I should leave, and in this kind of weird jujitsu, made it sound like I volunteered. Before I knew it, he escorted me to the door and thanked me for quitting."

Marty shook his head. "You can't say that."

Fred said bitterly, "It's *exactly* what happened."

"I mean in the press release."

"Oh," Fred said. "No. Of course not."

"So, how do we want to talk about this?"

"Well. I don't think I can say I want to spend more time with my family. The kids have all grown up and moved away. God forbid I visit them. I'd pull up in the driveway and they'd pull down the blinds. They've got their own lives."

"With all due respect, Fred, nobody who leaves a company to—quote—spend more time with their family, has *ever* spent more time with their family. We say that sort of thing to provide a little cover for the dearly departed."

"Well I don't want to give that as a reason. My family would read that and freak out."

"Alright. How about this: You've decided to accept a new challenge. An announcement will come later, but you're very excited about it."

"*What* new challenge?"

"Something might come up. When headhunters learn you're on the market, odds are good they're gonna beat down your door with a hammer. I mean, c'mon. You're, you're..." *What?* There was nothing Marty could think of to recommend him. "You're *Fred*, for crying out loud."

Fred slumped. "I'm fifty-eight years old. I'm closer to the end of my career than the beginning. I have to doubt whether there's anyone out there looking for someone with my profile. The fact is, we have been losing money for some time and my name's on that. Of course, you know that was largely Tom's doing."

"Oh, right," Marty said. *Career-wise, this guy is toast.* "Is there anything else you've always wanted to do? It doesn't have to be a job. You could work in your garden. Play golf. Build an ant farm."

Fred threw his head back, looking up at the ceiling. "I don't have any hobbies. And I don't really want any. Do we have to decide this right now?"

Marty shook his head. "Nah. Of course not. Take all the time you need. I don't have to get the release out until tomorrow."

"*Tomorrow?*"

Marty nodded. "Believe me, it's better for you this way. Define your story before the rumor mill does it for you."

Fred grunted and sat sullenly, staring at Marty. He was apparently disinclined to move until Marty either gave him better direction on what he should do with the rest of his life or the janitorial crew eventually turned out the lights. "You know what?" Fred said. "I'm kicking myself right now."

Marty checked his watch. "Why's that?"

Fred sighed. "I ran into Digby Pierrepont at the Metropolitan Club a month ago, right after Walker left Crowe Power. He said I should come in and talk to Robbie Crowe about a job at his shop."

"*What?* Are you kidding? That's great!"

Fred winced. "No, it's not. I turned him down." Fred shook his head wistfully. "God, I wish I'd taken him up on the offer. If only I'd known."

Suddenly, the clouds parted and it all became clear to Marty. If Staminum could not only whack this loser but stick him with a competitor, it would make his firing doubly valuable for Staminum. He slapped the desk and leaned in. "Fred," he said. "Call Digby."

"What?"

"I know I shouldn't tell you this, Fred, because you should never send such a valuable asset to a competitor. But this is about you right now, and I want to help."

"What would I say?"

"Send him a note. Say you've been thinking about your conversation and, after some reflection, you'd like to talk to him further."

"What if he calls? What do I say then?"

"Tell him you're considering a change and you really like what's going on at Crowe Power. Throw a few bouquets Robbie's way, too, and if you have to, dump on Staminum. It won't hurt your cause, I promise you."

For the first time all day, a craggy smile emerged between Fred's red splotches. "I like that."

Marty clapped his hands together. "Better move fast, okay? I'll try to delay this press release as long as I can, but Walker's gonna be on my ass soon to get this thing out."

Fred practically leapt from his seat. "I'm on it."

Marty stood and shook his hand. "Can you imagine? What a huge win! You'd be a real catch for Crowe. They'd love to stick it to us. And for you? Talk about vindication. *Man!*"

"Thank you, Marty. *Thank you!*"

Marty slapped him on the back, like a trainer might hit the hind of a quarter horse to make it run. "Go, Fred, *go!*"

17. GREENERON: THE OTHER SIDE

Walker ran his usual early-evening bed check through the Staminum C-suite as the sun set over the Palisades, illuminating the dust particles floating about the empty offices like miniature satellites.

As in previous stints piloting companies through the darkness, Walker made it his mission to orbit his executive world late in the day, surveilling through doorways and windows to see who was keeping office hours and who wasn't, and dropping in on the few who hung around for the chance at a little face time with the boss. The best time to catch up, he thought, was when the chores were finished and the day was nearly done.

By six-thirty, most of Staminum's leadership team had already beaten a retreat to Westchester, New Jersey, and the Upper East Side, but Walker was pleased to see a few executives still had their butts firmly affixed to their Aeron chairs. Whether they were working or merely updating their financial portfolios with the day's stock gain was impossible to tell. Were they making plans to buy a mansion on the Jersey Shore? Perusing yachts to sail to Martha's Vineyard? Acquiring a pig farm in the Berkshires? It always amazed Walker how many senior executives quickly outspent their capital gains, making them captive dependents on the company, stuck in their jobs longer than they wanted. Walker, on the other hand, wasn't much of a spender. He kept his expenses low, living in a rental apartment downtown. The larger significance of his fat pay package was as a means of keeping score. His compensation totals were a measure of his achievement, a reflection of his worth, and a way to compare his value against all other CEOs out there.

As he padded down the hallway, Walker saw the back of Marty McGarry sitting across from Maria Territo in her office. He caught Maria's eye and put his finger to his lips as if to say *"Shhh!"*. Then he quietly crossed the threshold and clapped Marty hard on the back.

"What the fuck!" Marty blurted as he jumped out of his chair. He turned to see Walker and blanched. "Oh. Hello, Walker."

Walker brushed it aside. "How's that press release on Fred comin'?"

Marty winced. "Getting there. Just not quite finished."

Walker clenched his jaw, annoyed. "No sense keepin' last night's fishbones around the kitchen. Let's get that thing out on the curb before it stinks."

"I'm holding it because we decided he's leaving to pursue new opportunities. Now I'm waiting to see if he might actually have one."

Walker guffawed. "Fred? Naw. Who'd hire him?"

"Someone's interested. You're not going to believe who."

Walker's eyes darted back and forth as he thought. Then it hit him and he nearly spat. "*No!* Seriously?"

"He might —*might*—get a big job at Crowe Power."

Walker laughed. "You are pullin' my leg!"

"He's talking with Digby tonight."

Walker clapped his hands together and twirled around in a hillbilly happy dance, as if he heard some jug music in his head. "Good for him!" He sat on the edge of Maria's desk, where she was pouring another packet of sugar in her coffee and stirring it with her pen. "Of course Robbie would hire him," Walker said, bobbing his head as he ran through the scenario in his mind. "Tim's been CEO for about a month. Stock's dropped like a rock. Robbie's probably sick of him already. He'd love to think he's stealin' one of our guys."

"That's the idea," Marty said. "I'm helping him with his message points."

"Best news all day!" Walker reached over and lightly rapped Marty's knee with a knuckle. "Love the way you're thinkin', Marty. You might turn out alright, despite my reservations." He turned back to Maria. "Now—tell me about Greeneron. What did you find out?"

"Let me show you around the swamp." Maria led Walker and Marty to a conference table, where she unfurled a five-foot long roll of paper diagramming Staminum's Greeneron subsidiary: an incomprehensible conglomeration of twenty-one companies focused on energy technologies. Most were little more than concepts, while a couple—a solar power company in Nevada and wind farm in Iowa—were up and running and bleeding cash.

"The losses are even worse if you count expenses they bury under general administration for the whole company," she said.

"Any chance of a profit?" Walker asked.

"I have better odds at winning Powerball. And I don't even buy tickets." She looked over her shoulder to see if anyone had crept up on them. "Do you mind if I roll this up? I don't want anyone wandering in here and seeing this. I think they know what I'm up to and they don't seem to like it. And when I tell you about this, you'll understand why."

She explained that every one of the Greeneron companies was created in similar fashion. A consortium of venture capital firms, led by Winesta Capital in Boston, would license an early stage energy technology from the laboratories of a leading research university, such as MIT, Stanford or CalTech. License in hand, they would build a start-up around it and dress it up. Winesta added staff and advisory boards of distinguished scientists to build credibility, and spent liberally on websites, marketing, and PR to raise the company's profile.

"VCs do that all the time," Walker said.

"Right," Maria conceded. "But here's where it gets slimy, and I'm not talking pond scum. By amazing coincidence, every one of these companies was purchased by Staminum for just under one hundred million dollars. That just so happens to be—"

Walker interjected, "—the limit of Steady Stamper's spending authority."

"Exactly," Maria said. "Any acquisition above that price would have to go to the board for review and approval."

Walker nodded. "So all these purchases were made without any oversight."

"That made me wonder why," Maria continued. "Winesta is privately held and they have next to nothing on their website. So I called on some of my old 'dark arts' friends to help me with research. Don't ask me who they are or where they are."

Walker smiled. "Or you'd have to kill me."

"No," Maria said. "They would."

Walker dropped the smile. "Gotcha."

"These guys were able to get their hands on all kinds of interesting documents: a private prospectus, an investor presentation, and some other insider materials, none of which can be shared outside this room. All the research pointed in the same direction."

Walker shook his head. "Let me guess: Steady Stamper."

"And Kip Stamper. And Fritz Stamper. And his wife, Alice Stamper. There are Stampers stamped all over this thing. Throw in a few close friends, too. Like Margaret Hathaway."

Walker nodded. "That explains a lot."

"And a woman named Elise Barreau."

"Steady's personal trainer."

"She's got a piece of the action, too." Maria sat at the conference table and folded her hands together. "Legally, we can't pierce the veil of Winesta without filing a lawsuit, which we obviously cannot do. But we know what happened here."

Walker sat down and propped a foot on the table. "So let me get this straight. The Stampers put up a little bit of money to create a bunch of small companies at a relatively low cost, knowing every one of them would be sold to Staminum at a high price. Guaranteed."

"Yes. At roughly a hundred times more than they put in."

Walker's jaw dropped. "No."

Maria nodded. "They've made almost two billion dollars so far, all of it by fleecing their beloved Staminum."

"No wonder they weren't worried about earnings. They were gettin' their money out the back door." Walker leaned back, putting his hands behind his head. "People go to jail for stuff like that."

"Do you want to prosecute? I'm not sure we'd get anywhere. The Stampers are huge political donors. Steady's been a bundler for every office in Manhattan— city, state, and fed. And we can't use any of this material as evidence. It would point directly to my sources."

Walker exhaled. "So what do we do?"

Maria shrugged. "I don't know. We can't keep carrying Greeneron on our books at its current value. At some point in the next year, we're going to have to take an impairment charge. And that leads to other problems."

Walker blew out his cheeks and looked up at the ceiling, thinking. "Unless..." he said.

"Unless what?" Maria asked.

Walker looked back at Maria. "We sell it."

Maria shook her head. "That's not gonna happen. What kind of idiot would buy it?"

Marty laughed. "I think that's a question that just answered itself."

Maria slapped the side of her head. "Robbie! Of course."

Walker nodded. "He'd love Greeneron. He'd see all his dreams come true."

Maria asked, "How do you get him to bite?"

Marty hit the table with his open hand and stood up. "Fred."

Walker cocked his head. "How?"

"He's our Trojan Horse. Load him up with all kinds of Greeneron crap and roll him downtown. He can whinny to Robbie that you hate to part with it but you're desperate for cash. Fred can plop the whole steamy pile onto Robbie's desk. He'll smell opportunity."

Walker regarded Marty with a sliver of admiration. "I don't believe I've fully appreciated until today, Marty, what a devious pot licker you are."

"Walker, please," Marty said. "I'm the comms guy."

Maria sat up straight and took a serious tone. "We all need to be careful about what we say. We can't make any misrepresentations of the value."

"I'll walk the line," Marty said. "I won't cross it."

Maria said, "None of us can."

18. TWENTY-ONE SKIDOO

L indsey grabbed the handrail and descended the steps from 52nd Street to the 21 Club, the former speakeasy that was once the haunt of Homer Crowe and his leadership team. They would pile into cars and head uptown to blow their expense accounts on whiskey and cigars at dark corner tables on the main floor and private rooms upstairs.

Lindsey found Maria checking her phone in a red leather chair next to the fireplace in the paneled lounge at the front of the club. At the sight of Lindsey, Maria rose to greet her, and on instinct, the two of them embraced lightly and awkwardly before taking chairs across from one another with a serving table between them. For once, Lindsey was certain she wasn't imagining that the woman in front of her had slept with her husband.

"Hope you don't mind. I started without you," Maria said, raising a vodka martini glass by the stem.

"You go right ahead," Lindsey said. "I need to notch it back a bit."

Maria sighed. "It's just one for me. I've got to go back to the office." The waiter delivered a sparkling water with lime for Lindsey, along with a snack caddy with mixed nuts, wasabi peas and cheese crackers. Maria quickly snatched up some of the peas and gobbled them down. "Dinner," she said with a shrug.

Lindsey smiled, uneasily. "Thank you for meeting me," she said. "I know how busy you must be in your new job."

"It's alright. I need the break. It's only day nine and I can't even see over the papers on my desk."

Lindsey nodded. "I wanted to ask you a bit about Crowe Power."

"I'd rather forget about it. But, okay. Shoot."

"This may sound funny, but... what does Robbie actually do at the company? I mean, I know he's the chairman, of course. But how does he, you know, spend his time?"

Maria chuckled. *Robbie Crowe. International Man of Mystery*, even at home. "He never talked about it?" Maria asked.

"Only in broad strokes. Occasionally, he'd talk vaguely about some grand vision for the company. Or, when he was frustrated, he'd complain about the people who reported to him, especially Walker. He didn't seem to think anyone was any good. According to Robbie, he was the hardest working person at Crowe Power."

Maria sipped her drink, leaving a perfect crimson lip print on the glass. "Except that he hardly works at all."

"He goes to the office, right?"

"Sure. When he feels like it. But he doesn't work, not in the conventional sense. He plays around with his Fantasy Baseball roster. He calls his friends to gossip about the people they knew from school and who was doing the best in terms of jobs and fortunes and wives and homes. He'd chat with his in-house cronies, like Digby and Howie-Do-It, who have to listen to all of Robbie's 'poor, poor, pitiful me' nonsense. His interest in the company is pretty much limited to a few things that pique his interest, like acquisitions, and alternative energy, and executive hirings and firings. And he worries constantly about how others view him. Is he admired? Is he respected? Does he get the credit he deserves for... whatever. He looks at Twitter about fifty times a day and the answer's always the same: no."

"People don't respect him?"

"Why would they?"

"So that's his day. Doesn't sound like much."

"He chases women."

"Like you."

"Sometimes," Maria said with a shrug, "he catches them."

Lindsey squeezed the lime in her water. "The company paid him nineteen million dollars last year. That's an enormous amount of money for somebody who doesn't do any work."

"Much of that was in stock appreciation, which I'm sure you know was largely driven by Walker. But still, it's a lot of loot. I calculated it once. He makes about two hundred and sixty-five times the average worker at Crowe. And he works about half as much."

Lindsey shook her head. She was not opposed to making money, even big bags of it. But there were right ways and wrong ways and amounts that were appropriate to one's contribution. She, like Robbie, came from a privileged upbringing, but her Midwestern family always stressed the value of hard work. She was required to do household chores for her allowance, which was miniscule compared to the family fortune, and to do volunteer work through her church. She asked, "Is Robbie worth that kind of money?"

Maria laughed. "Are you kidding me? He would tell you they don't pay him enough. *Oh, the sacrifices I make! The hours I put in!* Yada, yada, yada. After a while, the poor little rich boy schtick is a bit much to take, you know?" She looked at Lindsey: her exquisite tailoring, her perfect manners, and quiet confidence. "Or maybe you don't."

Lindsey shrugged. "Try me."

Maria sipped her martini, warming to the topic. "It was amazing to me how somebody with so many advantages in life could always act like a victim. You'd think he was under siege, with everybody trying to get something from him. His money. His job. His time. His privacy. Even his identity as a Crowe. I guess that's why he ate his lunch alone most days. Somebody might try to steal his peanut butter sandwich."

"So why does he want to do it?"

"Don't get me wrong. He loves *being* chairman. He just hates *doing* chairman. It's hard work and he doesn't have the patience, or the interest or, frankly, the experience. This is just my opinion, but I think he skipped too many rungs on the ladder on the way up. He never learned from his successes or his failures. He doesn't know the organization. He doesn't know the people. He doesn't know how to direct anybody. Deep down, I think he realizes that he's completely inadequate for the job, which makes him very insecure. That's why he's so sensitive to criticism. And, at the same time, such a bully. He beats people up for no reason at all. Yells at them. Screams at them. Humiliates them in front of their colleagues and tells them they're worthless. It makes him feel like he's in control, I suppose, especially when he's not."

"That's a terrible way to behave. I'm embarrassed to hear it."

"You must have seen some of this yourself."

"Oh, I've seen lots of histrionics, but he was never bullying with me or the kids. It was worse than that, in a way."

"How so?"

"He was indifferent. He just didn't care. When the going got tough, as it does sometimes, he got going—off to do his own thing, escaping situations without resolving them."

"Sounds like you're resolving them now."

Lindsey sipped her water. "I'm trying."

"So, tell me," Maria said. "How did he get like that? I've wondered many times why someone with all his advantages never seemed at ease. Was there someone in his life who was hard on him? His father, maybe?"

"His father had passed by the time we met, but yes, from what I've heard. Les Crowe was a very emotional man, probably bipolar, although it was never diagnosed, and a heavy drinker. He thought Robbie would never measure up to his forebearers and he told him so many, many times in very belittling ways. The Crowes who are in the company portraits in the Hall of Fam become larger-than-life legends and demi-gods. It's been hard for Robbie to live up to the mythology."

"That explains a lot."

"Given all that," Lindsey said, "why were you attracted to him?"

"Do you really want to go there?"

"I missed a lot living in my own bubble. I want to understand."

Maria set down her empty glass. "I come from very modest circumstances in Brooklyn, alright? My dad was a captain in the fire department and my mother washed floors. I left home when I was seventeen and made my own way through Stony Brook and Fordham Law. When I first met Robbie, I was a junior partner at a law firm that served the Crowe family. I was in a bad relationship at home and feeling pretty sad. Along comes this rich man with a big name from a big company, paying attention to me, flirting with me, making me feel like maybe I didn't deserve my crappy husband and that maybe there really was something bigger and better out there. What can I say? It turned my head."

Lindsey nodded. "Understandable."

"Robbie can be charming when he feels like it, and he was charming with me initially. He got me a job at Crowe Power, brought me into his inner circle and shared his problems. Oddly enough, I felt sorry for him. I thought I could help. He seemed so isolated, so lonely. I wanted to be someone he could trust. But, in the end, I realized he couldn't trust anybody. I certainly didn't trust him." She leaned forward and softly touched Lindsey's knee. "And, I'm sorry, I didn't even think of you. I guess I pretended you didn't exist, even though it was always in the back of my mind. *Robbie's married.* But since I didn't know you, I let it go. You see things a little differently in hindsight." She looked down and sighed. "I'm deeply ashamed of what I did. And I feel very foolish."

Lindsey patted the back of Maria's hand. "If it helps, I forgive you."

Maria looked up. "Thank you," she said, tears welling in her eyes. "I don't know if I could do the same."

"Hopefully, you'll never have to. I forgive him, too."

"You *do?*"

"Yes."

"Why?"

Lindsey shrugged. "It's the only way I can get out of bed in the morning. After something like this, you have to face the truth, hard as it is. You can wallow in your own bitterness or you can begin to move on."

"I'm sure it's not easy. But it looks to me like you're doing a pretty good job. I'm relieved. It would be worse for me if you looked miserable. But you look... happy?"

"That's a stretch," Lindsey conceded. "But I'm getting there."

Maria checked her watch. "I need to get back."

Lindsey stopped her. "Can I ask you one more thing."

"Okay."

"How do you see that role?"

"Which one?"

"Chairman of Crowe Power. What's the job description, in your view?"

Maria laughed. "That's *way* above my pay grade."

Lindsey scoffed. "You know more than you're letting on."

Maria appraised Lindsey's businesslike demeanor. Was she going where she appeared to be going? Maria took a deep breath and leaned in. "Alright. It's pretty simple, really. You don't need to be the so-called 'face' of the company, like Robbie tries to be. Let the CEO handle that. You also don't need to pretend you're the all-knowing, all-seeing expert on everything. That's why you hire experts on your team. Ask them questions. Hold them accountable for everything—not just what they do, but how they do it. That goes for your board *and* your senior management." Maria stood. "I really gotta go."

Lindsey said, "Would you ever work there again?"

"Not under the current circumstances."

"You mean if Robbie's in charge?"

"I wouldn't go near the place."

"And if he weren't?"

Maria smiled. "Call me."

$$* \quad * \quad *$$

After stopping in the ladies' room and heading for the exit and her waiting car, Lindsey encountered a familiar face coming through the door of the 21 Club: the flight attendant from Crowe Bird I. *What was his name?*

"Charles!" she cried, partly in relief that she remembered it. "How lovely to see you."

He blushed. "You too, Mrs. Crowe."

She regarded his suit and tie. "Don't you look nice."

"I'm applying for a job," he said.

"No," she said, disappointed. "You've left Crowe?"

"Actually," he said, sheepishly, "it left me."

She took his arm and pulled him out of the entranceway. "How so?"

Charles explained the lunch mix-up, Robbie's volcanic reaction, and his abrupt dismissal on the tarmac.

"Oh, my word," Lindsey said, shaking her head. "I'm deeply sorry."

"Don't be," Charles said. "Please. It wasn't you."

Lindsey fumed at the thought of Robbie's bullying. "That is no way to treat people. Especially someone as positive and helpful as you. I can't believe Robbie would do such a thing." She paused, reconsidering. "Actually, I can."

Charles shrugged. "It's sad. But... I'm adjusting. Or trying to."

She reached out and touched his arm. "Are you okay? Do you need anything?"

He smiled. "A job."

She searched through her purse for a personal card with her contact information and handed it to him. "Please. Use me as a reference. Here or anywhere else. I'll be happy to tell them you provided nothing but outstanding customer service. You were always so polite. So professional. From my vantage point, you were the best attendant we ever had."

Charles nodded. "Thank you, Mrs. Crowe. You're very kind."

Lindsey left the club and headed up the stairs to the street level and her car, reflecting on her conversations with Maria and Charles. Clearly, they left the wrong person on the tarmac in Chicago.

It should have been Robbie.

19. THE IDOL RICH

Robbie rode the elevator downstairs to the cocktail party exhausted from his afternoon. Had he been in the whirlpool too long? He examined his pruney fingers, which looked like the hands of a man twice his age. Once again, he had pushed himself beyond all human endurance.

Now, he'd prefer a snooze to a drink, but he'd have to suck it up because, as Dr. Kristi Kramer might say, he was summoned here for a higher *purpose*. He must persevere and fight through his fatigue. Tim made it quite clear that if Robbie missed everything else on the afternoon agenda, which he had, he should still— please, please, *please*—show up at the cocktail reception before dinner. As a direct descendant of Homer Crowe, Robbie was important not only as the company's current chairman, but as something of a mascot, like the Michelin Man, Mr. Peanut, or Sparty. Everybody rallied around him, Tim said, and mixing with the regular folks showed a certain bonhomie. Surely, it would buoy their spirits after a day of difficult breakout sessions to see a genuine Crowe in the flesh.

In return for making his celebrity appearance, Robbie tasked Tim with fetching him drinks, since it would be difficult for him to do with people mobbing him for handshakes and a bon mot or two. It was incumbent upon Robbie, as the inspirational leader, to motivate these poor schlubs in their menial labors with stories of his own arduous efforts and derring-do. *See, people? Even the giants put their shoulder to the wheel from time to time.* As Tim delivered Robbie a gin and tonic, the chairman was patiently listening to Phil somebody-or-other talk about shutting down a refinery on the Gulf Coast because of a safety issue. Naturally, the story triggered memories for Robbie of his own battle experience on the front lines.

"You're not going to believe what happened to me," Robbie said, as the executives pulled closer, slurping their beers and scotches. "It was my first day at the company, right? They parachute me into the refinery down in Aruba to do a little troubleshooting. I mean, this thing hasn't been running right and they want me to check it out. So I go into the control room and I look at this one dial and I could sense immediately—hey, something isn't right here. The needle's in the red. I went straight up to the general manager, this grizzled old dude, and told him maybe he ought to shut the damn thing down. He said, 'What the fuck do you know about it? Get the hell out of here and don't come back.' Just like that. I couldn't believe the attitude."

"Wow," Phil said. "Like *you're* the problem? What did you do?"

"I said, 'Look, *sir.*' Just like that. 'Look, *sir.* That's not your call.'"

"Unreal!" exclaimed *Hello! My Name Is BRIAN*. "Where were you working? The cat cracker?"

Robbie paused. Cat cracker? *What the hell was that?* "In that area," Robbie said, draining his G&T.

"Oh man," Brian said. "You don't mess around with the cat cracker."

Robbie nodded. "Damn right."

"Whole place could go kerblewy."

"That's what I was trying to tell him. Guy wouldn't listen."

Phil was amazed. "Given your family heritage and all, I wouldn't think they would make you, you know, work that hard."

Robbie shook his head. "You have no idea. Some people want to kiss your ass; some want to kick it. But hey. We all have to pitch in and earn our stripes around here, right?"

"So what did you tell him?"

Robbie shook the melting ice in his glass and sipped the water. "I said the same thing I told a thousand different people as I worked my way up the ladder. 'I don't want any special treatment. Just because my name's on the building doesn't mean you should treat me differently than anyone else.'"

"Wow," Phil said. "That's so cool."

Lucy Rutherford, a fast-rising executive who was running the company's largest and best-performing division, stepped closer in the circle, intrigued by Robbie's tale of personal heroism. "That's quite a story, Robbie. I was down in Aruba at the same time as you, and I remember hearing you were there, but I never saw you. Why did you think there was something wrong with the cat cracker?"

For a moment, Robbie had the stunned look of someone who felt a wet surprise in their shorts. "Oh, *shit*. Wouldn't you know?" He reached into his pocket, pulled out his phone, and looked at the blank screen. "Sorry, Lucy. I've gotta take this." He slapped the dead phone to his ear. "What is it?" he said loudly. "You're kidding!" He slipped around a corner, found Digby in another grouping of executives, and whispered to him. "Digs, what the fuck's a cat cracker?"

Digby swigged his scotch. "I give up. A snack for the kitty?"

"What?"

"How the heck do I know? I'm a lawyer, for God's sake."

"Then don't give me some bullshit answer. Find out. It's possible I had a job in one. I need to know what I was supposed to be doing."

"Aren't you a little late?"

"Lucy Rutherford's all over my ass."

Digby stared at him. "I'm trying to follow—"

"Just fucking *ask* someone, will you? Clearly, I can't ask somebody a question like that. I'd look like an idiot."

"But you're okay if your general counsel looks clueless?"

Robbie shrugged in a way that said, *Of course*. "Why should I care about that?"

"Robbie..."

"*Do* it," Robbie barked. "I don't have time to fuck around."

Digby saw Chief Engineer Elmer Schatz waiting in line for a drink and made a beeline for him. He sidled up behind him and gently pulled his arm. "Elmer," he said, "can you help me with something? How would you define a cat cracker? I want to be sure I explain it right to somebody."

Elmer nodded. "I'm sure you know it's the guts of the refinery, right?"

"Who doesn't?"

"I'd put it this way: it takes crude oil and breaks it down, turning it into gasoline, gases, and other products. Our company wouldn't be in business without it."

Based on further intel, Digby reported to Robbie that if he had shown up at the refinery for more than his first day, he would have worked with a variety of electrical, mechanical and process engineers like Lucy in a control room. While there was no job involving the cat cracker for which Robbie was remotely qualified, a princeling like him would merely be expected to hang around, look interested, soak up a little knowledge, and check a box so he could be "qualified" for the next promotion. Digby recalled that Robbie didn't even do that much; the key achievement of his six-month tour was the best tan of his life.

"So what the hell am I supposed to say to Lucy?" Robbie asked. "She's grilling me about this. It's like I'm talking to *60 Minutes* or something."

"Why don't you tell her you were just there to observe?"

"I can't say that," Robbie said. "I'd lose my street cred."

Digby blinked. "You have *street cred?*"

Robbie paced in a little circle. "Let's think this thing through. If we fire Lucy right now, before dinner, she'd have to leave immediately, right? She could just pack up her things and go."

"Oh yeah," Digby said. 'That's a great idea."

"Then I wouldn't have to answer her stupid questions."

Digby squared his shoulders with Robbie and looked him in the eye. "You can't fire her," he said, "especially for that. She's a star performer—probably the most promising executive talent we have in the company. You do recall that Tim wants her to be the next Chief Operating Officer."

Robbie ran a hand through his hair. "Okay. Fine. *Fine.* Then you have to keep her away from me. The chairman of this company doesn't need the third degree from some COO wannabe. All I was doing was trying to tell a little story. Maybe I exaggerated a bit. She comes on like Torquemada." He looked up to see Lucy walking his way, her eyes fixed upon him. Robbie turned his head and spoke into Digby's shoulder. "Oh my God. Here she comes now. Go talk to her."

"What?"

"*Go!*"

As if hit by an antiballistic missile, Lucy was intercepted by Digby and shot off course, splashing harmlessly back into the cocktail crowd, protecting the chairmanship from a social catastrophe. Robbie heaved a sigh of relief and took off safely in the opposite direction. Now... *where was Dr. Kristi Kramer?*

20. ROBBIE, UNPLUGGED

Robbie found his prized consultant at the head table in the banquet room, patting the seat of the chair next to hers and looking at him like a carny eyes a corn dog. "You," Dr. Kristi Kramer commanded, "are sitting right here with me."

Robbie gladly obeyed her command, as others on the leadership team found their seats and waiters delivered salad courses and poured wine. Much to Robbie's annoyance, they were soon joined by the pestilent Tim, who took the seat on Robbie's other side and stashed his massive binder under the chair.

"Digby's sitting there," Robbie said.

Tim protested, "My name tag is here."

"That's a mistake."

"But... I *put* it there."

Robbie reached over Tim's flatware and his charger, across the bread plate and butter dish, and around the wine glasses and water glass to snatch the name tag away. He placed it on his plate and folded the corners like a paper airplane, then sailed it across the table, where it landed on a beet.

"Looks like you're over there," he said.

Tim sighed and pushed back his chair, taking a piece of the tablecloth with him, sending a pair of wine glasses crashing onto his plate, and creating a clatter. Robbie slapped his forehead as wait staff rushed over to assist. How long was he going to have to live with this wad of gum on his shoe? As he watched Tim leave, Robbie turned his attention back where it belonged: on the divine Dr. Kramer.

"So," Robbie said, "what did I miss this afternoon?"

She rolled her eyes in wonderment. "Where do I start?" Kristi said. "We had the most *amazing* breakout sessions. I know you were super busy, but I really do wish you could have been there. Everyone was so bought in."

"And what exactly were we selling?"

Kristi explained that the first portion of the retreat was dedicated to deciding whether the company would define a mission, a purpose, or a vision. Following two hours of vigorous debate, they concluded that they couldn't decide. So they smooshed it all together into a formula that incorporated all three concepts: they would use Robbie's grand *vision*—they were a little fuzzy on the details—to frame a *mission* that, in turn, carried a sense of *purpose* that was all wound up in a powerful new slogan that would inspire the masses. And while nobody was quite sure what the slogan meant, everyone agreed the process was first-rate executive entertainment that fully justified the massive expense of the offsite. Time to *par-tay!*

"So, what did you come up with?" Robbie asked.

Kristi nodded toward the stage, where uniformed attendants were on ladders hanging a banner. "There it is," she said proudly.

We Will be the Most Responsible Energy Company in the World!

Robbie shrugged. "That's... it?"

"Don't you just *love* it?"

"I don't know. Don't you think slogans are kinda cheap?"

"This one wasn't."

"What's it mean? 'Responsible?'"

"It means we do things the right way."

"And what does *that* mean?"

"That's up to us to define. It's our aspiration as one global team."

"Uh-huh."

"When it all came together, it was the most *wonderful* moment of community," Kristi said, her eyes moistening. "Everyone was on the same page about where we need to go and who we want to be." Sensing the needle on Robbie's give-a-shit meter trending toward zero, she quickly spotted an opportunity to re-engage him. "Is this your napkin?" Whether it was or wasn't, she picked up some linen and placed it discreetly on Robbie's lap, with her hand underneath it. Patting Little Robbie, she said, "I hope you aren't too exhausted from your work today to deliver the goods tonight."

Robbie smiled. "You bet."

"I mean your speech."

"Oh. That? Easy peasy," he said. "I've given this speech a million times. I could do it in my sleep."

Kristi admonished him with a look. "After the day we've had? No! This is no time for the same old, same old," she said, sharply. "We are agents of change, my friend. That's what this whole conference is about. We're going to be the most responsible energy company in the whole wide world. It's your turn to show your support. Wave the flag. Tell us how we're going to do it." She squeezed him beneath the napkin. "Go big or go home."

Robbie sucked in his breath as Little Robbie got littler. What could he say that was different from what he had said a thousand times before? "I've had a few ideas floating around my head," he said. "Maybe I'll test one of them on the crowd tonight."

She leaned close to his ear. "Blow me away tonight," she cooed, "and I'll do the same for you."

Tall order, Robbie thought, but surely an effective incentive.

As others around the table began to look their way, Kristi pushed back to a respectful distance and summarized for Robbie the afternoon session, which centered on ways the company could recruit more millennials and Gen Xers. Aging baby boomers were leaving the energy business faster than a gas leak, and Crowe Power needed fresh blood to take their place. To foster the executives' understanding of the younger generations—species more exotic to this crowd than leafy sea dragons and pink grasshoppers—Kristi said she had arranged for a real live teenager to speak to the gathering during dinner.

Right on cue, Tim stood at the lectern on a stage at the front of the room and began to introduce the widely celebrated Rainwater Jones, a 15-year old high school student from Seattle who rode a donkey for part of her 800-mile trip to Berkeley to symbolize the urgent need to end the world's dependence on fossil fuels. Rainwater, who donated half her speaking fee to environmental advocacy group the Planetistas, explained to the executives that she regarded them all as devil spawn. It was well past time for them to repent, renounce their role as drug pushers feeding the world's sick addiction to oil, gas, and coal, and provide bona fide green alternatives. While she mercifully did not advocate for donkey transit systems as a way for people to get around—the waste disposal alone would be horrendous—she did allow that her generation would hold them personally responsible for their momentous failures and, in all likelihood, throw them in jail.

"You... *you*," she sneered over the clatter of flatware as people dug into their petite filets and mounds of fluffy potatoes, "you'll all go down in history for despoiling the planet with your greed and your oil and your dirty cars. You plunder the earth, emitting gazillions of tons of CO_2 emissions and destroying the future. *Our* future! *My* future! Do you have no alternatives? Is this the best you can do? Could you think of nothing else over the past one hundred and five years besides more of the same?" She scanned the sea of faces before her. "On behalf of my generation, I would like to say in closing that you all *suck.*"

The assembly applauded and tapped their wine glasses with their forks in polite acknowledgement of, if not agreement with, the courageous young Rainwater. "Wow," Tim said, thanking her for her remarks. "Serious food for thought. Whether you agree or disagree, I think it's important to get outside our comfort zone now and then and hear from people who have a different point of view. Thank you so much, Rainwater. Hope you have a good donkey ride back to Seattle." He clapped for her as she left the stage before returning to the next order of business. "Okay, then. On to dessert. Believe it or not, we're having Baked Alaska."

As the audience laughed, Robbie whispered to Digby. "What did that girl say? I was completely zoned out."

"She wants us all in prison."

"I'll take jail over another offsite. Do you have my speech?"

"You're using a script?" Digby asked, stabbing his last bite of steak and swirling it in the peppercorn sauce. "I thought you were just going to tell them what you always tell them. Hard to believe they'd be sick of it after five short years."

Robbie nodded in the direction of Kristi. "Apparently I need to kick it up a notch."

"Want to impress your girlfriend?"

"I just need a prop. Do you have any paper? Doesn't matter what's on it."

"Sorry. I don't," Digby said. "There's a survey about the offsite under your plate."

Robbie pulled out the survey—*GIVE US YOUR FEEDBACK!*—and glanced over it. "Much as I hate to pass up an opportunity to anonymously rate Tim a big fat zero, this will have to do."

On stage, an increasingly intoxicated Tim waxed weepy over the wonderful learnings of the past twenty-four hours and how they were all united in their common mission, which was to become really, really responsible about something. He said he hoped everyone would return to their respective offices energized by a profound sense of shared purpose, and commit to working together for the common good of their employees, communities, the environment, activists, customers, all earthly creatures, as well as any inhabitants of distant solar systems and galaxies who may be tuning in via interstellar transmitters. And now, without further ado, what better to top off this fantabulous conference and send everyone hurtling into the afterglow of scotches and brandies at the post-dinner cocktail reception than a few words from the esteemed chairman. "Ladies and gentlemen," Tim slurred, "let's hear it for *Lester Robertson Crowe... the Turd!*"

Booyah! The inebriated crowd, still cognizant that next year's executive bonus pool formula was under board review this month, thundered its approval as Robbie bounded onto the stage, grinning, nodding, acknowledging various attendees he didn't know with a cocked finger, and finally, shaking hands with Tim, smiling as if he liked him, and leaned close to his ear.

"Did you say 'turd?'"

"What?" Tim said with an exaggerated grimace. "*Noooo.*"

"You did."

"Did not."

"Did too."

"Did *not!*"

"Well, listen, buddy boy. It's Lester Robertson Crowe the *Third.* Got it?"

"I *know* that. Sheez."

"Well, say it clearer next time. Or just call me Robbie. You might find that easier."

Together, they turned to the assembled executives who were rising from their seats, offering a standing ovation so rousing it could have been mistaken for sincerity.

"Wow," Robbie said, looking over the bleary-eyed people wobbling at their tables. "I really appreciate that." He motioned for them all to sit. Considering how hammered they were, it was for their own safety.

"Alright," Robbie said, clapping his hands together, "let's give it up for Tim. I mean, did he do a fantastic job putting all this together or what? Incredible program!" Tim stumbled forward and waved and smiled with a decidedly crooked face, looking like he might shower the people nearest the stage with grateful tears, urinate, or simply fall off into their laps. "And let's also show our appreciation for our special guest and, I can happily say, a long-term partner for the Crowe Power Company, Dr. Kristi Kramer. What an honor and privilege to have her on our side."

Kristi turned from her table and blew kisses to the crowd while Robbie nudged Tim offstage with a firm knuckle in the small of his back. Robbie then walked to a small round high-top table, sat down on the stool next to it, uncapped a bottle of water, swigged, and looked toward his flock, struggling to see beyond the glare of stage lights. He had to know *somebody* out there. So many faces had changed since the last offsite he attended that he barely recognized anyone. Maybe he really should attend a management meeting once in a while. After all, as executive chairman, actively participating in management was part of his performance contract.

He pulled a folded copy of the event survey from the breast pocket of his coat and flattened it on the table, as if it were his prepared text. As the crowd settled in, Robbie pretended to scan the paper before him until the room was completely quiet. At last, he shook his head, looked up, grabbed the paper, and held it aloft.

"You know, the people in our communications department gave me this text to read to you with all the so-called 'approved' corporate messages," he said in a tone of complete disdain. "Well, guess what? *I* didn't approve them! These were all written *before* we had the presentation from Kristi this morning, and the breakout sessions today, and the wonderful talk tonight. Sometimes, it takes a smart, conscientious young woman like little, uh... Groundwater there to challenge us so-called 'adults' on our assumptions. She said we need to rip up the script, and that's exactly what I'm going to do." He theatrically shredded the event survey, balled it up, and tossed it off stage as the crowd roared its approval. "Let's talk about how we, the agents of change in this room, are going to approach things very differently from here on out to reinvent Crowe Power as—" He paused to look behind him at the freshly-printed sign. "The most responsible energy company in the world."

The applause enveloped Robbie like a coating of fire-retardant foam. He raised an eyebrow toward Kristi, then looked back to the broader group. "For too long at this company," he said, "we've worshipped the false god of profits, as if simply meeting the quarterly numbers makes everything alright. Well, you know what? It doesn't. That may be okay for those short-term investors on Wall Street who really don't give a damn about us and our company. All they want to do is make a lousy buck."

Executives whispered among themselves as they clapped. *This doesn't sound good for our stock options.* Robbie continued, "From here on out, we're in it for all of our stakeholders, who stick with us for the long-term because they're the ones that really matter—our communities, our employees, our customers, our suppliers, even the people outside our headquarters every day chanting 'Death to Crowe Power.' If we all work together, we can save our one and only planet. Isn't that more fulfilling than some joyless, mind-numbing march to improve net income? To those who say that all we need to do is make money, I say: *not on my watch!*"

Kristi watched in rapt attention while executives clapped tepidly, desperately hoping he wasn't serious, but reasonably secure in knowing that anything he said would never be executed anyway. Robbie bathed in the applause, which emboldened him further. "There's no reason in the world why we can't have it all. We can be green *and* profitable. We can provide energy to the world *and* emit far, far fewer greenhouse gasses. We can live up to the principles of my great-great-grandfather, Homer Crowe, who said, 'Don't just generate power. *Be* the power.'" Robbie paused to let that sink in. He also wondered whether Homer Crowe ever said such a thing.

"You know, a lot of companies are out there now promising they're going to be carbon-neutral at some distant date decades in the future, long after many of us have passed from this earthly realm. Well, I say, that's not good enough! Let's be bold. Let's lead the world. If we're going to be the most responsible energy company in the world, let's stake our claim to become the *first* carbon-neutral energy company in history!"

The assembly rose to its unsteady feet. Kristi looked like she might jump up on stage and beat him with her tits again. "Go Crowe! *Go!*" she cheered. As Robbie saw the ravenous look in her eyes, he knew it was high time to get this over with and move on to the reward of his private afterglow.

"I know it's dangerous to be standing between this crowd and the after-dinner drinks," he said, as the audience chuckled, "but I just want to say one more thing. I know you all read the papers—or your phones or tablets or whatever it is you use to get your news. And I know you've seen reports suggesting Walker Hope is going to make a run at us now that he's running Staminum. Well, all I can say is: *Let him try!*" The executives cheered, on cue. "One of the wonderful things about my family's continuing involvement in this company is that nobody can get away with something like that unless *I* say so. And I'd rather tear the place down than give it to some son of a bitch who doesn't have our best interests at heart. This isn't *his* company. It's *ours*. And it's gonna stay that way as long as I have something to say about it."

Thunderous applause rained down on the stage while Kristi fixed Robbie with a come-hither look and licked the corner of her mouth. *Was she blown away?* He'd soon find out. As Robbie locked eyes with her and stepped off the stage in her direction, his path was rudely obstructed by Tim, who swallowed him up with a bear hug. "That was *so* freaking great, bro," he said.

Bro? What possessed this man? Robbie stepped hard on Tim's foot, prompting him to stagger backwards. "What the hell are you doing?" Robbie demanded.

"I, I'm sorry," Tim said. "It's just that, that—that was the greatest damn speech I ever heard. We are so on the same page. You and me. We are an incredible team."

Robbie looked at Tim with astonishment. Didn't this sad sack know they weren't a "team" in any sense of the word, and they were not engaged in some kind of bromance? "Team" suggested an equality that simply did not exist. Robbie was a royal and Tim was a commoner, a hired hand, like the coffee lady and the janitor and the guys at the front desk. To insinuate himself onto the same exalted plane as Robbie—a *direct* descendant of Homer the First—was ridiculous, a concept beneath contempt. "Stay in your lane, alright?" Robbie said. "We've got a big job ahead of us."

"I hear you, chief," Tim said, swaying. "There's just one thing I want to ask you."

"What?"

Tim wobbled, trying to remember his question.

"*What?*" Robbie demanded.

"Oh. Just this: do you have any thoughts on how we're going to do that?"

"Do what?"

Tim scratched his head. "You know. What you just said up there."

"What'd I say?"

"We'd become the first carbon-neutral energy company in the world. How do we do that *and* still make money? I'm a little concerned about that."

Robbie struggled for patience. *Was it always going to be like talking to a child?* "Tim, I just gave you the marching orders, which is my job. Your job is to..." He made a rolling gesture with his right hand.

Tim looked baffled. "To what?"

"*March*, man. What is it you don't get?"

Tim nodded dutifully. He was going to have to work awfully hard to better understand this complicated man and his incredible vision. Robbie *must* have more answers than he's sharing. He's so smart, he *must* have thought this through. Otherwise he wouldn't have been so bold and emphatic, right?

As Tim watched Robbie saunter back toward the elevators with Dr. Kristi Kramer, he realized he was on his own. At times like this, leaders must lead. And so he went, off to join his troops as they pushed ahead to the next front—a poolside Tiki Bar, where they would begin their campaign of corporate responsibility with a few more belts.

21. PROMISE KEPT

True to the importance of Keeping Promises, a chapter in the upcoming blockbuster *Goodness Greatness*, Dr. Kristi Kramer had blown Robbie away following his thrilling speech, and he had reciprocated in his own way. Now, in the soft glow of the Presidential Suite, she laid back at the end of the living room sofa wearing a fluffy white robe and sipping a glass of Marcassin Chardonnay, which, like her, was known for a "slightly smoky edge." Eyeing her vanquished prey at the other end of the couch, she extended her right foot between Robbie's knees and probed under his robe with her talented toes, searching for signs of life. Finding no survivors, she withdrew her foot, pulled out her phone, and trained it on her new client. Time to get to *work!*

"What are you doing?" Robbie asked wearily.

She pressed the red button on her screen. "I want to interview you."

"In my robe? Surely, neither one of us needs a record of this."

"I do. If I'm going to make my publishing deadline, I need to start capturing your thoughts, and I mean *A-S-A-P*, darlin'. Don't worry about the camera. It's just the way I take notes." Holding the phone in one hand, she used the other to reach out and pat his leg. "So, c'mon now. Tell me. How is Crowe Power going to become the first carbon-neutral energy company ever? *Dazzle* me!"

He rubbed his hands together, as if he were summoning a genie. "I still have a few details to work out."

"That's fine. Which ones?"

"Well. I guess you'd have to say... all of them."

"*Pshaw.* You must have some notion of how you're going to do this."

"Of course, I have ideas. I mean, I think about this stuff all the time. It's just that now we have to work out the particulars." He pointed with his thumb toward the window, where the executive team was partying below. "That means getting these people off their dead asses."

"What exactly do you want them to do? My readers *crave* stories about processes they can put to use themselves. What's your M.O.?"

Robbie sighed. "Well, I typically give a speech that lays out the big vision."

"Right. Got that. Then what?"

"Then it's up to the rest of these people to execute."

She looked dumfounded. "That's it?"

He sipped his wine. "Pretty much."

"But you give them guidance, right?"

"Well, yeah. Of course I do."

"So what do you want them to do now?"

"They should look at everything. Biofuels. Hydroelectric. Wind. Solar. All that stuff people have been working on for years. But don't be limited by that." He sat up, warming to the topic. "Find the wildest, craziest forms of energy anyone can think of and look into it. Honestly, I don't care if they squeeze electricity from a turnip. Tell me: How much juice could you get? Could you scale it up? How much would it cost?"

"Oooh! Turnips!" she squealed. "I *love* this."

He sat back again, smiling. "That's just how my mind works. I'm very creative that way."

"Okay. So. What's your guess? If you only had a dollar to invest right this minute, which technology would you bet on?"

"It could be solar, I suppose. Maybe offshore wind…" He sat up, aggravated. "But I can't do *all* the work. My job is to give them a sense of the possibilities, to open their minds to new ideas. We have a climate emergency on our hands, and I don't see anyone at our company doing anything about it except me. Every time I talk about it, they look at me all cross-eyed. I want them to get *moving.*"

She put her camera down. "I know what you need to do."

"I'm all ears."

"Issue a press release."

"On what?"

"On this! Tomorrow. I mean it! You could make it a letter to shareholders. Proclaim your goal. Draw a line in the sand for everyone to see. It will be totally unexpected, like a tobacco company saying they want people to stop smoking. Or a car company telling people they want them to start riding bicycles instead of driving SUVs. It's groundbreaking. And, once it's out there, it will put the pressure on your team to go, go, *go!* You don't move people with small ideas. They need big, inspiring, *Robbie-palooza* ideas. If you're going to go down as one of the greatest leaders in business history—and, I must say, you're well on your way—then you need to lead! Tell people where you want to go and show them the way."

Robbie scratched his chin. "I don't know. I need time to organize my thoughts."

"Don't worry about it. I'll do it. It's all covered by my retainer."

Robbie poured another glass of wine, a Sine Qua Non Syrah from 2003. He had no idea it cost $1,100 a bottle, nor did he care. He'd never see a bill, and why should he, considering his massive contributions not only to the Crowe Power Company but to human progress. "I think we're getting ahead of ourselves. Maybe I shouldn't have said anything yet."

She put the camera back up. "I inspired you."

He winced. "Put that thing away, will you?" He reached for the camera and she pulled it back, away from his grasp.

"Don't," she said sharply.

"Do you want a spanking?" he asked with a mock serious expression.

She fluttered her eyes. "Another one?"

He reached again to grab it from her, prompting her to laugh, turn it off, and put it in the pocket of her robe. "Alright, alright, *alright!*"

They sat in silence a moment and Robbie sank back into the sofa, drifting off. Why did he make that stupid fucking pledge? Did he really commit the company to some preposterous goal just to get a blowjob? *I really am an ass...*

"Look," Kristi said. "I have seen this problem many times before. Everyone in a position of awesome responsibility feels the burden of doing it all sometimes. But you can't. Once we issue this release, you need to assign responsibility for implementing your vision to a leader on your team and hold them accountable. Don't carry this weight on your shoulders, big and broad and burly as they are." She winked. "Delegate. If they get it done, great. You still get all the credit. And if they don't, you cut their balls off."

Robbie crossed his legs. "Who would I delegate to? You've seen what I have to work with."

"Start with Tim. He's your CEO."

Robbie rolled his eyes. "He'd never figure it out."

"Then assign someone else. You can't let this just drift."

"I don't know who."

"Robbie Crowe," Kristi said sharply. "Do you want to change the world or not? This is your chance. You have to seize it. And I mean right away. Strike while that iron of yours is hot, hot, *hot.*"

Robbie stood up and walked to the window, peering through the curtains at the gathering below. "I look at this team and I wonder," he said, shaking his head. "Do any of them get it?"

"You're forgetting something," she said. "They came up with the idea of becoming the most responsible energy company in the world. That's their dream."

He turned back to her. "You sure you didn't write it?"

She demurred. "All I did was lead them where they wanted to go. Just like you're doing now." Kristi joined him at the window, where she could pick out Tim, walking around with a drink, mingling with the other executives. "I think you may be underestimating him," she said. "He hangs on every word you say."

Robbie shrugged. "Well, that's understandable, I guess. I am his boss."

"Damn right you are. All you need to do is tell him what you want him to do and see how he responds."

$$* \quad * \quad *$$

After they dressed, Robbie and Kristi took separate elevators to the ground floor and joined the poolside party a few minutes apart, lest the more sober executives put one and one together and accurately conclude they were two.

While Kristi made her typical grand entrance with all eyes turning her way, Robbie waited in the shadows behind a potted palm, texting Digby to confirm that he was there and Robbie would have someone to talk to. God forbid he should suffer some awkward moments standing alone. He sent his message, then peered through the fronds, spotting Kristi smiling and nodding and waving, working her way through the crowd like Miss North Carolina courting votes on a pageant stage. Tim, meanwhile, was making love to the karaoke mic, eyes closed, belting out "Sweet Caroline" in a pitch that suggested he might have never heard the song before. The assembly chimed in on the chorus. *"Good times never seemed so good! So good! So good! So good!"*

Robbie slipped quietly into the crowd and made his way toward Digby, who was standing among a group of executives posing with flaming blue shots under the banner, *"We Will Be the Most Responsible Energy Company in the World."* Robbie stood back and watched as they yelled "Cheers," clinked their glasses together, and threw back the liquor. Some of them casually tossed their glasses in the flower beds, others turned to pee in the bushes, and several of them ordered another round. Robbie snatched a glass of wine off a serving tray and nodded to Digby, who sauntered over.

"Impressive display of responsibility," Robbie said.

"They're still getting up to speed on the concept."

Robbie nodded toward Tim, his singing CEO. "How are we going to do this with him leading the charge? If *America's Got Talent*, it's not evident here."

"You're giving up on him already, aren't you?"

"What am I supposed to do? This whole thing rests on his shoulders and he seems to have no fucking clue. He doesn't even know the words to the song." They turned to watch Tim, who was waving his arm to lead his leadership team through a chorus of "Don't Stop Believin'." "Is there some way to get him to stop? He's embarrassing himself."

Much to Robbie's horror, Kristi approached with Lucy Rutherford, the devil herself, who had accosted him so disrespectfully at the earlier reception.

"Robbie," Kristi commanded, "Lucy and I need your view on this."

Robbie drank some wine, shoved his free hand in his pocket, and braced himself. "What's up?"

Lucy said, "I'm sorry to drag you into this, Robbie. But I'm just trying to understand why we have to be so grandiose. If we continue to convert our old plants from coal to natural gas, we'll make steady progress on our carbon reduction goals."

Kristi shook her head, annoyed. "Steady progress? Crazy, she talks! Nobody gets any credit for that! We need to go big! Grab some attention! That's where our new mission comes in."

As Robbie listened quietly, Lucy said to Kristi, "How did this company stay in business for a hundred and five years without knowing its mission? We provide energy to people who need it and we do it in the cleanest and safest way possible. Same as when Homer Crowe cranked up his first generator in 1915. What's the difference?"

"But, see! That's just it!" Kristi implored. "Now we're going to do it *responsibly.*"

"Homer Crowe didn't?"

"Not enough, in my book!"

"Yeah," Lucy said with a shrug. "I read it."

"It's like little Rainwater said. We should do it in a way that requires no trade-offs. Zip. Zero. Nada."

"There are *always* trade-offs, Dr. Kramer," Lucy said. "Rainwater's fifteen years old. She doesn't know her ass from a wall plug. I don't care what kind of energy it is. You put up a windmill, you kill bats and birds. You build solar reflectors, you've gotta get rid of the toxic waste at some point. Either way, you still need conventional energy as a backup because sometimes the wind doesn't blow and the sun doesn't shine. Where do you think the juice for electric cars comes from? Most of it's from fossil fuels. Just because the more virtuous among us like to think it comes from pixie dust doesn't make it so."

Kristi, out of platitudes for once, was nearing the end of her expertise on the matter. She looked to Robbie for help, but he was staring up over the trees at constellations, tilting his head from side to side. *Was that Perseus? Or Gemini?* She turned to Digby, who suddenly scampered off, talking on his phone. Finally, it was Tim who saved her. Standing on a chair to make another toast to corporate responsibility, he lost his footing and tumbled into the pool like a cannonball, sending a geyser of water over the party, provoking howls of laughter from his leadership team. As he floundered in the deep end, it appeared that Tim was once again in over his head, this time dangerously so. Lucy quickly handed her glass to

Kristi and made a lifeguard leap into the water, coming up behind Tim, sliding an arm over one of his shoulders to pin him across her chest and drag him into the shallow end, where he found his footing, spitting out streams of water and struggling to catch his breath. The executives applauded and whistled as he waved and slowly climbed out of the pool, followed by Lucy.

Robbie leaned toward Kristi's ear. "This is our leader?"

Kristi sighed, recognizing this wouldn't work. "Do you have a Plan B?"

Digby returned, holding his phone, a look of urgency on his face. "I might have one."

Robbie said, "Seriously?"

Digby nodded. "Can I have a word?" Together, they left Kristi and stepped away from the crowd. "I just heard from Fred Crispin," Digby said. "He's thinking of making a change and he wants to explore possibilities with us before he talks to anyone else."

"What? *Fred Crispin?*" Robbie threw his hands up over his head, as if he were signaling a touchdown. "Oh my God. Are you shitting me?"

"I just talked to him. He's really excited."

"Oh, that's great!" Robbie dropped his hands to his side. "Who is he?"

"He's Walker's number two at Staminum."

"Ah. That's right. *Right!* Well, what are we waiting for? Let's go get him."

"For what?"

"He can replace Tim."

"You can't replace Tim yet. Tim just started."

"Oh, so what. Christ almighty. Who cares about Tim?"

"It will look bad for you."

"Hmm."

"It's got to be something else."

"Fine. Make him COO."

"You can't do that, either. Tim wants Lucy Rutherford."

Robbie pointed toward the pool. "Lucy Rutherford just pulled that lunkhead out of the drink. That alone is grounds for firing her. Let's bring in Fred and in six months, he can have Tim's job and we can broom her out, too. It's a win-win."

"If you hire Fred, Tim might quit on us."

"Then we win *again!* Oh my God! This is too good to be true. Can you imagine the look on Walker's face when he hears I've stolen his top guy? He'd crap his pants."

"What do you want to do?"

"Arrange a meet," Robbie said. "As soon as we get back to New York. No, sooner. I want to move on this as fast as we can. Have him call me before we get on the plane tomorrow. I can't wait!"

22. SPINNING CLASS

Marty's wake-up call came at 6 a.m. with a buzzing phone on his nightstand. He rolled over and saw Fred Crispin's name on his screen. Feared dead less than twenty-four hours earlier, Fred was not only alive, but awake at an ungodly hour.

"I hope you don't mind me calling you so early," Fred said.

Marty quickly cleared his throat, if not his head. "Quite alright," he said.

Fred's excitement could hardly be contained. "You nailed it, Marty. Crowe Power is *very* interested. I'm speaking with Robbie Crowe by phone in a few hours. Unless I'm completely misreading the signals, it looks like there's a very good possibility I could become their next Chief Operating Officer."

Marty swung his legs up and sat on the edge of the bed and blinked hard. "That is so great, Fred. I couldn't be happier for you."

"Don't worry, Marty. I won't tell anybody you encouraged me. I'm sure the idea of me going to the competition would not set well with Walker."

"I would expect an emotional reaction," Marty said. "But you know what? Let the chips fall where they may. Sometimes, we just have to put our company loyalties aside for a moment and think about people."

"You're a true friend, Marty."

Marty popped AirPods in his ears to continue the conversation while he moved, and headed for the kitchen, where he switched on his Keurig coffeemaker and warmed a mug with hot water from the tap. He took a seat on the kitchen's only stool, looking out at the darkened courtyard separating his building from the apartments on LaGuardia Place and Thompson Street. He was the only one in the neighborhood up. "What can I do to help?"

"You know Robbie Crowe far better than I do. What do you suggest I say to him?"

Marty thought back to the few encounters with Robbie that had gone well and the many more that had not. "Well, first of all, know that it's not possible to blow too much smoke up his pantleg. He enjoys nothing more than a good lickspittle."

"I should flatter him?"

"Love him up, Fred."

"What would connect with him? Can you give me an example?"

Marty popped a cartridge in the coffee maker and hit the button for a large cup. The machine gurgled to life, dribbling his coffee into a mug and spattering the well-worn countertop with brown spots. "The old standby is to talk about how you've always admired his vision. That's a surefire applause line. You might also want to express your astonishment that a man so far above the station of ordinary slobs like us continues to work as hard as he does. He loves that one."

"Good stuff, Marty. Just hold on a sec. I'm in the kitchen writing all this down and my damn pen stopped working. Hold on." Marty heard the clatter of Fred rummaging through a drawer. "Okay. Here we go. *Great vision, so far above slobs... like... us.* Got it."

Marty poured milk in his coffee and sat down. "Be sure to say you really love the way Crowe Power takes the long view and doesn't give in to the extreme greed you see elsewhere. Tell him it's obviously a company of high-minded ideals and you love that. He'll get a big boner."

"*Long view, high ideals, boner.* Uh-huh. Anything else?"

"This is important: make sure you tell him Walker's an asshole."

There was a pause at the other end. "I don't know, Marty. Believe it or not, I have a lot of respect for Walker, despite what he did to me."

"Fred. Listen to me. Do you want the job or not?"

"Yes."

Marty commanded. "Do as I say."

"Okay. Walker's an asshole."

"Good. Glad we got over that. Please don't confuse what you think with what you might say. It won't help, alright?"

"Got it."

"You'll want to stay away from certain topics, too. No small talk about wifey-poo and kids. He's on the outs with Lindsey. And don't press him for details on any topic whatsoever. Not the company. Not his strategy. Not the weather. When he feels cornered or pressured in any way, he tends to get nervous and that makes him lash out. He won't want to hire somebody who doesn't know their place."

"This is so helpful, Marty. Anything else I should avoid?"

"Just the obvious."

"What's that?"

"You know. Staminum's top-secret project."

There was a long pause. "Not sure what you're talking about there, Marty."

"Oh, c'mon, Fred. *Project X.* You know...."

"Hmm. I, uh. Maybe by another name?"

"I'm sure you've heard about Walker working furiously to raise cash. Word is he's selling Greeneron."

"No! Really?"

Marty sighed. "I'm not privy to all the details, but he's thinking it might fetch... three billion."

"No kidding. You know, now that you mention it, I guess I've been picking up bits and pieces. I didn't realize Walker was moving that fast."

"Well, he is. From what I gather, it's looking more and more like Greeneron's going to sell quickly. And here's the sad thing for people like me who are still stuck at Staminum. Whoever gets their hands on Greeneron will hold a portfolio with incredible technologies. This could define the future of energy. Can you imagine what a guy like Robbie would do with something like that?" *Why, he'd blow even more money out his ass!*

Fred whistled. "It would probably cement his reputation as a bold visionary, dontcha think?"

"Absolutely!" Marty said. "Why, he could be hailed as one of the great business leaders of all time, just like his great-great grandpappy. Responsible. Foresighted. Caring. It would be an incredible personal coup. And imagine this: all it would take to bolster his personal reputation would be a few billion dollars. A small price to pay, considering."

"I have to mention this to Robbie, don't I? I mean, what if he missed out? He could blame me for not telling him."

Marty sighed. "Gosh, Fred. I'd hate to see you traffic in inside information. But you know what? The rumors are starting to get out there. Hell, I heard somebody talking about it just yesterday."

"So what do you think? Fair game?"

"I probably shouldn't tell you this, Fred. But if it helps you close your deal, then I'd say use it. And Fred? You didn't hear it from me."

"Of course."

"Godspeed, my friend."

* * *

Marty donned his corporate uniform—a navy pin-striped suit from Hickey Freeman, a light blue shirt, a red Hermes tie with little blue fishes on it—and carefully stepped down three long flights of concave stairs, passing bearded neighbors in hoodies and ripped jeans heading in the other direction, before emerging into the long, early-morning shadows on Bleecker Street. Turning onto LaGuardia Place to grab another coffee, he was met by a battalion of stroller moms, Panzer Division, plowing through the pedestrians in their path. *Outta my way! I got a baby heah!* There were the usual gaggles of NYU students, walking blindly as they typed on their phones, and dog walkers in their sweatsuits guiding rescue mutts to pee on the signs that read, "Please Curb Your Dog." Marty stepped around and over the familiar cast of professional beggars marking off their sales territory for the day with blankets and pillows, stuffed animals, pets, paper cups padded with a few starter bills, and hand-printed cardboard signs. *God bless!*

As he crossed through the center of Washington Square Park, passing the demented Pigeon Man tossing handfuls of corn on the walk while the grateful fluttering birds covered him in shit, a familiar voice called from behind. "Nice suit."

Marty turned to see Howie-Do-It, Robbie's trusted henchman, closing fast. Marty kept walking, but Howie caught up and sidled up beside him, reeking of weed. "Jesus, Howie. You stink," Marty said. "You're blowing pot already?"

"Just a little somethin' to calm me down so I don't kick your ass."

"Ah," Marty said. "Well then. Please feel free to have some more."

"You seem to be in quite a hurry."

"It's not that I'm not delighted to see you, Howie. It's just that I've got to go to something we call 'work.'"

Howie scoffed. "You sayin' I don't work?"

"I don't know. Is beating people up work?"

"With some people, I'd do it just for fun."

Marty stopped and assessed Howie-Do-It, a stumpy block of steroidal muscle who resembled a stop on the evolutionary journey from monkey to man. As if Howie's physique weren't menacing enough, Marty suspected he also carried an assortment of concealed weapons. He was not someone with whom one should trade insults, although Marty could think of a cutting remark or two. "Is there something I can help you with, Howie?"

"Tell your dentist to back off."

"My *dentist?*"

"You know what I'm talking about."

"I do?"

"Come on, Marty. Fess up, man. You're in on this, too."

Marty shook his head. "Sorry, Howie. I left the Robbie Crowe School of Melodramatic Arts a month ago. I don't know what 'this' is. Maybe your boss is just a little too paranoid for his own good." Marty shook his head and resumed walking toward the subway.

Howie followed after him. "You know a Dr. Stuart Littmann?"

Marty laughed. "Don't tell me—"

"He made a threat against Robbie."

"Oh, c'mon. That's nuts."

Howie flushed red. "You know he did."

Marty looked at Howie, incredulous. "Have you seen Dr. Littmann? He couldn't stop tooth decay."

"He said you were a patient."

"I was. No longer. Not after he jackhammered my jaw like he was ripping up asphalt on Third Avenue."

"He's upset with his investment in Crowe Power."

"Who isn't? There's a lot of that going around."

"He's taking it out on the boss."

"And you're out to protect the boss." It occurred to Marty that this encounter, played right, could actually prove productive. "Really wish I could help you, Howie, but I've got an emergency meeting with Walker at nine. We've already got a crisis on our hands."

"What's going on?"

Marty resumed walking. "You know I can't talk about it."

"C'mon, Marty."

"Right. Like I can trust you, Howie. First thing you'd do is call Robbie."

"Only if it's juicy."

Marty scoffed. "It wouldn't matter anyway. He already knows."

"Knows what?"

"Just ask him." Marty shook his head gravely. "And tell him we owe him one for sticking it up our ass."

23. SOAP BOX

Robbie emerged from the shower and was toweling off his hair when he was startled at the presence of another person, causing him to skid on the wet bathroom tiles. As he regained his balance, he found Dr. Kristi Kramer sitting on a bench, completely dressed, coiffed, and made up, holding a document in her hand. Did she *ever* stop working?

"Jesus!" he exclaimed. "You scared the shit out of me."

She placed a hand to her cheek. "I am so sorry!"

"I thought you left already," he said, wrapping the towel around his waist, struggling to close it over his male baby bump.

"Heading back to Chapel Hill in a bit," she said. "I just had to get this draft of a press release in your hands before I go. It's so important that it goes out today. You do not want to lose a minute of momentum out of this conference. We need to let the world know where you stand!"

"Absolutely," he said. "Where is that?"

"This will tell you."

Robbie reached out for the paper and skimmed its contents, heralding the big news that Crowe Power Company Chairman L. Robertson Crowe III was announcing a bold new initiative: to become the first carbon-neutral energy company. It provided no date for this magnificent achievement, nor did it articulate a strategy for getting there. It did, however, mention that the objective was aligned with Crowe Power's mission to become the most responsible energy company in the world, a mission which might include some sacrifice of profitability, if necessary. It was also pointed out that these goals were a reflection of Robbie Crowe's lifelong commitment to environmental stewardship.

Robbie sat down on the edge of the jacuzzi. "Good to mention my lifelong commitment to the environment," he said, softly hitting the paper with the back of his hand. "People forget I was on this enviro jazz *way* before anyone else. Nobody even heard about carbon footprints until I started talking about them."

"Really?"

"Well, actually, I think it was the Planetistas who started the conversation. But they pointed to me as an example."

"In a positive sense?"

"Well, not at first. They used to criticize me for having six homes, as if that's not normal for someone with a little bit of money. But then I told them why that's actually a very good thing. 'Hey,' I said, 'by owning a half-million acres of land around my cabin upstate, I'm actually *preserving* it as a carbon sink. All those trees absorb carbon dioxide from the atmosphere.' Those idiots hadn't even thought about that."

"I bet that shut 'em up!"

"Not exactly. They thought I should build windmills on it."

"Did you do it?"

"Hell no," he said, recoiling. "It would look like total crap."

"Oh."

"I said, 'Look, people. I'm keeping this land in its natural state.' I mean, aside from the main house, and the pool, and a couple of golf holes and a tennis court and a guest lodge and a caretaker's home, it was pretty much just as God made it. There's also a long driveway and some landscaping and some very tasteful lighting, but that's it. Nothing more. It's pristine. And we keep it that way with barbed wire fencing."

"No wonder they call you an environmental guardian. I take it they backed off."

"Not immediately. But it didn't take long before they realized nobody was going to push me around. People don't understand that about me. They think, 'Oh, he's rich. He's soft. He's probably a pushover.' They have no idea what they're up against—until they tangle with me." Robbie paused to appreciate Kristi's fawning expression, her understandable admiration for such a stand-up guy. And this from a best-selling author of books on business leadership! She knew a titan when she saw one. "I don't mean to brag," he said, "but the fact is, I don't take shit. From *any*body. I was going to fight to the death, and I did."

Kristi fluttered her eyes, batting out *I love you!* in Morse code. "Oh my goodness!" she squealed. "What did you do?"

"I sat them down and said, 'Alright. How much is it going to take to make you stop protesting?' And they said, 'A million bucks.' I said, 'No way.' Just like that. 'No way!' Oh, you should have seen them. They pounded the table. They bitched. They moaned. But ultimately, all I did was write them a check for a measly hundred thousand bucks. That's it. I said, 'No more. Take it or leave it.' It wasn't what they wanted, but they knew I wasn't going any further. So they cashed the check and they shut up, at least for a while." He sighed. "Now, they're coming after me again. I have no idea why they're back so soon."

"Do you think maybe they just want more money?"

Robbie rubbed his chin. "Possible, I suppose."

Kristi shook her head at the wonder of another Robbie miracle. "You know, Robbie, these are amazing stories I need to capture in my book. Real-life profiles in courage." She held her hand in the air, looking at something she pictured in her mind. "I can see a chapter entitled 'Taking a Stand.' You can be such an inspiration to others."

Robbie nodded. "Aw. I don't know about that. I just try to do my part. I like to say, 'A man who stands for nothing will fall for anything.'"

Kristi slowly turned her head from side to side. "That is so profound."

"Well, I didn't make it up actually. Might have been Malcolm X. But I was thinking it right around the same time."

"You would have been how old? Three?"

Robbie shrugged. "Something like that." Eager to change the subject, he returned to the document. "What's this line that says the initiative is consistent with our company's 'cherished values?' What are those?"

"Oh dear." She winced. "We should take a minute to review. I'd hate for someone to ask and you don't know."

"Just give me a minute." Robbie handed her the paper. "I'm at a critical hair moment here. Let me put some pomade in it." He nodded toward the living room. "I'll join you in a sec."

As Kristi left, Robbie turned to the mirror and assessed his image. Clearly, a couple of days romping about with Dr. Kristi Kramer in the Presidential Suite had put some color back in his cheeks. He dipped into a jar of pomade, spread it across both palms, and worked it into his thinning hair. Then he smoothed his hair over and smooshed some of it forward, covering up the balding areas in the front. He cocked his head to one side, then the other, then struck a thoughtful pose, glancing back at the mirror to see how it looked in profile. *Oh yeah! You've still got it all going on!*

He slipped on a bathrobe and slippers and sauntered into the dining room, where Kristi was at the table, typing on her laptop. Robbie grabbed the coffee carafe from a serving tray in the center of the table, poured himself a cup, and sat down. "So where did you find this crap about our values?"

"I pulled them right off your company website." She typed on her laptop, her eyes scanning the results on the screen. "According to the 'About Us' section, it says your values are honesty, respect for people, protecting the environment, providing value to customers, commitment to diversity, and passion for work."

Robbie shrugged. "Does anyone believe this stuff?"

"Of course they do! Your values speak to who you are as a company and how you deal with everyone who has a stake in it. They're like that goo you just put in your hair: the common bond that holds everything together and makes it look real good. Your signature's at the bottom of the values page. Don't tell me you never even read it?"

Robbie leaned back in his chair, looking up at the chandelier. "Wait a second," he said. "I seem to recall the head of HR saying if we handed employees a bunch of company values, we'd get ten percent more work out of them without giving them a raise. So they built a program around that. Lasted about a week. There was a nice colorful brochure that went out, and we had a town hall about it and I told some stories about my great-great-grandfather that might have even been true. But once the show was over, I don't think anyone ever mentioned the values again. And I can tell you for damn sure I never saw anybody working any harder. After the presentation, everyone headed to the bars on Stone Street to celebrate our virtue."

"Just as it should be!"

"I thought the whole thing was a complete waste of time."

Kristi looked perplexed. "You talk like that, you're gonna kill my business. I make a small fortune helping companies identify the values they didn't even know they had. We have to have something about Crowe Power values in my book if you're going to be on the cover. And you're going to be quoted as saying you think about them every single day."

Robbie laughed. "Okay. Fine. *Fine.* Knock yourself out. What the hell do I care?"

She leaned back in her chair and used both hands to seductively smooth back her hair. "You need to take this more seriously."

"What was that last value? A passion for work?" He leaned forward and rubbed her knee. "What do you say we put that into practice."

The shake of her head said no, but her smile said yes. "There are other values, you know. Like respect for people." She pulled away, but not far. "I've got to go."

He laughed. "Isn't another one about providing value to customers?"

"Yes."

"Aren't I a customer?"

She let her hair fall down over her shoulders. She looked at him and addressed him in the voice of a call center employee. "And how can I help you today, Mr. Crowe?"

24. HITCH IN THE SWING

The press release announcing Robbie's bold new initiative for the Crowe Power Company hit the wires at midday and sent CRO shares reeling another five percent as investors absorbed its implications for profitability. While the press lauded Robbie for his courageous stand and moral leadership, a half-dozen analysts read it as confirmation that Robbie was driving the company into a ditch and issued recommendations to sell Crowe Power stock as fast as they could.

The news hit family patriarch Charles Francis Crowe II, Robbie's Uncle Chuck, while he was teeing off on the fourteenth hole of the Sebonack Golf Club in Southampton, New York. He had just reached the apex of his backswing when his phone alarm beeped, causing him to bring down his club with a riffle that shanked his shot into the trees. He cursed the interruption and snatched up his cigarette from the tee box.

"Sorry, Lloyd," he said to his golfing partner, Lloyd Lundquist, the retired chairman of LT&T Insurance. "I keep my phone on only for emergencies. Apparently, I've got one now." He picked up his phone and peered at it. "Our company stock is tanking for some reason." He scanned the phone again, punched a button, and scowled, muttering, "Robbie."

Lloyd chuckled. "Hard to believe all the drama down on Broad Street. I thought your stock was for widows and orphans."

"My wife will be a widow before too long. Robbie's going to give me a heart attack."

Lloyd teed up his ball and practiced a few swings. "Surprised you let him drive the family business. He seems to keep wrapping it around a tree. Hope you're insured!" Lloyd looked behind him at an approaching foursome. "You want me to let these guys play through after I hit?"

"Go ahead," Chuck said. "I've got to make a call and find out what the hell's going on. This might take a minute."

Lloyd waved at the approaching group while Chuck walked toward the crest of a small hill and spoke quietly into the phone. He reached Robbie as he stood with Digby outside the lobby of the hotel, waiting for their luggage to get loaded into an SUV for the ride to the San Francisco airport.

"Uncle Chuck," Robbie answered cheerfully. "Always good to hear your voice."

"Maybe not today, Robbie."

"What's the matter?"

"You tell me. Our stock is cratering yet again, this time because you issued some sort of news release?"

Robbie explained the gist of his initiative, then said, "I don't know why everybody's freaking out."

"Well, Robbie," Chuck said, exhaling a line of blue smoke, "shareholders tend to take it seriously when you signal your intentions for the future of the company. They wonder if you're out on some ideological bender. You do recognize investors have lots of other choices out there? There's no requirement to invest in us."

Robbie quickly grew impatient with his octogenarian uncle. People in that generation would never understand enlightened leadership like his. "Fine. *Fine.* Let the short timers get out. We don't need them. I want people to invest in us because they see we're doing things the right way."

Chuck flicked his cigarette into the sand and stepped on it with his heel. "Robbie, we've been over this before. There are a few of us in the family who don't happen to have a long term. All of our estate planning is tied to Crowe Power hanging around for a while. That doesn't work if you run us out of business."

Robbie shook his head. "No, no, no. It's just the opposite. This is all about sustainability, Uncle Chuck."

"Right. I hear that term bandied about a lot. I'm not sure anyone knows what the hell it means. But I'll tell you something your cousins and aunts and uncles and nieces and nephews are all going to understand: their net worth. And that's been dropping like a rock."

"I know you're concerned. But I see no reason why we can't be the world leader in environmental responsibility and make money at the same time."

"Okay," Chuck said. "How?"

Robbie gulped. "Well... I'm working on that. I hope to have something for you and the board to consider very soon."

Chuck looked at his watch. "When are you back in New York? I think you and I need to have a little quality time together."

"I'm flying back today. How about next week?"

"How about tomorrow. I'll see you at HQ at eleven."

"I'll have to check my calendar, Uncle Chuck."

There was a pause. "I know all about your calendar, Robbie. See you tomorrow."

Chuck hung up and shook his head, trudging through the grass to rejoin Lloyd. "I'm not sure Robbie's ever going to grow up. We should have given him a coloring book and a box of crayons instead of our business."

"Could he stay within the lines?"

"Never has," Chuck said. "That's the problem."

"I've been hearing a lot about him lately from the guys at Staminum."

"Can you fill me in?"

"Strictly on the q.t."

"Of course. I've already hit enough shots for two games. Let's play the nineteenth hole."

✳ ✳ ✳

Dr. Stuart Littmann was injecting a patient with Novocaine when Chanisse came to his door. "Dr. Littmann, Peter Berkov is on line two for you. He says it's urgent." Littmann carefully withdrew the needle and put it on a tray. "Be right there."

The dentist sighed. Calls from Peter were typically not good news, especially since Stuart had put all his chips on CRO. He stood up from his stool, removed his blue latex gloves, and headed to his small, cluttered office off the lobby. He shut the door behind him and punched the button for line two. "What's going on, Peter?"

Peter sounded grieved. "Stuart, I know I sound like a broken record, but your Crowe Power stock is tanking again."

The dentist shook his head in despair. "What is it this time?"

Peter explained the circumstances. "It's the idiot chairman. I don't think there's any chance this guy is going to move things in the right direction. The consensus is that Robbie Crowe's in over his head, focusing on some pie-in-the-sky bullshit. Painful as this is, I recommend you cut your losses and get the hell out of there."

Littmann rubbed his forehead hard. "I can't do that."

"Stuart. Please. I beg you. There are a million better places to put your money right now than CRO."

"That money is from my parents, God rest their souls. They worked hard their entire lives to get me through school and to save up a little for a rainy day. Then I just blow it? That's a desecration of their memory. I can't live with that."

"It's only going to get worse."

"It will get better if somebody holds Robbie Crowe to account."

"And who's going to do that? You?"

"I'm trying."

"He's not listening. And neither are you. Get out of CRO and it won't be your problem anymore. You'll live longer."

Stuart hung up and fell back in his chair. He'd ridden this lame horse this far. Worse, unbeknown to Peter, he'd borrowed against his stock to pay off his apartment. If Crowe didn't rebound, he could lose it all: his Crowe investment, his apartment, even his practice. There was only one way out: To push Robbie Crowe as hard as he possibly could.

* * *

In a booth in a dark corner of Café Che across from Crowe Power headquarters, Natalia scrolled through the glowing news coverage of Robbie's release. At Café Che, the vibe was even warmer. Ernesto, the café's assistant manager and the comandante of the Planetistas' field operations on Wall Street, brought Natalia a cup of tea and a grudging smile. "This one's on *la casa*," he said.

"Gracias," she said, with a smile. "We're making progress."

Ernesto slid into the booth. Dressed in Café Che's uniform of jungle fatigues and black beret, he wore a patchy five-day beard that befit his revolutionary struggle. "Is Robbie Crowe for real?" he asked, scratching his stubble.

She nodded. "He is very determined to make a difference."

Ernesto sighed. "Some people in the movement aren't convinced. We had a meeting this morning. They aren't satisfied with press releases. They want action. Or else."

"Or else what?"

"We're going to occupy Crowe Power."

Natalia scoffed. "How would you do that?"

"Take over your lobby. Live there until you meet our demands."

Natalia collapsed back in her seat. "I don't think you could get the dinosaur through the revolving door."

"It's inflatable," he said. "We blow it up when we get inside." He reached over and patted the top of her hand. "Look, Natalia. You know how I feel about you. You know I appreciate all you're doing to change hearts and minds over there. But some of the people in our group... they're hard-core. I'm doing my best to contain them, but—" He looked away for a moment, then turned to her and spoke in a near whisper. "Here they come now."

Two Café Che workers, whom Natalia knew from her time working behind the counter, appeared at their table: pink-haired Oksana Kirinsky, First Secretary of the Planetariat, the governing body of the Planetistas, and a reputed wizard at the espresso machine, and her boyfriend, Gazi, a busboy, and by the looks of him, a possible member of the Taliban. "We are joining you," Oksana announced. Natalia and Ernesto each moved over to make room as they slid into the booth.

"I hope you saw the news from Robbie Crowe today," Natalia asked. "He's one of the few leaders in corporate America taking a stand."

Oksana shrugged, unimpressed. "He's rich. He's powerful. He can say whatever he wants. Why should I believe him?"

Natalia looked exasperated. "What else do you expect?"

"More."

"More?"

"Whatever he *said*, whatever he *did*, whatever he *does*, it does not matter." She dropped a fist on the table. "He can do more. And we will hold his feet to the fire of our burning planet until he does. You understand? You exploited our earth's resources that belong to The People." Oksana pulled a crinkled piece of paper from the pocket of her apron and handed it to Natalia. "These are our demands. We will accept nothing less."

Natalia unfolded the document and read it: "This Week Only: Fifty Percent off a Poquito Soy Latte."

Oksana reached over and turned it over. "Other side."

"Ah." Natalia looked down the list, a smorgasbord of revolutionary aspirations scrawled in red ink under the heading "PLANETISTA MANIFESTO:" Immediate cessation of energy production from fossil fuels, plus a universal basic income, six months off from work each year, free rent, health care, college, child care, drug clinics, pet-sitting, breakfast, lunch, dinner, Sunday brunch, and beer. "This is well outside the scope of Crowe Power."

"Stop with the corporate propaganda already," she said, sneering. "Your company is worth billions."

It was worth more than sixty billion, actually, but Natalia recognized it was not the time to say so. "What if we start on one issue first? Like climate change. Let's see what we can do about that. Working with you, of course."

Oksana turned to Gazi. "What do you think?"

Gazi said, "It's time we get out the guns."

Oksana nearly melted. She smiled at him lovingly and reached out to stroke his arm. "You're the best," she said.

Ernesto glanced nervously around the shop, which was filling up with customers from nearby office buildings. "Gazi, did you put out that cheesecake like I asked?"

Gazi shook his head. "Not yet."

"Take care of it, will ya? Now."

Gazi sighed and departed for the cooler. Natalia said to Oksana, "There's no way you're going to get everything at once. A more realistic plan would focus on what Crowe Power can actually do. What if we commit to transitioning to alternative technologies over a measurable time frame that gets us to our goal?"

Ernesto rubbed his chin. "I like that." He cast a glance to Oksana.

"That's okay, but not enough," she said. "We need money to finance our revolution."

"We've just donated a hundred thousand dollars. How much do you need?"

Oksana said, "More."

"More?"

"It will never be enough."

25. A FINE BROMANCE

In the back seat of a Chevrolet Suburban making its way toward the San Francisco airport, Robbie dreamily closed his eyes, warmed by the memory of one last tune-up with Dr. Kristi Kramer and soothed by Fred Crispin's balmy response to the question of why he wanted to join Crowe Power.

Everything Fred said not only sounded so right, it made Robbie feel really *good*. There wasn't another person around him these days who knew how to do that. Here, at last, was an obviously smart, insightful person, deeply respectful of Robbie, his heritage, and his groundbreaking leadership. How could Robbie get Fred to start tomorrow?

Through the phone, Fred's voice piped in. "Sorry to repeat myself—"

"No, please," Robbie said. "Go ahead."

"I've always admired the way you've led Crowe Power. This week is just another example. I mean, your press release blew me away. So many leaders talk about values. It's obvious that you actually live them."

Robbie swooned. He didn't want just Fred. He wanted an *army* of Freds. "That's something I take very seriously," he said. "That's why I need people at this company who can make sure we all live my values every single day. It can't just be me."

"I'm totally on board with that," Fred said. "It's obvious, even from the outside, that nobody loves Crowe Power more than you. And it's not just love, but tough love. You know that if the company's going to survive and thrive in a difficult industry, it must commit to change. Some people will resist, but you keep pushing because you know it's the right thing to do."

Damn! This guy gets me! Robbie looked over to Digby, the other passenger in the back seat. He pointed to the phone and mouthed the words: *The real deal!*

Digby nodded and returned to working a word puzzle on his tablet.

"That's why I'm working around the clock. Because it's right," Robbie said. "And I absolutely won't rest until we get it done. You know, I'm just coming back from an offsite where I told the leadership team that I want us to become the most responsible energy company in the world."

"That's one reason I'm thinking of leaving Staminum," Fred said. "Under my direction, we've made incredible progress on finding new energy solutions through our Greeneron subsidiary. Have you heard of it?"

"Of course."

"It's a really impressive portfolio of technologies, right? Any one of these could break through and become a game changer as far as the environment is concerned. And if that happens, Staminum could move away from carbon completely. But are we investing in them the way we should? No. Quite the opposite."

"What do you mean?"

"This is strictly confidential, Robbie. And I tell you only because I think you could save Greeneron. Walker wants to sell it."

"Really? Which part?"

"The whole thing."

Robbie bolted upright. "*The whole thing?* That's crazy. Why would he do that?"

"As you may know, Staminum's been in a rough patch profit-wise for some time, due to a variety of reasons outside of our control."

"Headwinds, right?"

"Exactly. Now Walker comes in, completely oblivious to the great progress we've been making on every front. He's desperate for cash and selling Greeneron is the way he wants to get it. I objected, of course, but he doesn't want to hear it. He doesn't get that the world is changing. You know how stubborn he can be. I hate to say it, but he's kind of an asshole."

Robbie reached over and grabbed Digby's arm, then frantically waved a thumbs up. "He has some redeeming qualities, I suppose," Robbie allowed. "My feeling is this: Let him hit singles at Staminum. We're swinging for the fences at Crowe Power. I want home runs. Grand slams. I want to lead the entire league in clean green energy."

"You want Greeneron."

"I'd love Greeneron. How about this? Let's get you on board to run it, huh?"

"Why, Robbie," Fred said, choking up. "I would be honored."

"With some real leadership, who knows? There could be more than one of those technologies taking off. There could be two, or three, or maybe even all of them. Crowe Power could become the undisputed leader in clean energy. Oh my God!" Robbie was talking himself into a frenzy. Fred *and* Greeneron? Holy shit! He needed to calm down.

Fred continued. "It all sounds so exciting, Robbie. I can see how it could all come together in an incredible way. But you'll want to move quickly. I'm hearing Greeneron could go for three billion dollars."

Robbie sighed. *That's a big lift.* He would have to take an expenditure like that to the board for approval. Fortunately, his board was a collection of washed-up executives, cabinet secretaries, foundation chiefs, and university presidents, all of whom were beholden to him. The real challenge was convincing his former CEO. "Would Walker actually sell it to me? I think he hates me."

"Robbie, you know all Walker cares about is the bottom line," Fred said. "If you give him a high enough bid, you'd get the deal."

Robbie thanked Fred and promised him a formal offer when he and Digby got back into the city. As the car crossed over the Bay Bridge, Robbie fantasized about the bright future ahead. If he could land Fred and Greeneron, Crowe Power would have an unbeatable one-two punch. Better yet, everyone would know that it was he who had brought in a top Staminum talent *and* the company's most consequential acquisition in decades in one fearless—and bold!—stroke. There would be no mistaking who gets the credit for Crowe Power's success this time around. Not Homer Crowe. Not Charles Crowe, Les Crowe, or Walker Hope. Everything would have Robbie's unmistakable green thumbprint. Dr. Kristi Kramer would tell the inside story of Robbie's crowning achievement through her book, guaranteed to be a best-seller because Robbie would buy a hundred thousand copies for every employee, the news media, Congress, you name it. Even the ever-elusive Natalia might be impressed as Robbie was hailed far and wide as a hero of the planet. The protests on Broad Street would disappear. In their place: a parade up Broadway, with Robbie riding a zero-emission scooter, showered with love and admiration and biodegradable ticker tape. This was going to be *so great!*

Robbie laid back in his seat, happier than he'd been in weeks. "We've got our guy," he said. "And, potentially, a lot more than that."

Digby dropped his tablet in his lap. "Uh-oh."

"Imagine this. Rather than Staminum buying us, we buy the only part of Staminum that's worth a crap."

"Greeneron."

"Walker wants to sell it."

"No doubt. It's a money pit."

"After the run we've had, we can handle it."

"And you want to blow our cash on that?"

"We're not blowing money, Digs. We're blowing away the competition by placing a highly strategic bet on the future. How do you put a price on that? A hick like Walker is not sophisticated enough to get it. I'm more than happy to take Greeneron off his hands. Won't he be sorry after he sees what we do with it?" He rubbed his hands together in gleeful anticipation.

Digby was feeling worn out. What was the use of fighting Robbie? He'd get his way, regardless. "What about Fred?"

"I want you to draw up an offer for him today and get it signed tonight. Whatever he's making at Staminum, I say double it. We're so close on a deal, I don't want to leave anything to chance. There should be no doubt in his mind that this is the right move for him."

"What about Tim? Don't you think he should interview Fred?"

Robbie looked at him, incredulous. "Why?"

"Seriously?"

"It's not his call, Digs. It's my call." Robbie looked out the window as San Francisco Bay again came into view on his left. "You know what's so great about all this? Crowe Power is finally my baby. I never felt that way when Walker was here. I do now. This is my chance to put my mark on this company—and maybe on history. I know you're going to think this sounds grandiose, but I can change the world. It's like Kristi said: this could be a revolution."

Digby sighed. "That's fine. But Tim is still your CEO. And you can't pretend he isn't there."

They exited the bridge and continued down I-80 toward the airport. "You know who Tim reminds me of?" Robbie asked. "Wally Secrest. He worked for me when I was running Strategy. I don't know why, but Wally used to bug the crap out of me. I think it was the strange way he parted his hair." Robbie shook his head at the memory. "Anyway, he was just like Tim in the sense that he was constantly hanging around, seeking my approval. He kept insisting on having a meeting with me to discuss some idiotic idea. He'd wait outside my office for hours. I'd come out around five o'clock with my coat on and say, 'Sorry, Wally, but I gotta be somewhere. 'He'd say, 'I'll come back tomorrow.' I'd say, 'Fine. Suit yourself.' It went on like this day after day. I don't know how the poor bastard got anything done. His whole day was a complete waste of time." Robbie chuckled with delight at the memory.

"Maybe I'm missing something," Digby said. "He was wasting company time and that was *good*?"

"He wasn't wasting *my* time."

"And that made it okay?"

"It was a teaching moment."

"He learned what, exactly?"

"He wasn't the boss," Robbie said, folding his hands peacefully over his belly.

✳ ✳ ✳

The Suburban pulled through the security fence around the airport and sped ahead onto the tarmac toward Crowe Bird I, where the vehicle came to a halt at the foot of the stairs, which were lowered onto a red carpet. Tom Michaels, the company security chief, leaped out of the front passenger seat and scanned the horizon for terrorists, kidnappers, and crazed dentists. Finding the grounds safe for passage, he opened the rear passenger door to allow Robbie out the back. The driver opened Digby's door on the other side, and the Batman and Robin of the Crowe Power Company were escorted to the plane for their flight back to Gotham.

Safely ensconced in their customary seats, Robbie and Digby were immediately offered breakfast by Chad, the new replacement flight attendant, who'd been flown in from New York the night before.

"See?" Robbie said, nodding toward the galley. "An improvement in service already. All it took was decisive action."

While the pilots prepared for takeoff, Robbie checked on the previous night's baseball box scores before noticing a flurry of activity outside. Tim was walking out of the Signature terminal toward Robbie's plane, holding a bag of popcorn. What *now?*

Tim climbed the stairway and stepped into the cabin, huffing and puffing. "Robbie, there's a maintenance problem with my plane," he said, munching on the popcorn, a kernel of which tumbled down his shirt to the neatly vacuumed Broad Street Blue carpeting. "Mind if I hitch a ride home with you?"

Robbie, revolted by the notion of Tim riding along, had been looking forward to spending the long flight back to New York snoozing and watching a movie. Now he had to sit up and listen to Tim talk about objectives and metrics and report-outs and other boring shit? *Fuck me.* "I don't see how that's possible," Robbie said.

Tim looked puzzled. "Why not?"

Robbie was stunned. Nobody had ever even dared to ask him for a lift. "This plane is meant for only two passengers."

Tim glanced around the plane. "The capacity is nineteen."

"Yeah? So's a Greyhound bus. What difference does that make?"

"Robbie, I was just thinking—"

Robbie sat up, agitated. He said through clenched teeth: "Why is this my responsibility all of the sudden? It's your plane that's fucked up. Not mine. Why don't you just get our other plane?"

"I checked. It's not available."

"Why not?"

"Apparently your son has it," Tim said, sounding a bit more annoyed than he should have let on. "He and his buddies are flying back from vacation in Europe."

Robbie flushed red. "Who the hell told you that?"

"Robbie, I'm making no judgments. I just thought, if it were convenient..."

"Well, god*damn* it, Tim, it's not convenient. Alright? We're full." Robbie looked to Digby, who was hiding in his newspaper, which was pulled tightly around him. "Digby, will you be so kind as to help Tim find another plane? A charter, perhaps?" He looked out the window, then back to Digby. "This appears to be an airport. It looks like there are dozens of planes out there. Surely, we can find one for Tim. I don't want to sit here on the tarmac all day."

Digby sighed, put his newspaper down, and led Tim out of the plane toward the Signature terminal. Robbie returned to his phone, where a message from Howie-Do-It popped up on his screen.

HOWIE

Marty sez Walker scared shitless
top exec going to Crowe Power

Robbie laughed and hit the call button on his phone.

"Dude," Howie answered.

"Did Marty name names?"

"Nah. But it seemed like it was somebody really, really big."

"Well, yeah. We're about to steal their best guy. An absolutely huge win for us. Oh, man. Would I love to see the look on Walker's face? Tell me. What did Marty say about the nutty dentist? He put him up to it, didn't he?"

"I don't think so. Marty seemed totally surprised."

"You can't believe that. The guy's a professional bullshit artist."

"Whether Marty's in on it or not, Dr. Littmann is starting to ramp it up."

"What's he doing?"

"He's beating the hell out of you on Twitter. Good thing he's only got about six followers."

Robbie looked out the window to see Digby walking back up the steps to the plane. "That's still six too many," Robbie said to Howie. "I can't have somebody out there saying I've destroyed the company. What if others get the same idea? That could go viral. We've got to shut him down, pronto. I mean, what gives this guy the right to say anything he wants about me?"

Digby entered the cabin and sat down. "The First Amendment?"

Robbie waved him off with a scowl. "You need to make another run at him. Figure out where he's vulnerable and attack. Does he have a family?"

"Never married. Lives alone on the Upper West Side."

"Parents?"

"Dead. That's how he got the money to put into Crowe stock."

"What about driving? Does he have a car? Somebody, and I'm not saying who exactly, could maybe... slash his tires?"

Digby glared at Robbie. "I really don't want to hear this."

Robbie rose from his seat and walked to the back of the plane. "Howie, look. We can't allow this to stand. Somehow, some way, you need to make this guy stop. I don't want to be looking over my shoulder the rest of my life, worried about whether he's gonna kick up a shareholder suit. Have you thought about destroying his business?"

Howie sighed. "It's occurred to me. I looked at posting a bunch of crap about him on Yelp. You know, like he's got bad breath. He causes pain. He keeps you waiting. That sort of thing. Problem is, his ratings are actually pretty good. People seem to love this guy. I'd have to post a hell of a lot just to get him down to four stars."

Robbie propped a hand on the ceiling and looked out the window. "Alright. What about this: you somehow provoke him so that he reacts—a push, a shove— and you have to kick his ass?"

"I don't know. He's got this receptionist, Chanisse, who looks like Mike Tyson in a dress."

Robbie laughed bitterly. "You've got to be kidding me. You're afraid of a *receptionist?*"

"No. No! Of course not. I'm just sayin'. You should have seen her. Or he. Or zhe. Or whatever. This, this... *person* was built like a brick shithouse. And this day and age, you never know who's packin' heat."

"Okay. Fine. I tell you what. You just keep track of this crazy dentist. I want to know what he's doing, every minute of the day and night. Maybe we can get him away from the office and find a way to put him down."

"How do you want to do that, boss?"

"By any means necessary. You said he's pretty tiny, right?"

"Looks like the kind of guy everyone in school used to give a noogie."

Robbie liked the sound of that. He couldn't take on really big institutional investors, but he could surely make mincemeat out of this little pipsqueak. "Well," Robbie said, "this guy may think he's tough, hiding behind his nutty letters and his tweets. But let me tell you something. He's not going to want to run into me. He won't know what hit him."

26. AN APPEAL FOR MERCY

U pon his return to the city, Robbie's first order of business was to visit Lindsey to manage the marital damage. If he couldn't stop her from initiating divorce proceedings, he could at least try to slow her down. A division of assets now could imperil his control of the company at the very moment he stood on the cusp of business immortality.

Boris dropped him off in front of the townhouse on East 67th Street that Lindsey's parents had given them as a wedding present twenty-four years earlier. Frederick, the house manager, opened the door to the grand marble foyer, and the chef, Renee, who made the greatest chicken Caesar salad in the world, poked her head out of the kitchen in the back and smiled, albeit sadly. Robbie mumbled a hello and climbed the sweeping staircase to the second-story study, where he heard the familiar sounds of a television show, suggesting that at least one familiar routine hadn't changed: Lindsey's nightly spin of the *Wheel of Fortune*. Given their shaky relationship, Robbie reminded himself not to blurt out the answer when he entered the room. That could be the fatal blow to their marriage and everything that depended on it.

"The Drapes of Wrath," a contestant announced.

"No. Sorry," said the host, Pat Sajak. "Alfonso?"

Robbie bit his tongue as Alphonso offered, "The *Grapes* of Wrath?"

"That's more like it," Sajak said.

Robbie crossed the threshold to hearty applause and found Lindsey in her customary corner of the floral-patterned sofa, a glass of lemon water on the table where she typically placed a large glass of wine. Much to his surprise, she wasn't watching the show. Her head was down and she was peering through her reading glasses at a folder on her lap, scribbling notes on its edge. Catching a glimpse of Robbie out of the corner of her eye, she quickly closed the folder and turned it over onto a cushion.

"Hello," she said curtly.

"Hey."

Lindsey picked up the remote and clicked off the TV.

"Please," Robbie said. "Don't turn it off on my account."

"It's a rerun of an old show," she said. "Kind of like you just dropping in when you happen to feel like it."

Robbie feigned hurt. "I wanted to see you."

"All I ask is that you respect my privacy and call first. Have Winnie do it if you're tied up... to a bedpost or something."

Robbie let it go, determined not to argue. "Sorry. I ran out of time. I've been in California for a few days and there's a lot going on at the company." He looked around and was struck by the abundance of fresh-cut flowers in the room. There were nearly a dozen arrangements on end tables, the credenza, the windowsills, even the floor. "Who died?"

"Some of my friends apparently think our marriage did," she said. "The orchids are from Karen. The pink peonies are from Charlotte. The tulips are from Bits. Three dozen roses from Mitzi."

"The real estate broker?"

"I think she smells a commission."

"That's *way* premature."

Lindsey shrugged. "I was impressed, actually. Seemed like a shrewd business move to me." She looked at him quizzically. "So, what's on your mind?"

He sat down on a chintz ottoman. "I'm worried that you've already made up your mind about where all this is going."

She looked up at the vaulted ceiling and ran the back of her fingernails up the side of her neck a couple of times, then turned back to Robbie. "I don't think it's really 'going' anywhere, Robbie. It's simply... gone."

Robbie sagged. "Lindsey. Please. There's absolutely no reason to rush into any of this."

She looked at him as if he were kidding. "I've had twenty-four years to think about it."

Robbie found her resolve unnerving. This was not the passive, foggy, go-along Lindsey he thought he knew. He scooted the ottoman a little closer to the sofa. "I know you probably don't believe this, but I'm going to say it anyway. I can change. As a matter of fact, I *have* changed."

She regarded him skeptically. "Changed what? Your socks?"

"My *behavior*, of course. I know I haven't been a model husband. I messed up. I'll be the first to say so."

"Actually, you're the second. After me."

"Whatever. You can't let a few past indiscretions get in the way of our life together."

She laughed, mirthlessly. "Robbie, all those women you got involved with weren't simply 'indiscretions.' Nor were they a 'few.' Chasing women is your lifestyle, your hobby. Some men collect postcards or stamps. You collect girlfriends, and you acted for years as if our marriage were of no consequence whatsoever. And you know what? It took some doing, but you finally convinced me. It doesn't matter to me anymore, either."

He recoiled, looking at her bitterly. "You say that like you had nothing to do with it."

Lindsey leaned forward, incredulous. "This should be interesting."

Robbie stood, kicking back the ottoman, and slowly paced, idly picking up framed family photos he'd never noticed before and examining them like artifacts from an ancient civilization. "You were never there when I needed someone to talk to."

"There... where? If you'd come home, you'd have found me here."

"No. Not always. You had your friends, and your boards, your events with the kids. And let's face it. Even when you were around, you were in the bag half the time."

"Oh my," she growled. "If you think insulting me is the best way to persuade me, you might want to think again."

"I'm serious. There were plenty of times I needed to let my hair down."

"Your hair? Or just your pants?"

"You have no idea what I've been through." Robbie felt his eyes welling. Was it her cutting commentary? Her cold demeanor? His sense of the impending loss of a critical relationship? The fact that maybe he really did love her more than he realized? *No*, he thought. *It can't be that…* "Everyone assumes it's easy being me," he said, sadly shaking his head. "They have no idea how difficult it is to carry the burdens that I do. To run the company. And the board. And the family voting bloc. And, at the same time, to find a sustainable pathway for the future before we're driven out of existence. I think about these things twenty-four seven, but you never showed the slightest interest in any of it."

Lindsey nodded. *Uh-huh, uh-huh.* Then she spoke, forcefully. "Let's get something straight, Robbie. Whenever I asked about the company, you told me you didn't want to talk about it."

He waved her off. "It's too complicated."

Her voice rose. "For me, or for you?"

He set down a family photo and sat back on the ottoman. "What's gotten into you?"

She picked up the folder from the sofa cushion and held it up. "I've been learning a lot about Crowe Power lately. And I'll tell you something: I'm very concerned with what I see."

Robbie sucked in his breath, bracing. "Like what, exactly?"

"Like executive performance."

He dismissed that notion with a wave of his hand. "Don't worry about that. Tim's already on his way out. It's just a matter of time."

"I'm talking about you."

"*Me?*"

"From what I understand, the company is seriously undervalued because of you."

Robbie flushed red. "Where'd you get that idea?"

"My advisors, among others."

Blue-blooded veins popped out on Robbie's forehead. "Like who? Bentley Edwards? Poundstone Bank? What a bunch of *crap*. That's *outrageous!*"

"Wall Street applies a 'management discount' to the stock because they don't think you know what you're doing. They believe you've stacked the board with lackeys who won't hold you to account, and you've put Tim Padden in the CEO job because he won't challenge you. Investors have no confidence in either one of you—certainly, nothing like they did in Walker Hope. My advisors tell me the best thing that could happen to Crowe Power is for you to be removed as chairman and take Tim with you."

"And you actually believe that?"

For the first time since they were married twenty-four years ago, Lindsey felt the power in their relationship shifting. She stood and faced Robbie, her chin raised, boring in on his weakness. "It's not what I believe, Robbie. It's what the market believes. They don't trust you any more than I do."

Robbie looked around, as if searching for a place to hide. "Anyone who thinks that just doesn't understand. I'm in the process right now of bringing in some top talent and reinventing this company for the twenty-first century. And we're this close." He held his thumb and index finger a quarter inch apart. "I'm sure you've heard of Dr. Kristi Kramer. She's going to write a book about it. The world is going to see us as the model for what a modern company should be."

"Really? We were doing just fine until you drove out Walker. From what I've seen and heard, it was nothing more than a fit of jealousy. That's an awful reason to make such an important business decision."

Robbie stood up and leaned against a table, adopting a rope-a-dope defense. "I had to get rid of him."

"Why?"

"He... thought he was me," he said quietly.

"He *what?*"

"He went out every day and ran the company like I wasn't even there," Robbie said. "He wouldn't bother to ask for permission or show any kind of respect for me or for our family. He just went out and... did stuff."

"What stuff?"

"All kinds of stuff."

"Wasn't that his *job?*"

"Yes, but it was like he was the Crowe, and I was some schmo."

"How did you arrive at that conclusion?"

He waved her away. "It's hard to explain."

She folded her arms across her chest. "Try me."

Robbie staggered toward her. "In the press releases for our earnings? He was always quoted first. Over me, the chairman! For him, it was always 'me, first.' Our employee town halls? Someone would ask a question. He'd jump in and answer before I even had a chance, like he knew more about everything. When he started, I thought, 'Fine. *Fine.* We'll show everyone there are no egos here. We're a team.' So we'd go down to the lunchroom together, in a show of unity. You should have seen him walk through the line. He was a fucking showboat. He'd shake hands with everyone he saw, right down to the cashiers and busboys, acting like he was a candidate running for office. He was gripping. He was grinning. It was ridiculous."

"What's so awful about that?"

"It was embarrassing, like I wasn't even there."

"What did you do about it?"

"Well, naturally, I never went again."

"You didn't say anything?"

"No."

"How many times did you go to the lunchroom with him?"

"Just the once."

"And then you drove him out."

"Don't you see? He deserved it."

Lindsey shook her head in wonderment. After all these years, she was finally beginning to understand. "I'm curious, Robbie. Did your girlfriends buy this nonsense? Did they actually listen to this and say, 'You poor baby?' Because you're right. I wouldn't have had much patience for it."

Robbie shrugged and leaned against the credenza. "I don't know what you mean by 'girlfriends,' as if there were a lot of them or something. But I would say the people who worked with me over the years certainly saw the challenges I was facing every day and respected what I was trying to do."

Lindsey saw Robbie as she had never seen him, shrinking before her eyes. She stood up, walked over and patted him on the shoulder. "Robbie. In a certain way, I kind of feel for you. You are a child. You have no business being in such a commanding position in a company with the responsibility for so many lives."

Robbie sniffed, weakly. "That's hardly your call."

"Don't be so sure."

27. THE PRIZE PACKAGE

R obbie recruited top executives like he seduced his girlfriends, with one important distinction. After the initial burst of romance, recruits were invited home to meet his wife, to see how the other one-tenth of one percent lives and consummate the agreement over port wine and cigars in the third-floor library.

Just as he romanced each new girlfriend, Robbie insisted to each prospective executive that they would be inseparable, a formidable team, bonded by a sense of common mission and mutual respect. Robbie's door would always be open, welcoming them any time, even if only to check in and say hello.

It was never an intentional deception, since Robbie always meant it at the time. He would be infatuated at first. It's just that once he realized he could win someone over, he began to lose interest quickly. *If they're such hot shit, what are they doing here?* He never loved them quite as much in the morning.

In romancing Fred Crispin, there was no home or family to use as props. Robbie needed to haul in his Next Great Catch from an unadorned meeting room at the New York Athletic Club. Far from ideal, it was at least private, away from prying eyes at the office. And, regardless of the venue, Robbie was quite confident he would get their partnership off on the right foot by impressing Fred with a charm offensive.

Taking the elevator to a meeting room on the fifth floor, Robbie found Digby and Fred working through the lush compensation package, which laid out Fred's salary, bonus, stock options, retirement plan, various perks, and, vitally important for anyone working for Robbie, severance terms. All told, it was nearly double what Fred had made at Staminum, but surely it was worth it for Robbie to snare such a prize.

Robbie bounded into the room. "You must be Fred!" he said, excitedly.

"I sure as heck am," Fred said, jumping out of his chair to pump Robbie's hand. "Gosh, Robbie. It's such an honor to meet you in person."

"The honor is all mine," Robbie said. Looking Fred up and down, Robbie had to admit the man did not cut an impressive profile at first glance. In person, Fred was rather schlumpy, wearing a weird shirt-and-tie-color combination that didn't quite work. And what was with those red splotches on his face? *Did the dude have leprosy?* Still, Robbie, in his eminently fair and open-minded way, decided to overlook such superficial concerns and consider more important issues. He reminded himself that he cared far more for what was inside a person's head and heart than what kind of rash they had on their face. Didn't Fred say during their telephone interview that he had always admired Robbie? *Yes, he did.* And didn't Fred say that Walker was a jerk? *Emphatically so.* Clearly, Fred was a man of good, solid judgment.

"How do you like the package?" Robbie asked as he sat down at the table.

"I'm delighted," Fred said, resuming his seat.

"Glad to hear it," Robbie said. "Do we have a deal?"

"Signed and sealed."

"Excellent!" Robbie reached over and patted him on the shoulder. "I can't wait to get started."

"Me neither," Fred said.

"Tell me more about your background. How'd you get where you are today?"

Fred launched into his life story, a pedestrian tale of a suburban upbringing, education at state schools and a long, boring climb up the corporate ladder at Staminum in tandem with some guy named Tom. As Fred droned on, Robbie found himself drifting off. Was that a nose hair emanating from Fred's right nostril? It was extraordinarily long. Every time Fred breathed or said a word that began with a "p," it shot in the air before settling down again over his lip. Couldn't Fred feel that or see it? Why hadn't anybody bothered to tell him? You'd think he'd look in the mirror once in a while. Or maybe that was too scary. Not that any of this should make Robbie rescind the offer, but still... It was distracting.

"—and so that's how I ended up as COO."

What had he said? "Wow," Robbie said. "What an incredible story, Fred. Thanks for sharing."

"My pleasure," Fred said. "I'm impressed that you would show such an interest. My background was nothing like yours, I'm sure."

No, and thank God! How do people like this bother to get out of bed in the morning? "So tell me, Fred. What else do you need from me to get started?"

"I guess I'd like to know a bit more about your expectations for the job. I want to make sure we're completely aligned so that I can hit the ground running."

"Great!" Robbie said. He explained that his plan for where Fred would fit in had evolved significantly since they talked over the phone. With the possibility of landing both Fred and Greeneron, Robbie had decided to reorganize the company in two parts. Old Crowe, which would comprise the company's traditional power-generating operations, pipelines and refineries, would be run by Tim. New Crowe, which would focus on developing Greeneron's alternative energy technologies, would be run by Fred. Virtually all of the company's efforts, and its capital, would be plowed into New Crowe, while Old Crowe would get just enough to keep it going until it could be dismantled, shut down, or sold off.

"I love it," Fred said. He didn't know anything about alternative energy but thought it best not to volunteer that information. He'd figure it out, sooner or later.

Digby eyed Robbie. "What if we don't get Greeneron?"

"That's not possible," Robbie said. "I'll do whatever it takes."

Digby squirmed in his chair, clearly uncomfortable. "We can't afford a bidding war."

"We have plenty of money," Robbie said, impatiently. "It's all just a question of how we choose to spend it. Do we just keep plowing money into the same crap in Old Crowe or do we build the future with New Crowe? Seems pretty obvious to me. Right, Fred?"

"Oh, yes," Fred said.

Robbie looked at Digby with a raised eyebrow. *See?*

Digby ignored the message and pressed ahead. "Suppose you're bidding against one of the big dogs. The price could go north of three billion."

Robbie scowled. "Read my lips, Digby: I. Don't. Care. I want this deal."

Digby threw up his hands. "Your call."

Robbie shot out of his chair. "Damn right, it's my call," Robbie said, annoyed. "Fred, I hate for you to see this little family squabble right out of the box. I'm sure you understand why I'm so high on this."

"Of course," Fred said, grandly. "It looks to me, Robbie, like Greeneron is the missing piece in the Crowe Power puzzle. It's totally consistent with your vision for where you want to take this company. And, really, it's more than that. It's about how you want to lead the world."

Ooooh, yeah! Robbie sat down and kicked back, smiling broadly and putting his hands behind his head. "You're exactly right, Fred. *Exactly* right!" What did Shakespeare say? *Some men are born great, some achieve greatness, and some have greatness thrust upon them?* Robbie was starting to thrust greatness upon himself! God, he loved being L. Robertson Crowe III right now! "I want to get this done sooner, rather than later. It would be so cool to announce your hiring and the acquisition of Greeneron at the same time. We will shock and awe!"

"Well," Fred said, "this is very, very exciting. What is my title?"

Robbie said, "I think we should call your position what it is: President of New Crowe. You'll still be an officer of Crowe Power, a member of the leadership team, and you'll have a dotted line to Tim. But you'll have your own sandbox, and you'll have direct access to me. We'll be in lockstep, I assure you, working as closely as two people can be. I want you to call me anytime you have a question. Day or night. Will you do that, please?"

"I sure will," Fred said, reaching for his phone. "What's your number?"

Robbie waved him off. "Don't worry about that right now. Digby always knows where to track me down."

Digby rolled his eyes. "Right."

"There's one other thing," Robbie said. "A huge problem we have at the company right now is that nobody tells me anything. I find out more through the media or the rumor mill than I do from my own team. That's got to change. We're never going to succeed if everyone's keeping secrets. So I'm going to count on you to keep me apprised of anything and everything I need to know. Promise me no surprises, and I'll do the same for you. I want to build a culture of absolute transparency."

"That's wonderful to hear," Fred said. "I fully support that."

"Excellent."

"So... how much does Tim know about me?"

Robbie shrugged. "Nothing."

"Is, um, somebody going to tell him?"

"He'll find out soon enough."

Digby interjected. "Robbie. Didn't you just say—"

Robbie sighed, impatiently. "We're on a need-to-know basis only, Digby. Do you want Tim asking a bunch of irrelevant questions right now and slowing things down? We don't need the distraction and neither does he."

They shook hands and Fred departed, delighting in his new opportunity. As he took the elevator down to the ground floor and headed out to the bustle of Central Park South, he couldn't help feeling unsettled by some of Robbie's comments, especially about Tim. *If he treats his CEO like this, how will he treat me?*

28. STRAINED BEDFELLOWS

Digby emerged from his dressing room in his pajamas, robe and slippers. He might be the last man in America to wear clothing specifically designed for sleeping, but Digby found great comfort in traditional rules and standards.

After another adventure with Robbie, there was a calming familiarity to Mozart's Piano Concerto No. 15 playing softly on the sound system, the sight of Bits propped up in bed reading, and the backdrop of dark windows overlooking Central Park. He silently kissed his wife on the forehead, then dropped into an overstuffed chaise in a corner, opening his iPad to scan his mail and messages for the last time that day.

Bits looked over her reading glasses. "Did you get your yes-man?"

"Yes, ma'am," Digby sighed. "Robbie's next victim is Fred Crispin, a thoroughly unimpressive executive from Staminum Energy. If he were as good as Robbie would like to believe, Walker would never have let him slip out of his clutches."

"Is there any possibility it could work out?"

"About the same as finding green cheese on the moon. We didn't take the time to do our due diligence on Fred lest we—quote-unquote—'lose out.' Robbie has assigned him to lead a division that doesn't even exist yet, at least at our company. We still have to acquire the whole shebang from Staminum, but Robbie has that gleam in his eye. There's no denying him."

"That sounds awful."

"And awfully expensive. This has all the hallmarks of another Robbie Special, where he follows a hunch. No time for due diligence! We've got to hit the gas. It's like watching a car wreck in slow motion. You know there are going to be casualties, yet there's nothing you can do but wait, and watch in horror, and call for ambulances when it's all over. He wants Fred and this Greeneron subsidiary, and that's that."

Bits put down her book. "How did this happen?"

"Which part?"

"The part where Robbie gets to do whatever he likes with the company. That's our company, too."

"Who's going to stop him? The board? If he told them to jump, by God they'd try, even with their walkers and canes. The family won't do anything to stop him, since they find everything about the energy business highly distasteful, except for the dividend checks. The market has sent an unmistakable signal to Robbie that it disapproves of his leadership, but he interprets that as a sign that he simply hasn't gone far enough. So he doubles down on his worst instincts, as if another shot of bad medicine will do the trick."

Bits patted the bed. "Digby. Come here."

Digby dutifully got up from the chaise and walked with floppy feet to sit on the edge of the bed. She hugged him, kissed his cheek, and held him close for a moment. Then she sat back, holding his hand. "I'm sorry you're going through this."

"No sorrier than I am."

"Thank you for taking that job. I thought it would help to have an adult in the room with Robbie."

"I've tried. Lord *knows* I've tried," he said, exasperated. "There's only so much I can do. You disagree with him, and he cuts you off and looks at you like you're stupid. You propose a different course than what he has in mind, and he ignores you and changes the subject. You suggest taking more time to study options and he thinks you're some corporate dinosaur who can't keep up with his torrid pace. The man can't be helped."

"He's always been a spoiled brat. I guess this is what happens when you always get your way your entire life. Nobody ever told him 'no.'"

Digby sighed. "The frustrating thing is that the company can be only as good as he is. And the plain truth is that he just isn't very good. Now, Walker was good. In fact, Walker was great. We had a heck of a chance with him to put this company on solid ground for a generation to come. But competence was too threatening to Robbie. He had to run him out and bring in someone he could push around. And even that wasn't enough. He's going to let Tim twist in the wind while he brings in another lapdog. But that's not the scariest part."

"What is?"

"I've seen this movie before. My father and grandfather managed to squander our entire family fortune with their impulsive, stupid behavior. Now here we go again. He could blow it all."

Bits sank back into her pillows. "Any chance we'll get lucky?"

"He could get hit by a bus." His eyes widened and he put his hand over his mouth. "Did I say that?"

"I understand. You're frustrated."

He looked on the nightstand. "What are you reading?"

"Believe it or not, the annual report."

"For Crowe Power?" He picked it up and glanced at the cover, which showed cows in a green pasture under a web of power lines. The headline:

Peaceful Coexistence
The Crowe Power Company
& Nature

"I'd never read one," she said. "Now I know why. It's spectacularly boring."

"It's supposed to be," Digby said. "We don't want to encourage any interest in our 10-K. God forbid somebody actually reads it. Why are you interested all of a sudden?"

"I'm wondering if we can't do better. I hear from you and Lindsey about Robbie's behavior and then I read here that the chairman of Crowe Power is a magnificent visionary. I can't believe we're talking about the same person."

Digby stood from the bed. "We're not. One is Robbie Crowe. The other is the fictional character he'd like to be."

"Do you think he should run the company?"

"Absolutely not. But it doesn't matter what I think."

"What if others started thinking the same way? I know one large shareholder who's starting to think Robbie needs to go."

"You and Lindsey get into the sauce?"

"She's not drinking."

Digby snickered. "There's the problem."

"Digby, listen. If they divorce, she has more votes in the family than anyone."

He shrugged. "That's not enough."

"Which is my point."

"I don't follow."

"If we join her, it wouldn't take a whole lot more to change things."

"Why would we do that?"

"That's what I'm asking. Should we join a revolution?"

"And overthrow King Robbie?"

"Why not?"

"I would lose my job, pathetic as it is."

"Yes. And gain a fortune." Bits explained the scenario that Bentley Edwards and his team had laid out for Lindsey. "He's costing us. And not just in terms of money. I see the toll it's taken on you. You come home beaten up every day. This is a chance for you to stand up to him."

Digby took a deep breath. "It's not enough to go after Robbie. You have to take him down. Otherwise, a wounded Robbie is even more dangerous. Does Lindsey have it in her to challenge him?"

"I think it will take some time. But she is deeply motivated."

"A woman scorned?"

"A woman reborn, with eyes wide open."

29. POTATOES AND LEAKS

Marty found *Buzzniss* reporter Tilda Ecklund seated by the windows at a coveted corner table at Bubby's in Tribeca, where she was wedged between a gaggle of nannies and their young charges on one side, and a couple of bleary-eyed TV stars with bedhead and a baby on the other. Outside, beyond the life-sized plaster cow in front, the wealthy downtown neighborhood of cast-iron buildings was slowly stirring to life at a pace befitting its rich and somewhat famous denizens from the worlds of entertainment and publishing. Marty slid into the banquette next to Tilda: a trim, elegant woman, dressed in layers of charcoal gray, with rustic wooden eyeglasses, long silver hair, bright blue eyes, and a ready smile.

"So good to see you again," Marty said.

"You say that almost as if you mean it."

He nodded. "Then I haven't lost my touch."

They ordered breakfast and sipped their coffees as Marty assessed his adversary. Tilda had made her reputation breaking big stories, and the idea that Walker Hope was running into resistance from the founding family at Staminum would certainly qualify, reverberating in concentric circles: the C-suite, the rank-and-file, the stock market, and the media. This made her dangerous—to Walker, to Staminum, and, most worrisome, to Marty. If he wanted to move Tilda off that story line, he would need to dish up more than blueberry pancakes.

Tilda poured almond milk into her coffee. "I've talked to my editors, Marty. I'm writing tomorrow whether I have Walker's voice in it or not."

Was she bluffing? It was hard to tell without knowing her sources. "I'm trying like hell to get you on Walker's calendar," Marty said. "As you can imagine, he's incredibly busy."

"I can stop by his office, if that's helpful. Even a phoner would do. This is my story. I don't want to read it somewhere else first. I'd kill myself. Right after I killed you."

Marty fiddled with his flatware. "What will it say?"

She looked around to see if anyone might overhear. "The story's about the culture clash between Walker Hope and Steady Stamper. Walker's hick schtick against the WASPy ways of Staminum's founding family, members in good standing of the New York establishment. They're from two very different worlds and these worlds are colliding with potentially violent results."

"Wow," Marty said, leaning against the wooden slats on the back of the bench. "That's a pretty juicy story. If it were true."

"You can deny it if you like. I know it's true."

"I think, at best, that's a wild exaggeration, Tilda. Of course, there's going to be resistance. Staminum is the Stampers' baby. It's their heritage, their sense of identity. Their entire family history is all tied up in it. But here's the thing: their family fortune is also tied up in Staminum. And the fact is, Walker drives share value. Period. He did it at BFC Energy. He did it at Goliath Industries. He did it at Crowe Power. He's already doing it here."

"At what price, Marty? That's the question. The book on Walker is that he's really good at the nuts and bolts of running a business. He can drive results in the short-term, but they don't last after he's gone. Look at Crowe Power. Its share price has tanked since he left."

"That's not on Walker."

"He left the cupboard bare, Marty. And there are some people around Staminum who are very worried he's going to do the same thing to their company."

"How?"

"By selling Greeneron."

So she'd heard. Marty paused, thinking. This story could actually work to his advantage. "Where did you get that idea?"

"Is it for sale?"

Marty shrugged. "Everything's for sale at the right price."

Tilda, suddenly impatient, pressed. "Is Greeneron for sale, Marty?"

Marty sighed. "Let me put it this way. There's a lot of value in Greeneron that somebody's going to unlock. Who knows what some of those technologies could do with the right amount of investment? The brutal truth for Staminum right now is that we just don't have the capital to develop them all and run our core business. We're going to have to make some tough decisions on what stays and what goes. Hate to say it, but imagine what would happen if Greeneron were in the hands of someone willing to really invest in it?"

"Like your old boss, Robbie Crowe?"

"Maybe. He's already said Crowe Power is going to be the first carbon-neutral energy company in the world. I suppose this could be the way to do it." The waiter delivered their breakfasts and Tilda carefully poured a few drops of maple syrup on her pancakes. Marty dug into his Overstuffed Green Omelet, which struck him as an accurate metaphor for Greeneron. "I don't think anyone has ever put together such an extensive collection of promising technologies. Every possible source of alternative energy is covered. It pains me to say it, but I love the creative vision for Greeneron. It's not just a possible leg up on everyone else in our industry. It's bragging rights for whoever has it. A lot of people talk about carbon-neutrality these days. The question is: who's going to get there first? I wish it were us, but I think we're going to have to settle for steady progress."

"Okay. If, *theoretically*, you were to sell Greeneron, who else might bid? Are you talking to anyone else?"

"I can't name names, obviously, but I think you're safe to assume the usual suspects. Everyone will deny it and say they never comment on speculation. But you know Greeneron is a big prize, especially for the companies that are ambitious in the alternative energy space. Just don't say you heard the term 'bidding war' from me."

"Ooooh," Tilda cooed. She dispensed with her pancakes and pulled a notebook and pen from her bag. "Marty, I've gotta run with this."

"Tilda. Please. This was off the record."

"You didn't say that."

"I'm telling you now."

"I won't attribute it to you," Tilda said. "What if I say 'a company source'?"

"How about 'a source with knowledge of the situation'?"

"I can live with that."

"You don't need Walker for this story?"

"Not if you're confirming Greeneron is on the block."

Marty took a deep breath. "You drive a hard bargain."

"Deal?"

"Done." He looked at her plate. "Would you like some more butter?"

30. EXIT PLAN

Marty entered his office suite to find Fred Crispin standing in the reception area, engaged in an animated conversation with Brenda, who was seated at her battle station but roused from her usual torpor to exhibit surprising verve, chatting amiably and smiling. Was she batting her eyes at Fred? This was deeply unsettling, like coming across a rhinoceros mating at the zoo.

"Hey, Marty," Fred said, turning around. "Got a sec?"

"For you, Fred? Always."

They walked to a small glass-topped conference table by the window overlooking the western Manhattan skyline, the Hudson River, and the bluffs of New Jersey. A morning sun reflected off the skyscrapers across the river and flooded the room.

"Marty, you've been so good to me that I don't know quite how to tell you this," Fred said, fidgeting.

Marty shrugged. "I've been in this business a long time, Fred. Nothing you could say is going to shock me."

"I'm in love with Brenda."

"I take it back."

Fred leaned forward, his elbows on his knees. "I know. How could an incredible woman like her fall for a guy like me, right? But the fact is, we've been together for some time. Very quietly, of course. My wife has no idea. Neither does her husband, which is good, since he's a bit of a gun nut. But now that I'm going to Crowe Power, we're going to have to tell them. And I want to take her with me down there. I'm really, *really* sorry about that, because I know how much she means to you, even after such a short time. She tells me how much you rely on her for just about everything. I'm sure you're finding her quite indispensable."

Actually, Marty thought, he'd never had an assistant quite as dispensable. In fact, he'd rather handle the incoming calls himself than trust her to scribble out a coherent message. "Obviously, from a selfish perspective, a guy like me would be very sorry to hear that, Fred. I mean, in the short time we've worked together, I've learned she's, she's... *Brenda*."

Fred nodded, ruefully. "Isn't that the truth?"

"There's nobody I've ever worked with quite like her."

"Believe me, I get it."

"I don't know how she does it day after day... after freaking day."

"Amazing," Fred said, shaking his head in wonder. "She was my assistant for a couple of years, which is how things got started. She was just so quick to anticipate things, so responsive to my needs. I couldn't help myself. One day, we finally bonded in the pantry, right next to the toaster oven. I remember removing her tuna melt so I could stick in my grilled cheese." He paused. "Funny how such an ordinary moment like that can change your life."

"That must have been something," Marty said. "Why didn't you keep her as your assistant?"

Fred sighed. "Every time she came into the office, we ended up closing the door. It was just wild, crazy, manic sex. On the desk. On the conference table. On the couch. Against the bookshelf. Anywhere and everywhere. We couldn't get enough." He chuckled at the memory.

"How'd you get any work done?"

"I didn't," he said with a shrug. "She liked to play 'Hide the Memo.' The little minx! Eventually, I figured we better separate to avoid arousing suspicion. And it worked, right? You didn't figure it out, and you're with her every day. But yeah. She's one of a kind. God knows I can't leave her here with a single guy like you. You'd be hiding memos all over the place."

"You flatter me, Fred. Another dream dashed I suppose." Marty slapped the table. "So tell me about Crowe Power. I can't believe how fast you made it happen."

"It was unbelievable. I had the most wonderful conversations with the chairman. What a charming man."

"You *are* talking about Robbie, right?"

"Yes. Of course. He's so *human*."

"I've heard people say that."

"The good news is, I got my offer right away and it was very, very generous. Now I'm wondering. How should I handle things with Walker? I'd rather just slip out the back but it's really important for me to help Crowe Power get a bid in for Greeneron, if it's not too late."

Marty pondered the thought before answering. "I think there's still time."

"Do you think Walker would sell it to Robbie? He's concerned there may be some bad blood there."

"When it comes to business, Walker's blood runs a bit cold. If Robbie offers enough, he'll win the prize."

"Oh, that's great to hear," Fred said. He looked around, then dropped his voice. "What about me? This could be very awkward. Will Walker be furious that I'm going to his old company?"

Marty shook his head. "It's not your fault you're a guy in demand. Of *course* the competition would snap you up. Robbie Crowe's a lot of things, but he's no dummy. He knows talent when he sees it. And, if you can make the case to Walker that you're going to Crowe Power to help Staminum raise cash in its time of need, I have to believe he'd be more than grateful to you. Hell, he might tack on another half-hour for your goodbye party."

Fred looked at Marty in surprise. "Do I get one?"

"It's possible."

"So. I should just lay my cards on the table with Walker?"

"You're holding all the aces, my friend."

"Alright." Fred stood and hitched up his pants. "Marty, you haven't steered me wrong yet. By the way, did you get the press release finished?"

"It's down in Walker's office, awaiting his sign-off."

"What did we decide to say?"

"You're leaving for exciting new opportunities."

"Fantastic! And it has the virtue of actually being true!"

"I love when that happens in a press release. Makes it so much easier to write."

"I'm going to push him to get it out tomorrow morning. Can we say I'm going to Crowe Power?"

"I don't know. Tell Walker that's what *you* want. Don't take 'no' for an answer."

Fred took a deep breath. "I won't. I'm actually feeling very good about all this. It will be nice to speak to Walker on *my* terms for a change. He didn't seem to think I was worth much. I wonder what he'll think now when he hears the news. It will be kind of fun, in a way, to see the look on his face."

Marty stood and shook Fred's hand. "Wish I could be there to see for myself. *Vaya con dios, mi amigo.*"

Fred sucked in his breath. "Thank you."

Marty leaned close to his ear. "If you start to feel a bit rattled, just think of Brenda and your wonderful future together."

Fred nodded. "You're an inspiration, Marty."

Marty shook his head and pointed a thumb toward the outer office. "No, no, no. That woman out there. *She's* an inspiration."

* * *

As word leaked out on the fifty-first floor that Fred was leaving, he quickly became Dead Fred Walking. His calendar was instantly depopulated as he was quietly uninvited to standing meetings. Office doors that used to open to him when he walked by stayed closed. Colleagues who were usually quick with a hello and a smile breezed past without making eye contact. He had nothing left to do but pack his personal things, download a confidential file or two, and talk to Walker.

Fred managed to book eight minutes before Walker's last scheduled pee of the afternoon and was ushered in to see Walker at precisely ten minutes to five. There he found the CEO beaming from ear to ear. *Why's he so happy?*

"I understand congratulations are in order," Walker said, offering a hearty handshake. "So glad to see you landed somethin' so fast."

"I'm more surprised than anybody," Fred said.

Walker sat down and Fred followed. "Well, I'm delighted for you. Truly. Even if you are goin' to my old stompin' grounds. I guess that means this is your last day here."

"Is it?"

Walker looked up at the ceiling a moment, then back to Fred. "Yessir. I believe so."

"I don't have to go just yet. I'm can stick around a couple days and help with the transition."

Walker shrugged. "Nah. That won't be necessary, big guy." He stretched and put his hands behind his head. "Time to go."

"Okay." Fred slumped. "I'll say my goodbyes to the troops at the going-away party."

Walker nodded. "Yeah, well. That's not happenin'."

"It's not?"

"You're goin' to a competitor, Fred," he said, slapping him on the knee. "We can't celebrate defections, especially when I've got a cash crunch here. We'd look pretty stupid, don't you think? Whoopin' it up while Rome burns? C'mon, man."

"I understand," Fred said, dejectedly. "Marty said you have the press release?"

"Yeah. I do. But we're not doin' that, either."

"You're not?"

"Crowe can cock-a-doodle-do about you all they want. But here, we're just gonna pretend you never existed. Hate to say it, but odds are good your name will never be mentioned within these walls ever again. I think you understand how it works."

"Well, I—"

Walker looked at Fred with a squint. "Is there somethin' else? Much as I'm fond of you, I got to get to work on Staminum business."

"Yes. There's just one other thing, Walker. I've heard through the grapevine that Greeneron might be on the block."

Walker smiled coyly. "Aw, Fred. You know I'd love to comment, but I can't. You're not an employee anymore."

"I'm not?"

He looked at his watch. "As of fifty-five minutes ago. That reminds me." Walker leaned forward. "Can I have your security badge?"

"Sure. I guess so." Fred pulled his wallet from his pants, fished through the credit cards and ID cards, pulled out his turnstile pass for Staminum World

Headquarters, and placed it on the table. "Don't I still need it to get out of the garage?"

"Nah! The guards who walk you out will take care of that. Is there anything else?"

Fred found himself once again up to his neck in Walker's quicksand and sinking fast. If he didn't help Robbie get Greeneron, he'd have nothing to do but play Hide the Memo with Brenda. "I understand that you can't give me inside information about Greeneron. All I wanted to say is that it could be a win-win for both of us."

"How's that, Fred?"

"Well. I know you want to raise money. Robbie Crowe wants to get into alternative technologies. Maybe there's a transaction there that makes sense for both sides."

Walker looked Fred in the eye. "You know nothin' would tear my guts out more than helpin' a competitor like Crowe Power. But that goes out the window if it helps Staminum even more. And if ol' Robbie Crowe is the highest bidder, so be it. Tell him to go ahead. Bid. But he shouldn't dilly dally. Things are movin' pretty fast around here. Price is going up even as we speak."

"Then I better get going."

"Do what you gotta do, Fred."

"Have you set a price?"

"Can't say exactly. But you can assume the bids start at three billion dollars."

Fred shrugged. "You get what you pay for, right?"

"Sometimes," Walker said with a laugh. He stood and clapped Fred on the shoulder. "I know how much Robbie cares. He deserves somethin' like Greeneron. And you know what? I'd love to see him get it."

"You would?"

"Sure!"

"So there's no hard feelings?"

"Nah! Not at all. If he's the highest bidder for Greeneron, that will more than even the score."

31. A SIGNATURE MOVE

After taking the red eye back to New York, the still-reigning CEO of the Crowe Power Company was back in his new lair, the corner office opposite the chairman. Despite the rocky start with Robbie, Tim was feeling very good about the direction he'd established in California. The company had a mission now, and they were getting damn close to a plan. It was on his shoulders to see it all through. He'd prove to Robbie he should have no regrets whatsoever. He picked the right person for the job.

Tim leaned back in his massive leather executive chair—*dang, this is comfortable!*—and propped his right foot on the desk, a massive, custom-made slab of dark walnut in the shape of an aircraft carrier. During the years he slaved for Walker, Tim had imagined himself behind the big desk, and now at last he was here, taking his one-time champion's place, grabbing the reins of this storied company and driving it into its future. What was the old saying? *With great power comes...* something. More power? More money? A bigger office? Whatever it was, he'd look it up, and make darn sure he got all of it.

He drummed his fingertips together, contemplating his next orders of business while his executive assistant, Anna, sat in the chair across from him with pen and pad in hand, staring blankly and awaiting direction. Strange, but he felt an awful lot smarter since his promotion to the corner office. Despite Robbie's tantrums, the chairman and the board of directors had seen something in him— a certain genius for getting things done, perhaps—that even he hadn't fully appreciated until his promotion.

There was so much to do, too much for ordinary people to get their head around. And Tim was not ordinary, not anymore. He was a—say it slowly—*C-E-O*, with no one to answer to but Robbie and the board. There were no fool's errands to run for Walker Hope, no more grunt work for which others get credit. He had the corner office and an eye-watering compensation package for a reason. He had arrived.

"The first thing I'd like to do," he said at last to Anna, "is get a fireplace."

"Excuse me?" she said.

"Nothing too elaborate," he said. "Something modest, but nice, maybe with tiles in company colors. You know, show the flag. I bet Robbie would like that."

"A real fireplace? Not an app?"

"No. A real working fireplace."

"You want to put it in *here*?"

"I'm thinking over there, actually," he said, pointing toward a space between the picture windows overlooking New York Harbor and the Statue of Liberty. "It would warm up the place a bit. You know, make it not so corporate. I fully expect Robbie will be coming in for conversation from time to time to discuss our progress. I'd like him to feel relaxed, so he can really focus. Sometimes, he gets distracted by the damndest little things, and I don't want that to happen in here."

Anna took a deep breath. "I'll get with our building people and check into costs."

Tim shook his head. "No, no, no. This isn't like the old days, Anna. We've climbed to another level now. We've got a five-billion-dollar operations budget. And Robbie said very plainly out in California that money didn't matter so much anymore. I'm more concerned with *speed*. We need to get things done as fast as humanly possible."

She sighed. "Anything else?"

"Yes," he said, standing and gesturing with his thumb toward the wall behind his desk. "I notice the storeroom next door isn't used for much. I'd like to put a bathroom in there. Maybe cut a passageway in the corner. Given everything I've got to do, I really don't have time to waste walking all the way down the hall."

"And back."

"Exactly."

"That's got to be almost ten minutes a day," she said, drolly.

"Multiply that by every working day of the year."

"You're talking hours. Days, even."

She was playing him for her own private laughs, but he failed to notice. "I bet it's a week!" he asserted. "We can't stand for that kind of inefficiency around here. Every minute counts."

"I hate to be a wet blanket, Tim, but I'm not sure building a bathroom is allowed."

"Why not?"

"That space actually *was* a bathroom when Les Crowe had this office," she said. "Robbie had it ripped out before Walker started. Apparently, there are rules about who gets a loo."

Tim scoffed. "I'm sure that was just because it was Walker. Robbie couldn't *stand* him. This is a different deal altogether. Robbie and me... we're not exactly simpatico just yet, but we're definitely finding our way together. He told me to do whatever it takes to get this company on the right track."

"So, a fireplace and a bathroom," she said, stabbing an exclamation point on to her notebook.

He walked around behind her, his hands clasped together, deep in big thoughts. Clearly, he could not afford distractions at home if he were to nail this new job. His wife, Michelle, would need to share in the spoils of his victory. It's like Li, his new driver, told him: *Happy wife means happy life.*

"Check into the repairs on Crowe Bird II, would you? I'd like to know when it's coming back."

"Where do you want to go?"

"Me? Nowhere," he said. "I want to send Michelle on a little shopping spree in Paris as a thank you for putting up with all that's happened over the past few weeks. Can you arrange that?"

"Of course. Lucky girl."

"There's just one other thing."

"Yes?"

"I'm not sure how to put this exactly, since this is something clearly not in your job description." He looked at her tentatively. "As a person I trust, I need you to call me out if you think I'm coming down with, you know... the disease."

She covered her mouth in alarm. "What disease?"

"CEO disease."

"Oh. I thought you were talking about something serious."

"I *am*. It's what happens when you get a little too big for your britches."

She waved him off. "That's not you." She looked at her notepad. "Although I see how somebody might get that idea."

Tim shook his head, deeply concerned. "It's happened before. A lot of people get jobs like this and they immediately start thinking their stuff doesn't stink. I don't want to be that guy, alright? I'm still just a regular ol' boy from Purdue, regardless of this big title and the vast global responsibilities. All I want to do is keep my head down and stay humble, hard as that may be under the remarkable circumstances. I need you to tell me if I'm getting a little too lofty or isolated in my own bubble, out of touch with what's going on around me." He turned away, lost in a big thought.

Anna nodded. "I'll do my best."

He turned back to her, puzzled. "I'm sorry. Did you say something?"

"I said, yep. Got it."

"I mean it," he said, pointing a finger in her direction. "You get in my face. Anytime. Understood?"

Anna stood, looking again at her notepad. "Well. Since you mention it, you might want to think about—"

Tim held up a hand and shook his head. "No. Stop. Thanks for that, but there's no time for that right now," he said as he hurriedly sat down at his desk. "I've got an incredible idea and I've got to write it down right away."

She sighed and turned to leave, while Tim grabbed a shiny gold pen from its holder and an embossed, personalized notecard from a wooden bin. He peered at the card, which suddenly hit him in a deeply satisfying way.

Crowe Power Company
OFFICE OF THE CEO

Wow, he thought. *That's me!* Just as quickly as his brainstorm had come, it petered out in a fog of self-congratulation. He focused instead on practicing his signature on these lovely notecards, trying different iterations as he went. Should it be *Timothy J. Padden?* That was rather formal, but fitting, given his august position. Or should he adopt a more casual mien and just sign everything *Tim,* maybe with a lower case 't'?

Yours,

tim

Oh, yes. That had a nice understated style to it! He could be one of those one-name people, like Elvis, or Fabian, or Sparky. Or perhaps he should go completely formal and include his middle name. *Timothy James Padden.* The First! Progenitor of a new industrial dynasty! *Oh, yeah,* he thought as he scrawled it out. *That looks pretty good....*

"Knock, knock."

Tim looked up to see Digby in his doorway. "Digby, my dear fellow," Tim said, grandly. He gestured toward the visitor chairs in front of his desk. "Please."

Digby took a chair and a deep breath. "I need to apprise you of a couple of things."

The pained look on Digby's face suggested this would not be good news. Tim felt his heart flutter as Digby got right to the point. "The first thing you need to know is we're bringing in somebody to oversee our push into alternative energy."

"Oh."

Digby nodded. "Yeah."

"Do you have someone in mind?"

"It's gone further than that," Digby said. "We've made an offer to Fred Crispin."

"Fred... *who?*"

"Fred *Crispin*, from Staminum."

Tim was shaken. "I, I—I've never heard of him.

"He was Tom Flaherty's number two for years."

"I see." Tim's eyes darted around as he tried to comprehend what was happening. "So he's got experience. Is he some kind of expert in alternative energy?"

"We'll find out soon enough."

"Wow," Tim muttered. "Always good to bring in more talent, I guess. But, honestly, Digby, shouldn't I have been consulted about this in advance?"

"Things moved rather quickly, Tim. Fred became available and Robbie wanted to grab him before anyone else got the chance."

Tim sat back in his chair, absorbing the news. "I respect Robbie's wishes, of course, and his skills at evaluating talent. I mean, after all, he promoted me." He laughed, nervously.

"Of course."

"But I would think I'd at least get the chance to interview a direct report."

"Actually, it's a dual reporting thing. Fred's reporting to Robbie."

"*Directly?*"

"Yes. Robbie has decided to break the company into two divisions. You'll run the traditional operations. Fred will oversee the alternative energy space."

Suddenly, Tim didn't want a fireplace. He wanted an oven so he could stick his head into it. This clearly limited his authority, especially in an area that promised the most growth. "What's going on here, Digby? Is there something I need to know?"

Digby sighed and put his hands on his knees. "All I can say, Tim, is that this is the way Robbie operates. He moves fast, and he doesn't always ask for input or advice. The people who survive around here are the people who understand that and just go with the flow. I recommend you do that as best you can."

Tim held up the palms of his hands to indicate he was compliant. "Believe me. I'm not trying to rock the boat here."

"I'm sure you're not. That's not you, and I know that."

"Thank you." He looked out the window and softly shook his head. *Why does Robbie make things so difficult?*

Digby continued. "There is one other issue I need to surface with you."

"What's that?"

"We're making a bid for Greeneron."

"The Staminum subsidiary?"

"Yes."

"So that would comprise our alternative energy division."

"Right."

"Okay. I'm getting the picture now."

"Here's the other thing. We're bidding three billion dollars."

"Three *billion?* In stock, I hope?"

Digby shook his head. "Cash."

Tim sank in his chair. "Where in the world would we get that? I was just going over the budget on the plane."

"That's what Robbie wants you to figure out." Digby stood. "Sorry to be the bearer of bad tidings, but he wants it tomorrow. He's meeting with Walker in the afternoon to make his pitch."

"Digby, our entire capital budget is five billion. We need that to maintain our pipelines, buy new equipment, and convert some of the older power plants from coal to gas."

Digby shrugged. "You might want to think about how you can do that with two billion dollars instead, maybe less. Robbie wants this deal, badly. I've seen him like this before. Once he has it in his head, nothing—and nobody—will stand in his way."

32. BRAKING NEWS

Tilda Ecklund's *Buzzniss* story that Staminum Energy was putting its Greeneron subsidiary on the block broke just as the stock market opened, sending Staminum shares sharply higher in early trading. Walker reviewed a print-out of the piece in Marty's office, where he ran his middle finger across every word. As he eyed Walker across his desk, Marty wondered: *Was that finger a message?*

Staminum To Sell Greeneron Subsidiary
Walker Hope's need for cash puts green biz on the block

The story reported that several big-name global companies were interested in Greeneron, although their spokespeople denied it or declined comment. It also stated that a likely bidder was the Crowe Power Company, whose chairman had a well-known passion for low-carbon energy.

"Everybody's gonna expect that Robbie will buy it, right?" Walker said. "There's no backin' out now."

"That's what I'm thinking," Marty said with a smile.

As Walker continued reading, his expression changed into a scowl. The story claimed unnamed Staminum "insiders" questioned if Walker was selling Greeneron out of desperation and whether his carpetbag of tricks may have run out of magic. "What the heck does this mean?" Walker asked, angrily eyeing Marty. "'Some wonder if this is Walker Hope's Waterloo.' Like Napoleon? Is that what she's sayin'? *Defeat?*"

Marty leaned across the desk. "Walker, she has sources inside the company who want to sabotage this move," Marty said.

"Stampers?"

"Gotta be."

"Well I don't care for that at all. How did you let her write that?"

Marty winced. "She didn't ask my approval, Walker. I shaped the story as best I could. It's not perfect, but on balance, this is a huge win for us—and especially for you. We've got Greeneron for sale and the story suggests there are multiple bidders. That will surely help the price."

Walker was paying no attention. He was continuing to pore over the parts about him and becoming more incensed. "And what's *this?*" Walker demanded. "'Hope's well-known playbook of cutting costs and boostin' profitability may come at the long-term expense of the companies he leads.' Whose opinion is that? *Yours?*"

"Of course not!"

"Marty, I *save* companies. I don't destroy them. How am I gonna send a story like this to Mamaw in Detroit?"

Marty's energy for his job drained out of him into a little puddle of resentment under his desk. *What a fucking ingrate!* Marty weighed a response that began with the word, "eat" and ended with the word "me." Instead, he gathered himself. "Difficult as it is to see in print, Walker, we have a few critics. It goes with the incredible success you've had. Best we can do, I think, is to get our side out there, which we did."

"Best we can do? That's not the standard," Walker said. "It's not about effort, Marty. It's about results. *Results!* I have to say I'm very, very disappointed in you."

A knock came on the doorframe, prompting Marty and Walker to catch a historic sighting: a visibly agitated Margaret Hathaway, who had never been seen in the office before ten o'clock. "May I have a word with you, Walker? Privately?"

Marty gladly took the hint to leave. "I'll get a cup of coffee," he said.

Margaret took the chair next to Walker and held up her phone. "Is it true?"

Walker couldn't resist playing with her. "Is what true?"

She shook her head and glared at him. "You have no idea what kind of beehive you kicked over, do you? The family is furious. Mr. Stamper is flying back from Switzerland today. He wants to see you ASAP."

Walker nodded. "Why, that's wonderful news. It'll be so nice to see him."

She laughed bitterly. "No, it won't. It will be one big slice of fresh hell. I tried to warn you, Walker. There are certain parts of the company you simply do not want to touch. Greeneron is No. 1 on the list. How could you put it up for sale without approval from the Stampers?"

"Who said I put it up for sale?"

"Buzzniss. And now Bloomberg. And Reuters. And every news site in the world."

"Amazin'," he said, shaking his head as if mystified.

"If you're playing dumb, Walker, you're more convincing than you realize. This is an incredibly stupid move."

Walker's eyes narrowed as he leaned forward. "I'm a little confused here, Margaret. Did you see me quoted anywhere about this?"

"It said…" She slipped on her reading glasses and looked at her phone. "It said 'a source with knowledge of the situation.' I take it that's your bag man here." She nodded her head toward Marty's desk. "Mr. Stamper is going to want to know what the situation is exactly."

Walker's tone turned decidedly icy. "I'd be happy to tell him what I know. Maybe he ought to call me first instead of you."

"I am *only* trying to help you repair some of the damage before it's too late. Is Greeneron for sale or isn't it?"

Walker collected himself. He leaned back in his chair and put one foot on the edge of Marty's desk. "Let me put it this way, Margaret. Greeneron can't be sold unless somebody wants to buy it."

"It also can't be sold unless you get approval from the board. And all I can say is: Don't count on it. The Stampers have taken a very personal interest in Greeneron. They've spent years building it. It's their baby and they will not want to see it trundled off to a competitor. Is it possible you'd even think of offering it to Crowe Power? That would be the frosting on the cake. The Stampers and the Crowes are like the Hatfields and McCoys. They hate each other. They have for generations."

Walker could hear the phones ringing in Marty's outer office, undoubtedly from reporters. "Margaret, I know these are unsettlin' times as we try to get this company on the right footin'. I really appreciate your efforts to help with the

Stamper family, who are essential to our success. But I don't think the situation is goin' to be helped by a game of telephone. Do you? There's way too much misinformation and speculation out there already. And while I know you may have a personal concern in the matter, it's probably best that I speak to Mr. Stamper directly when he gets here. I'm sure that when I do, he'll understand everything perfectly."

Walker's unflappability irritated Margaret even more. Her breaths came in heaves. "I hope you know what you're doing, Walker. This could get very ugly very fast."

Walker nodded. "I appreciate your concern, Margaret. Have a lovely day."

33. STEADY, AS SHE GOES

Walker pushed through the glass door to his outer office, where he was met by his assistant, Barbara, who stood as he entered and anxiously wrung her hands.

"Walker, Mr. Stamper's office just called," she said. "They asked me to notify them the minute you arrived. Mr. Stamper wants to see you immediately."

Walker, unruffled, nodded. "Alright."

"What shall I tell them?"

"I'm on my way."

As he turned to leave, Barbara added, "Digby Pierrepont from Crowe Power called three times while you were gone. He says Robbie Crowe wants to meet with you about Greeneron as soon as possible."

Walker grinned. "Any other calls?"

"None."

"Find a neutral site, a place where we can have some privacy. I'll see Mr. Crowe at five-thirty."

Walker bounded up the stairs two at a time to the building's top floor, epicenter of the Stamper family empire: the Stamper Foundation, the family's philanthropic arm; Stamper Holdings LLC, the family's investment company; and a warren of private offices for day use by family and friendly board members if they happened to need space for a few hours. Walker stepped quickly through a darkened, spot-lit gallery of portraits, artifacts, and mementos on his way to Staminum Energy's Office of the Chairman, which occupied the southwest corner above his own office. He opened the door to the reception area and encountered Steady's frosty assistant, Gloria. She appraised him from head to toe and sniffed.

"He's expecting you," she said with a slight nod toward the door.

Walker slipped past her to the inner sanctum, a massive space configured like a mid-century modern apartment, with a living room at the center, a dining area off to the side, a full kitchen, a bedroom, and several bathrooms. Floor-to-ceiling windows faced New Jersey to the west and the World Trade Center and the rest of downtown to the south. Steady, in an open-collar dress shirt, sat glumly on the living room sofa, reading. He peered over his glasses at Walker, but otherwise didn't move.

Steady commanded, "Have a seat."

"Hope you had a nice vacation," Walker said cheerfully as he took a leather Eames chair next to the sofa.

"I cut it short," Steady said. He regarded Walker with an icy glare and held up a sheaf of printouts. "On account of this."

"Sorry to hear that," Walker said.

Steady took a deep breath. "If these reports that you are attempting to sell Greeneron are true, then you and I have a serious problem. Is it possible you ignored my directive?"

Walker feigned confusion. "Which one? The one to fix this company?"

"You know damn well what I'm talking about." Steady slapped the printouts on the sofa. "*Who* in God's name do you think you are? Is there something you don't understand about the chain of command around here?"

Walker shook his head. "No, sir."

Steady visibly shuddered, struggling for the words to express his frustration. "Then, then—*why*? Oh, good lord." He rubbed his forehead, then looked up at Walker. "I'm beginning to see now why you wear out your welcome at every stop. Do you always act in such a presumptuous manner?"

"I do."

Steady laughed bitterly. "You admit it!"

"Steady, you hired me to turn around a company that's been losin' money for years. There's no way to do that without addressin' the serious problems we have."

"And you think Greeneron's the serious problem."

"It's not the only one. But it's a biggie. We've sunk two billion dollars into it, the losses are mountin', the capital requirements are huge, and there's not a snowball's chance it's goin' to make a profit in my lifetime or yours. If we can get somethin' for it, then *dang*. We owe it to our shareholders, includin' you, to sell it."

Steady stood up and walked toward the windows, composing himself as he looked out, then turned and sat on the sill, facing Walker. "Do you have any idea what Greeneron means to my family?"

"Probably more than you think."

"I doubt that," he grumbled. "Four years ago, before we started Greeneron, we had protesters outside our office every damn day claiming we were destroying the environment. Have you heard of the Planetistas? Horrible, vicious people, calling us vile names. Trailed us everywhere we went, even banging on the window at Jean-Georges while my wife and I were having dinner. Can you imagine?"

"I'm sure it was unsettlin'."

"Practically destroyed my taste for foie gras brulée. But it was worse than that. In the midst of all the hubbub, Alice and I decided to donate one hundred million dollars for a cancer wing at our hospital. And do you know what happened? They turned us down *flat!* Under pressure from the Planetistas, they said they wouldn't accept our, quote, unquote, *dirty* money, even to treat cancer! After a hundred years of contributions to this city's museums and theaters and hospitals and libraries, the Stamper family had become pariahs. It was utter humiliation."

Walker nodded, sympathetically. "I'm truly sorry you went through all that."

Steady sighed. "We considered just chucking the whole damn thing—selling our shares in the company, moving permanently to Ouchy, and assuming a low profile for the rest of our lives. But that would leave our children and grandchildren to fend for themselves. And we knew that would mean the end of our family's involvement in the company. After a great deal of soul-searching, we decided to stay and fight. Not for us, mind you, but for them, and for our family's reputation. We would turn this deeply unpleasant experience into a positive. That's when we came up with the idea of Greeneron."

"So," Walker said, scratching his chin, "the idea was to protect your family's good name."

"Absolutely. We recognized the world was changing. We needed to change with it. Greeneron is the Stamper family's way of demonstrating our commitment to finding new and better ways to provide energy to the great masses out there." He waved in the general direction of Hoboken.

Walker stood and shoved his hands in his pockets, slowly approaching Steady. "And you did all this with no sense of when or how the company would make any money?"

Steady raised his chin and sniffed the rarified air. "We based our decision on an age-old principle: virtue, as they say, is its own reward."

Walker shook his head. "Except in this case."

Steady eyed Walker warily. "I don't follow."

Walker continued, "How do you think people would regard your family if they knew how you built Greeneron?"

Steady felt the moral high ground shifting under his feet. "What could you possibly mean?"

"I'm talkin' about the way these Greeneron companies were created. The way Staminum bought them at inflated prices. The evasion of board scrutiny on every one of the purchases. The profits that were made at our company's expense by certain people."

Steady gasped. "I'm not sure what you're suggesting here, Walker, but I resent the hell out of it!"

Walker said somberly, "It gives me no pleasure to say it."

Steady, cornered, looked about him, breathing hard. What else could he do? He stood up from the windowsill and nodded in Walker's direction. "You're fired."

Walker shook his head. "I don't think so."

"I'll—" Steady's mouth went dry. "I'll advise the board immediately."

"No, you won't."

Steady wobbled, as if Walker had hit him in the gut. He stared at Walker slack-jawed, then staggered over to the dining room table and sat down. Walker joined him at the table. "I don't know every detail about what happened here, Steady, and I really don't want to know. But if we're going to discuss this any further, I'll need our General Counsel in the room. And, if we go down that road, I think you'd be well-served to have a lawyer present, too."

Steady licked his lips and gulped. "I hardly think that's necessary."

"Then let's take a look at our options, shall we? I can turn my findings about Greeneron over to the Board of Directors. I'm sure they would be quite alarmed by the way you kept them in the dark."

"Nonsense! This matter hardly seems to merit their attention."

"In that case, I could leave it to Maria to decide. Her preference is to bring in an independent counsel to investigate and issue a report. At that point, it's very possible we would be obligated to alert the SEC."

Steady's guffaw lacked conviction, but he gamely pushed back. "You're making a mountain out of piles of bullshit, Walker."

Walker winced. "Really? You want to test that theory? I'll do it."

Steady took a deep breath and slumped in his seat. "What do you want?"

"I want to sell Greeneron. If we're lucky enough to find a buyer, we can make all this go away."

Steady's eyes darted back and forth. At last, he sat back and eyed his CEO. "Your insinuations are absolutely unfounded, Walker. I'm sure that any independent review would agree with me. But the last thing I want to do is drag my family's name through the mud. Under the circumstances, I think a sale is a sensible option." He took a deep breath and recovered his sense of authority. "Approved."

34. THE ROAD TO GLORY

Robbie and Digby rode in the back seat of the Lincoln Navigator as it plowed its way up the FDR before exiting at 61st Street, where they came to a halt behind a long line of red taillights. Robbie, squirming with anticipation over his upcoming meeting with Walker Hope, took out his anxieties on the back of the driver's seat, slapping it hard.

"What the hell's the matter with you, Boris?" Robbie called. "Why did you go this way?"

Boris leaned over his console, studying the Waze app on his tablet and mumbling to himself in Russian, then looked up into the rearview mirror. "I'm sorry Mr. Crowe. I don't see no good way to go right now. Every street: red." He held up the tablet for Robbie to examine for himself.

Robbie pointedly refused to look. What did he care what the map said? "Go up First Avenue," he barked.

"One second, Mr. Crowe."

"Don't take Second!" Robbie hit the back of Boris's seat again. "Are you out of your *mind?*"

"No, no. I say, *ONE* second. You know?"

"We don't *have* a second, Boris. Go up First, like I said!" He slapped the back of Boris's seat with both hands.

Boris held up the tablet again. "What if we...?"

"Goddamnit, Boris! I don't care *which* way you go. Just keep us moving, alright? We've got to get there." Robbie sat back and looked over to Digby. "Can you believe this *shit?*"

Boris backed up a foot, then carefully turned to his right, climbed the curb, and lurched onto the sidewalk, rocking the vehicle back and forth. He pulled out a blue bubble light and placed it on the dashboard, drove around a fire hydrant and squeezed past the buildings, squeezing angry pedestrians into doorwells.

Digby watched with astonishment. "He's driving on the sidewalk."

Robbie shrugged. "So?"

Digby sighed. "Well, you know, if we had left on time...."

Robbie glared at Digby. His brother-in-law was becoming increasingly impudent. "I was *waiting* for my *cappuccino.*"

"Yeah, well," Digby said. "Now we're up against horrendous traffic. Pretty sure Boris didn't arrange all this. It's rush hour. It's Manhattan. What did you expect?"

Robbie looked at his watch and collapsed back in his seat. He was spent and he hadn't actually done a damn thing all day but stew about getting his hands on Greeneron. He looked out the windows at the buildings that were now a foot from his face and gamed out his encounter with Walker.

The last time he'd seen his former CEO had been at their impromptu meeting in the pantry next to the Crowe Power board room, where Walker agreed to leave the company. Robbie hoped then that he'd never lay eyes on the son-of-a-bitch ever again. Would Walker still wear that annoying shit-eating grin? That was probably unlikely, Robbie mused, considering Walker was now the captain of a sinking ship. Staminum was listing so badly, it couldn't even hang on to Greeneron, the crown jewel in its treasure chest. Nor could Walker keep a hotshot like Fred Crispin on board. The poor bastard must be getting very, very desperate. And you know what? *Tough shit.* Walker's weakness gave Robbie an opportunity to get what he wanted. This meeting shouldn't intimidate Robbie in the least. Not at all! He should regard it as a victory lap, a triumph over his more celebrated rival.

Calmed slightly, he allowed himself to imagine the pot of glory at the other end of this rainbow. With Fred at his side and Greeneron in his pocket, Robbie would build an enterprise that would become the envy of the industry, a model for modern business, and a darling of the activist crowd. The Planetistas would deflate their saggy dinosaur and fold up their picket signs. Natalia would regard him with adoring eyes, and who knew where *that* could lead? Under Robbie's guidance, Crowe Power would not simply exist as some run-of-the-mill energy company, pumping out profits and pollution in equal measure. It would become a... *technology* company! *Yeah!* That's the ticket! Tech would put Crowe Power stock in an entirely different classification, with a far better multiple. And, by virtue of its clear progress toward carbon neutrality, it would attract sophisticated new investors from the ESG crowd in Europe and the American coasts who put a premium on what's really important about a company—its social and environmental impact. And, in case anyone failed to notice this new-age enterprise, the whole magnificent story would be chronicled for the entire world to see in Dr. Kristi Kramer's upcoming best-seller, *Goodness Greatness*.

How would they position him on the cover? In profile? A three-quarter shot, showing off his jawline? Should he wear a tie? Or affect more of a Silicon Valley look, befitting Crowe Power's status as a tech company? He definitely wouldn't pull a Steve Jobs with a black mock turtleneck, but he wouldn't model the old "Dress for Success" styles of Jack Welch, either. He'd seek a middle ground, and push for a line on the cover like, *"Goodness Greatness,* with Robbie Crowe." Better still, *"Goodness Greatness: The Robbie Crowe Story."* Ah! Yes! His name probably ought to be as big as Dr. Kristi Kramer's, and—Boris drove back over the curb and lurched ahead onto First Avenue, jolting Robbie back to the present and the task at hand. *Shit!* None of these plans would matter if he failed to close the deal for Greeneron.

"Digs."

Digby sighed. "What?"

"Just so you're not crabbing at me about this later, the price tag for Greeneron could go higher than three billion."

Digby declared, "Fine. We walk away."

Robbie shook his head. "Not a chance."

Digby shifted in his seat to face Robbie. "We don't have the money."

"What's the big deal? If we have to, we can sell some of that other shit we've got."

"What shit?"

"You know, pipelines, power plants, refineries."

Digby said, "You mean the 'shit' that makes money?"

"Whatever."

"Robbie, do you have any idea what Greeneron is even worth?"

"I read the filings."

"Seriously? The 10K? The 10Qs? The proxy statements?"

"Parts, yeah."

Digby sighed. "I'm not comfortable with this approach at all. We need more than a casual reading. We should at least see a data room."

"Data, schmata," he huffed. "What the hell's that going to tell us? These technologies aren't profitable yet? *Duh!* Like we don't know that? Jesus, Digby. Show a little imagination."

Digby shrugged. "Maybe we can imagine some profits."

Robbie heard enough. He put his back to the window to face Digby. "What more do you need to know than the fact that Exxon and Dupont are also bidding for Greeneron?"

"We don't know that. You're going to believe the rumors?"

"We have to assume they're true."

"And bet the company in the process?"

"It's bet-the-company if we don't!"

Digby turned away. "I give up."

Robbie sank back in his seat and looked straight ahead. "You see, Digs, this is exactly why I'm the chairman of this company and you're not."

Digby swallowed his tongue along with his pride, resisting the impulse to point out the obvious: *It's not because you're a genius. It's because of your DNA, dummy.* Someday, Digby was going to have to let Robbie know what he really thought, but this was not that day. To escalate as they were about to enter an important meeting would be malpractice for a general counsel. Better to keep Robbie reasonably calm and argue later, if necessary.

Boris pulled the Navigator up to the side entrance of the Pierre Hotel and hustled out to open the door for Robbie. Digby managed to open his own door all by himself and, per custom, trailed Robbie by a respectful half-step. They buttoned their suit coats as they stepped smartly onto a red carpet laid over black-and-white tiles on the sidewalk and entered the hotel lobby, where an elevator whisked them up to a suite on the top floor. There, they were met by a well-muscled Staminum security agent standing guard in the hallway, who instantly recognized them and waved a key card at the lock to let them into a spacious suite overlooking Central Park. They found Walker standing in the middle of the living room, hands in his pants pockets, grinning as always. *What's the deal with this guy?* Robbie wondered. *He should be depressed as hell.*

"Hey, Robbie," Walker said, offering a firm handshake. "So good to see you. I've missed you, buddy."

Buddy? The suggestion that they were on some equal plane awakened all of Robbie's resentment of Walker's blatant disrespect for the social order. Still, with his eyes on the prize, he kept his cool and summoned the manners that were drilled into him as a child but deployed only sparingly since. "A pleasure to see you, as well, Walker."

Maria Territo emerged from a hallway. The sight of her, so smartly attired and self-possessed, aroused Robbie's memories of other pleasures past, and thoughts of payback. Given how rudely she'd treated him by spurning the lovely parting gifts he'd offered her following their long affair, this meeting would be his chance to show her what she was missing by going with Walker to Staminum. She picked a loser this time.

"I'm sure you remember my general counsel," Walker said.

"I certainly do," Robbie said with a faint leer.

Maria nodded a hello and the four of them settled into a conversation area. Robbie took a chair across from Walker, with a coffee table and a tray of refreshments separating them. Digby and Maria sat on the adjoining sofa, each poised to take notes on the conversation.

"Thank you for meeting with me on such short notice," Robbie said, pouring ice water for himself.

"Always happy to see old friends," Walker said. "You know, I've still got a soft spot in my heart for Crowe Power. So many warm memories."

Ha! Maybe for you, Robbie thought. "It is a special place," he allowed.

"I understand congratulations are in order?"

"For?"

"You have a new addition to your leadership team."

"Oh, yes." Robbie couldn't help but break into a grin. "Fred? Sorry to steal him away from you, but we think he'll fit perfectly into our plans."

"Can't win 'em all, I guess," Walker said, with a wistful shake of his head. "So. I understand you're interested in Greeneron."

Robbie looked at Digby, then back to Walker. "We're intrigued by the rumors. I thought perhaps there's a way we can help each other out."

"I appreciate that so much, Robbie," Walker said. "All I can tell you is that we are willin' to listen to offers." He explained that Staminum had lost too much money for too long of a period of time. The company's debt levels were unsustainable, and it needed cash to improve its balance sheet and run its operations. He hated to part with Greeneron and all of its highly promising technologies, but he had no other choice. "I'm in a pickle," he said.

Robbie listened to this sob story with barely concealed glee: Walker B. Hope had finally hit the wall. The world was soon going to realize that Walker was a fraud, a hatchet man who could cut costs to squeeze out short-term profits but failed to build the kind of solid foundation that would last beyond his tenure. And here was indisputable proof! Walker had treated Robbie with such disrespect over the years, with his false assumptions about who was who in the pecking order. Now here he came, hat in hand, practically *begging* his old boss for help throwing away Staminum's future just to fix his bottom line. What an *idiot!* Robbie crossed one leg over another, sat back in his chair, and pressed his fingertips together. Clearly, when all was said and done, history would judge Robbie more favorably than this flame-out. Why, it could be an entire chapter in *Goodness Greatness*: How Robbie Bested Walker. *Damn, it feels good to be a gangsta!*

"So," Robbie said, "what are you looking for?"

Walker said, somberly, "My best hope for Greeneron right now is that it gets the most appropriate home. A lot of thought and care went into buildin' this part of the business. The Stamper family would hate to see all the promise of Greeneron somehow squandered. Wouldn't you agree, Maria?"

"Oh, yes," she said, casting a glance toward Robbie. "It's not just the money that will cinch this deal. It's our desire to see that Greeneron ends up in the right hands."

Robbie wondered: did that mean they were leaning toward him? He recalled that the last time he'd seen Maria, his former mistress, she had been stuffing a non-disclosure agreement in his mouth and telling him she'd ratted him out to Lindsey. Perhaps she'd gained some perspective since they stopped seeing each other, and she had new respect for him. If not, she should be gaining it now. He said, grandly, "I don't think there's any question that Crowe Power would be the right fit. We have a vision around social responsibility that is, I think, unparalleled in the industry."

"Don't I know it?" Walker said, raising his hand as a witness. "It's *so* remarkable that you keep talkin' about your vision year after year. And you stick to it, regardless of what anyone else says. That takes some guts."

Guts! Damn right! "I can't say it's been easy," Robbie said, appraising his fingernails. "From time to time, there have been skeptics who say it can't be done. But you know what? I could care less what anybody else says. I follow my own instincts and do what's right."

"Don't you though," Walker said with an admiring tone. "Personally, I don't know anyone who thinks quite the way you do. Once people see your vision all come together, I predict they're going to be absolutely stunned at what you've done with Crowe Power."

Maria privately recalled her last day at Crowe, when she met Natalia, Robbie's latest recruit, whom she suspected he was grooming as a potential mistress. "No doubt, certain people will see you as a genuine hero."

"Maria, please," Robbie said, putting his right hand over his heart. "You know me well enough to know: It's not about me. It's about our *planet.*"

Maria nearly burst out laughing, but she contained herself and nodded in solemn agreement. Once he got going on his soapbox, he really was a sucker for his own bullshit. "That is so... what's the word? Righteous?"

"That works," Robbie said, nodding thoughtfully. "So tell me. What's it going to take to make this happen?"

"That's the hard part," Walker said, sitting back. "I wish I could tell you."

"What do you mean? You don't *know?*"

Walker shook his head. "No."

This was the last thing Robbie expected. "I'm hearing three billion," Robbie said, his eyes glancing back and forth between Maria and Walker. "I would think that's more than enough."

Walker glanced to Maria, then back to Robbie. "Beauty's in the eye of the beholder," he said, with a shrug. "And if you have several beholders..."

"How many 'beholders' are there?"

At last count, Walker thought, *none*. But there was no reason to let Robbie know that. Walker merely wanted to lead Robbie to the conclusion he had already reached: that he desperately wanted Greeneron. Walker's job was to continue pushing all Robbie's buttons: his vanity, his manhood, his craving for admiration and respect, and get him to bid against himself, upping the price along the way. Walker wouldn't lie, but he surely didn't need to volunteer the whole truth, either. "Robbie," Walker said, "I'm sure you understand that all our conversations on sensitive topics are held in the strictest confidence."

"I've heard Exxon and Dupont. Maybe others."

Walker cast a glance to Maria, who showed no expression, then back to Robbie. "I can't confirm that."

Robbie snapped his fingers. "I knew it."

Walker said, "All I can say, Robbie, is that I'm sure that you, of all people, can imagine the incredible halo effect Greeneron could provide to big companies under pressure from activists. Greeneron would offer relief from the criticism, and maybe even a chance to lead the world in a new direction. How do you put a dollar figure on that?"

Robbie nervously licked his lips. Was this transformative prize slipping away? "I don't want to beat around the bush here, Walker. How about three-point-five billion?"

Walker grimaced, as if it physically hurt him to respond. "Look, Robbie. You and I have a lot of shared history. You know I'd love for you to get Greeneron. But..." He sighed.

Robbie leaned forward, his impatience rising. "But *what?*"

"If you can't afford it, it's okay. There's nothin' to be ashamed of. I know it's a *lot* of money."

Robbie glanced at Maria and suddenly felt as if his pants had been pulled down around his ankles, and not for the right reasons. He looked down momentarily just to be sure they were still up. "I can't *afford?*" He was practically spitting. This was an affront to his manhood! "I guarantee you I can afford it, Walker. And I want it."

"Oh, you've made that part quite clear." Walker noted: *He's spiraling out of control again. That's a very good thing.* "And I wish like the dickens I could say you're biddin' enough for it and that Greeneron is yours. I just can't."

Robbie slapped the arm of his chair and blurted: "Four billion."

Digby leaned over and grabbed Robbie by the arm. "Robbie, can we have a moment?"

Robbie yanked his arm away and scowled at him. "No!" He turned back to Walker. "How about it?"

Walker liked the bid very much: four billion dollars would recoup Staminum's investment in Greeneron, make up for its losses, and clear a good-sized profit. But with a desperate Robbie playing with house money and bidding against his earlier offer, odds were favorable that Walker could extract even more. It sure wouldn't hurt to try. He picked up a folder from the coffee table, opened it, and scanned its contents, which happened to be the Pierre Hotel's late-night snack menu. He sighed, closed the folder and looked across the table at Robbie with a pained expression. "That doesn't quite get it," he said.

"Walker," Robbie said, throwing up his hands. "What the hell?"

"Robbie, I am sorry. But it's my solemn duty to the Stamper family and to all our shareholders to realize Greeneron's full value."

Robbie wagged a finger. "And I'm telling you I'm not walking out of here until we have a deal. Name your price."

Walker looked at Maria, who shrugged. He turned back to Robbie. "I don't know what to tell you."

Robbie said, "Four and a half."

Walker blew out his cheeks. "How about giving me a day or two to think it over."

"That's a good idea," Digby said, starting to get up.

Robbie glared at Digby, forcing him to sit back down. "No, it's *not*," Robbie said through clenched teeth. He turned back to Walker. "Five billion dollars. Final offer."

Digby said, "Robbie. Please. Let's regroup."

Robbie stood up and faced Walker. "I want the answer now."

"Robbie. *Dang.* You drive a hard bargain. I mean, given my situation." Walker shook his head. "All I can say is, you got me."

"And?"

"I think... we have an agreement in principle."

Robbie slapped his hands together. *"Yes!"*

"I'll take this to my board as soon as possible. That's probably not a concern for you."

Robbie scoffed. "A formality."

Walker stood up to shake Robbie's hand. "Congratulations, Robbie. I can't say it won't hurt to see Greeneron leave the Staminum family. But I sincerely hope you derive all the value from this that you so richly deserve."

35. CRYING UNCLE

As always, the arrival of Charles Francis Crowe II on the twenty-fourth floor of the Crowe Power Company headquarters generated a buzz among the huddled masses, yearning to break free from the mundane.

The last of his generation, Uncle Chuck was an iconic figure, the patriarch of the company's royal family, the closest link to its storied past, and the only member of the family who had actually known Homer Crowe, the deified founder. Chuck's presence hearkened back to Crowe Power's post-war glory days of unmitigated growth and prosperity, when America's unquenchable thirst for the energy provided by fossil fuels spurred relentless demands for more. The most persistent criticisms of energy companies then were the ever-higher prices they charged for their products, "obscene" profits, and their contributions to air and water pollution. Over lunches of vodka martinis and sole meuniere fileted tableside at Luthece and La Grenouille, Chuck and other Crowe Power leaders easily dismissed the critics as radical riffraff. Then it was back to the office, more often than not, to resume the long march toward record earnings and stock splits.

At 82, Chuck still retained the executive style from the bygone era: a pin-striped suit, black lacquered wingtips, hair precisely parted with a fine-toothed comb. He carried himself with a natural authority, secure in his place among the carefully illuminated portraits in the somber corridors of the twenty-fifth floor and its "Hall of Fam." He made no apologies for his wealth, nor insincere deflections of being just like everyone else.

As he made his way off the executive elevator, the security guards in reception rose in unison to greet him, stopping just shy of salute. He nodded hellos and moved on to his office, which was permanently staffed for his rare visits by his ancient assistant and caretaker, Greta, who busied herself with magazines and online shopping when he wasn't around. She shakily rose from her chair and cast a welcoming smile on her adored boss.

"Mr. Crowe," she said, clasping her hands together. "So wonderful to see you."

"I'm not sure Robbie will agree with you." He handed a briefcase to Greta and looked at his watch. "Guess I'm about to find out."

Greta reached for her phone. "I'll let Winnie know you're on your way."

Uncle Chuck returned to the hallway and headed toward Robbie's office, where the chairman was busy at the desktop computer on the credenza behind his desk, scanning Twitter for the latest libels and defamations against him. Finding nothing new, he turned to his next most pressing issue: tallying the effects of the previous evening's box scores on his Fantasy Baseball stats—*he had zoomed up to third place!*—when Winnie buzzed him on the intercom. "Mr. Crowe, your Uncle Chuck is on his way down."

"Oh, shit," Robbie muttered. He hurriedly closed the window with the baseball standings, and his Twitter feed, then wheeled around and grabbed a random folder off the top of the many piles around the perimeter of his desk, arranged as a defense against visitors who might assume he did nothing all day. He cocked his head to see the folder's label, "Q4 Financials," and opened it for the first time. Just the sight of the balance sheet elicited a yawn that he managed to suppress, lest Chuck pop in and detect Robbie's utter boredom with the details of his job. He spread the folder contents across his desk, picked up a pen, and poised it as if he were about to correct the numbers, zeroing in on the sheets as if he knew what they meant. At the sight of Chuck crossing the threshold, Robbie fell back in his chair and exhaled hard. Clearly, he was exhausted.

"Just in time," Robbie said, wearily. He gestured toward the piles of unread files on his desk. "These reports are killing me."

Chuck said, "Are you able to tear yourself away for a few moments?"

"Absolutely. I'm glad to take a break." Robbie wearily pushed himself out of his chair and nodded toward the grouping of sofas and easy chairs in the corner of his office. "Let's sit over there. I've been in the same damn chair for hours."

"Really? Winnie said you just got in."

Robbie scoffed. "It might seem that way to her. Sure doesn't feel like it to me."

"I know it must be grueling." Chuck took a seat on the sofa and looked around at all the greenery: pots of tropical plants, a pair of palm trees, and a humidifier to keep everything looking green and lustrous. "Looks like you're running an outpost of the Bronx Botanical Garden around here." Chuck pulled out his cigarette case and held it up for Robbie to see. "Do you mind?"

"Not at all," Robbie said. "These plants absorb toxins."

"I hope they leave a little bit for me," Chuck said. "It's kind of the point."

Robbie opened a drawer in his bookcase, pulled out an ashtray commemorating the 1965 Golden Jubilee of the Crowe Power Company, and placed it on the coffee table. Chuck torched a filtered cigarette with his silver lighter and snapped it shut with a loud click, then sent a small cumulus cloud toward the ceiling. He turned his gaze toward Robbie.

"I haven't seen our stock drop like this since the Arab Oil Embargo."

Robbie shook his head. "I know," he said. "People just don't get what we're doing here."

"You think that's the problem?"

"Absolutely."

"What if they actually do?"

"What do you mean?"

"What if they see what you're doing and they just don't like it?"

"Possible, I suppose. They just haven't seen it all yet. But everything's starting to come together incredibly well. Once we let the world know about our plan, I think everyone will be amazed."

Chuck blew a gray-blue stream of smoke toward the Weeping Fig. "Why don't you amaze me first."

Robbie began by telling him that, by virtue of his own considerable charm and powers of persuasion, he had pried the incredibly talented Fred Crispin away from Staminum and made him Crowe Power's CEO-in-waiting.

"What about Tim?" Chuck asked, pulling a stray piece of tobacco off his tongue. "I thought he was your guy."

"Yeah, well." Robbie sadly shook his head. "He's a bit of a problem."

"How so?"

"He just hasn't risen to the occasion. I thought if, you know, he had the right opportunity, he'd seize it. But I get nothing out of him. I never see him. I have no idea what he's up to. At the very least, you'd think he'd want to pick my brain a little bit, make sure we're on the same page."

"Look, Robbie. You know he wasn't my choice. He was yours. But it doesn't sound to me like you've even given the guy a chance. He's been in the job for what? Two months?"

"Not quite. But you can tell pretty quickly about a guy. And I'm just not seeing it."

"You see it in Fred."

"Absolutely."

Chuck lit another cigarette. "I wonder why Walker didn't."

"Didn't what?"

"See the magic in Fred."

"What do you mean?"

"He fired him."

Robbie's jaw dropped, with spittle showing in the corner of his mouth. "He, he—*what?*"

"Just a few days ago. Walker whacked him."

"Oh, *no, no, no.* That has to be a misinterpretation. Fred *quit* Staminum to come here."

"Not the way I heard it. Walker fired him first. Word is that you picked him up out of a Sixth Avenue dumpster and gave him a pile of money, double what he was making when he walked the plank."

"How do you know all this?"

"I was golfing yesterday with Lloyd Lundquist, who's on the board over there. He said he was surprised we were taking on Fred. Of course, that was news to me, since you've never mentioned him to me or anyone else on the board. Lloyd tells me Fred wasn't much more than a glorified go-fer for their last CEO."

Robbie shook his head. "No *way.* That's just sour grapes. Fred's a star."

Chuck nodded. "Uh-huh. Like Tim?"

Robbie simmered. "I'm very sure I've got the right guy this time."

"Gotcha. What else do you have in your bag of tricks?"

Robbie explained his deal to purchase Greeneron, which provoked a coughing fit from Uncle Chuck. "You—" *cough,* "want—" *cough,* "to buy that—" *cough,* "piece of shit?"

Robbie was mortified. "Why on Earth would you call it that?"

Chuck recovered his breath and stuffed out his cigarette. "Are we talking about the same thing? The Staminum subsidiary, right? The one they call 'Greeneron the other side?' It's a grab bag of the Stamper family's alternative energy wet dreams. From what I heard, not one of them is worth a poop."

Robbie shifted in his seat. "Not yet."

"Maybe not ever. Nothing's panned out. They were readying an impairment charge to write off the whole damn thing for two billion dollars. How much do you propose to pay for it?"

Robbie felt the room starting to spin. Should he pretend he had another call to take? Say he had to go to the bathroom? Pull the fire alarm? He took a deep breath. "Five."

Chuck leveled a look at Robbie. "Five... what?"

Robbie cleared his throat, then, in a near-whisper, answered, "Um, billion."

Chuck sat back in his seat. "And you... negotiated this all by yourself?"

"No. Digby was there. He did most of the talking. I said we ought to go slow, but he was worried that Exxon or Dupont were going to grab it away."

"I see. And where did you guys get that idea? That story on *Buzzniss.com* the other day? Lloyd tells me that was a little chum tossed in the water by Marty McGarry. He and Walker were hoping you'd bite."

In a surge of panic, Robbie considered abandoning his plan entirely, rescinding his agreement with Fred and withdrawing his offer for Greeneron. All he could think of were the reactions if he retreated. The Planetistas would redouble their protests. Natalia would probably join them. And what about Dr. Kristi Kramer? What would happen to her book? How could he lay claim to greatness without making some bold moves? He couldn't lose his nerve now. It was time to double down and press ahead. "Uncle Chuck, I think you're getting a very distorted view from Staminum. They've always hated us, and they especially hate me. And now that they're in such terrible shape, they're trashing me to deflect attention away from their own problems. It's nothing but propaganda. We can't fall for that."

"What do you propose to do?"

"I say we take this to the board. Lay out the whole plan. When they understand everything, I think they'll see why this all makes sense. We've had a good run for a few years, but we're building this company for the future, not the past." He studied Chuck's dubious expression. "Will you at least support me that far?"

"Robbie, as I've said many times: I'll back you as long as you maintain the support of the family. I've told you my concerns. Take them for what they're worth. If you still want to press ahead, that's your call. I won't stand in your way."

"Thank you, Uncle Chuck. I really appreciate that."

Chuck leaned forward and looked at Robbie. "But I should warn you. Whatever you decide, you'll live with the consequences, for better or worse."

36. BOARD OF POWER AND LIGHT

A ssembling the Crowe Power Company's aged Board of Directors for a special meeting via the mystifying technology of videoconferencing proved quite a challenge for Winnie. The directors were long past their career heydays, when the cutting-edge tools of the trade were fax machines and car phones. They were completely unfamiliar with the concept of cameras and microphones on their computers. *What in tarnation are they going to think of next?*

Willard Clark, the ninety-one-year-old former Secretary of the Interior, who suffered from creeping dementia, showed up on camera on his patio in West Palm Beach wearing a wifebeater. Frantic efforts to alert him to the video nature of the call failed, since he had not turned on the sound, nor did he know how. Winnie finally reached his nursing aide, who helped him through the particulars of a video connection, and his housekeeper brought him a button-down shirt, which she was able to put on him after several tries against his stiff resistance. Semi-dressed, Willard remained baffled by the proceedings and irritated by the change in routine. "Why the hell is this meeting on TV?" he bellowed. "I thought our meetings were private."

Robbie, surveying the video grid from the mahogany-paneled boardroom in New York, assured him that everything was confidential, but Willard's eyes narrowed and he shook his head, unconvinced. Was somebody trying to pull something over on him? *He was on to these guys...*

Virginia Einholz, the director who green-lighted every pollution permit Crowe Power requested during her eight-year tenure as governor of Delaware, connected by phone from a golf cart in Tucson, where she periodically smiled and waved to her friends on the course and offered shout-outs for good tee shots. "You *go*, girl!"

Melvyn Somers, the former CEO of Appalachian Coal Corporation, a longtime Crowe Power supplier, could only figure out how to display his forehead on camera, despite repeated instructions to adjust the angle. And Tommy MacDonald, a former Wall Street CEO who served as a trustee of the charitable Crowe Family Foundation, had no idea his four-year old grandson had sneaked into the background and was scratching his armpits, imitating a monkey.

As Uncle Chuck took his place next to a glum Tim Padden across the conference table, Robbie said, "I think we're all here. I'd like to bring this meeting to order." He glanced over his shoulder to Digby: *is order even possible?* He looked out the window, across the East River, toward the sparkling Atlantic Ocean and the distant Hamptons. If he weren't so selflessly dedicated to leading this company, he could be in East Hampton now, jogging along the beach, checking out the talent. He reminded himself that he was on a mission, and he had to stay focused on the task at hand. He turned back to the screen, where the collection of silver, balding, and frosted heads bobbed up and down, to and fro in the video boxes, like lottery balls awaiting release.

"I have a question," Willard said.

Robbie nodded. "Please, Willard. Go ahead."

"Do we get our usual meeting fee? You don't rip us off because I'm doing this from—" He turned to someone off screen. "Where are we, anyway?"

Robbie looked behind him to Digby, who piped in. "Of course, Willard. All the directors get their standard fee for remote meetings, just as you would if you were here."

Willard said, "Are you serving any food?"

Robbie rolled his eyes and again turned to his uncle, who had known Willard for decades. "Uncle Chuck, can you handle this?"

Chuck looked toward Willard's box on the video grid. "Only what you can serve yourself, Willard."

"You didn't send anything in advance?" Willard said. "I really like those rice crackers we get in New York."

Chuck said, as patiently as he could, "How about this, Willard. We'll ship you a box as soon as we can. We'll throw in some cookies, too. Alright?"

Willard smiled. "I'll keep an eye out for 'em."

Robbie looked to the screen where directors were sheepishly raising their hands. *Can't we have some too?* "How about this?" Robbie said. "We'll send them to everyone." As heads nodded in approval and Winnie delivered Robbie his customary cup of Bolivian Jungle Roast from Café Che, he said, "I think, at last, we're ready to get started."

Behind Robbie, Natalia slipped into the room and took a seat along the side, outside of camera view. Robbie nodded and smiled knowingly, then held up a sheaf of papers for the directors on screen. "I hope you've all had a chance to review the deck we sent you regarding Greeneron..."

Thump! An errant tee shot bounced off the roof of Virginia Einholz's golf cart, prompting her to yell, "Call *'FORE'*, you *jerk!*" She looked off-screen and shook her head. "What an asshole."

Robbie looked up from his notes. "Excuse me?"

"Oh, I'm sorry," Virginia said, looking back at the camera. "Did you hear all that?"

Melvyn called to someone off-screen: "Louise. Get me a Coke, will ya? With ice—wait. *No* ice. Wait, ice. Ah, hell. I don't care."

Digby leaned in. "We're getting a fair amount of side conversations on the call. I'd like to ask everyone to please go on mute unless you have something you want to add to the discussion." He sighed and nodded to Robbie.

Robbie continued. "Alright. Regarding Greeneron:" He went on to explain its many splendors: whiz-bang technologies fresh from the research labs at leading universities; exciting replacements for oil, gas and coal; and the promise of enabling Crowe Power to become the undisputed leader in the bold new world of alternative energy, a carbon-neutral powerhouse that would serve as a beacon of enlightenment and help Crowe Power demonstrate that it was truly the most responsible energy company in the world. All for the low, low price of just five billion dollars.

"And, best of all, we have just the person to lead it," Robbie said. While Uncle Chuck watched skeptically, Robbie extolled and embellished Fred Crispin's credentials. Fred, he said, was intimately involved in Greeneron's development and understood every nook and cranny of its portfolio. In addition to his background in petroleum engineering, Fred just happened to be one of the world's pre-eminent experts on alternative technologies. As an added bonus, he was one of Staminum's most highly regarded executives, whose loss would be deeply felt by Walker Hope as he tried to keep his sinking ship afloat. Fred was, in a word, a catch, and Robbie had caught him by virtue of his own remarkable charm and persuasiveness, not to mention a large bag of cash, and Fred's desperation for a job with real meaning. He would work closely with Tim, and the two of them would comprise a leadership dream team for the foreseeable future. Or, at least, until Tim could be dumped.

As he finished his pitch, Robbie surveyed the Hollywood Squares grid of boxes for a response and marveled at their somnolence. Couldn't they at least fake some interest, as they did when they attended meetings in New York?

At last, Waylon Frazier, Chairman of the Africa Electrification Project, who depended on the Crowe Corporate Fund for the majority of his budget and his salary, gestured and mouthed some words on screen, but no sound came through.

Digby leaned toward the screen. "Waylon," he said. "*WAYLON!* You're on mute."

Waylon nodded and pushed a button. "Sorry," he said. "I just wanted to say, bravo, Robbie. Bravo! Very exciting."

Ah. Now that's more like it, Robbie thought. *C'mon guys. Some support would be good here.*

Tommy McDonald would not be outdone by Waylon in his enthusiasm for whatever Robbie, his benefactor, wanted. "I have to agree. This sounds like a real game changer for our company."

Robbie couldn't help but smile. *Game changer! Yeah! I like that!*

SuretyTrust Group chairman David Padgett, who sensed a business opportunity to finance the acquisition of Greeneron through his bank at a hefty commission, turned verbal handsprings. "Such an impressive coup, Robbie. Greeneron *and* Fred Crispin? Why, that's the very definition of leadership in my book. I'll absolutely support in every way I can."

Barbara Butler, the former CEO of the old Mid-Atlantic Power & Light, who had sold her company to Crowe Power many years before and profited handsomely from the stock she earned in return, offered her obligatory salute, as she did in every meeting. God knows there was no other way to make this kind of money per minute. "I have one word, Robbie: *bold.*"

Robbie was euphoric with this bootlicking, because he knew in his heart of hearts that this was hardly sycophancy. These were accomplished people, just a hair or two past their prime, and they would never put their august reputations at risk behind a lousy strategy. The fact is, this *was* bold. It *was* a coup. Robbie deserved heaps of praise. And when the word got out, the positivity would reach a crescendo with the people who mattered. Like Dr. Kristi Kramer and her millions of readers. Like the Planetistas, who would have to give him credit. Like Natalia, who was watching him with, what? Admiration? Maybe, after the meeting, she would finally reward him for making good on his promises...

Robbie's reverie was broken by creaky old Melvyn Somers, who saw the future of his old coal company continuing to whither as coal fell further out of fashion. He cleared his blackened lungs with a rumbling phlegmy roar. "Five billion dollars sounds like an awful lot of loot, Robbie, especially when our facilities are working perfectly fine right now," he said. "Can we afford to do this?"

Robbie was ready for this. He looked over to Natalia, then leaned forward and folded his hands in front of him, comfortable in his growing certainty. "It's my view, Melvyn, that we can't afford not to. Alternative technologies are the wave of the future. And we can ride that wave, or we can fall under it, and get crushed. Either way, it's coming. And if I have anything to say about it, we should get on top of it."

Robbie looked to Uncle Chuck, who watched the proceedings with an expression of fatalistic detachment. He could resist further, but what was the point? The board was a reliable rubber stamp, especially after the departure of Moe Klinger's proxies, and the family was in no position to intervene. What option did they have besides Robbie? He was their only choice as long as Homer Crowe's descendants wished to retain control. He was their best option, and maybe their last.

Virginia Einholz, eager to tee off at her tournament, moved for a vote, which was quickly seconded by Waylon. Support for both the acquisition of Greeneron and the hiring of Fred Crispin was swift and unanimous, as was the eagerness to end the call and get on with the day. Robbie practically leapt from his chair as the meeting concluded, ready to start spreading the news.

Tim, sensing the kiss of death on his tenure at Crowe Power, brushed past Robbie without saying a word. Uncle Chuck noticed his demeanor as he gathered his things.

"Tim does not appear to be taking this very well," he said to Robbie. "He didn't say a word."

Robbie shrugged, and looked over to Natalia, who was leaving. "Fine," he said, hurriedly. "Let him quit."

Robbie made a move to catch Natalia, but Chuck came around the table and blocked his way. "You need to keep him."

"Tim?" Robbie said. "Why?"

"I've seen these kinds of grand plans go cock-eyed before," Chuck said. "Sooner or later, you're gonna need somebody to fire."

37. VICTORY LAP

A s he left the boardroom, Robbie paused in the Hall of Fam, the wall of spot-lit portraits of those company chairmen and CEOs whose last name had been Crowe. For the first time in his adult life, Robbie could look at them all without shrinking from a sense of inadequacy. With a bold stroke, he had put his unmistakable thumbprint on the company. He belonged with the giants.

The first portrait in the corridor was of Homer Crowe, the illustrious founder, an uneducated tinkerer, inventor, and entrepreneur with far-sighted vision, standing in front of a giant dynamo. Next was Lester Crowe, his capable, diligent, and over-educated son, who led the company to its post-war heights of growth and prosperity. He posed in a suit in his office with the backdrop of Midtown Manhattan in the distance. Charles Crowe, who throughout the 1980s and '90s effectively battled antitrust suits and Congressional criticism, was portrayed next to a large globe festooned with stars where Crowe facilities were situated around the world. Fourth in succession was Les Crowe, Robbie's father, a belligerent drunkard who couldn't keep his pants on, but somehow managed to keep the company afloat and independent during a time of rampant consolidation. Les was captured at his desk, a piece of furniture with which he had kept little acquaintance. Last, and now far from least, Robbie was portrayed in front of a wind farm that later went bust, with beams of sunlight smiling on his shoulders and an angelic expression on his face.

What would all the greats of Crowe Power's past think of Robbie now? He suspected they would be very pleased indeed that he had accurately sensed a change in the wind and adapted to it. Better still, he had swept away the last vestiges of Walker Hope's heretical regime and restored the crown. Walker's tenure would be regarded forevermore as a mere interregnum, a dark age best ignored, despite its profitability.

After his deals were approved and announcements were sent out over the PR Newswire, Robbie found his office a more welcome place, too. He was setting up goals and knocking them down, accomplishing things that could be attributed to him and him alone. There was no Walker Hope to steal the credit this time around. There was only Lester Robertson Crowe III to take the bows. Was it too early to commission a bust for the reception area? Maybe he could get Digby to propose it, in which case, he would reluctantly accept.

In the meantime, there was nothing left for him to do but to bathe in the glory of it all. Pacing in front of his desk, he leaned over his console and pushed a button.

"Winnie, I would like to see Natalia as soon as possible."

A voice came crackling through the speaker. "She's not here, Mr. Crowe."

"When is she expected?"

There was a pause. "She's never actually *expected*, Mr. Crowe. She comes and goes as she pleases. She left right after your meeting."

"Well, see if you can track her down and find some time on my calendar for us to get together. I need to see her."

"Do you have a preference? Your calendar is wide open, except for your two-hour block for lunch."

Robbie was losing patience. "Just make it as soon as possible, alright?" *Damn!* He punched the button to end the discussion. Talking with Winnie was not an efficient use of his time. Perhaps he'd have to broom her out, too, as part of this new golden era. Maybe he could find some younger chick with a little more pep in her step. Natalia might know somebody. Perhaps she could bring in a friend, and the three of them could have a little welcome party in the office. They could have a few drinks, get all warm and gooey, and then move the festivities to the bedroom and—

The intercom buzzed. "Mr. Crowe, I found Natalia over at Café Che. She's on her way back to the office."

"Send her in as soon as she arrives."

"Will do."

Robbie clapped his hands together. He couldn't wait to hear her review of the board meeting. She had to be impressed with his tour de force! He hit the button again. "And have her bring me a Bolivian Jungle Roast."

"Yes sir."

Robbie looked around the office. Did this set the right mood? He looked at the bookcases filled with framed photos of Robbie and his father with presidents and dignitaries, awards from various foundations for being a Crowe, and books on climate change and the environment, some of which he'd actually opened. He pulled out *Broiled Alive* by the noted thinker Mac McGowan and placed it perpendicular to the other books so that it faced out. He also adjusted his trophies and citations so that the Inspired Leadership Award from the Peoples Environmental Front, for which he'd paid two hundred and fifty thousand dollars in donations, was most prominent.

The electronic door swung open and there she was, Natalia, holding a cardboard tray with two coffees and a small paper bag of pastries.

"I thought you might like a vegan bar," she said sweetly.

He smiled. "You know what I like!" he said. *What the hell was a vegan bar?* Oh well. He'd eat it and love it, even if he had to gag it down. He walked over to the sofa and sat, leaving plenty of room for her to join him. She selected, instead, a chair.

"So," she said. "You've had quite a day."

Robbie sipped his coffee and exhaled, shaking his head at the wonder of it all. "Amazing day, really. I think, finally, we've got a really good story to tell the Planetistas."

She nodded. "I've already told them."

"You did?" He leaned forward, excited. "What did they say?"

"They said you're walking the talk."

"They *did?*"

"Well, actually, I said that. But they agreed. And, better still, they said they would stop the protests in front of our building."

"Really? Oh my *god.* It's all coming together!"

She paused. "There's a cost. We'll have to donate another hundred-thousand dollars to the cause. They need to buy a new dinosaur and some better noisemakers."

"Fine," Robbie said grandly. "That's a small price to pay."

"I thought you would be pleased."

"You have no idea." He leaned over the armrest, so close that he could reach out and touch her, his eyes locking with hers. He wanted nothing more than to take her in his arms right now and show her exactly how much he adored her. "You deserve something special for your efforts. A celebration of some sort."

She leaned forward, eagerly. "I couldn't agree more."

"What would you like to do?"

She reached over, placed her hand on his knee and looked into his eyes. "Well, if you don't mind, I was thinking of getting out of here early today."

Oh yeah! *Let's go!* "Of course," he said, warmly. "Where would you like to go? Just name it."

She withdrew her hand. "My boyfriend and I are going to Le Bernardin."

Robbie was crushed. "You... have a boyfriend?"

"Julius Holiday."

Robbie's lip quivered. "The hedge fund guy?"

"We're kind of having a double celebration."

"For what?"

"Well, for one: Me getting the Planetistas off your back, which I'm very happy about." She raised her coffee cup and touched his in a toast. "Cheers."

"Cheers," Robbie said glumly. "What's the other celebration?"

"Julius has made so much money shorting your stock that he's bought me a new apartment in Gramercy. I get a key to the park and everything." She giggled and sunk into the couch. She noticed Robbie was dead still, his mouth agape. What was wrong with him all of the sudden? He looked so saggy.

"Robbie," she said. "You should really try the vegan bar. It has lots of protein."

PART TWO

Sparks Fly

FEBRUARY - MARCH

38. CACHE COWS

I n the rolling hills of the Berkshires in western Massachusetts, Robbie, wearing a blue denim jacket, leaned over a split rail fence, one boot up on a slat, his arms resting casually over the top rail as he squinted in the bright orange morning sun. The camera pulled back to reveal Robbie ruminating beside a field of cows enjoying their breakfast.

Over a soft bed of lilting pastoral music, Robbie addressed the future. "Some people," Robbie said, "see problems in the carbon emissions that emanate from this beautiful landscape. I see solutions." Robbie turned to the camera and talked as he walked. "I'm Robbie Crowe, chairman of the Crowe Power Company. Every day, the scientists at Greeneron are finding new ways to generate energy that reduces our planet's output of greenhouse gases. We're harnessing the power of the sun, the wind, the tides…" He gestured behind him. "Even these cows."

The camera cut to the interior of a barn, where white-smocked scientists were strapping large plastic containers onto the backs of cows and connecting tubes to their stomachs. The double doors to the barn opened and the cows moseyed outside to the pasture, as Robbie explained the process. "These lightweight containers capture the methane gas from each cow's digestive system, which we then convert to life-sustaining energy that heats our homes and turns on our lights." The camera showed Robbie in the barn sipping a glass of milk. He turned to the camera and smiled. "That's an idea we all can live with."

The next shot was back outside in the sunshine, where Robbie beamed with satisfaction over the herd of backpacked cows, as the symphony of violins and cellos gathered in volume and pace. "My great-great-grandfather Homer Crowe launched our company's push for responsible energy more than a century ago, a tradition we honor today with our development of twenty-one renewable power sources, each one a possible breakthrough in ending our world's addiction to fossil fuels." As the music reached its crescendo, Robbie said, "Just one more way in which the people of Crowe are powering our future… together."

The last shot in the commercial showed a close-up of a cow chewing contentedly, while an announcer said: *"No animals were harmed in the filming of this commercial."*

The lights came on in Robbie's private conference room off his office, where he sat at the head of the table, grinning from ear to ear and shaking his head in wonder at his incredible acting abilities. Why, if he weren't busy running this company, was it a stretch to think he could be a movie star?

He looked around the conference table at the puzzled expressions of Tim, Fred and Digby, then to Hatch Peterson, the creative guru from Plan9 Interstellar, who was sitting anxiously on the edge of the windowsill while his retinue of account executives, writers, and producers awaited a verdict from stiff chairs along the back wall.

Robbie didn't care what any of them thought. "I absolutely *love* it!" he said.

Hatch clapped his hands and stood. "Awesome!"

"Brilliant. Just *brilliant!"* Robbie turned to Digby. "What do you think? I looked pretty damn good, right?"

Digby crossed his arms over his chest and raised an eyebrow. "Are you kidding?'

Robbie sighed. "You don't like it."

"Cow farts?"

"No, you ninny. Not cow farts." Robbie stood up and walked toward Digby. "That's the thing, Digs. It never gets to that stage. The tube goes right into the cow's stomach before the gas can even come out of the cow's ass. It short-circuits the whole digestive process. Right, Fred?"

Fred nodded, unconvincingly. "I believe so."

"Okay. Even if you accept that idea," Digby continued, "what about our investors?"

Robbie waved off the idea. "Seriously? You think I give a crap about them?"

"They're going to look at this and say, 'This is what Crowe Power got for five billion dollars? Cow poots?"

"You aren't *listening,* Digby. It's not an actual poot."

"People may interpret this in unkind ways."

Robbie threw up his hands and turned toward the windows. "You know what? Fine. *Fine.* If people are that narrow-minded, fuck 'em. I know a few people who are going to be mightily impressed. What did you think, Fred?"

"You come off really, really well, Robbie."

Robbie turned to Digby. "See?" Then he looked over at Tim, who slumped in his chair. "What about you, Tim? Do you finally get what we're doing here?"

"Absolutely. We got a helluva commercial for five billion dollars."

Robbie seethed, turning to the broader group. "Cost be damned. This is exactly the kind of thinking I want people to associate with the new Crowe Power. We're thinking way outside the box."

Digby sniffed. "And the barn."

"Whatever," Robbie said. "Hatch. Tell Digby about the other commercials we're talking about." He turned to Digby. "Listen to this."

Hatch, dressed in his usual Brooklyn creative regalia, picked up a folder from the conference table. "We want to do one around algae, and how we're converting it into biodiesel for tractors and, you know, whatever mechanical stuff they use on a farm."

Robbie looked at Digby. "Is that cool or what?"

Hatch continued. "This one's a bit out there, but the team *really* loves it. Now, stay with me, alright? We open on a frog."

Digby sighed. "Of course. It's green, right?"

"Yes, submerged next to a lily pad. The frog slowly emerges from the water and faces the camera. And then, magically, it speaks. 'Some people call it scum. The scientists at Crowe Power call it life-giving energy.' Then we cut to Robbie, crouched near the water's edge, his hand reaching into the muck." Hatch picked up a piece of paper and read from it. "'There's a lot of natural goodness in this pond. And we at Crowe Power are finding ways to capture it as an energy source for our future.'"

Robbie clapped his hands together. "How about *that!*"

Digby smoldered. "A talking *frog?*"

Robbie looked offended. "Ever heard of Kermit?"

"This isn't a puppet show, Robbie," Digby said sharply. "We're spending billions of dollars on this stuff. You want to look like *Robbie in Wonderland?* People will think you're dropping acid."

Robbie looked at the team around the conference table. "Hatch. Fred. Tim. Could you wait for us outside a moment?" Robbie waited for the door to close behind them, then turned back to Digby. "What the fuck, man. Why are you so negative? The frog thing is just an idea at this point. You want the same old time-lapse shots of lights coming on in cities, and traffic swirling around freeways, and airplanes taking off? Nobody cares about that stuff anymore."

"They might if they're sitting on a runway," Digby said, standing up. "Look, Robbie. I'm telling you this as your counselor, a family member and, I think, as your friend. The knock on you as chairman is that you're out of touch with the guts of our business, that all you care about are fanciful new energies, and that it's killing our stock and hurting our profitability. Now we're going to show you hanging around with cows and talking frogs? You're not Doctor Doolittle. You're the leader of a serious global business."

"Digs, I know you're trying to help. But we've got to change the conversation around this company. It's embarrassing that the only thing that people associate with us is fossil fuels. We have to be more than that."

"Totally agree. Except we're not, just yet." Digby paced. "I understand that lots of companies are out there trumpeting their good intentions through their science projects. This just seems disingenuous to me. There's no chance that cow... vapors are going to become a real business for us. I'm afraid you'll get more ridicule than admiration, especially after our earnings come out next week."

Robbie grimaced and rubbed his forehead. "That's why I want to get ahead of it now. Who cares where we are as a company right this minute? Earnings are a snapshot in time, that's all. So let's carpet-bomb the Sunday shows this weekend. Get people looking beyond the present to the future. I bet a pile on Greeneron. We need to show people it's paying off." He rubbed his hands together anxiously. "It's got to."

He walked over to a credenza and hit the intercom. "Winnie, send in Natalia."

"She not here, Mr. Crowe."

"Where is she?"

"Haven't seen her today."

"Let me know when she shows up. I want to show her something."

"I bet you do," Digby said, standing to leave. "This is all about impressing Natalia, isn't it?"

"What's wrong with that?" Robbie said.

Digby paused at the door. "It's a fool's errand, Robbie. Odds are good that if she likes it, lots of other people are going to hate it. You might win her over and lose everyone else."

"She's a skeptic, and that's what I love about her," Robbie said, leaning back on the credenza. "If I can convince Natalia, I know this: I can convince the world."

39. DIMINISHING RETURNS

As soon as he entered the conference room known as The Homer, Robbie had the foreboding sense he was descending into the valley of death. The team assembled to prepare for the fourth-quarter earnings call with investors and the news media was decidedly grim, with hunched shoulders, clenched jaws, and eyes sullenly cast on the binders of information in front of them.

Robbie took a deep breath and steeled himself to take his chair at the head of the table next to Digby. Robbie leaned toward him and spoke in a low voice. "Jesus. Where's the corpse?"

Digby looked at him. "Just arrived."

Robbie scanned the faces of the people around the table, none of whom looked in his direction. Tim sat on his right, avoiding eye contact by studying his briefing book, with Fred doing likewise next to him. To Robbie's left after Digby was Chief Financial Officer Anna Pachulski; Lucy Rutherford, head of the Americas; the new Chief Communications Officer Yvonne Jackson—or was it Johnson?—and her assistant, Rafael something-or-other. At the other end of the table, in the shadows, was a cadre of staff people who clearly didn't have any standing, or they wouldn't be kept in the dark. They were known collectively as The Mushrooms.

Anna, the tightly-wired CFO who crackled with nervous energy, said, "Alright, people. Are we ready to get started?" Nobody responded, but she took a sip of water to clear her throat and plunged ahead anyway. "The first thing I want to draw your attention to is the draft of our press release, which will go out tomorrow, before the market opens. You'll note, Robbie, that we are posting a loss, our first in five years." She waited a moment for that to sink in. "As you'll see in the script, we attribute the loss to headwinds."

Robbie nodded. "Headwinds," he said. "Okay. Makes sense to me."

Anna said, "That was a suggestion from Fred. Very helpful, I think."

Robbie nodded approvingly to Fred, who exhaled with relief.

Lucy wasn't as sanguine. She flipped the release over, then back again. "Shouldn't we acknowledge that the chief reason for our loss was that we deferred maintenance on our facilities? That's what caused downtime for repairs and lost production."

Anna cast a glance toward Robbie, who shifted uncomfortably in his seat, then back to Lucy. "I don't think that's something we want to say."

"I don't *want* to say it either," Lucy said, "but it happens to be true. Since we started plowing all of our money into Greeneron, we've starved operations. I don't know how many more cutbacks and layoffs we can afford. If we don't resume a normal maintenance schedule soon, one of these facilities is going to blow."

All eyes turned to Robbie. Greeneron was known to be his baby. Did Lucy just call it ugly? He snapped, "We just said it was headwinds, Lucy. That's all we have to say. Move on." He cast a sharp glance at Anna, who picked up the cudgel.

"Lucy, we hear what you're saying," Anna said. "But, as Robbie has said, criticism of Greeneron is short-term thinking. We *know* that our investment will pay off, eventually. For now, we just have to tighten our belts. Right, Fred?"

Fred nodded. "Oh yes. A lot of things have to come together, but we're very upbeat about Greeneron's potential. *Very* upbeat." He looked to Robbie and smiled confidently, his splotches glowing a fiery red.

Tim looked at Fred skeptically. "You have a path to profitability?"

"Sure," Fred said. "All we have to do is prove out the technologies, lobby various governments for subsidies and tax breaks, and create a massive worldwide infrastructure to enable consumers to have access. Once we do that, we're minting money."

Tim, increasingly embittered by his hopeless mandate to operate without money, bore in. "When?"

Fred offered a shrug. "We could see a profit from one or two of these technologies in, oh... five years?"

Tim sighed and shook his head. "Five years."

"If everything goes according to plan." Fred bobbed and weaved. "Could be four, if we get extremely lucky."

"And if we don't?"

"Could be six years, seven. I don't know. It's hard to say, exactly."

"So it could be eight, nine, ten..."

"Possible."

"Maybe we should license a technology that harnesses moonbeams that we can shoot out our butts."

Robbie felt the blood rush up his neck into his face. "Alright. Enough!" Tim might have directed this particular assault at Fred, but he knew it was really aimed at him. What had gotten into Tim? Just because he was a dead man didn't mean he had to act out and force a premature dismissal. Didn't he know this wasn't the place to challenge Robbie's infinite wisdom, right here in front of everybody else? If he had to bitch about Greeneron, he should get on Robbie's calendar, provided there's an opening, and register his objection privately. "Tim," he said, "you're missing the point."

Tim turned to Robbie. "I confess that I am. I don't know what we're accomplishing with all this spending on speculative businesses while we're starving the core of our existing one."

The fucking *nerve* of this guy! The point was... Hell, Robbie didn't know the point exactly, but what difference did it make? It's Greeneron! Robbie's signature initiative! Who was Tim to question it? Some fucking goober from Indiana? *Fuck him!* Robbie caught Anna's glance and pointedly looked up at the clock.

Anna picked up on the cue. "Tim, we all appreciate your question, but would you mind if we tabled this discussion? I'm mindful of our time and we have a lot to get through to prepare for this call."

Tim knew further resistance was futile. "Of course."

"Great. I want to turn to the Q&A, which is the second tab in your binders. These are the questions that could come up, and we want to be ready for them." She looked to the back of the room, where one of The Mushrooms trudged through dreary explanations about losses, layoffs, and the forecast.

Digby leaned over to Robbie and whispered: "You know this is going to be a fucking bloodbath, right?"

Robbie said, "Better not be my blood. Can't they come up with any better answers than these?"

"That would require better results."

Robbie pushed back his chair. "I don't think I should even be here for this. We should march Tim out there. Let him take all the crap. It's his part of the company that's failing us."

Digby looked at him, incredulously. "Are you serious?"

"Why not? Somebody's got to take the heat."

As they reached the binder's last section, labeled STRATEGY, Anna said, "Robbie, we think this next question goes to you. 'Given the sharp loss and the bleak outlook, are you considering a change in strategy?'"

Robbie looked at Anna as if she had suddenly sprouted antlers. "What kind of bullshit question is that?"

Anna said, "I'm sorry, Robbie. This isn't us asking. It's a question we expect from Evan Marshall at Citi. He always goes for the big picture."

"Evan? That guy's a pain in the ass. He's never liked us. Why don't we just keep him off the call? Let him sit in the queue all day."

"We could, but the same question might come from any number of people."

"Then cut the damn call *short,*" he said with a snort.

Anna looked for help from Digby, who intervened. "We have to answer the question sooner or later. The group discussed this yesterday and we decided the best place to do it was on tomorrow's call."

Robbie shook his head with disgust and dismissed him with a wave of his hand. "Okay. *Fine.* Whatever."

"So," Anna said, "how would you like to respond?"

Robbie looked at her sharply. "You want *me* to answer that?"

She looked at him pleadingly. In a trembling voice, she said, "It speaks to the overall direction of the company."

Robbie exhaled. All the crap he had to do… "The answer is no. *No!* We're *not* changing our strategy. And, Evan, by the way, fuck off, thank you very much."

Nervous laughter rippled around the table as Anna plunged ahead. "I believe the next question is also yours, Robbie."

Robbie looked at the binder and read it, his annoyance rising. "Would I consider stock buybacks to shore up the share price? *No!* We don't have the money. Next question."

Anna took a breath, then said, "I assume, then, that this is a 'no' also, but investors are asking us: 'Would you consider suspending the dividend to conserve cash?'"

Robbie went ashen and sat back in his chair, as if he'd been told he had six weeks to live. "What?" he asked.

Anna said, "I hope you saw the briefing paper we gave you on the issue."

Briefing paper? "What briefing paper?"

"We delivered it to your office last week."

"Well, I sure as hell didn't see it. Somebody fucked up here."

"I'm very sorry about that, Robbie. The paper laid out our choices for cash. It pretty much comes down to a choice between funding Greeneron or continuing to pay the dividend. We can't do both."

Robbie sank back in his chair. He knew he would have to face this question sooner or later. The dividend was sacrosanct to the Crowe family, and it was the only reason for anyone to buy the company stock right now. Given these dire results, and the need to continue pumping cash into Greeneron to justify the acquisition, what choice did he have? Quietly, almost inaudibly, he said, "Suspend the dividend."

Digby looked at him in astonishment. "*What?*"

Robbie took a deep breath. "We have to."

Digby looked to Anna. "Let's hold off on that answer for now."

As the meeting concluded, Robbie dashed for the door, eager to escape the meeting, the questions, and the accountability. *Where was Natalia when he needed her?* Or Maria, Priscilla, Janet, or Laura, or any of those other paramours who had signed non-disclosure agreements when he had tired of them? Maybe Dr. Kristi Kramer was in town. If only he had somebody with whom he could lose himself for the rest of the day.

Digby gathered his materials and quickly followed Robbie, chasing him down the hall to the chairman's suite, where he caught him fumbling at the ID reader next to the glass doors. Robbie was starting to hyperventilate. "They're going to crucify me."

"Who?"

"Who do you think? Wall Street. The press. Twitter. Everybody."

Digby knew this had to be handled delicately. He held up both hands, palms facing Robbie. *Calm down; I come in peace.* "You can take some short-term grief in the press. You can take it from Wall Street, too. And a little heat on social media won't kill you. But you cannot lose the family. That's your last refuge, your one safe harbor. Which means you can't touch the dividend."

Robbie sagged. "What else am I gonna do? You heard Lucy. If we don't maintain our facilities, they could blow up. People could die. And who do you think they'll blame for that? Some stupid plant manager? No! They'll blame *me!*"

"Alright. I hear you. Let's talk about our options."

"I already know what they are. I've been dwelling on this for weeks. We can't borrow any more money; we're heading for junk territory again. And I sure as hell can't starve Greeneron if we're ever going to see a payoff. Something's got to give."

"If that 'something' is the income of your cousins and aunts and uncles, that's going to be a problem. You know the kind of lifestyles they lead."

Robbie eyed Digby suspiciously. Was Bits behind this? "What about my sister?"

"She won't like this either."

"Then here's the deal." Robbie stuck a finger in his chest. "You need to manage her."

Digby scoffed. "Oh, really. Why don't you try it sometime?" He turned to walk toward his office.

Robbie called after him. "How do you think Staminum's going to do?"

Digby stopped and turned around. "They're reporting today."

"I *know* that, numbnuts. That's why I'm asking."

Numbnuts? Digby thought, *now I'm 'numbnuts?'* Just another useless idiot? He looked at his phone as he walked back toward Robbie. "Press release just crossed the wire. Looks like—" He paused, reading.

"What?" Robbie pressed. "*What?*"

"First profit in four years. Improvements in every sector." He stifled a laugh as he read. "You want to hear the quote from Walker?"

"No. But tell me anyway."

"CEO Walker B. Hope said, 'The significant windfall we received from the sale of Greeneron has enabled Staminum to fully fund its operations across the board for the first time in years. By reinvesting in our facilities and adding top talent in our company from the shop floor to the C-suite, we've been able to improve our efficiency, productivity, profitability, and balance sheet.'"

Robbie felt like he'd been stabbed. "I can't take this."

"There's more," Digby said. "Mr. Hope said, 'It's also enabled us to complete the conversion of all of our coal plants to natural gas and make a significant investment in renewable energy. We fully expect to become carbon-neutral in ten years or less, which will make a major contribution to the health of our planet.'"

Robbie fell back against the wall. Was he having a stroke? "They're going to beat us to carbon neutrality? When we have Greeneron?"

Digby said, "Apparently, that's why."

Robbie balled his fist and scowled. "That fucking Fred."

40. ILLIQUID

D r. Stuart Littmann laid in bed, staring at the ceiling of his apartment on the Upper West Side, running through various scenarios in his mind, all of which ended in financial ruin. By sticking with his investment in Crowe Power, he was nearing a catastrophe. Crowe's first loss in years, bleak outlook, and suspension of its dividend sent more investors running for the exits, leaving him with a rapidly depreciating asset. Stuart's original million-dollar investment was now worth five hundred thousand, and falling.

With his pulse racing, Stuart rose from his bed and walked to a small desk in the corner of his living room. He turned on his laptop and sorted through the mail he had purposely avoided looking at during the day. Amidst the spammy pitches for storm windows, home security systems, and penis enhancements were a series of notes from his bank, reminding him that the payment on his loan was now seriously in arrears and that his account would soon be transferred to a collection agency unless immediate steps were taken. What steps, he wondered, were left to take?

He pushed away from the desk, walked to his spare bedroom, and flicked on the wall switch, illuminating his shrine to vintage TV shows, comic books, and baseball cards from the previous century. The walls were lined with posters signed by cast members from *The Brady Bunch*, *Charlie's Angels*, *The Six Million Dollar Man*, and his favorite, *Honey West*. A display case featured collector dolls: a Mego Elastic Batman, an original Superman, and a GI Joe. He had a *T.V. Guide* from 1953 with Lucille Ball on the cover, the very first *People* magazine from 1974 featuring Mia Farrow as Daisy Buchanan, and a 1970 bobblehead of Colonel Sanders. Every item in this collection represented some happier moment in a safer, more sheltered time. It was his escape from the modern world, and it was about to be closed off. All of these things, he realized, would have to go. Aside from his six-year-old Volvo, they were the only assets of value that he could sell.

He slumped sadly against the wall. What, he wondered, did Robbie Crowe have to sacrifice for his disastrous leadership? Did he have to give up anything that touched him personally? Did it even bother him that many of the people who invested their money with him were not wealthy like he was, nor insulated from financial shocks? Stuart sighed, turned off the light, and shut the door behind him. He would need to get used to the idea that these things no longer belonged to him. It was just stuff.

He returned to his computer and sat down, as his cat Felix twirled around his ankles, looking for attention. Stuart reached down and stroked his ears, thinking about what he would sell first. The Angels? Lucy? GI Joe? It was like selling his children. The guilt was overwhelming. He was a bad dad!

Stuart buried his head in his hands. If only Crowe Power would get rid of Robbie Crowe, maybe his stock could miraculously rebound and spare him the agony of bidding farewell to his little family. Before he signed on to eBay, he'd make one last stand on Twitter.

❋ ❋ ❋

A couple of miles to the southeast in a suite at the Peninsula Hotel, Robbie Crowe was awake, too, laying in bed with his iPad and scrolling through his Twitter feed, where public opinion was cleanly divided. On the one hand, Robbie was lauded for his company's innovative efforts to find new energy alternatives—in tweets largely written by contractors hired by the Crowe Power PR department. Those voices, however, were drowned out by the critics who were not on the payroll. They hammered him for the falling stock, the poor financial performance, and the success of his rival, Staminum.

Dr. Stuart Littmann was, as usual, blunt.

Stuart Littmann, DDS @$crewedByCrowe 7m
Robbie Crowe is a disgrace! He has two
honorable choices. 1: Resign. 2: Sell the
company. Shareholders must be served!

Good lord! Was somebody going to do something about this? Where the hell were his defenders? Yes, it was two a.m., but they should be on guard twenty-four/seven. What the hell did he pay all these people for? Did he have to take care of this himself?

Seething, Robbie walked to the living room where his phone was charging and dialed Howie-Do-It.

After three rings, Howie answered. "Yo. What up?"

"Are you seeing this *shit?*"

"Twitter?"

"Of *course,* Twitter. What the fuck, man! Is anybody going to push back on this guy?"

Howie sat up and swiped his screen to call up the Twitter feed. "Oh yeah," he said. "I see what you mean. That kinda sucks."

"*Kinda?* This dentist is out there calling for me to lose my job. He already has nine likes and three retweets. Where are my people? Why's everyone dead on their ass?"

"Dude. It's the middle of the night."

"The critics are awake! Why aren't we? We're a global company, for crissakes. Why don't we have a team of people in India or Singapore on this? They should be monitoring this and responding in real time."

"I hear you, boss. Let me make some calls."

"Make them now. I don't care who you have to wake up. This can't continue."

"Got it. I'll spread the word."

"And, come tomorrow, I want to resume full-time surveillance on this Dr. Littmann prick. We need to track his every move. Where he goes in the city. What he does online. Who his friends are. Everything. He needs to know he can't fuck with me."

41. PAYBACKS ARE HECK

Walker slid his plastic tray along the lunch line in the Staminum employee cafeteria, picking up a cup of chicken noodle soup and half of an egg salad sandwich, offering howdy-dos to everyone he encountered, and asking how they liked their jobs. The response was unanimous. Why, they all *loved* their jobs! Was there any other answer to give the CEO?

"Wonderful to hear!" Walker would say. "Thank you for *all* you do!" And it didn't matter what they did! *It was somethin'!* Gosh, he loved these people! Workin' so hard!

"Isn't it *fun* when you see results?" he'd ask. One and all nodded most assuredly. Making profits for Staminum Energy was practically a dream come true! None of the secretaries, bookkeepers, lawyers or technical support people seemed the least bit concerned that Walker made four-hundred-and-eighty-six times as much as they did. They were glad to play a part on a winning team for a change. And if that's what they paid the coach, so be it! Let the news media try to stir up resentment on issues like that. Walker knew: he had *value.* And the proof was right up there on the scoreboard. First profit in years! Vastly improved operations! Better emissions profile! Walker picked up a carton of skim milk, paid eleven dollars and two cents for his lunch with his credit card, and carried his tray through the crowded lunchroom to a table in a corner where Marty and Maria were sitting.

He slid into his chair and beamed a winner's smile. "It's *so* darn good to see everybody so excited about our company."

"Oh yeah," Marty said on cue.

"For sure," Maria croaked.

Walker leaned in. "You feel it, too?"

Maria said, "I'm pretty giddy about the beatdown we gave Crowe Power."

Walker winced. "Things sure have turned all catawampus down there. Looked to me like their only good news is their carbon emissions were down."

"That's because their plants were shut down for unscheduled maintenance," Maria said.

"That's one way to lower carbon output," Walker said.

Marty said, "Paybacks are—" He glanced at Walker. Had this man ever uttered even a borderline curse word in his life? "...heck."

"Aren't they though?" Walker shook his head, solemnly, and took a moment to say a silent prayer before eating. At last he looked up. "I take no satisfaction from their misery."

Marty looked at him skeptically. "Not even a little?"

Walker held his thumb and index finger a quarter-inch apart. "Well. Maybe just a tiny bit. I mean, we left 'em the playbook: a plan, processes, a path forward. Why Robbie chose not to follow it is beyond me."

Maria scoffed. "That's easy. It wasn't his idea."

"You think?" Walker said, munching on his sandwich.

"Of course," Maria continued. "If he doesn't think of something first, it's stupid. He has to be the expert on everything. Which is why he doesn't attend any management meetings. He's afraid somebody might actually know what they're talking about."

Marty shrugged. "She's right."

Walker put down his sandwich. "The shame of it is they have so many good assets and such wonderful people. It's so sad to see it all wasted."

Maria leaned in. "Let's put them out of their misery."

Walker cocked an eyebrow. "By taking them over?"

"Why not?"

Walker said, "You know, the funny thing is, Robbie's no dummy. He's fast on his feet. He's had a great education. And he's right about many things. Like carbon emissions, renewables, and alternative energy. But he wants to make changes for the wrong reasons."

Marty chuckled. "So he can get the credit."

"Exactly," Maria said.

"Everyone's got an ego," Walker said. "I get that. I might even have a little myself." Marty and Maria looked at him blankly. *Walker has an ego? What ego?* "But if you're in it for the personal glory," Walker continued, "you can blow a lot of money on vanity projects that have no hope of returning your investment."

"Like Greeneron," Marty said.

Maria said, "*Caveat emptor.*"

From outside, they could hear a gathering hubbub on the street below. Other diners began to walk to the windows to see what was going on. Walker decided to see for himself, and Marty and Maria followed him. Looking four floors below to the plaza on Sixth Avenue, they saw about fifty protesters wearing jungle fatigues and black berets, holding signs, banging on plastic drums with wooden spoons, and placing an inflatable dinosaur outside the headquarters' front door. A man with a scruffy Castro beard was speaking into a megaphone but whatever he was saying could not be made out. A banner held aloft near the curb said:

HEAVE HOPE

Walker was puzzled. "Now why would they do that? We're makin' progress."

Maria shook her head. "Robbie sent them."

Walker was dismayed. "You think?"

"Oh yeah. Classic move."

"Let's go down and say hello," Walker said brightly. "Looks like they're workin' hard out there. Let's take 'em some sandwiches. Get a handful of our Sustainability Reports, too. Do we have any left?"

Marty shrugged. "Only about forty boxes."

"How many did we print?"

"Forty-one, I believe."

A few moments later, Walker pushed through the revolving door to the plaza in front of headquarters trailed by Maria and Marty, a couple of servers from the kitchen carrying trays of sandwiches and cookies, and employees from the Office of Corporate Citizenship with armfuls of Sustainability Reports, the company's report card on its environmental progress. At the sight of Walker, the group pumped up the volume of their chant: *Hey, hey, ho, ho. Walker Hope has got to go!*

It was a mild day for late February, and the sun that peaked over the skyscrapers was warm. Walker cast an eye toward the signs. One bore his likeness and said: *Staminum Board: Send Walker Walking.* Another had Walker's picture in a red circle with a line through it and said, *Nope to Hope.*

Walker strode up to the man with the microphone and offered to shake his hand. "I'm Walker, that fella you're talkin' about there," he said with a grin. "Really pleased to meet you!" Ernesto looked at him in shock but shook his hand. "Would you mind if I get a picture of me with your dinosaur? My grandkids would be just *tickled.*"

Ernesto stepped back as Walker instructed Marty to take a couple of shots with him next to the inflatable dinosaur, which was fifteen feet high and listing toward the Radio City Music Hall across the street. Far from menacing, the dinosaur looked more like a roadside attraction announcing a sale on big-screen TVs.

"Say, 'gas,'" Marty called.

Walker smiled broadly for one shot, then called Maria over. "C'mon. Let's get you in the shot."

Maria took the other side of the dinosaur, and Marty snapped another photo as the puzzled protesters looked on and stopped their chanting. They were supposed to rattle this guy's cage. This wasn't working out too well…

Walker turned to the protesters and waved them over. "C'mon!" he called. "Let's get a group shot!"

As the protesters looked at each other, then wandered over, they were joined by a costumed Elmo, who had been harassing tourists for photos, as well as a woman dressed as the Statue of Liberty. Onlookers lined up next to Marty to snap their own photos of the unlikely throng of corporate executives, protesters, and costumed characters.

"This is *so* cool!" Walker said.

As the photo-taking ended, the cafeteria workers handed out sandwiches, some of which were accepted, and Ernesto turned to Walker. "I know what you're doing, man," he said. "You're trying to show everyone you're a nice guy, when in fact, you're destroying the environment."

Walker, distracted, looked away for a second. "Aw. Ernesto, is it? I wish your people wouldn't drop their sandwich wrappers on the sidewalk like that." Walker went over and chased a couple of stray wrappers blowing around on the ground. He picked them up and took them to a trash can, where Ernesto followed him.

Ernesto said, "I'm talkin' to you, man."

Walker turned and faced him. "I know. I hear you." He waved over a Staminum employee with the Sustainability Reports and handed one to Ernesto. Then he leaned in closer. "I recommend you read this, and then maybe we can talk sometime."

"I'm not impressed by your corporate bullshit, man," Ernesto said, holding up the report. "I'll never believe your lies."

Walker nodded. "Alright then. If you won't read it, please dispose of it responsibly and recycle it, okay?"

Ernesto stalked off as the protest fizzled and the activists junked their signs in garbage cans and headed for the subway. Walker watched them walk away and waved when one of them turned back for a moment. Marty and Maria joined him and waved, too, like a family bidding goodbye to relatives pulling out of the driveway.

Suddenly, Elmo accosted Marty, pulling him away by the arm.

Marty listened, then turned back to Walker, shaking his head. "He wants ten bucks."

Walker nodded. "That's alright. Give it to 'em."

I'm supposed to pay him? Not Mr. Fifty-Million-Dollar Man? Marty sighed, pulled a bill out of his wallet, and handed it over. Elmo then slid his arm around Marty, suggesting another photo. "Get the fuck outta here," Marty said, squirming out of his grasp.

42. OFF HIS NOODLE

D r. Stuart Littmann trudged up the stairs from the Times Square subway station, trying to shake the idea that somebody was following him. Perhaps it was his imagination getting the best of him. Since the rapid escalation of attacks against him on Twitter, glancing over his shoulder had become an unfortunate habit.

He emerged on 41st Street near Broadway, collected his breath, and walked east to Bryant Park. On an unseasonably warm late-winter morning, the first signs of outdoor life were reemerging, with people enjoying coffee at chairs and tables under leafless sycamores. He passed the main branch of the New York Public Library and crossed 42nd Street, and was struck again by the feeling he was being watched. Was he paranoid? He looked around and spotted a plain sedan with two men wearing sunglasses facing his direction. One of them was talking on a phone.

Walking hurriedly up Fifth Avenue, Stuart caught a reflection of Howie-Do-It in a store window, walking behind him. Panicked, Stuart began looking around for a cop. What would he say? *People are after me?* He'd sound like a nut. He picked up his pace, threading his way through a throng of people before making a left on 43rd Street, cutting through an office building to reach 44th Street, and dashing into his building, furiously pumping the elevator button while keeping an eye on the revolving door for possible pursuers. At last the elevator car arrived, and he entered alone and fell against the back wall, breathing hard. He exited on the nineteenth floor and entered his office, where he was met by Chanisse, who stood up behind the reception counter, alarmed by his evident distress.

"Dr. Stu, are you okay?"

"Yes," he said, leaning on the counter and closing his eyes. "I'm fine."

"You don't look fine."

Littmann sighed, opened his eyes again, and stood up straight. "I was followed."

Chanisse came around the counter and looked at him. "Oh no. Not that Mr. Doolin again."

"Him, yes. Maybe others. If he shows up here, I want you to call the police immediately."

"I certainly will," Chanisse said. "And if I have to, I'll take care of him myself."

He waved her off. "No, no. Please don't. I don't want you getting in trouble with these terrible people. They have lots of money and lots of time and they could destroy you. But I'll tell you one thing: after what I've been through, I've got nothing to lose. They're not going to intimidate me. My dear mother and father, bless their memory, survived the SS. I can survive Robbie Crowe and his henchmen."

Littmann went to his office and sat down at his desk and logged onto his computer to check on his shrunken stock holdings. Crowe Power had plunged another dollar-fifty since the market opened, costing Littmann another thirty thousand dollars. He pulled out his phone and called up his Twitter app. He wrote:

Stuart Littmann, DDS @$crewedByCrowe
I won't back down from @CrowePower goons!
They need to extract Robbie Crowe now! He is
like a bad cavity, causing shareholders great
pain & infecting the company with terrible
ideas. Root canal needed!

Stuart hit the button to post his tweet and sat back in his office chair. This would no doubt provoke Robbie Crowe further, but he didn't care. It was time to take a stand.

❊ ❊ ❊

Downtown at Crowe Power headquarters, Robbie Crowe was at his desk, staring at his phone and watching the spiraling number of retweets and likes of Dr. Littmann's post with growing alarm. How could anyone agree with that pathetic loser? Some of the other commentators were even meaner, calling Robbie a dilettante and a dabbler, thrust into an exalted position by virtue of his bloodline, despite being deeply unqualified and unsuited for the job. Every insult lashed his psyche, already haunted by the suspicion that he was only in this job because of some Crowe-mosomal fluke. Was he really that bad of a chairman? *No.* He *couldn't* be! They were all just jealous! Wait until all these whiny bastards realized that he was simply ahead of his time. Eventually, they would see the truth when he was celebrated in Dr. Kristi Kramer's book for both goodness *and* greatness. *When was that damn book coming out, anyway?*

He wheeled around in his chair to his desktop computer and tried to exorcise the social media drama from his fevered brain by preparing for his Fantasy Baseball draft. That was no help at all: there were way too many statistics to consider. He sighed and clicked on Outlook to check his calendar and found it was vacant as usual, except for the standard two-hour block for lunch. Maybe he should grab Digby and head over to Commie Coffee for a little break. Those people loved him now. Or maybe he could summon Natalia and talk about his courageous decision to continue funding Greeneron, even at the expense of the dividend. Wouldn't she be impressed?

He punched the button on his console. "Winnie. Send Natalia in, will you?"

"She's not in yet, Mr. Crowe. It's only eleven."

He angrily punched the button again. Was there no relief anywhere? Maybe he should pop in his earphones and stream a TV show on his phone. *What was that show about the thing with that guy?* He was going to look it up on his browser when he found himself reflexively clicking on Twitter again. Dr. Littmann's original tweet had been shared or liked three hundred times, and was spawning spinoff threads including #RobbieSucks and #CroweMustGo. Time to check on Howie's progress in shutting this guy down.

"Howie," Robbie said into his phone. "The asshole dentist is going viral. Where are you?"

"I'm at his office building, watching the entrance. We've got some other guys covering the back," Howie said, as he stood in a doorway across the street. Howie covered the phone and spoke quietly. "Tom from Corporate Security's nearby, so I've got to watch what I say."

"What's your plan if Littmann comes out?"

Howie sighed. "I dunno. Tom says we can't do anything."

"Nothing at all?"

"He says we can stare at him. Try to give him the heebie-jeebies."

"Oh, for crissakes. Fuck Tom! That's why I want you there. You outrank him."

"He's the head of company security."

"Yes. But you report to me."

Howie sighed. "What do you want me to do?"

"I want one of you guys to kick his ass. I really don't care who. I just want him stopped. Will somebody please get off their dead keister and help me? Jesus. What does it take?"

"I'm doing what I can for now. I'm watching the door. And Tom's watching me."

"Howie," Robbie said in a strained voice reeking of self-pity. "This man has humiliated me in front of the entire world. And nobody's going to do anything about it? I can't believe it."

"Robbie. If I kick his ass, that's a parole violation. I'm back at Rikers."

Robbie leaned back in his chair and slapped his forehead. "Alright. You know what? Fuck it. I'll handle it myself."

"How?"

"I'm coming up there."

"No, no. Boss, please. Don't do that. We'll take care of it, somehow."

"You're obviously *not* taking care of it. Once again, it's all on me."

Robbie hung up, jumped out of his chair, and headed for the door. He yapped at Winnie that Boris needed to bring the car around and pick him up on New Street. He grabbed the express elevator, stepped quickly through the corridor to the rear entrance, and climbed into his waiting Batmobile, which quickly reached the FDR and headed north. Robbie put his head back on the seat. At last, *somebody* was going to do *something* about this. And that somebody was him.

* * *

Dr. Stuart Littmann completed four examinations, filled three cavities, prepped two molars for crowns and performed one root canal before finally taking a break. He stripped off his mask and his blue rubber gloves, removed his white lab coat, washed his hands, and announced to Chanisse that he was going out to grab some lunch.

Chanisse rose from her seat looking mortified. "Dr. Littmann, are you sure you want to do that? What if those men are still following you?"

"What can they do to me?" he said. "How much more can they get? They've taken my money. Now my freedom, too? No. I can't let them dictate how I live my life. If I do, their victory is complete."

"But doctor—"

"Don't worry about it, Chanisse. Really. There should be some safety in crowds."

Not enough, Chanisse decided. Her brother had been beaten to death in broad daylight outside a Bronx bodega by the MS-13 gang while dozens of people stood by, hooting and cheering and recording videos. She couldn't let something like that happen to Dr. Littmann, who had treated her with nothing but patience and kindness, especially during her gender transition. She would stand by him as he had stood by her. As he left the office, Chanisse asked Emilia to cover the phones while she went out to keep an eye on things. Staying back a distance so that the doctor didn't see her, she followed him to his go-to lunch destination: the Great Chengdu Noodle Bowl on 45th Street. As Littmann took his place in line just inside the restaurant door, Chanisse spotted Howie-Do-It lurking nearby with another man, who had the clipped and cropped appearance of a cop. Two other men similarly-fashioned were ominously watching from a car across the street.

As Chanisse ducked into the shadows, a Cadillac Escalade came speeding down the street and slammed to a halt in front of the noodle shop. A driver jumped out and opened the rear door for a man who looked remarkably like Robbie Crowe.

Robbie, wearing sunglasses as a half-hearted effort at disguise, collected himself at the curb, adjusting his suitcoat and cuffs, as Howie joined him and pointed out the perpetrator inside the restaurant. Robbie nodded, then headed into the shop alone, while Howie and the security platoon waited outside, shuffling nervously.

Chanisse crossed the street and crept up to the storefront window, then slipped inside the door, where she saw Dr. Littmann carrying an orange plastic tray toward a communal table. Robbie eyed the dentist from the line before giving his order and stepping aside to wait for his food. Dr. Littmann, oblivious to the gathering threat, unwrapped his chopsticks and squirted a pouch of hot sauce on his Spicy & Tingly Noodles, then blindly scooted over a bit as someone tried to sit next to him. He glanced up briefly, then did a double take as Robbie took the seat beside him and put his own bowl on the wooden table.

"You got some kind of problem?" Robbie asked quietly.

Littmann gulped, struggling for air. "What do you want?"

Robbie continued to speak under his breath. "You're looking for trouble."

Littmann's fear suddenly turned to anger. "You know what? You're right. I do have a problem. *You* are my problem," he said. "You are destroying a perfectly good company and taking me down in the process."

Robbie seethed and twitched. "What right do you have to say anything about it to me, you insignificant little fuck? Who the *hell* are you?"

"I'm a shareholder in your company. Doesn't that count for something? What's the matter with you? You're supposed to be looking out for us."

Robbie tried to control his anger. "I don't answer to you."

"That's the problem. You don't answer to anybody. And you don't give a damn about who you hurt, either."

"I sure as hell don't care about you," Robbie said.

"Why are you following me?" Stuart demanded, his voice rising. "I want you to stop harassing me. Now!"

Robbie looked around, and noticed that, in typical New York fashion, nobody was paying attention. But he could contain himself no more. "Okay. I'll stop. Just remember this." Robbie turned his head away from Dr. Littmann but shot his elbow into his ribs, sending the dentist backward on his stool and knocking the wind out of him.

"Ooof!" Stuart wailed.

As other diners rose and pointed their cameras at the sudden fracas, Chanisse came swooping in behind Robbie, grabbed his head from behind, and slammed it into his bowl of Bang Bang Noodles. Chanisse pulled Robbie's head up by the hair and shoved it down again into the soup. Robbie yelped in pain as the red-brown pepper sauce flooded his eyes and nose. Suddenly, he was back at Harvard, getting a swirly at the Porcellian Club from the upperclassmen, the smell of Comet cleanser replaced by garlic and onion and chili. "What the *fuck!*" he cried, as he came up for air.

Chanisse ignored Robbie and checked on the dazed Dr. Littmann while Howie and the security team came rushing inside the restaurant. Robbie sat dazed on his stool, blindly grabbing for napkins to sponge the steaming sauce off his face and picking chives out of his ears.

Tom said, "I'm calling the cops."

"No! *Stop!*" Robbie commanded. "Just get me out of here."

Howie threw a coat over the chairman's head, lifted him from the stool, and guided him through the door to the Escalade. Boris came hobbling around the car from the driver's seat and opened the rear door. "Oh my gosh, boss! What happened?"

Howie shoved the chairman into the back, slammed the door, and told Boris, "Get him out of here, now. *Go!*" He slapped the back of the car and turned to see that half the restaurant had come to the curb to watch and record the activities. "Nothing to see here, folks," Howie said. "It's all over."

At that moment, Chanisse escorted Dr. Littmann out of the restaurant. Seeing the diners' cameras trained on him, the dentist paused to address the gathering. This, it appeared, was his moment. "My name is Dr. Stuart Littmann. I am a shareholder in the Crowe Power Company who has lost a fortune because of the poor leadership of chairman Robbie Crowe. Now, to add insult to injury, I was attacked today by Mr. Crowe himself. Why this man continues to have a job is a complete mystery to me. He should be fired. Thank you." As Chanisse pulled the doctor away from the crowd, the dentist turned back and waved to the cluster of people still holding their phones aloft. "I should also mention that we are running a special on whitening. Twenty percent off through the end of the month. Go to DocStu.com."

43. PLEADING INNOCENT

Winnie called Digby's mobile phone shortly after Robbie's return from the Great Chengdu Noodle Bowl showdown.

"Can you come over?" she asked somberly.

Digby looked to his team, assembled in the Lester conference room for their weekly meeting. "Can it wait?" he asked. "I'm in the middle of something."

"So's the boss," she responded. "You'd better come."

Digby excused himself and headed down the hall toward the chairman's suite. He entered the inner sanctum to find Winnie standing outside Robbie's bedroom at the rear of the office. The chairman emerged barefoot, wearing fresh suit pants and an open-collar shirt, his hair still damp from a shower. Robbie handed a pile of soiled clothing to Winnie. "I don't know if these can be saved," he said.

Winnie shook her head. "I'll do what I can."

Winnie departed and shut the door behind her, leaving Robbie alone with his general counsel. They circled one another, warily. Robbie said, "What?"

Digby moved in closer. "I'm afraid to ask," he said.

Robbie held up his index finger. "Before you start: it wasn't my fault."

"Of course not," Digby said. "It never is."

Robbie retreated into the bedroom to retrieve shoes and socks, returned to the sofa in the living room, and sat down on a footstool to put them on. "That motherfucker attacked me, right out of the blue. Completely unprovoked."

"Who?"

"That crazy dentist. Littmann."

Digby folded his arms across his chest. "He did, did he."

"Well. Not him, *exactly*. Someone who works for him."

"You didn't provoke him in any way."

"Of course not! What do you think I am?"

Digby flopped down into the club chair. "I've got a pretty good idea."

Robbie explained that he just so happened to be in Midtown when he decided to stop for lunch.

Digby nodded. "That sounds plausible. You're hungry. So you skip right past your usual haunts La Grenouille and Jean-Georges to go to the... what is it?"

"The Great Chengdu Noodle Bowl."

"Uh-huh. And you just randomly picked that out of nowhere."

Robbie snapped, "I heard good things about it, alright?"

Digby sighed. "Then what happened?"

Robbie continued in wide-eyed wonder. "Suddenly, this guy sitting next to me starts jabbering at me about our stock price. I try my best to ignore him, but he won't let up. He just keeps bitching about this and that and the other thing, saying I ruined the company. And then I realize: it's fucking Littmann!"

"How did you realize that? Was he wearing a name badge?"

"No. I just... you know, had a sense. He was saying a lot of the same crap he writes on Twitter."

"A lot of people are saying similar things on Twitter, but okay. You realized it was your nemesis, the abominable Littmann. Go on."

"So I just said very calmly—"

"I'm sure."

"I said, 'Excuse me, Dr. Littmann. I understand you're frustrated. But this is not the time or the place. Please just let me enjoy my lunch while you enjoy yours. I'd be happy to speak with you some other time and listen to your concerns.'"

"Uh-huh."

"So I'm just sitting there, listening to all this crap, when completely out of the blue, this gigantic person comes in, attacks me from behind and slams my face in the soup."

"And what did you do?"

"What could I do? I couldn't see. I couldn't breathe. I'm blinded by this spicy sauce in my eyes. Thank god Howie was around, and Tom and a few of his guys. They wiped me off and got me out of there and put me in the car."

Digby rubbed his chin. "And you were saved."

Robbie seethed. "You don't believe this, do you?"

"Of course not!" Digby said. "That's an absolutely ridiculous story."

"It's the truth!"

"No it isn't. You'd never stop for lunch at some random noodle shop without sending in a hazmat team first. You'd never sit at a common table; there are commoners there. You'd never just accidentally run into your most vociferous critic, sit there and listen to him chew you out, and then politely respond, 'I want to finish my lunch.' Nor is it even remotely possible that Howie, Tom, and his guys just so happened to be there."

"Yeah?" Robbie said, flushing red. "What do you think happened?"

"I *know* what happened. You were stalking the guy."

"Why would I do that?"

"Because you're obsessed with your critics, especially this guy. You wanted to shut him up. Intimidate him a little. Show him some muscle."

"Oh, *come on!* That is such bullshit."

Digby stood up. He was as angry as Robbie had ever seen him. "You might pull this Mr. Innocent crap with somebody else and they might even buy it. But I know you. And I know exactly how you'd end up in a situation like this. The good news is you're likely to get the benefit of a doubt."

"Why?"

"Because nobody is going to believe you're that stupid."

"You think?"

"A man with all your advantages in life? Of course you wouldn't risk it all to attack this poor schmuck who has no standing at all. That would be absolutely insane."

Robbie stood up and they walked toward the outer office. "Well here's the thing, counselor. Regardless of what you think you know, you have to fix it."

Digby fumed, but followed Robbie to the reception area, where Winnie held the telephone receiver in her hand. "Mr. Crowe, a producer from Fox is on the line. They'd like you to come on the air."

Robbie turned to Digby. "No way I do that, right?"

Digby took a deep breath and collected himself. "You may want to define the story before the dentist does."

"You think?"

"If there's one thing you know how to do better than anyone I've ever known, it's to sound sincere even when you don't believe a word you're saying. That alone gives you a fighting chance."

44. BOOK HIM

F acing a fast-approaching deadline for her manuscript, Dr. Kristi Kramer was in her office at the Mission Institute for Higher Corporate Purpose on Franklin Street in Chapel Hill transcribing video recordings of Robbie when a text from her agent popped up on her phone.

MANDY

Put on Fox Business.

Kristi grabbed the remote and found the channel. There, on the screen, was a slow-motion video taken by a patron of the Great Chengdu Noodle Bowl, featuring Robbie Crowe getting his head dunked in a bowl of noodles, with a crawl at the bottom of the screen: CROWE POWER CHAIRMAN ATTACKED, followed by BANG BANG TAKEOUT IN MIDTOWN.

As the video ended, the host said, "Crowe Power chairman Robbie Crowe was assaulted today in a noodle shop on 45th Street in Manhattan by Chanisse LaBelle, a receptionist at a dentist office in the area. LaBelle, known as Tyrone Bellingham when she starred in football at Fordham, told police she was defending her boss, Dr. Stuart Littmann." A headshot of Littmann displaying his gleaming white teeth appeared briefly on the screen. "We have Mr. Crowe joining us now from his headquarters on Broad Street to tell us about this bizarre incident. Robbie, what the heck happened out there today?"

Robbie, adopting his most innocent and wide-eyed expression, shook his head and chuckled. "Honestly, I have no idea. It was so strange. All I did was stop in this little shop for a bowl of noodles. I sat down with my lunch and this guy next to me starts jabbering away. I couldn't even understand what he was saying. Next thing I know, somebody else comes flying in from behind me and slams my head into the bowl of noodles. Weirdest thing I've ever experienced in my life." A new headline went up at the bottom of the screen: ENERGY KING KUNG POW'D.

"So," the host said, "you didn't initiate this confrontation?"

Robbie laughed as if that were the most ridiculous idea in the world. "Heavens no! I don't go around randomly picking fights with people. I've got enough to do watching over this company. The attack was completely unprovoked."

A co-host jumped into the questioning. "Robbie, we've learned that Dr. Littmann is a disgruntled shareholder of Crowe Power. He's been attacking you on Twitter for your company's poor stock performance. It's kind of an amazing coincidence that you ended up in the same restaurant at the same time."

Robbie shrugged. "Doesn't seem so unusual to me. I run into shareholders on a regular basis all over town. Some of them express opinions about the company that I may not like, but I always listen carefully. It's just part of the job. You have to be humble and more than a little thick-skinned. You can never take it personally. I know where the buck stops."

"The bucks have certainly stopped flowing through Crowe Power. You're showing losses for the first time in years."

Robbie dismissed the idea. "As you well know, that's no indication of where we're going as a company. Our future is very, very bright."

The anchor jumped back in. "Your stock shot up briefly this afternoon when early reports of the incident suggested you might have been incapacitated. That suggests some investors agree with Dr. Littmann."

Robbie flushed red but collected himself. "I'm sure there are always opportunists out there who prey on bad news. That reflects more poorly on them than it does on me. As my daughter says to me sometimes, 'haters gonna hate.' I don't pay any attention to them at all."

"Are you going to press charges?"

Robbie shook his head. "No. None of us needs the distraction of something like that. We're simply going to move ahead, guided by our company values, and keep building Crowe Power into the most responsible energy company in the world. That's our goal and we won't be satisfied until we get there."

"Yeah, well. You know, a profit might be nice, too. Thank you, Robbie Crowe. More on this story as it develops. In the meantime, CRO is down another two dollars this afternoon—"

Kristi's phone rang as the interview ended. It was Mandy. "This is the guy who's going to lead your book? I'm struggling to see the goodness or the greatness."

"It's a *journey*, Mandy," Kristi said. "And that's what makes it so interesting: the progression from dud to stud. We still have a ways to go, but I'm confident we're going to get there."

"Really? Have you checked Twitter? They're going nuts out there. It's torches and pitchforks for Robbie Crowe, except when they're ridiculing him. They have photos of him with hot sauce all over his face and a headline that says, 'assault with a deadly noodle.' They're billing this as the Great Noodle Bowl Smackdown and demanding a rematch at Katz's Deli, where they can duke it out with pastrami and matzo balls. Listen to these hashtags: #RobbiesLimpNoodle, #EatingCrowe, #CroweToGo."

Kristi rubbed her forehead. "Oh, lordy. That's not good."

"Not good? He's a joke. How do you expect anyone to take *Goodness Greatness* seriously? And you want to put him on the cover?"

Kristi sighed. "He screwed me."

"Not surprising."

"Mandy," she sighed. "What am I gonna do?"

"I don't know. Is there a way to turn this on its head?"

"To what?"

"What else have you got?"

Kristi slumped in her chair. "All I've got is a deadline staring me in the face. You know better than anybody that I tried dozens of CEOs and chairmen before I settled on Robbie Crowe. He wasn't exactly my first choice."

"No, but he's certainly well known, especially after this. For once, he actually seems relevant," Mandy said. "There has to be a way to exploit that. What about a tell-all?"

Kristi sat back in her chair, thinking. If she couldn't frame *Goodness Greatness* around Robbie Crowe, she didn't have a hook for her book. And if she didn't have a book, she would have to forfeit her advance. Robbie's stupid altercation threatened everything, including her future speaking engagements, her consulting fees, and the Mission Institute itself. That simply could not happen. She idly hit the button on her phone, continuing the video she had been transcribing. There was Robbie, in a bathrobe, leering at the camera. *"Do you want a spanking?"* Whoa! Now *there's* a thought. She said to Mandy, "He sexually harassed me."

"You're kidding."

"I have it on video."

"No!"

"He demanded sex in return for a contract."

"Tell *that* story!"

"Held up my deal until he got what he wanted."

"I'm getting *chills.*"

It wasn't her fault Robbie hadn't lived up to his end of the bargain in making a good company great. If he was going to get into stupid fights with shareholders, then he deserved a good public spanking himself. And she'd let him have it. She could go on TV right now and start banging the drum by beating his ass. The publisher might even bump up her advance. When life hands you lemons, why not squeeze out a little pulp?

Kristi snapped her fingers. "New title," she said. *"Power Down: How Good Companies Go Bad."*

"I *love* it!"

"Right?'

"Give me the story line."

"Well, let's see. It's like this: Crowe Power was doing just fine under Walker Hope. Then Robbie Crowe couldn't keep his mitts off it. So he drives out his rival, brings in a toady he can blame for any failures, and uses his position to extract sexual favors from poor people like me who depend on him for our business."

"To which you can personally attest!"

"Absolutely! Are we still believing all women?"

"I think we're down to 'most women' at this point. But it really doesn't matter. You only need to convince enough people to sell your book. I'm sure you can do that."

"In my sleep, girlfriend!"

"Whatever it takes."

"That's my motto!"

45. EATING CROWE

Moe Klinger scanned the menu at Del Frisco's Double Eagle Steakhouse with a mixture of amazement and longing. "Listen to these appetizers. Bacon au Poivre. Duck Confit Meatballs. Crabcake with Cajun Lobster Cream Sauce." He shook his head in wonder. "Lots of ways to firm up those flabby arteries."

Walker shrugged. "Have 'em all. It's on me today."

"No can do. My cholesterol's ticking higher than the NASDAQ. I'll get the sea bass. Hit me upside the head if I agree to a side of creamed corn." He slapped the menu shut. "So tell me. Are we ready to move on Crowe Power?"

"I am," Walker said, closing his own menu. "I think it's just a question of timin'." He rested his arms on the table in the cavernous main dining room next to the two-story picture windows on Sixth Avenue. What privacy wasn't granted by the hostess in seating them was afforded by the rapidly-advancing coronavirus. Government officials were still proclaiming that all was well, but Moe said he wasn't buying it, and neither were restaurant patrons, who were beginning to shy away from crowds.

"I think the time is drawing near," Moe said. He leaned closer and spoke in a near-whisper. "I talked to Senator Peabody yesterday. He sits in all the government briefings in Washington and he tells me this virus going around is gonna be a shitstorm. People in the know are dumping equities as fast as they can. I figure it's gonna whack hotels, theaters, and cruise lines like a goddamn tsunami. That means travel and tourism will take a beating."

"And that means prices for energy will fall hard."

"Right. Which makes this a buying opportunity."

A waiter came by for their orders. Moe stuck to his original intention and skipped the creamed corn, and Walker asked for a salad topped with grilled shrimp.

Moe continued. "CRO is already sinking like a stone, thanks to Robbie. As this bug takes hold, you know their stock's going to tank even more. I think we put in a bid at a small premium—say, twenty-five percent. It'll still be a bargain compared to where it was when you were running the show."

"You realize Robbie would lay down on the tracks to stop us."

"Yeah? From what I hear, even the Crowe family wouldn't tap the brakes. They'd run right over his sorry ass. A lot of these people are more broke than woke, and they're pissed at him for not helping them make some dough. They may not show it, but Crowe progeny have blown more fortunes than a prizefighter. They need the cash, even if it means selling their beloved candy store."

"Kind of sad, in a way."

"Are you kidding? It's a good thing. We're doing them a favor, putting them out of their misery," Moe said. "So tell me, now that you're settling in: would a combination of Staminum and Crowe Power make enough money to make it all worth our while?"

Walker grinned. "Absolutely."

"Tell me how."

Walker placed his left hand over his right and meshed his fingers together. "When you look at our footprint and theirs, it's a terrific fit. A Staminum-Crowe combination could cover ninety percent of our target markets. We'd be number one or two in almost every one. And where we weren't, we'd sell our properties or close 'em, and plow the money back into the best assets. I'd even place a bet on one or two of those Greeneron technologies."

Moe nodded. "I like it."

"There are a few redundancies, too, which is an opportunity to cut costs," Walker said. "I could see fifteen thousand jobs goin' away along with half the management, maybe more. I've already got my list of who needs to go."

"Starting with your old buddy Fred?"

"Hate to fire a guy twice, but yeah."

"What about Tim?"

"Only if Robbie doesn't fire him first."

"I hear that could happen any day now."

"Maybe the best thing about acquirin' Crowe Power," Walker said, "is that taking them out allows us to raise prices and improve margins. All in all, it's a combo that can't miss."

"Except with the Justice Department. They might see it as a violation of antitrust." Moe broke off a piece of bread with sesame seeds, glanced at the butter, and sighed. "All the more reason to move on this while we have a friendly administration."

"Will Steady support us?"

Moe snorted. "Are you kidding me? He'll do anything we ask. I haven't seen him since your surgical removal of his nuts over that Greeneron business left him whimpering in his suite. I think he's hanging out in countries that don't have extradition treaties with the United States, just in case you decide to blow the whistle."

"What about the board? Where do you think they land?"

Moe gave into the butter and spread a thimble of it on his bread. "We'll let 'em think they'll get seats on the new board. They always roll over and play dead when they expect treats."

Walker said, "So what's our next move?"

"Let this coronavirus bug hit the windshield. A lot of investors won't be able to see straight. That'll drop the price a bit more. Then we wait for CRO to hit bottom. Maybe we'll get lucky and Robbie will do something else that's colossally stupid, like that noodle shop brawl. Can you believe that idiot?" Moe shook his head. "If there's a rematch, I've got my money on the dentist." He made a karate chop motion with his right hand. "Take that." He roared with laughter.

"Hey Moe," a voice said. They looked around to see David Mandelbaum, a young private equity trader, passing by their table. After a few pleasantries, David asked, "You see the latest on Robbie Crowe?"

"Don't tell me he fucked up again," Moe said, dabbing his mouth with the linen napkin.

"He's having his #MeToo moment. Dr. Kristi Kramer. Know who she is?"

"Vaguely. Some kind of business guru?"

"That's it. And pretty hot, actually. She's saying he forced himself on her in exchange for a contract."

"I hope she got a good deal."

"Three million for a consulting gig."

Moe scoffed. "Jesus. That guy overpays for everything, including ass."

"He's not much of a corporate chairman, but he's a terrific entertainer," David said. "CRO's down another five percent. You dumped it at the right time."

"Trust me," Moe said, "I sold high."

"You always do."

David moved on, leaving Moe and Walker to their lunch, and their plan.

Moe said, "The time is now."

46. TABLOID FODDER

A ttempting to sleep was futile. Sooner or later, Robbie knew that he'd have to get up and face the day's new horrors.

After Dr. Kristi Kramer issued a statement through her agent alleging he had extorted sex from her, the media had been hounding him for a response, with paparazzi lurking outside his hotel and his office. Digby offered a categorical denial on Robbie's behalf, but why would anyone believe him? Robbie had already exhausted his credibility on the noodle fiasco. Now, as a man of extreme privilege, he was presumed guilty until proven innocent. Equally troubling, Robbie suspected more allegations could be forthcoming as other women emerged from the woodwork of his bedroom. Non-disclosure agreements provided little protection in this environment, with #MeToo activists clamoring to release all allegations against accused predators.

Robbie stared at the ceiling, considering his dwindling options. He could lay in bed all day and hope everything would just go away—an unlikely outcome. He could change his appearance in some way so that no one would recognize him on the street. If he stopped coloring his hair, how long would it take to grow out in white or gray? Groucho glasses wouldn't look very realistic, but what if he grew a beard like David Letterman? It worked for him for a while. How long would that take? Months? Years? Or... maybe there was a way to launch a counter-offensive. He could ask Digby to sue Dr. Kristi Kramer for defamation. *Yeah!* And maybe send Howie out to beat up people who sided with her. There would be blood all over town and, and... Ah, *shit.* That was a terrible idea, too.

He roused himself from bed and wandered into the living room, where his breakfast awaited on the dining room table, with the day's newspapers next to his coffee service. He picked up the *New York Times* and scanned the front page, which carried a slew of analyses and memos gravely asserting that the president was worse yesterday than he'd been the day before and that experts and insiders believed he would be even more terrible tomorrow. Mercifully, there was no mention of Robbie or Dr. Kristi Kramer until the Business page, where it merited a brief story. The tabloid *New York Post*, however, was another matter: a photo of Kristi, at her sultry best in a plunging neckline, alongside a separate photo of a cowering Robbie, shielding his face from photographers as he entered Crowe Power headquarters. The headline slapped the chairman harder than Kristi ever did:

HANKY SPANKY
- **Big Whack Attack at Crowe Power**
- **Randy Robbie a hit with the ladies**
- **Limp Noodle Boy stiffs reporters: "No comment."**

Robbie buried his head in his hands. What an embarrassment. He could never go out on the street again. Ever! And it was all such *bullshit!* Why were his press people so dead on their ass? What was the PR lady, Yvonne what's-her-face, doing about this? And where the hell was Digby? He was supposed to be here an hour ago. If Digs weren't his brother-in-law, Robbie would fire his ass right now. He had no one to talk to but Winnie, his ever-loyal executive assistant. He dialed her number and—*hallelujah!*—she answered. He'd never been so happy to hear her voice.

"Winnie! Hey!"

"Good morning, Mr. Crowe."

Hmm. Was she a bit more distant today? Or is that the way she always was? He couldn't tell, since he'd never paid attention until now. "Just checking in," he said, innocently. "Anything going on?"

"Oh, yes," she said. "Yvonne's been trying to get in touch with you. She's getting lots of calls from reporters and TV producers. She said CNBC asked if you wanted equal time after Dr. Kristi Kramer goes on the air today."

"She's going on TV?"

"That's what they said."

"Well, that's a 'no,' obviously. I can't go on there again," Robbie said. "Have you seen any of the, uh, coverage so far? I hear there's a lot of nonsense in the papers today."

"Honestly, Mr. Crowe, I haven't had a chance. Phone's been ringing off the hook. And even if I had the time, I wouldn't pay any attention."

"You wouldn't?"

"Trashy gossip like that. No, thank you. I don't think it's right."

Atta girl! Stout, steadfast Winnie! God bless her! She was still with him. At least somebody out there was. He made a mental note to give her a raise at some point. No rush, of course. "I appreciate that, Winnie."

"We're behind you, Mr. Crowe."

Robbie felt his eyes welling, awash in gratitude for her and sympathy for himself. "Thank you so much. You have no idea how much that means to me."

Fortified by Winnie's support, Robbie summoned enough courage to turn on CNBC, and quickly wished he hadn't. "CRO stocks plummeting again this morning on more tumult at the top of Crowe Power," said host Joe Kernen. "Just a week ago, Chairman Robbie Crowe was caught up in a fracas at a Midtown noodle shop. Now come bombshell allegations from noted author and consultant Dr. Kristi Kramer that Mr. Crowe sexually harassed her. She joins us now from her office at the Mission Institute for Higher Corporate Purpose in Chapel Hill, North Carolina. Good morning, Dr. Kramer."

Kristi sighed and shook her head gravely. "I've had better mornings, Joe."

"Apparently. We saw the video of Robbie Crowe in a bathrobe threatening somebody—we assume that was you—with a spanking. What the heck was going on there?"

"Well, as you know, Joe, I've been an adviser to top executives around the world for more than a decade. In very typical fashion, I met with Robbie Crowe to discuss ways in which I might help him achieve his vision for Crowe Power. Sounds simple enough, right? Well, that vision turned out to be a nightmare. At least for me."

"How so?"

"First of all, he insisted we discuss an arrangement in his hotel suite. I should have known right then and there that something untoward was afoot. Then, when we get to his room, he said he wanted to change his clothes. Much to my surprise—*horror,* actually—he comes out in a bathrobe. And he insists that sex was a pre-condition for any kind of agreement with him and his company. And, as you saw on the video, he threatened violence if I didn't comply."

"A spanking."

"Sadism!"

"Okay, let's run that segment."

There on the screen was Robbie Crowe, frowning. *"Do you want a spanking?"*

The host continued. "That could be interpreted a couple of ways, Dr. Kramer. You sure that wasn't just playing around?"

"I don't know what kind of 'playing around' you might do, sir, but that was hardly fun and games to me."

"Did you tell him no?"

"Of *course,* I did. But here's the thing, Joe. He's a billionaire businessman, an heir to a colossal fortune. Money means nothing to him. It means a whole lot to me. I'm just an independent business owner, doing what I can to make a living. I'm not complaining, mind you—I've done extremely well with my best-selling books and my high-level consulting—but I'm not in his league. Clearly, he was at an advantage in our negotiations. He knew it and he used it against me. It was like the ol' Hollywood producer's couch. You don't get the part unless you play along."

"And you did."

"I'm ashamed to say so but yes, I did, and I regret it. And I don't want what happened to me to happen to other women, especially my daughters. What kind of world do we want them to grow up in? That's why I'm going public with this, painful as it is. People—and I mean everyone: men, women and in between—should not be treated like toys. We've got to stop allowing sex to be a trading currency in business. That's why I'm dedicating a new seminar at my Mission Institute for Higher Corporate Purpose to help women deal with sexual extortion like this. I'm also going to make it the subject of my next book: *Power Down: How Good Companies Go Bad,* which is now available for pre-order on Amazon."

"Okay. Thank you, Dr. Kramer." He turned away from the screen and back to the camera. "We've put in calls to Crowe Power for comment but have not been able to get a response yet." He turned to his co-host. "Maybe Robbie Crowe's still laying in bed having a cigarette. What do you think?" He turned back to the screen. "Coming up: Senator Peabody says the coronavirus is absolutely nothing to worry about. It's like the common cold, he says. We'll hear from him after this—"

Robbie clicked off the TV and fell back on the couch. They were gleefully ridiculing him! Was anyone going to defend him? He called Winnie and asked to be put through to Yvonne, his new head of communications. She answered after one ring and Robbie jumped hard. "Yvonne? What the hell are you doing about this?"

"Robbie. Hello. So glad you called. I've been trying to reach you all morning."

"You apparently aren't trying very hard."

"I'm so sorry, but you weren't in the office and Winnie wouldn't give me your number. It appears I'm blocked."

"So you just gave up? C'mon. You're a senior executive at this company. I hope you're more creative than that."

Pause. "Understood."

"Alright. I want you to get in touch with everybody running this story and tell every one of them that it's bullshit, okay? A complete fabrication. This is not what happened."

"I've been working on a statement, Robbie, but I'm missing some critical information. Do you mind me asking: what *did* happen, exactly? Reporters want to know."

Robbie rubbed his temples. Was this really necessary? He had to relive this nightmare?

"Fuck them," he said. 'We don't owe them any explanation at all."

Another pause. "With all due respect, Robbie, it's not about the reporters. It's about you and your reputation. If this story is wrong, please help me knock it down. I want to defend you. I need some ammo."

A rap on the door. "Hold on," he said. He put his phone on mute and walked to the foyer, looked through the peephole and saw a very solemn-looking Digby. "Digs," he said, motioning for him to come in. "Where have you been, man? We've got a hell of a situation here."

Digby winced. "I stopped to watch the coverage in the lobby."

"Oh, Christ. They're showing it here?"

"It's everywhere, bro. TV. Radio. The marquee in Times Square."

"*No...*"

"You're the story of the day."

"Oh, for crissakes. I don't know why somebody can't put a stop to this. I've got the new communications lady on the line. She's apparently as useless as Marty was. Doesn't anybody know how to do their job around here?" Digby followed Robbie back to the dining table. "Yvonne. I've got you on speakerphone with Digby. Read the statement you have so far."

"Okay. 'Crowe Power Company Chairman L. Robertson Crowe III vigorously denies the allegations made by Dr. Kristi Kramer. The charges are baseless and completely without merit.'"

Robbie shook his head in disbelief. "That's it? That's all you're going to say? You know she's not even a real doctor. She's got some bullshit degree she gave herself. We need to go after her. Hard."

Digby mouthed the words: *Call her back.*

"Yvonne. Hey, listen. Just stand by. We'll get back to you."

Robbie hung up and collapsed in his chair.

Digby leaned forward, trying to get Robbie's fullest attention. Was he listening? "We're not going to attack her."

Robbie raised his chin, defiantly. "No?"

"Did you not learn from the noodle shop? You can't keep attacking your critics. You don't have the resources. And, frankly, you don't have the skill. You sound like a whimpering rich boy, which you are."

"You realize this charge is all bullshit, right? *She's* the one who used sex to get a contract from *me*."

Digby shook his head. "Do you think for a minute that's an argument you can win?"

"Why not? It's the truth."

"You want to debate the particulars of this in public? 'I didn't want to spank her to hurt her. I just wanted to make her squeal a little bit?' That's nuts. Bottom line is you'll be perceived as the powerful one. You had an advantage."

"She had me pinned down! She was whacking the shit out of me with her tits!"

"I really don't want to hear it. Neither does the rest of the world."

Robbie blew out his cheeks and stood up. "Do I survive this?

"In what sense?"

"Do I keep my job?"

"You have a bigger challenge than Dr. Kristi Kramer."

"How so?"

"I just got a courtesy call from the general counsel at Staminum Energy. Maria Territo. Remember her?'

"What about her?"

"They're making a bid to buy our company."

Robbie slumped. "There's no fucking way."

"You think?"

"I can block a sale."

"You have ten percent of the family's votes. You don't have fifty-one."

"Oh, c'mon," he scoffed. "They always side with me."

"We'll find out soon enough if they still do. Uncle Chuck has called for an emergency family meeting."

47. A MURDER OF CROWES

Robbie slouched on a green velvet loveseat in the living room of a Turret Penthouse on the top floor of the Beekman Hotel in New York's Financial District, nervously sipping from a plastic bottle of water and privately bemoaning his predicament.

Downstairs, in a private room, his family was gathering for an emergency meeting and, for all he knew, planning a funeral. The view outside his windows offered a spectacular view of the Brooklyn Bridge, but it held no charm for Robbie. He was concerned about the imminent "Murder of Crowes," as Uncle Chuck tagged their family gatherings. Today, it was possible that an execution might actually occur. His company could die.

As Digby entered the room, Robbie declared, "I'm not going down there."

Digby responded nonchalantly. "No?"

"After all this crap in the media, they must hate me."

Digby nodded thoughtfully. "You may have a point."

Robbie popped his head up and glared at Digby. "So you agree. You think this is all my fault."

Digby, wearing a tweed sportscoat, gray flannel slacks, and an open-collar shirt for the family meeting, sat down in a leather lounge chair next to a stone fireplace and hunched forward. "I'm the company's lawyer, Robbie. As far as I'm concerned, it's never your fault. But that doesn't mean they think that. A few of your cousins might need convincing."

"About what?"

"That we should keep the company and that you should still run it."

"Oh." His eyes flashed. "Really?"

"Would you prefer that I tell you only what you want to hear? Or should I say what they're really talking about out there?" He shrugged. "It doesn't matter to me. I get paid either way."

Robbie regarded Digby with an accusing look. "Here's the problem, Digs. You're getting way too much enjoyment out of this. Why don't you stop looking down at me from your high fucking horse? I don't need a lecture. I need support."

Robbie was right: Digby couldn't help but enjoy watching Robbie squirm. Still, he protested. "I'm not sure what else I can do. I've prepared all the materials for the family to review. I've laid out the key message points for you, the answers to expected questions, and the recommendation that you wanted. At this point, Robbie, it's up to you. Should they cash in their chips or not? Make your case."

Robbie leaned forward, rested his elbows on his knees, and furiously massaged his forehead with the fingertips of his right hand, as if he were rubbing out a stubborn spot. "It's outrageous it has even come to this. Why is this on me? It's like nobody who ran this company before me had anything to do with these problems. I inherited one hugely fucked-up business, you know. I come in and try to modernize it and what do I get? Nothing but *crap.* From them. From you. The board. Everybody." He looked up and stared at his brother-in-law. "You know what? Fuck it. Maybe I should just toss the keys to that hillbilly and say, 'All yours. Good luck with my idiot family.' Fucking Crowe-mosomes! I gave them everything I could and this is how they treat me. They blow."

Digby had participated in this ritual so many times that he knew its arc by heart. Robbie had to first scrape the emotional bottom and marinate in the juices of self-pity before he could rise to the occasion. Digby's job was to hold his hand through the darkness and eventually pull him out. "Let's not concede just yet," Digby said. "We haven't even voted."

"Oh, don't give me that. I know these people better than you. I've lived with them my entire life. They like the prestige and the money and that's all they care about. Nobody wants to do any hard thinking or, God forbid, some actual work. They see Walker Hope coming along with his bags of cash and they drop their knickers just like that." He snapped his fingers. "I should have had Howie shoot that bastard back when he offered to do it. *Shit.* It makes me sick."

Digby pushed himself up. "Don't be so sure it's over. The attendance is very good, so clearly there's interest. Aunt Lizzie is here from Boca. Jack Dilworth from

Maine. Trip's here. Topher. Every one of your cousins, except Achala. We couldn't reach him in Tibet. Apparently, he's walking the Kora."

Robbie shook his head sadly. "A hundred years of family ownership down the drain," he said, choking back a tear. "I can't believe it's come to this."

"It hasn't yet. And if you hold the family together, it won't. But, damn it, man, you need to get a grip."

Robbie looked up in shock. "Digby. Did you just swear?"

Digby blushed. "Sort of."

Every bone in Robbie's body seemed to creak and yaw as he rose slowly from his chair, buttoned his navy-blue blazer, took a deep breath, and left the penthouse for the main event. He and Digby took the elevator to the Kelly Room in the 1883 hotel's cellar and emerged into the elegant catacomb, where spotlights illuminated the aged brick walls and modern chandeliers dangled down between tubes and pipes and rebar. With Digby at his side, Robbie was quickly immersed in the swirl of aunts and uncles and cousins and nieces and nephews, who were attended by a battalion of white coated servers with platters of hors d'oeuvres and trays of champagne. They had come from across the country and, in some cases, the world, for the most significant family gathering since Homer Crowe died in 1955. Robbie worked his way through the crowd with ready smiles, handshakes, and flattering comments, offering friendly greetings to everyone he met and promising to get together sometime.

As he exchanged air kisses with the ancient Aunt Lizzie and gave a clap on the back to the ne'er-do-well Trip, Robbie's anxiety morphed into a strange sense of relief that the long-anticipated battle with Walker Hope over control of his company was now here. There were no more worries about when the attack would come or how it would be prosecuted; the details were explicitly documented in a filing with the SEC and the Crowe Power Company board of directors. The only question was how the family would respond to his pitch. Did they still care about having control of their historic company? Did they want to fight for the right to another hundred years? Did they care about Robbie's green agenda? Or did they want to move on, take what they could get, and focus on tending to their wineries, galleries, foundations, investment funds, homes, boats, planes, movies, and medical marijuana operations?

Despite his charm offensive, Robbie sensed the reception was decidedly cooler than it had been at the family gathering the past spring, when shares were rising and money was flowing. Were they keeping their distance because of growing concern over the coronavirus that was suddenly in the news, or was it him? How much, he wondered, had his messy publicity around the noodle shop and harassment charges made social distancing a convenient excuse to avoid getting too close? Hard to believe any of those issues would be a major concern in this family, given the sordid histories of other company leaders—ones that everyone in this room knew too well.

Homer Crowe had cultivated a public image of a simple, God-fearing, up-by-his-bootstraps engineering genius and family man, but he built a mansion for his mistress upstream on the Hudson River from his own estate, worked closely with the mob to keep unions out of his plants, hired party buses for his all-male management teams to go on outings to whorehouses in Jersey City, and bribed numerous public officials to secure government contracts. His obituary from the wire services characterized him simply as an industrial pioneer and philanthropist. Homer's son Lester operated his own secret police who spied on company executives, bullied critics, organized heavily-armed militia to guard plants and pipelines, and extorted favorable supply contracts from vendors. By virtue of the record profits and global expansion under his command, Lester was widely commended as the rightful successor to Homer's august throne. And Robbie's own father, Les, was known inside the family for his serial philandering, including an affair with Robbie's nanny, Brielle, and long stays at Hazeldon. His public reputation was neatly sanitized in his later years by building wings on libraries, endowing chairs at universities dedicated to high-minded research, and providing hospitals in third world countries. By comparison, Robbie's deviance wasn't in the activities themselves; it's that he had been caught.

Stepping onto a podium with Digby, Robbie noted that Lindsey was working the room, chatting amiably and shaking hands. *What the hell is that about?* Robbie liked the clear-eyed Lindsey even less than he liked the bloodshot, bleary, and bloated version. At least a drunken Lindsey never wanted to engage in the family business.

Uncle Chuck, wheezing from his lifelong cigarette habit, labored as he climbed onto the dais and looked around the room. At the sight of him, the family began gathering at the tables and taking their seats. Robbie approached Chuck cautiously. "What's your read on the vote?"

Chuck put his hand on Robbie's shoulder, partly to steady himself. "Ask me after you make your spiel. Not to put too much pressure on the moment, but when all is said and done, this is pretty much a referendum on you." As Robbie sagged, Chuck said, "Want me to kickstart this party?"

Robbie nodded, and Uncle Chuck walked to the front of the platform, where a lectern had been placed. "Good afternoon," he said, to a babble of greetings back. "I want to welcome you all to this special meeting of our family. Before I turn things over to Digby for the business at hand, I'd like to offer a couple of comments." Chuck took a deep breath as he considered the moment, and his voice quavered slightly. "First of all, I want to say once again what a distinct privilege it has been to be a part of such a great company. It is not an overstatement to say that Crowe Power has played an essential role in the development of our country and of our world. People often take for granted the energy that powers their lives. They flip a switch or turn a key and think nothing of where it all comes from or how it was generated, or all the people who made it happen. Well, I tell you what: Crowes—the people in this room and the people who came before us—made it happen."

The family members set down their drinks and finger foods to applaud, and Chuck continued. "Secondly, as you know, everything we've done as a family over the years has been geared toward maintaining our company's continued independence. Other shareholders come and go, but we have been steadfast. Crowe Power is more than a company to us. It's our heritage. It's our identity. It supports how we live, and how our children and their children live. Now, we're at a crossroads in our long family journey. Is Crowe Power as it's presently constituted the right vehicle to sustain our family for generations to come? Or do we take the opportunity that's been presented to us to change course? That's the question before all of you this afternoon."

Chuck cast a sideling glance to Robbie, who was rocking back and forth on his feet, lost in his own thoughts of what he intended to say. "Before I turn this over to Digby, I would be remiss if I did not express my personal gratitude to Robbie," Chuck said. He looked over to Robbie, who showed surprise at this generosity.

Chuck continued, "Robbie stepped in as chairman five years ago to keep our family's guiding hand on the tiller and lead it through significant change. As I witnessed first-hand with my uncle and my brother, it's an extremely difficult assignment to be placed into the top job with so many expectations from so many people: our family, our employees, investors. Robbie has operated in a spotlight that can be very harsh and unforgiving. But I have no doubt that he has done his best to act on behalf of the interests of our family, which is all we can reasonably ask. So to Robbie, I say: thank you." Chuck stepped away from the lectern and applauded as the family members rose to their feet, clapping dutifully, if not enthusiastically.

Robbie didn't know how to take that. Was this Uncle Chuck's way of saying it was over? He grimly stepped forward and acknowledged their salute with a nod, a tight smile and a wave. "Thank you," he said.

Digby stepped up to the lectern to detail the offer from Staminum Energy. Should they accept the bid, the family would receive cash payments as well as common shares in Staminum in return for all of Crowe Power's assets around the world, from the headquarters in Manhattan to the pipelines in Peru. Crowe designees would obtain five seats on Staminum's fourteen-member board of directors—enough to annoy, but not govern—and Robbie would become vice-chairman, which everyone recognized was a face-saving but meaningless position that would phase out within a couple of years.

"While all of our company's shareholders will be entitled to a vote on the offer," Digby said, "the decision is in your hands. Our family bloc is enough to swing the outcome in either direction." He explained that if the Crowes did not come to an agreement by acclamation this afternoon that a formal vote would be held, and that the majority view would determine the family's position. He turned behind him, where Robbie was continuing to fidget. "With that, I'd like to turn the meeting over to our chairman."

Robbie stepped tentatively to the front of the dais, unnerved by the sudden dead silence. Not a chair moved. Not a plate clattered. Not a glass clinked. One hundred and forty eyeballs —one hundred and thirty-nine, if you considered Uncle Dink, who lost one in a fly-fishing accident—were trained on him. It was one thing to speak to employees or common shareholders or analysts he didn't know. It was quite another to address his social peers, who had as much claim to this line of American nobility as he did.

He struggled to control his emotions as he began, his eyes downcast. "I never wanted this job," he said, quietly. "I took it out of an overwhelming sense of responsibility to you to watch over our family's interests and protect our name. Somebody in my generation had to, and, well, I felt it was my duty.

"Like each of you, from the time I was a small child, I have been defined by our company and its history. People would meet me and say, 'Oh. You're a *Crowe* Crowe.' That meant something to them, and I was never sure what. Did they think I was rich? Spoiled? Connected? Smart? Or, in the word of our times, privileged? To varying degrees, all of us in this room are probably at least a little bit of all of those things."

His voice picked up as he warmed to the topic. "Here's what I wanted them to think. That Crowes are *responsible*. That we care about our planet. That we're not in it just for ourselves, but for our world. Maybe that sounds a little airy-fairy, and maybe it is. But I felt strongly that we had to try to change perceptions about who we are. The world in which Homer Crowe operated is long gone. He could generate energy and throw the waste in the nearest river or bury it in a field. Nobody particularly cared. They care now. So do I. And, I know, so do you."

He walked across the dais, thinking. He had bared this much. He may as well go all the way. "Have things turned out the way I hoped? No. I'll be the first to admit it. We had a good run there for a few years, but I knew in my heart that it could not be sustained. We were living off our past glories, squeezing the last bit of efficiency and profit out of our aging legacy assets. We weren't doing nearly enough to compete in the coming age, and to get ahead of all the opposition that was coming our way. We needed imagination. A willingness to take a risk or two. And we needed change—big, serious change. That's why I bought Greeneron. It's not all going to work, but somewhere in that incredible portfolio are the seeds of technologies that will grow our company for the next hundred years. Can I prove it? No. But I firmly believe it.

"And now, because we're in a period of transition from the old Crowe to the new, there are people out there like Walker Hope who want to take advantage of our momentary vulnerability. They see that our stock is down and they pounce. I get it; that's capitalism. The same system that allowed us to flourish might also kill us. I've heard a few of the commentators on television cheer for this. 'Creative destruction,' they call it. 'Survival of the fittest.' 'Dog-eat-dog.' Well, it doesn't have to be that way. Not if you think the name Crowe still means something."

He walked to the front of the podium and his voice rose, his face flushed. "I oppose the sale of our company with every fiber of my being. We did not come this far for this long to simply surrender when an offer to sell comes along. Crowe Power is not just a company. As Uncle Chuck said: it's who we are. And while we haven't always been happy about the associations that have come along with that, we are making tremendous progress in finding new technologies that will define the future for our company, and our country, and the world. I truly believe we are on the precipice of a new era for Crowe Power that will be better than anything in our storied past."

Robbie went back to a table to retrieve his water bottle. He sipped, put it down, then turned back to his family and resumed. "I've heard some people say that this offer is an embarrassment, a sign that we can't manage our company any longer." He paused and looked out over the assembly. "I don't see it that way at all. To me, this offer is a testament to our worth. Let the critics call us 'Crowe-mosomes.' The hell with them! We have built a grand and great company, and we should be proud of our place in history. This family—*our* family—built a worldwide enterprise of enduring value. The bid from Staminum isn't a repudiation. *It is a validation!* Now the question is: who should reap the reward? The Stamper family? Walker Hope? Or us?"

The applause seemed genuine, Robbie thought, but it was brief.

"Now," he continued, "I will be the first to admit: I've had a rough couple of weeks. It's been no fun to be the focus of such awful publicity. I will also admit: I have my weaknesses. I'm only human. But let me assure you: while there is a lot more to these stories than what's reported out there, it would be even more damaging for me and for the company to respond tit-for-tat to every ridiculous allegation. I believe it's all generated by people who'd like to see our company damaged so that they can take advantage. And while I accept that this sort of nonsense goes with the territory, I encourage you to consider the sources. We can't be fooled by the hecklers and the critics, or let them guide our judgment on the future of our business.

"Let me also acknowledge that our company has just had a very tough quarter. But let's be clear: We expected that. We did not acquire Greeneron with the idea it would become a cash cow overnight. It takes time and investment and a bit of sacrifice. With patience, I have absolutely no doubt it will provide fabulous returns to our family, in terms of income as well as our reputation. It will also— and I firmly believe this—help Crowe Power have as much impact on the century ahead of us as we did on the century prior. So please. Bear with me and stay the course and you will be rewarded. Say 'no' to those who want us to check out and end our family's incredible run. I promise you: the best days for our great company are still ahead."

Robbie walked off to the side and grabbed his water bottle as everyone in the room rose to their feet and clapped. Robbie turned back and waved to them as Digby approached and talked to him quietly.

"Great job," Digby said.

For once, Robbie valued Digby's opinion. "I did okay?"

"You did."

"Really?"

"*Yes*. Jesus."

Robbie exhaled. "Did I sway them?"

"That, I don't know."

Digby walked to the lectern and glanced at his watch. "Before we call for a vote, we have time for your comments and questions. If you have something you'd like to say, please just raise your hand."

Jack Dillworth, Robbie's fortyish cousin who ran a money-losing bed-and-breakfast in Camden, Maine, held his hand aloft. Digby nodded to him. "Jack, I think you're up first."

Jack stood up at his table. A regular at these gatherings, he wore the ragg wool sweater, slacks, and rubbery shoes that made him look like a paid spokesmodel for L.L. Bean. "Thanks, Digby. Helluva speech there, Robbie. Really good comments. Helps me appreciate where you're coming from." He cleared his throat. "You know, I think all of us in this family like to see ourselves as different from the unwashed masses out there, but I've realized for a long time that we're like everyone else. Like you said, we've all got our flaws. That includes me." He looked down at his twenty-one-year-old girlfriend, whose long tresses covered her face like Cousin It. "Right, honey?" She nodded back, possibly smiling under there. "She knows. Anyway, I can overlook a lot as far as behavior goes. My problem is this: while all of our company leaders in the past generated some bad publicity from time to time, none of them ever eliminated the dividend. That, to me, is what hurts more than any of those crazy stories in the papers. Based on what I'm hearing from people today, we could all use the money."

Family members looked to each other and whispered. *Uh... yeah!* Jack had struck a nerve, and Robbie sensed it. "Believe me," Robbie said, stepping toward the front of the stage. "Suspending the dividend was the last thing in the world I wanted to do. I know how difficult that is for you all. But when we made the difficult decision to transition our company from old energy to new, we knew it would come at a cost. I had cut everything else I could, even my salary, which I voluntarily took down to zero. There was really no other option. But I promise you: It's temporary. We will get it back."

Jack remained standing. "Do you know when?"

Robbie blew out his cheeks. "I wish I could say," he said. "It might be a year, or two years, or... more. I just don't know. Obviously, we'll do it as soon as possible." He paused and looked around the room, which suddenly felt a lot smaller.

As Jack sat down, Digby called on Topher Crowe, a sixth-generation millennial running a marijuana concession in Massachusetts. Wearing a wooly beard worthy of a Barbary pirate and a manbun the size of a baseball, Topher was too mellow of a dude to stand. He remained casually slouched in his seat as he spoke. "Uncle Robbie, I really appreciate how hard it is to run a business. Like you, I run one, too. Mine's just a little smaller." He laughed and cocked his head. "What I don't get is how we went from record profits to these *huge* losses in such a short amount of time. It was kind of a shock to all of us. I mean, I read about it and went, *Whoa!* When do you think the company starts making money again?"

There was a low murmur in the crowd. "You see, Topher, it's like the dividend," Robbie said. "It's impossible to predict exactly." Robbie could see the Crowe-mosomes growing restive. Maybe he should try his new theory on them. "You know, Topher, there's actually some very, very *good* news about these losses that I think few people appreciate."

"That's cool. Like what?"

"You see," Robbie said, "at some point in the future, when we start making money again, the year-to-year comparisons will look fantastic. They'll say, 'Wow. Crowe earnings are *way* up over the prior year.' That will generate some serious buzz around our business. I mean, not like the kind of buzz in your business. But still. It will be very good for our share price, our dividend, everything."

Topher tried hard to comprehend. "So, you're saying, like, the more we suck right now, the better we'll look... eventually?"

Robbie nodded. "Exactly."

Topher scratched his head. "Did you, like, plan it that way?"

"No, but you see how it could work out, right?"

Topher shrugged. *Not really.* "Never heard that one before, Uncle Robbie. But, okay. I guess it's like banging your head against the wall. It feels good when it stops." He chuckled to himself and figured he'd have to fire up a little doobie on the car ride home to cogitate on that one.

Digby hesitated to call on Homer Crowe III, a dweeb known as Trip, but he could not be ignored. since he was squarely in the middle of the front row, waving his hand as if he were an eager student in math class. Trip had pestered Robbie for a job at Crowe Power for nearly a year and had been weeks away from taking on an amorphous role in Strategy until the Staminum offer came in. Now he faced the prospect that Crowe Power might cease to exist, foreclosing any possibility of employment, from Crowe or anyone else, probably forever.

"Digby," Trip said, rising to his feet, "I think this question's actually for you."

"Shoot," Digby said, peering over his reading glasses.

Trip plunged his hands into the pockets of his pleated khakis. "If Staminum buys us, is there anything in the agreement that guarantees jobs to members of our family? Are we, like, great-great-grandfathered in?"

"Other than Robbie?" Digby shook his head. "No. But they have promised they will give all of our current employees full consideration for jobs there."

Trip looked like he might cry. "But... I was just about to *start.*"

"I don't know what to tell you, Trip. I think we could make a case for you, but I can't say how much sway we would have. If you were still interested, you might have to actually apply for a job there."

Trip looked stricken. *He'd never done that before!* "Do we have people who can help with that?"

Digby smiled sympathetically. "I'm sure we can find someone to assist. That said, all of us might have to learn a few new tricks."

Trip, distraught, sat down, shaking his head. *Tricks? What kinds of tricks?*

Robbie pulled Digby aside. "End this fucking thing. I see where it's going. I didn't budge them an inch. All these selfish bastards care about is their own goddamned income. They all just want to take the money from Staminum and run. I can feel it."

"Should I call for a vote?"

"Go ahead. Just fucking sell it. I'm through sticking my neck out for these assholes."

A woman's voice came from the back of the room. "Excuse me." Digby and Robbie turned to see Lindsey, standing at her table in the back next to Bits. "May I make a comment?"

Robbie leaned into Digby. "Oh, for crissakes. This is all we need."

Digby ignored him and leaned into the microphone, "Of course, Lindsey."

Lindsey looked around at the faces that were all turned in her direction and took a deep breath to steady herself. "I completely understand the comments made by Jack and Topher and Trip," she said. "We *should* get more from our company than we are getting right now. If we're not drawing income and we're not seeing the value of our shares rise and we're not receiving any reputational benefit, what do we have, aside from vague promises of a better day? I hate to be so blunt, but let's call this what it is: failure."

There was a buzz in the crowd. Robbie leaned into Digby and spoke in an urgent monotone. "Where the hell is she going with this? Cut her off."

Digby shook his head. "I can't do that."

Lindsey continued, "Our stock is low because investors have lost faith in us. Like you, they can't see when we're going to generate a profit again or how we're going to do it. Our dividend is gone because we overspent on the acquisition of Greeneron. Five billion dollars got us... what? A magic-carpet ride into a fanciful future. Now our reputation is in tatters because of these hideous stories coming out about our chairman attacking a shareholder and assaulting a consultant. All this has left us weak, an easy mark. It's a fair question to ask the chairman: what have you done to our company?"

Robbie stomped to the front of the dais, enraged. "*Our* company? It's not your company. You're not even blood."

Lindsey stepped around the table and faced him. "This isn't about blood, Robbie. It's about brains. And backbone. And heart."

"As if you know anything about this business."

"More than you might think." Lindsey directed her comments to the people sitting at the tables. "I've been talking with a number of you over the past six months, and I know what you want from this company and how frustrated you are over what you're getting. I think a lot of it stems from the fact that we hold Crowe Power a little too closely. That's given license to certain people to treat the company as if it were their personal property, as if no other owners mattered. We dismiss 'outside investors' as interlopers who come and go. Those investors know we value them only when we want their money. So they've been voting with their feet—and their money—for months. And when those outside investors see our leaders act irresponsibly, the run for the exits turns into a stampede. Who does that hurt? Them? No. It hurts us."

Robbie pushed Digby out of the way and spoke into the microphone. "Stop this, Lindsey. You can't let your personal bitterness towards me drive this vindictive screed." He looked toward the others in the audience. "I think somebody's had too much to drink."

Lindsey nodded back to the glass on her table. "Iced tea."

"Long Island, I'll bet."

"Unsweetened. Like the offer from Staminum."

"You have to understand something, Lindsey. It's not personal. It's business."

Lindsey scoffed. "Yes, I saw that movie, too. But here's the thing, Robbie: it *is* personal for everyone in this room. That's our name on the building, on the stationery, on the payroll checks and stock certificates. As you yourself said, that name has meant something for more than a hundred years. And, on balance, it's meant something good. I don't accept the idea that because Homer Crowe or Lester Crowe or your father acted badly from time to time that it should excuse the behavior we've seen from you. We're supposed to learn from the mistakes of our forebearers, not repeat them."

Robbie said, "Your time is up."

A low rumble of disagreement came from the crowd. Did Robbie hear *booing?* Lindsey looked across the tables of people, saw the expressions of encouragement directed toward her, and turned back to Robbie. "I think, Robbie, you have that backwards."

Robbie turned to Digby. "Fucking *do* something, will you?"

Digby shrugged. "You don't want to hear what I have to say right now."

Bits stood. "Robbie, you're my brother and I love you. But there's no good way to explain your behavior or your track record. It's become an embarrassment. And it has to end."

Robbie stepped back, as if he'd been socked in the gut. Was no one going to stand up for him and defend him? These were his people, the source of his powers. He looked at Uncle Chuck, who sat impassively in the front row. Whatever he was thinking was not evident.

Aged Aunt Lizzie, sitting to his right, raised her hand. "I'd like to say something, but I don't want to stand."

Digby said, "That's quite alright, Aunt Lizzie. Please go ahead."

"Thank you." She stiffly turned over her shoulder toward the crowd. "I hope you all can hear me back there." She looked back to the stage at Robbie. "Robbie, dear, I've been a part of this company since I was born eighty-eight years ago. I've been through all the ups and downs and the personal struggles that some of our leaders have experienced, and we've had more than a few bumps along the way. When we turned to you five years ago to be the proxy for our family, we knew it would not always be easy, but I believe this is the lowest point that we have ever been. I can understand why some in the family think we should sell the company. They think this is the best we can do. But I don't think so. I think it's the best *you* can do, and maybe it's time to give someone else a chance. We could get our dividend back and become profitable again if we could stick to our knitting."

There was a smattering of applause.

Aunt Lizzie continued, "I don't know exactly how to do this, but I would like to nominate Lindsey to take your place. I've spent a good deal of time with her in recent months and I know how much thought and passion she would give this job. She has done her homework and she's very knowledgeable about this company and this industry, as I think many in this room can attest. The boys in this family have run this company since the beginning. By and large, they've had a good run. But I sense they've run out of steam. Strong leaders don't attack shareholders. They don't use our company funds to finance their liaisons. Maybe it's time to take a step back, give the ladies a chance to lead. Then support them. Help them. Act like a family that cares for one another. And then back up Lindsey when she tells Walker Hope: Thanks, but no thanks. We're keeping the damn company."

Thunderous applause echoed through the room, as Uncle Chuck stood and turned to Lindsey. "What do you say, Lindsey? Will you take the lead? If so, I'd like to make a motion."

Bits raised her hand. "Second."

Robbie shook his head in bewilderment. "What is this? Julius Caesar? Does everyone get to take a stab?"

Digby ignored Robbie and spoke into the microphone. "Lindsey?"

Lindsey nodded. "I'm all in."

As she walked toward the podium, the family members rose one by one, applauding and shouting encouragement. Even Aunt Lizzie pushed herself to her feet and clapped her hands. Ultimately, so did Digby.

Robbie turned to him. "Seriously?"

Digby nodded. "Sorry bro. It's time."

Robbie was paralyzed by a sense of cognitive dissonance. He couldn't square the euphoria and enthusiasm in the room with his overwhelming sense of defeat and humiliation. Suddenly, there was Lindsey, standing before him. As she grasped Robbie firmly by both shoulders and looked him in the eye, he couldn't help thinking: She got everything from their split. Not just their primary residence and half their marital assets. She got his job. His power. His standing. It might have been better to sell the company after all.

Her smile was warm and consoling. "Don't worry, Robbie. I've got this."

PART THREE

Rekindling

LATE MARCH

48. TRUTH TO POWER

At the conference table in his office, Walker put the finishing touches on his model for a global energy empire, then sat back in his chair and admired his handiwork: A worldwide network of refineries and pipelines traversing the Western Hemisphere and an expanding portfolio of power plants dotting four continents. And, at the very pinnacle of the org chart, the supreme leader of the new Staminum Crowe Corporation:

> Chairman & CEO
> WALKER B. HOPE

So well-deserved! With Moe's help, Walker would nudge Steady into retirement, add the duties of Chairman of the Board, and become the highest-paid CEO in the industry. The market value of this combination of Staminum Energy and Crowe Power would soar to extraordinary heights. Who could dispute that he was the best in the business, *THE* power in power? And while the offer to merge had not yet been accepted by Crowe Power, Walker could not imagine they would decline, given how far and how fast they had fallen, and how dim their prospects were for revival.

"Walker," his assistant called from the doorway. "Lindsey Harper Crowe is on her way up to see you."

Walker's head reflexively jerked. "*Lindsey* Crowe?"

"That's what Security said."

Just like Robbie, Walker mused. It was too humiliating to wave the white flag himself! He'd rather send his poor beleaguered wife. Let her accept defeat after he lost the war. People were right about him: he was a wuss.

As Heidi returned to the outer office to await Lindsey's arrival, Walker flipped over the diagram, straightened his tie, and walked quickly to his closet to retrieve his suitcoat from the Jos. A. Bank Signature Collection. Should he ask Heidi to take a photo of the two of them shaking hands to capture this historic capitulation? Moe would love that! Why, this would be like Washington and Cornwallis at Yorktown! Like Grant and Lee at Appomattox! And yet, the minute Walker saw Lindsey enter his office, so unexpectedly cool and composed and commanding, he recognized immediately that she was not there to carry a message from the Crowe Power boss. She *was* the boss.

Walker stepped up to meet her. "Lindsey. What a pleasant surprise," he said.

Lindsey, wearing a slim-fitting Alexander McQueen suit that flattered her newly toned figure, extended her hand straight out and smiled. "A pleasure to see you again, Walker."

They each took a chair at Walker's conference table overlooking the skyscrapers on Sixth Avenue and the bare trees of Central Park, and chatted briefly before Walker asked how the company was doing.

"There have been some changes at Crowe Power," Lindsey said.

Walker sat back, taking her measure. "Tell me, please."

She looked at her watch. "An announcement was released a few moments ago. Robbie has decided to leave the company."

"Really?" Walker said. "Never thought I'd see the day. Crowe Power has been his life. What's he gonna do?"

"He's... pursuing new opportunities."

Walker gleefully hit the armrests of his chair. "Oh, that's wonderful! He'd be great at that."

Lindsey was puzzled. "At what?"

"Doin' nothin'."

Lindsey winced. It annoyed her to hear such a cutting commentary from Walker, even though she thought the very same thing herself. "It's TBD what he's actually going to do. And, while that's not really my concern any longer, we wish him nothing but the best."

"Of course," Walker said, almost as if he cared.

"In his place," Lindsey said, "the board of directors has asked me to chair the company and I have accepted."

"Congratulations," Walker said, warily.

"Which brings me to the other news of the day," she said. "We're rejecting your offer to buy our company."

Walker sagged. "That's very disappointin'. May I ask why?"

Lindsey folded her hands over her lap, interlacing her fingers. "We think Crowe Power is worth a great deal more than you do."

"That's not surprisin'," Walker said with a roll of his shoulders. His tone turned pedantic. "I haven't met a top executive yet who doesn't think their company is undervalued. They all say, 'People just don't appreciate how good we are.'"

She was annoyed by the condescension. "I have no illusions of how good we are right now. We've made some bad decisions and we're paying for them. I'm determined not to make another one by selling our company at a time when our share price is well below where it ought to be."

"That's why we offered a steep premium."

She shook her head. "It wasn't steep enough."

Walker asked, "What if we sweetened the pot?"

"It's not just the price, Walker. Every member of the family feels strongly that Crowe Power has been an essential part of their heritage and it remains a critical component of their legacy going forward. They won't relinquish that just because we hit a bump in the road."

"Is that what you call Robbie?"

She smiled thinly. "Interesting that you could throw all our trouble on Robbie, Walker. You had a hand in it, too."

Walker flushed red, as if he'd been slapped in the face by Lindsey's finely-manicured hand. *"Really?"*

She leaned forward and looked into his eyes. "Really."

Walker retreated, folding his arms across his chest. "It wasn't enough that I saved your company?"

Her expression turned hard as she felt her own anger rise. "You mean, before you sabotaged it? You screwed us on that Greeneron deal, Walker, and don't think we don't know it. The price we paid for Greeneron is an anchor around our neck every single day."

Walker's eyes narrowed and his expression turned dark. "I didn't name the price. Your husband did."

"My *ex*-husband," she said hotly.

"Your chairman."

"Our *ex*-chairman."

"Lindsey, I'll admit. I led the horse to water. I had no idea how badly he wanted to drink. I might have gotten ten billion if I let him keep bidding. You should be glad he stopped at five."

"So... I should *thank* you?"

"I did what I could to help my new company."

"While you stuck it to your old one," she said, shaking her head in disgust. "We seriously considered suing you for fraud."

Walker put his hands up, in an expression of innocence. "Good luck with that. I never misrepresented a thing."

"Wouldn't that have been interesting to test in court?" she said. "A trial might have led to the discovery of how Greeneron was formed in the first place. We looked at the histories of these companies and found some interesting patterns. I don't believe Staminum could stand the scrutiny. Nor could you."

Walker looked deeply aggravated. "I trust you decided not to waste your time."

Lindsey continued. "We held off because we found that two of the Greeneron companies actually look very promising. We see spinoff possibilities that might even recoup the price we paid. We're in active negotiations to create joint ventures around nuclear fusion and hydrogen. If they work, who knows? We could redefine the future of energy in ways we hadn't imagined."

Walker said flatly, "Robbie did."

"Yes, he did. He was just reckless in how he went about it. But I can't fault his instincts." She leaned over and patted the back of his hand. "So in a way, Walker, we're grateful. You helped us set our sails toward a new horizon." She sat back again. "In the meantime, we're making Lucy Rutherford our new CEO. She intends to bring our traditional business back using many of the processes and procedures that you instituted. And, at the right time, we'll look for opportunities to grow. You made a very compelling case that our companies should be joined. We see how that could make a powerful combination."

He scratched his head, as Lindsey's intention finally became clear. "You want to buy us."

"Not today," Lindsey said as she stood. "And not tomorrow. But there will come a time, Walker, sooner than you might expect."

"You know we're not for sale."

"Start thinking about a price."

49. OVER THRONE

I f there was anything good to come from the coronavirus, Robbie thought, it was this: he got to wear a mask. Maybe, he thought, nobody would recognize him.

"Mr. Crowe?" the Delta flight attendant asked as she stood in the aisle, holding a coat.

Robbie, feeling a momentary sense of panic, looked around to see if anyone in the First Class cabin noticed. Nobody did, except for the middle-aged woman sitting next to him. She had ignored him the entire flight, but suddenly regarded him with alarm.

"No," Robbie said to the flight attendant. "Not me."

The attendant looked confused. "Really?" She glanced at her manifest. "I've got 4A here—"

Robbie cut her off. "Sorry."

The woman next to him relaxed and Robbie slumped back into his seat, adjusting the mask to make sure it was covering as much of his face as possible. Maybe he needed to wear a full hazmat suit or something, at least until the shitstorm raining down on his life blew over.

The jet pulled up to the gate at the Raleigh-Durham airport, where Robbie was the last to depart First Class. Nearing the doorway, he paused at the bridge, where the pilot and the flight attendant offered their obligatory smiles and thanks to the departing passengers.

"I have to apologize," Robbie whispered to the attendant. "I thought you said, 'Mr. *Snow*.' That actually is my jacket."

The attendant lost her cheery countenance and sighed. "I knew *I* wasn't crazy," she said. She reached into a compartment and handed Robbie his coat. With a smile that more closely resembled a sneer, she said, "Have a nice day."

Robbie was met at baggage by a driver holding a sign that said, "FLEBEETZ," which for purposes of this trip, was his undercover name. The driver escorted him to a waiting car, and they headed west on the I-40 expressway toward Chapel Hill.

Exiting at the NC-54 Bypass, the driver wound down Raleigh Road, then headed north through the tree-lined campus of the University of North Carolina before turning onto Franklin Street, the main drag, and stopping across from the Hemp Store. As Robbie remained seated in the back, the driver looked in the rear-view mirror.

"That's it," the driver said. "Upstairs over that jewelry store."

The driver wasn't going to open the door for him? Lord, this fall from grace was hard! Robbie looked around for a door handle—*where in God's name do they put these things?*—and finally located it. He successfully opened the door and crossed the street. In an alley next to the jewelry store, he found a lattice metal staircase leading to a second floor, and a dented steel door with a sign next to it on the brick wall: The Mission Institute for Higher Corporate Purpose.

Robbie dropped his mask below his chin and rang a doorbell, which was answered by Dr. Kristi Kramer. "Robbie, darlin'!" she cried. "You found me! Come on in!"

Robbie stepped tentatively into the office and looked around. A couple of desks. Some office equipment. A coffee maker that was frying some old brew into a smelly tar. A filing cabinet with a TV on top of it. "This is it?"

"Are you kidding? This is a step up! I started in a trailer," she said. "Have a seat."

Robbie took a padded metal chair next to her desk. "You hear 'institute,' you kind of think big red brick edifice and stone pillars. Especially in a college town."

"Exactly!" she said. "That's what I want you to think. All that stuff's across the street. This side is where the real world begins."

He scoffed. "Is that what you call it?"

"Close enough. Would you like some coffee?"

Robbie scrunched his nose. "Not that."

"I can make a fresh pot."

"It's okay."

She looked at him and began playing with her hair, pulling it up over her head and knotting it. "Thank you for coming down this morning. I frankly didn't expect I'd ever see you again."

"I had to see you."

She licked her lower lip. "I know what you mean."

Robbie shook his head. "Not that. I want to understand."

"What?"

"Why you did what you did. You know what you said about me wasn't true."

She dropped her hair back down and shook her head so that it settled on her shoulders. "Oh darlin'. I did you a *favor.* You were failing. You were going to get fired anyway. I gave you a platform."

"I don't follow."

"Redemption! You're a fallen man. A tragic story. It's Biblical. Shakespearean. You had it all and you blew it. Big time." She reached forward and patted his knee. "People love to see the mighty fall. But here's the thing. They also love a good comeback story. So..." She rolled her hand, indicating a forward motion.

"So, *what?*"

"Come back!"

Robbie sagged. "I have no idea where to even start."

Kristi walked to a file cabinet and fingered through some hanging folders, mumbling to herself. She pulled out a sheet of paper and returned to her desk. "I've done this a million times," she said, glancing at her sheet then handing it over. "First thing you do is repent. Admit the errors of your past." She adopted a preacher's voice and looked toward the heavens. *"Oh, Lord! Forgive me! I have sinned!"* She turned back to Robbie. "Then commit to doing better. Promise you'll devote all your time and resources to not only mending your ways but helping others avoid a similar fate. You can start a foundation. The Robbie Crowe Institute of Blah, Blah, Blah."

"Blah, blah, blah?"

"You'll think of something."

"An institute." He looked around at the shabby surroundings. "Like this?"

She waved her hand. "You can have a fancier office if you like. Get one of those marble palaces in Midtown. It doesn't really matter. It's all about perception. Come out with some high-minded principles. Do an apology tour. Write op-eds. Give lectures. I could easily see another TED Talk. You'll be rehabilitated in no time."

Robbie dolefully shook his head. "I don't see how that's possible."

"Of course it's possible! You're down in the dumps now. But the whole 'Robbie Crowe is a jerk' story will cease to be news after a while. People will get tired of it. They'll want something new. That's when you start to show them you've changed. And they'll go, '*Whoa!* I need to start thinking differently about this guy.'"

He shook his head. "I'm damaged goods. Not that it's my fault. At *all.* But still. Why would people believe me?"

"Because of third-party validation."

"What do you mean?"

"I will be the first to offer my public forgiveness for all your transgressions. And I will personally attest that you are a man *transformed.*"

"For a fee, I take it."

"Oh, you!" She looked away, shyly. "Nothing more than a modest retainer."

"I see."

"And rights to the book."

"Another book?"

"Are you kidding me? This would *surely* be a best-seller. You're a great cautionary tale to all the other corporate leaders out there. 'Don't be an idiot like this guy.' Frankly, I've already started to build a curriculum around it. I know lots of companies that would love to hear a powerful story of degradation right from the horse's mouth. You would command *huge* honorariums. I know a million places that would book you right now."

Robbie sighed. "I'll have to think about it." He stood up to leave.

She looked at him and took his hand. "Robbie. I know you've been through hell. You lost your job, your marriage, and your reputation. But here's the thing. Someday you're going to look back on this and realize: I saved your *soul.*"

50. FLIGHTS OF FANCY

A t the Raleigh-Durham airport, Robbie bought a Carolina blue baseball cap with "Tar Heels" on the front panel in the hope it would provide additional cover from the public. He was 500 miles from New York and a million miles from Dr. Kristi Kramer's promised redemption.

He settled into his seat in the back corner of First Class, drew down the window shade, and closed his eyes as an oversized man in an undersized shirt pounded his rollaboard into the overhead bin. The man flopped hard into the seat next to him, rocking Robbie's seat in the process. *Jesus, Fatso! Watch what you're doing!*

The man unpacked his laptop and glanced at Robbie fiddling with his AirPods. "Tar!" he said.

Robbie looked at him quizzically. "What?"

"Tar!" he said, more urgently.

Robbie shook his head, annoyed. "I don't know what you're talking about."

"Sorry," the man said. "Most people say, 'Heels.' I guess you're not a fan."

"Oh. You mean because of the hat," Robbie said. "Got it. I was just visiting."

"A souvenir?"

"I've got a few from here. More than I'd like, actually."

Robbie pounded the pillow and squished it into the dark corner. He pulled his hat low over his eyes, put his AirPods in his ears, and selected a calming app from his phone. As the plane climbed to its cruising altitude, Robbie drifted off, dreaming of Kristi and institutes and the life he used to lead.

* * *

Lindsey climbed aboard Crowe Bird I and found three other passengers spread out in the cabin to maintain a healthy social distance. Lucy Rutherford, the new CEO of Crowe Power, sat in the front section facing the galley. The new head of investor relations, Kathryn Keeley, was at the table behind her. And Digby was in the last seat in the back, his head buried in the Financial Times. He put the paper down when he heard her arrive and nodded a hello.

"Welcome aboard," Lucy said.

"I might say the same to you," Lindsey responded, cheerily. She took the seat formerly reserved for Robbie and sat back, looking around at her surroundings and colleagues. She reached into her briefcase, pulled out briefing materials, and set them on the table in front of her. "Thank you for these," she said, calling over her shoulder to Kathryn. "Very, very helpful. We have an excellent story to tell about Crowe Power."

"We do," said Kathryn. She leaned across and handed Lindsey a copy of *Fortune* magazine. "This is a very good story, too."

Lindsey took the magazine and looked at the cover, with her photo, taken in the Crowe Energy Company's Hall of Fam. Lindsey stood next to the portrait of Homer Crowe, looking very much like a woman in charge.

GIRL POWER
Lindsey Harper Crowe Rules Crowe's Nest

"Oh, my goodness," Lindsey said, putting her hand over her heart. "I'm not accustomed to this kind of publicity."

"It's a vast improvement over what we had before," Lucy said.

The galley door opened and the flight attendant emerged.

"Mrs. Crowe," said Charles. "Would you like some lunch?"

She looked at him and smiled. "What do you have?"

He bent at the waist and leaned forward so that only she could hear. "I have my *job* back. I am so grateful. Thank you."

"You're welcome." She took his hand and squeezed it. "I'm glad you're here."

He stood back up. "Would you like a Cobb Salad?"

"That sounds just fine, Charles," she said. "And please tell Captain Mark it's wheels up. Isn't that what you say?"

"It is."

She looked to Lucy and Kathryn, then back to Charles. "We're ready to roll."

✻ ✻ ✻

As Delta Flight 4709 began its descent into New York's LaGuardia airport, Robbie found himself, inexplicably, behind the counter of Café Che, wearing the jungle fatigues and black beret of his fellow employees. Ernesto, Oksana, and Gazi scurried around him fulfilling orders, urging him to move faster to manipulate the means of production. Robbie stood motionless at the espresso machine, holding a cup with the name "Natalia" scrawled across it.

"I have no idea what to do," he complained. "Why don't you just tell me?"

"You never push the right buttons," said Natalia, shaking her head in exasperation. She was his customer, regarding him with pity. "It's obvious you're not suited for this job."

"It's all your fault. I did it for you." He dropped the cup to his side. "All I want now is my coat."

"How about this one?"

What? Which one? He looked up and Natalia had vanished. Fatso was jostling his arm. "Hey buddy. We've landed."

Robbie shook the sleep away, trying to comprehend. "I'm sorry..." He looked up at the flight attendant standing in the aisle holding out a jacket. "Is this your coat, sir?"

Robbie nodded. "Yes. Yes, it is." He reached up and took it. "Thank you."

"We'll be at the gate shortly."

The big guy looked at Robbie, then looked away, and back again. "I can't help wondering. Are you, by any chance, Robbie Crowe?"

Robbie shook his head. "I wouldn't want to be that guy right now."

Fatso laughed as he stood up and reached into the overhead bin. "Isn't that the truth! Who would?"

Robbie slid out of the seat and into the aisle as the door opened and passengers began to file out. "I heard today he was attempting a comeback."

Fatso scoffed. "Good luck with that!"

Robbie shook his head in dismay. "I know, right? What are the odds?"

ABOUT THE AUTHOR

JON PEPPER is an entrepreneur, novelist, and consultant based in New York City. His company, Indelable, advises leaders on how to define, promote, and defend their businesses. He was previously an executive for two Fortune 100 companies, a business columnist and national writer for *The Detroit News*, a reporter for the *Detroit Free Press*, a magazine publisher, a radio talk show host, and an advertising copywriter. He and his wife, Diane, who designed this book cover, reside in Manhattan.

More about Jon and his novels is available at www.jonpepperbooks.com

The first book in this series, *A Turn in Fortune*, is available on Amazon.

You can learn about Jon's consulting firm at www.indelable.com

THANK YOU

This book would not be possible without the support, encouragement and, as needed, pushback from my wife and life partner, Diane Pepper. She is a creative spirit herself, as you can see from the design of this book's cover.

I also want to thank Nicky Guerreiro, whose thoughtful copyediting was extremely helpful in polishing my prose; Sarah Collier, my longtime colleague who served as a critical audience in the book's development; Dave Campbell, whose review of the first draft helped me know whether I was on the right track; and Michael Mullen, a skilled artist who turned Diane's cover design and drawings into a finished piece.

Lastly, I deeply appreciate the reviews offered both publicly and privately on *A Turn in Fortune.* Many readers told me they were eager to see what happened next. I wanted to know, too, which is why I wrote *Heirs on Fire.* Based on its ending, there's only one way to find out where things go from here.

Jon
September 8, 2020

P.S. I would be grateful for your review of *Heirs on Fire* on Amazon and Goodreads. Thanks!